DATE DUE

IN CAHOOTS

RANDOM HOUSE NEW YORK

IN CAHOOTS

A NOVEL OF SOUTHERN

CALIFORNIA, 1953

Malcolm Cook MacPherson

All rights reserved under International Pan-American
Copyright Conventions. Published in the United States
by Random House, Inc., New York, and
simultaneously in Canada by Random House
of Canada Limited, Toronto.

Grateful acknowledgment is made to Ken Nordine for
permission to reprint ten lines from his voice-over
to "Desolation Theme" from Walt Disney's *Pinocchio*,
recorded on the album *Stay Awake* (A & M Records).
Reprinted by permission.

Library of Congress Cataloging-in-Publication Data
MacPherson, Malcolm.
In cahoots : a novel of Southern California, 1953 / Malcolm Cook
MacPherson.
p.   cm.
ISBN 0-679-42204-8
1. Amusement parks—California—Garden Grove—Design and
construction—Fiction. 2. Environmentalists—California—Garden
Grove—Fiction. 3. Community life—California—Garden Grove—
Fiction. 4. Garden Grove (Calif.)—Fiction. I. Title.
PS3563.A3254I5   1994   813'.54—dc20   93-26884

Manufactured in the United States of America on acid-free paper
2 4 6 8 9 7 5 3
First Edition

Book design by Victoria Wong

For C.A.M. and M.A.S.,
Molly and Fraser, and Charlie,
and to the memory of my parents

In a very real sense the entire
society was a stage set, a visualization
of dream and illusion which was, like
film, at once true and not true . . . a
place where dream and fact energized
each other.

Kevin Starr, *Inventing the Dream:*
California Through the Progressive Era

Don't give up.
Just one more try.
Rainbows soon will fill
The sky.

Silly birds
Who should know better
Tell each young,
"Go and get her."
Lady Luck's the one they're after
Now and also ever after.

Ken Nordine

Garden Grove,
Orange County,
California
1953

1

Origin of the Species

It was a clear, even lucky day on land, but at sea the wind was raising a ruckus. Callum could see that much bouncing on the rumble-seat cushion as Bud shifted the old car up the last slope, where the temperature dropped and the funk of the Pacific came up like a fog. Edith squinted through her wire-rimmed glasses in the rearview mirror. "What's wrong now?" she shouted to be heard. Beads of sweat formed under her thick bifocals. "What on earth's the matter with you?"

"The Crown," Callum yelled, pointing ahead, toward the ocean, over the roof.

Edith looked across the empty landscape. "Well what about it?"

"Seals," he said, as if that said it all.

Bud chucked the gearshift into neutral and coasted the last mile with the downhill momentum of the car to save on gas. They were passing through the barren tracts of the Irvine Ranch. To the left out of sight was Laguna with its nudists, artists, and free-lovers—"Lagunatics," he called them. To the right was Newport Beach, with Errol Flynn's yacht, the *Black Swan*, tethered in the basin and the boat parade crouched in the harbor waiting for Christmas to come alive. Between these two glamorous places, the Crown hid behind a jagged dirt wall, a pocket beach that maps called Corona del Mar.

Edith squinted in the rearview. Then, without apparent reason, she laughed out loud, covering her mouth with her palm, which she raised like a semaphore whenever even the suggestion of humor hove into view. Edith could not grin, much less laugh, without exposing her buck teeth to the world. She told Bud she surprised herself that she laughed at all; her teeth gave her every reason to be as mute as Helen Keller.

She watched Callum, wondering what thoughts went on behind his curious brown eyes. Then she leaned her elbow on the sun-baked dash and stared at the deep ruts that Bud was negotiating down the dirt cliff road. He pulled into a parking slot and was yanking back on the handbrake when Callum leaped out of the rumble seat and ran for the surf.

"You gotta help," Blue screamed out the passenger-side window far louder than was necessary.

"Good girl, Blue," Edith said, eyeing her, hardly trying to hide the fondness she felt for her middle child. Blue was the picture of what she wished she'd been at her age—blond, blue-eyed, and cute, with a button nose, dark eyebrows, and an innocence that sometimes seemed contrived.

Blue's sister, Cloud, standing in the hot sand with her legs like a stork's, pursed her lips like a biddy. Cloud was dark and gawky, with freckles that dotted her face and arms in summer. Misery was as much a part of her nature as her curly brown hair and long, spindly legs. Life, Cloud seemed to have already concluded, was cruel. What saved her from having a personality gone wrong was cunning. Cloud was the type to settle even the smallest slight. Bud said she had the longest fuse he had ever seen. It was lit all the time.

The women, their arms folded like judges, watched Callum scruff back across the sand. He leaned into the rumble seat and filled his arms with an inner tube and the canvas umbrella and a blanket, thinking how for his sisters these things—ointments and oils and sunglasses, you-name-it, the junk that filled the garage all winter— *were* the beach. They could find no joy in the curl of the surf or the pull of the tide; the mystery of the ocean escaped their sense of what was important. *Their* beach consisted mainly of what they looked like in bathing suits and, this summer, guys too old for them, with dangerous ducktails and jeans slung too low for words.

Bud found a spot on the sand as though he were an explorer in a newfound land—not too close to the hot-dog and raft stands and other sunbathers but close enough to avoid a trek for a refreshment. He drove home the umbrella pole, looking remarkably like a Marine raising the flag at Mount Suribachi. Callum was spreading out the army surplus blanket and towels when a family violated an invisible boundary that Edith had drawn in her mind. And the whole family decamped to a position farther down the beach and repeated the rituals. Edith placed the wicker lunch basket in the shade of the umbrella and shook the tea jug for the muffled sound of rattling ice that made you thirsty all by itself. And she covered her dimpled thighs with a terry-cloth beach towel.

"You see the flag?"

The breeze had stiffened a bleached-out red warning flag flying above the lifeguard stand fifty yards away. It referred to huge, curling walls of green water that drove toward the shore and broke with a thunderous force. The waves had never seemed quite this murderous before; nobody was swimming, nobody was even wading, for fear of being sucked out and crushed by the combers. Callum sighed and hugged his knees to his chest while Edith poured him a glass of the tea.

Bud thumbed the pages of *National Geographic*, which he claimed was a source of inspiration. He said they wouldn't have come out here as a family like Okies if they weren't in search of dreams. The whole family was off in one corner or another of dreamland, it sometimes seemed. Edith and the girls wanted to become Job's Daughters. Edith said if that dream came true, the girls would meet nice boys and she could stop hiding behind her hand. Bud's dream was different. He no longer wanted to be like Errol Flynn in Pago Pago or Martin Johnson in British East Africa. He sought out practical dreams that stood at least a chance. These he called dream-schemes, to differentiate them from what went on in his head at night and, more often than he admitted, in daylight, too.

Looking up from his magazine he dug his toes in the warm sand and said, "Edith, I think I may be on the verge."

She unwrapped the cellophane from a brownie with the discipline of a thinner woman.

"Edith, are you listening?"

The surf womped so hard the land trembled, and everybody on the beach looked up. Mothers searched for their kids; some shouted at them to move inland. The surf rose to such a monumental height, the wind-feathered blue-green water looked like a romantic seascape that nobody was meant to believe.

"The verge of what, Bud?" she asked, inspecting the brownie again. By the tone of her voice she was asking less out of curiosity than marital duty.

"A dream-scheme," he said.

She held a morsel of the pastry on her tongue like a cough lozenge, letting it melt. "Oh, Bud," she mumbled.

"No, no, I mean it."

She sighed. "What? Minks again?"

Callum glanced at him with an expression of dismay. The breeding pair Bud had bought from the catalog a couple years ago had produced not a single offspring (and minks were known for doing it like rabbits). He had been in charge of cleaning out their cages, and didn't associate them with their satiny black pelts or with expensive women's stoles. Minks, as far as he was concerned, were a stink, and that was all, that strutted in his memory with the boldness of a drum major. He also connected them with Bud's dreams, which stalled so often the family hardly noticed anymore.

"Bigger," Bud replied.

"Not the night crawlers!" she said, keeping the conversation moving as she whisked her chin with the tips of her fingers.

"Bigger, Edith, much much bigger."

"But you haven't hit on exactly what, isn't that right?"

Bud shook his head. "Like I said, the *verge*, Edith. If you're like I am, the whole world's your oyster." He snapped open the *Geographic*.

Dreamily she said, "You're thinking of growing oysters?"

He wiggled his toes in the sand. "All I was saying, it's been a long time. I miss not having something on the agenda."

Callum snatched his Voit off the towel and walked down to the edge of the sea, kicking kelp leaves. He thought about Bud's verge.

Bud couldn't seem to understand that a dream that came true wasn't a dream anymore. What it became was hard to say. It was like imagining what happened to a soap bubble when it popped, all iridescent and suspenseful when it lived and simply nothing but invisible air when it was gone. He put his toes in the water and watched as several more bathers stood up and shifted their towels inland. A man with a wispy white beard walked by swinging the flat metal shoe of a mine detector, searching for buried treasure. A Pied Piper's line of kids Callum's age followed, shouting questions the old man could not hear for the pings in his ears. A boy in pale blue socks and droopy bathing trunks poked at the sand with a stick, while his mother watched him from under a broad-brimmed hat she held against the breeze. The boy rolled a white beach ball at Callum, inviting him to play. But Callum wasn't much for playing when he was on the Crown. He kicked the ball with all his strength. It arced in the air and landed on a wave. Undertow, like a miser with a stack of gold, snatched it out of his reach.

"Don't go after it, Bobby," the boy's mother shouted.

Callum tested the water up to his knees, pretending to get the ball. Bobby and his mother watched as though he were a thief. He glanced over at the lifeguard, who was concentrating on a girl in a two-piece suit. He slipped the Voit's cord up on his shoulder and settled into the sea, the pretense forgotten. He ducked under a low wall of bubbling froth and surfaced as the suck of the undertow drew him farther out. With strong strokes he pulled himself up and over that wave's falling crest. A few strokes more and he reached the zone between the foam and big, dangerous combers.

He bicycled with his legs, gauging a new wave that he either had to dive under or beat to its crested fall—or tons of water would pound him down and hold him under halfway back to the shore. It had happened to him once before, bouncing him off the bottom in a crazy world with neither up nor down. He had thought he was drowning and he felt himself go limp just as the wave had raised him to the surface for a breath of clean air. He now slipped the Voit over his right foot as though it were his armor and met the wave at the instant of its fall. Instead of crushing him it hugged him in its curl and pushed him up to its wind-feathered peak. For what seemed like a whole minute its green girth suspended him above the level of the sea; he *was* the wave as surely as anything he knew. Then it released him with a wicked hiss. He watched the shoreward roll of its hump before swimming out to where the sea darkened and was no more turbulent than a pool.

"I wish," he said out loud, and flipped on his back. "I'm wishing . . ."

He raised his head and caught a glimpse of the shore. Edith, shading her eyes, was surveying the horizon. Bud had left the shade of the umbrella and was waving for Blue and Cloud to follow him up the footpath on the cliff. Callum couldn't see the girls' expressions, but he knew they'd be muttering about why they couldn't just lay out in the sun. They trooped across the hot sand, and Edith headed toward the lifeguard stand with a stride that meant business. The guard had stopped talking to the girl in the two-piece and was reaching for a red torpedo buoy with which he saved lives.

Callum looked out to sea and made a full turn to try to discover what worried the landlubbers. At the level of the surface he saw the normal shoreward rhythm of swells. Nothing at all raised an alarm. A sailboat a couple hundred yards away made a sloppy tack; the red-and-black navigational buoys by the harbor entrance swayed under an empty washed-out sky. But that was all.

Just then a dark shape broke the surface about fifty yards farther out at sea. Then another and another followed that one. The things moved at an incredible speed, one instant visible, the next submerged.

A prisoner of panic, he thrashed at the water thinking, now that he needed a wave to speed him back to shore, not even a swell passed him by. One of the things brushed his foot. He was certain he felt it bump his Voit. It hit him again, nearly tearing the flipper off. He looked down into the water and stopped treading and waited.

Suddenly sunlight splashed like burst diamonds off the water as one of the things broke the surface in front of his face. He laughed out loud with relief and joy. "*Oo-ooo,*" he sang, the sound Edith made to soothe him when he was a baby. "*Oo-ooo. Come on, ooo.*"

He gulped air and dove headfirst with his eyes wide open. Just as he had wished, seals were soaring beneath him through the panes of dark and light water, dancing in a circle beneath his feet. One of them swam up close, around, and down again. Its flippers rippled water against his skin. He came to the surface with the seal, and they stared at each other in a kind of surprised wonder. The seal snorted and coughed. It had whiskers and a brown face and black eyes. A playful twitch of its mouth made Callum shout out loud for joy. At the sound of his voice the seal barked. With a flick of its flippers it dove under water, up again, down again, as though it were inviting him to come along.

He looked toward the shore. The lifeguard was in the water with the rope of his red buoy clenched between his teeth.

Callum called out, *"Ooo,"* then drove himself shoreward.

A ridge of sea gathered behind him like a fist, and Callum timed his strokes to match its speed. He picked up momentum and hitch-hiked on the water. The lifeguard measured the huge wave wrong, and he screamed, his mouth open wide. The wave shot Callum forward and fused him to its power. He flattened his arms to his sides and tobogganed down the slope. He hit the drop and flew right over the lifeguard's head. The pressure of the wave shot the red torpedo high in the misty air.

Callum controlled the wave and switched back and forth with a kick of his Voit, and near the shore he slipped behind it with a roll. The water frothed and popped as his feet gained purchase on the sandy bottom.

Edith was standing waist deep in the water with her hands on her hips. "Are you all right, sweetheart?" She started to cry and took off her glasses. "You scared me half to death."

The lifeguard floated up, a casualty of the surf, in front of twenty or so bathers who were standing around. He was breathing hard. Spume soiled his buoy.

"You little twerp," he shouted.

"You twerp . . . yourself," Edith said, turning angry with relief, then laughing at the sound of her own voice. She showed the lifeguard her back and marched up the beach. When she was out of earshot, she held Callum by the shoulders and asked, "What on earth were you trying to do, get yourself killed?"

"They weren't sharks, Mom."

She looked over her shoulder at the sea. "Sharks? What sharks? So what if they weren't? What does it matter what they were?"

"They were seals."

"No, I suppose it doesn't matter. The point is, they could have been anything."

"Seals."

She shook her head. "You and your father, I swear. I wonder where this dreaming of yours will ever end."

"Oo-ay, etts-oo-er," Bud shouted into his end of the Hoover vacuum-cleaner tube, sounding like he had a clothespin on his nose.

Callum hunkered down, fooling with the Hoover tube that snaked out the car window and back into the rumble seat. A tin funnel was taped on each end; it was supposed to work like a pilot-to-bombadier intercom, but it never did the way it was meant to. Bud insisted on using it, though, saying the idea was what mattered, and that was true.

He backed up the Ford, and it must have taken several whole minutes to cover the length of the driveway, long enough for Callum, bending over the side of the open rumble seat, to count the lines in the concrete. Bud jabbered to himself in his end of the funnel, not giving in to its inutility. Besides, it didn't matter to him that Callum could not understand what he was saying. Bud couldn't stay quiet for very long. He loved the sound of his own voice and would expound to a deaf dog as readily as the president of the United States. That was because he had a natural curiosity about things and people. It dictated a kind of leisurely pace. In the Ford it was thirty. He had to go slow. Otherwise, he said, he might as well stay in bed. His curiosity had produced dividends, too. Over the years he had found by the roadside one giant zucchini, a set of chrome hubcaps, one desert turtle, and one crate of Quaker State motor oil.

"Keep your eyes peeled," he said as they accelerated down the street.

For the sake of clarity, Callum leaned around the driver's side window. "Where're we goin'?"

Bud was making his rounds, which he did every Saturday. And making rounds was another way of saying he didn't know where he was going. He'd just set out in the hope of selling a pair of Knapp shoes, which he peddled with the casualness of a rich man. Weekdays he delivered Squirt and Hires and Nesbitt's from the back of a truck. It wasn't unheard of for him to drive away from a roadside café lighter several cases of pop *and* a pair of Knapps, thus performing what he called a double. On Saturdays he concentrated on the shoes. In this way he thought he was getting ahead. After a whole lifetime of slipping behind, Bud wasn't altogether sure of his direction anymore. He knew that he was tired of being poor. He said so all the time. He had not brought the family across the country from New England to get by with day-old bread, hand-me-downs, reclaimed oil, and retread tires. You could be an Okie in Oklahoma, he liked to say. He could have saved the gas if all he wanted from the Golden State was to get by.

"Where you want to go?" Bud asked.

"It don't matter," Callum said.

"Doesn't." And it didn't. "Let's head over to the grove," he said. "Oh, hey. Your mother says you were dreaming you saw seals the other day."

Callum dropped the funnel in his lap. He had not *dreamed* the seals. And even if he had dreamed them, they were *his* seals. That's how Bud was and it made him mad. Bud's dreams did not exist for themselves. They had to be *schemes,* which he used the same way a mechanic used a ball-peen hammer. What tempered his anger was the knowledge that nobody needed a dream as much as Bud. Time was no longer fully on his side. No matter if he acted half his age, his wispy hair, the veins like blue worms on his shins, the incipient hernia in his groin that felt to the touch like a plug of hardwood—these things told the truth that Bud no longer could count time among his few luxuries.

They rolled along the dusty two-lane road past the pink stucco county hospital, over the Santa Fe tracks. They skirted the Orange Drive-in Theatre and crossed the Santa Ana bridge that spanned a bone-dry riverbed, then past the dog pound behind a eucalyptus brake in a darkened grove. In the distance the gentle peaks of the Santa Ana mountains curved into a watery blue sky dusted by cirrus clouds. Orange blossoms, eucalyptus, and the funk of smudge pots scented the arid air. All around them, as far as the eye could see, were groves of walnuts and avocados, lemons and persimmons, almonds, peaches, nectarines, and bushy, broad-waisted orange trees. Orange County, after all, wasn't named for the color.

Callum spoke into the tin funnel. "Dad," he asked. "Why is he like he is?"

"*Ooooossssaaattttt?*" Bud asked.

"Mr. Wait."

"*Eeeeeuussenlipooop.*" Bud craned his head out the window. "Why don't you ride up here with me?"

"That's okay."

Bud put the funnel to his face. "*Eyefunkwagowatwanfst, howsst, sonnswaay, 'apppss, fruu, wnnwefushere, enwararisit, saristeraite-ome,*" he said and braked the car and threw down the tube. Like so much else Bud dreamed up, he did not discuss its failure, but it was there—a flopped idea. He pulled to a stop and ordered Callum to climb in the cab.

Under way again, Callum asked, "I said, Why does he live all alone?"

"How should I know?"

"Did he do something wrong?"

Bud hunched over the steering wheel. "He changed his name, as far as I know."

"Why did he choose what he did?"

"You'd have to ask him. I think it's why he reads his newspapers. He hasn't told me."

"That's a lot of newspapers, Dad."

Bud patted his knee. "That's a lot of something, son."

Bud braked at a sheet-metal mailbox on a four-by-four stump. He turned off the asphalt onto a tractor-wheel track and steered the Ford down a row of orange trees. Ripe fruit thumped on the windshield, and the sound of the engine scared up doves foraging in the furrows. Callum leaned out the window. He felt at home in groves like this one. He slept in them when he was tired and climbed in the trees and ate the fruit fresh from the branches. He could get lost in the streets of downtown Santa Ana but never in a grove. He knew them by how they were farmed better than most farmers, and this grove, Mr. Wait's, was the healthiest, most beautiful one around.

After a distance they entered a small clearing bordered by a

towering eucalyptus brake. The air was hot and dusty, and the
late-morning sun glinted off rusted hubcaps, scraps of chrome,
sheets of corrogated metal, and wind-pump blades cast aside in the
sere grass beside old tires, rotted cardboard boxes, citrus crates, and
smudge-pot parts. In the shade of the brake stood a shack with a
porch, a peaked tar-paper roof, doors, and windows. The place was
a dump that hardly looked fit for habitation. Old newspapers, thousands of them, stacked up ten feet high and containing millions of
stories chronicling California and the world beyond, formed its roof
and four walls.

"You stay here," Bud told Callum as he stopped the car in front
of the porch.

Callum climbed into the rumble seat and chucked pebbles at a
jackass standing like a lawn sculpture in a newspaper corral. Its
name was Bob. And Bob was not a mover. He neither flicked his tail
nor shimmied his skin. His most active trait was his odor. Oh, his
eyelids went up and down every now and then and his tail went back
and forth like sedge. Looking at Bob, Callum wondered if he had
ever been young. Bob was like a mirror. Looking at him you could
imagine the Nativity, *The Treasure of the Sierra Madre*, and *Death
Valley Days* if you wanted to. Whether Bob had his own real
agenda was also impossible to say. Even for what he was, Bob was
one dull honey.

The screen door screeched and banged shut. Bud and Mr. Wait
walked across the dirt yard. Mr. Wait's face was the color of old
newspaper and flat as a beggar's palm. He cut the strings on a hay
bale with his pocket knife and flung the hay into Bob's corral. When
he was done he dusted his smooth-pressed khaki pants and picked
loose straw from his threadbare shirt.

Callum joined him at the corral, leaning his elbows on the newspaper fence while watching Bob siphon water from a bucket. Mr.
Wait opened the gate and threw a rope around his neck. "It's time
he got rid of his last batch," he said. "You're welcome to come
along." He looked at Bud with a fixed expression. "You, too, Bud,"
and with the rope over his shoulder he walked toward the brake. At
the grove's edge, he hoisted Callum on Bob's bare back and set off
down a row of trees ladened with ripe oranges. Sometimes Mr. Wait

hired Mexicans for the picking and sometimes not. The fallen fruit replenished the soil, and Mr. Wait loved the soil as much as the trees it nurtured.

As if to make the point, he scooped an orange off the ground and, clucking his tongue, said, "These trees are like messy children." He creased the orange's spongy husk and handed Bud and Callum each a section, saying, "Eat 'em while you can." He looked at Callum. "Now you let me know if Bob backfires, hear? Then we'll turn him around and head back."

Callum pictured Bob exploding and slid off his back. He walked beside Bud, and they went deeper into Mr. Wait's grove, lost in the pleasure of a day with nothing to do. He loved it when adults validated nothing to do—it made doing nothing almost meaningful. The roar of passing trucks and cars farther on announced the boundary of the grove with the highway. The leafy branches had muffled the sound, but here on the edge conversation—even normal thought—was hard to achieve. Like a door opened to a noisy room, the highway was the portal to another world. They stood on an irrigation furrow watching people pass by in their cars.

"They used to crawl up and down here," Mr. Wait shouted. "They'd stop for a chat if they saw men they never saw before with a jackass and a boy. Now look at 'em hunched over like nervous rats. The beginning and the end, the start and the finish, that's all they care about anymore. Used to be the in-between was what people looked forward to."

"That's progress," Bud said.

"It's changing everything," said Mr. Wait.

"You're not worried, are you?"

"Who wouldn't be?"

Bob's backfire carried even over the traffic noise. Looking at him admiringly, they stepped smartly upwind. After a courteous few seconds, they tugged Bob back into the grove. Like he was weightless he skipped stiff-legged straight off the ground, once, twice, three times. Like a lot of things that summer, it was hard to figure out why.

Mr. Wait sat down on the front page of the *Santa Ana Register*, which was headlining John Walker Tailor throwing his hat in the ring for Orange County sheriff. Bud chose for his seat the nuptial announcement of Mary Alice Kellogg, the cornflake heir, to Earl "Wacky" Wicker, Garden Grove's used-car potentate. These recent editions, like cords of curing wood, would eventually be used in the construction of a new corral for Bob or an addition to Mr. Wait's house, but for now they were as comfortable as lawn chairs in the shade of the eucalyptus.

"Come over and sit with us," Bud shouted at Callum, who was gazing at Bob back in his corral.

"Sit down here, sonny," Mr. Wait said and dusted the headline HILLARY CONQUERS EVEREST.

For a long time they sat there in silence listening to the breeze in the trees and the swish of Bob's tail.

"Your paper collection is doing great, Mr. Wait," Callum said for something to say.

"Thanks, sonny. I appreciate that. I really do." Turning to Bud he said, "I've read every damn one of them." He spit near his toe. "Not much in 'em. These pecksniffs write about the whole rest of the world in one column. Imagine. The whole rest of the world."

As far as Callum was concerned, knowing about things brought changes that only worried him. He sometimes stayed awake nights fretting over what might happen to Edith and Bud and his sisters, but mostly worrying what change would do to him. He wasn't old enough to get along on his own. Until he was, he hoped changes stayed in Europe or China.

"Bud says the people over in Europe need to be saved from themselves," he said, recalling one of Bud's monologues. "The Asians, they're pitiful."

"I'm Asian," Mr. Wait said. "What do you think about that?"

"You're American," Callum corrected him.

"People didn't always see it that way."

They stared at the ground in embarrassed silence. Mr. Wait's personal life was not a topic they discussed, and broaching it now made them uncomfortable. The wind in the eucalyptus sounded like the blades of sharp knives. The silence this time went on and on. Silence was almost natural between Mr. Wait and Bud. They had met years ago when Bud spotted his mailbox out by the road. Before Mr. Wait could tell him to leave, Bud had started his pitch for Knapps—"Your feet, sir, will never complain again," right out of the Knapp sales manual. "I bet your feet will even thank you," and he'd held up a cross section of a real shoe. "The Knapp has come into your life. And what is a Knapp? It is the friend to the workingman's feet."

Bud had thanked Mr. Wait for his purchase of a pair of the shoes by returning the next Saturday with an angel food cake Edith had baked. They had been friends since then, sometimes with Mr. Wait coming to their house for dinner, sometimes their visiting him here.

Mr. Wait turned to Callum. "They teach you anything?"

"At school? Yes, sir."

"What?"

"Stuff."

Mr. Wait shouted, "Hard knocks," at his Knapps.

"Yes, sir," Callum said.

"I guess you know I live alone." He looked over at Callum. "When you live alone you can't disappoint yourself. People'll always let you down if you give 'em a chance, period and no exceptions."

"Mom and Dad haven't let me down," he said.

"They will, sonny, sooner or later, they will. No offense, Bud, but mark my words."

"But how?" Callum asked.

"Probably in the worst kind of way."

"Well, I don't know about that," Bud said.

Mr. Wait slapped the stack of papers loud enough to make Bob turn his head. "Oh hey," he said. He slipped off the stack, ran to the porch, and came back holding a newspaper. He sat back down, turning the pages. "Here it is here," he said. "Darned if I didn't see this the other day and I thought of you."

Bud smiled. "What is it, a stock market report?"

"You asked me to keep an eye peeled for stuff about Walt. Remember? Well, he's over in Denmark with his wife and little girls."

"What do you suppose he's doing over there?"

"Having fun. Rock candy, rides, a roller coaster, things like that."

"He could have *fun* at the Pike."

"He wouldn't go near it," Callum said.

The Pike in Long Beach, as far as Callum knew, catered to pickpockets, dope addicts, molesters, and nuts. Its best attraction, a roller coaster named the Cyclone, went off its tracks it seemed every other week. Each spring when it opened, the authorities talked about closing it down, but nothing was ever done. Teenage girls disappeared from the Pike into white slavery, and old folks got mugged in plain sight. Grandmothers were raped in front of their old husbands. Babies were eaten. The Pike was so scary kids had nightmares about it. Callum yearned to go there just to see if he could survive.

Bud said, "If I know Walt, he didn't cross the wide Atlantic to ride a whirligig."

"Maybe he's picking up a new dream," said Mr. Wait.

Bud faced him. His mouth was open and he let out a low sound. The look in his eyes, which opened wide and then squinted with the effort of thought, was altogether that of someone who had just had an idea but could not quite remember what it was. "You think so?"

Mr. Wait brought the paper up to his eyes. "It's just a bitty story, Bud, under the real estate column." He put down the paper and, staring at Bud, asked, "What, you forget something Edith asked you to do?"

"You're a pack rat," Edith scolded Bud, resting her hands on her hips. She was putting out a pie to cool on the back porch and was watching him. She fanned herself in the heat. "I don't see why you save those things. You never look at them."

"You do not throw away *Life*," said Bud as though it were a law. He was bent over binding *Life* magazines with bailing twine. The bundle would join the stacks of twelve years' saving in the garage. He had hauled the magazines out from New England; Bud had packed the *Life*s in the moving truck before the furniture.

"There won't be room in the garage pretty soon," Edith harped on.

Bud straightened up. "What's the matter with you? You sound to me like you need a back rub."

Edith smiled wanly. A back rub would be nice, she thought. She often asked Bud to give her one when the tensions got bad. "It's the waiting for the Job's Daughters, I guess," she told him. "Now, are you going to do something about those magazines?"

"Jeez, Edith, yes. But you don't know the sacrifice. They aren't just magazines. These are collector's items. Someday they will be worth . . . well, a lot."

Callum walked out the kitchen door following the scent of apple pie.

"One day these will be his inheritance," Bud said, meaning Callum. "How would it be, Edith, if he and I just sorted them?"

"Thank you," she said and suddenly was gone inside, yelling at Cloud and Blue to, pray God, stop doing nothing.

Maybe she had a point, Bud saw when he entered the garage a moment later. He looked at the *Life*s every time he started the car, but he had not really noticed how they had crept up the wall like a pulpy vine, year after year. In that sense the *Life*s were a kind of clock. And what had he done in all that time? For one thing he had brought the family out from New England, out of the cold and the old. He had worked hard. They owned their house, and there was food on the table. The kids were his pride, and he had cashed in his dreams to raise them. He knew he would never see Bora Bora or pan for gold in Alaska. He had settled on dreams closer to home, accommodating, simple, homespun dreams that still gave life zest.

Sorting the *Life* magazines did not mean tossing them out. He had to know what he was discarding, which meant perusing them one at a time. He told Callum to set aside the issues that dealt with World War II or had anything historical on the cover, and when in doubt, ask before throwing. It was a walk down memory lane, all those events that had slipped his mind, like the bombing of Nanking. Now there was something! Or Baldini's ride over Niagara in the rubber barrel. Or the brother-can-you-spare-a-dime photo of that poor bastard selling apples in the Depression. How about Winston Churchill with that Hav-a-Tampa touring the Battle of Britain grounds?

Bud was stretched out on the hood of the Ford with his back against the windshield. It was a cool place to spend an afternoon, in the shade, quiet, away from Edith and the house. "Pull down another bundle, will you?" he asked Callum, who was dawdling over a feature article on the cowboy entertainer Lash LaRue.

Callum stood on his tiptoes, and as he lunged at the uppermost bundle, the whole stack teetered and fell. A hundred *Life*s spilled over the car. Bud did not see the torrent of pulp until it was too late. Just as he was appreciating the regal profile of the Lion of Juda, he was buried in *Life*s. He started laughing as he pulled himself free. "Can you imagine the obituary?" he asked Callum, who had scrambled from under the magazines.

Bud rolled over on his side as Callum swept the hood of the car clear of the magazines.

"Hey, hold on a second," Bud said. He stared at a feature that had fallen open under his chin.

" 'Walt Disney toys with Kiddieland: Abe Lincoln and Granny's Cabin featured attractions.' "

Bud brought his face down close to the page. " 'Buddy Ebsen in a porkpie hat and suit and spats dancing in front of a mirror.' " The article was about the animation of miniature three-dimensional characters made of string and wires and gears and cams, called Audio-Animatronics. These robots were going to be an attraction at a place called Kiddieland.

"I don't remember hearing anything about that," Bud said to Callum. "It says here it was planned for a site by the LA Flood Control Canal and Riverside Drive. We've gone by there." Then he remembered. "That new state freeway was built instead right over the canal. That explains it."

"Kiddieland never got built?"

"Right," he said and hurriedly checked the issue date on the cover before tearing out the page. His face looked ecstatic, like it was split with a once-in-a-lifetime epiphany. "Walt," he said out loud, "why you sneaky son of a gun."

Callum, who felt like laughing just looking at Bud, thought, *Here we go again.*

2

Pow Wow Wow

"You probably wonder why I asked you by," Bud said to the group of friends and neighbors assembled that starry evening on his backyard lanai. He smoothed the crease of his twill pants to give his hands something to do. And while he waited for them to settle down, he appraised his heart's universe.

Japanese lanterns in pastels cast a warm glow on Edith, who looked lovely in a party apron bordered with ruffles. She thought enough about the importance of the evening to wear her special family brooch with the gold filigree and small diamonds, each of its five points representing a child, herself, and of course, Bud. She was holding an electric coffee percolator from which she had just refilled Gladys's cup. Gladys was in her pineapple muumuu. The pineapples looked like bombs. She pushed her sunglasses up on the bridge of her nose, then plucked a coconut Indio date off the milk-glass plate that Cheval passed her. Cheval was doing all she could to hold in her high spirits. She wore a halter top and short skirt as though she had no idea the effect she had on men even if she were dressed in a sheet.

Cloud and Blue stood near her, admiring Cheval's womanliness as something they instinctively wanted and hoped to achieve. They

studied her smoky laughter, secretly imitated her barroom vocabu-
lary, and tried to move their slender hips with Cheval's fetching
full-bodied rhythm. They looked up to her in every way, and when
the group gathered together like this evening, they were never more
than feet from her side.

Callum leaned against the wall, balancing in his palm an opened
spiral binder. He touched the end of the ballpoint to his tongue and,
as the evening's official secretary, worried that people would talk
too fast for him to record their words.

Bud crossed his legs at the knee. "Will the meeting please come
to order?" he asked.

Callum wrote down the words in the notebook.

The men, crowded on the swinging porch sofa and a couple of
metal chairs, did not hear. Each of them was Bud's close friend, but
only Milton counted as a relative, a brother-in-law. He was so unlike
his sister Edith it was hard to see how they were related; Milton was
odd and flighty and independent without meaning to be. He would
have hated to hear Bud call him an oddball. But how else to describe
someone who raised parakeets in a cage in his backyard and once
hypnotized himself into a trance that for a while seemed permanent?
He thought of himself as normal and would point to his uniform,
his Sam Browne belt and chukka boots, and his gabardine slacks
and shirt as signs. Milton did not want to be different. He simply
couldn't help himself.

Roland, who was whispering an off-color joke to Milton, was the
most flamboyant of them. He wore a silk foulard ascot, and his curly
blond hair was slick and smelled of lilac vegetal. He owned a shoe
store. That sounded like a boring job, but it did not describe
Roland's Buster Brown. Only last Christmas he had placed a naked
female mannequin in a porcelain bathtub crawling with live Mexican lobsters in the front display window. The lobsters attracted
crowds that the police were called in to control. It was inevitable
that the women of the Job's Daughters complained, and the police
chief had ordered Roland to dress the mannequin in a brassiere and
panties or face a twenty-dollar fine for cruelty to animals.

Mr. Wait had arrived wearing a silver bola tie set with a rough
turquoise stone. His khaki pants, stiff with starch, crinkled like

paper when he moved. Now and then he left his metal armchair to go out of the lanai with a treat for Bob, who made his presence known by his heavy breathing in the doorway.

P.O., their neighbor from three houses down (he was Cheval's boyfriend and, not incidentally, a hero of World War II), was holding out his plate asking Edith for another serving of her tamales. When he smiled he resembled a matinee idol, for his chiseled features were tanned a soft brown from his work under the sweet California sun as a land surveyor. His youthful good looks, however, stood in stark contrast to his gray dandelion-gone-to-seed hair, sticking straight out like he'd just been shocked. He said the hair was a legacy of the war, and nobody had ever asked him to elaborate, just as nobody had ever asked him what the letters P.O. stood for. Bud sometimes commented on how strange it was for him to have known P.O. for as long as he had without even knowing his name.

The women looked at their men with wifely love. Wifely love was altogether different from puppy or infatuated or especially passionate love, because it was tempered with equal measures of humor and an appreciation of weakness. When Edith pointed out to Cheval the workingmen's Knapps that unified their men, both women bent over at the waist with suppressed laughter, like mechanical birds on the edge of a drinking glass.

"I suppose you wonder why I asked you by," Bud shouted, and by the rosy color of his cheeks, he was mad. He pulled at the lapels of the tweed sport jacket he rescued year after year from Edith's Goodwill pile.

"For Edith's tamales?" P.O. asked. "*Muy excelente*, Edith"

Bud was already feeling like an animal trainer without having to shout like one. But getting this group's attention was like convincing seals to bounce balls on their noses. "No, the tamales aren't the reason, P.O. But they sure were good, Edith. The reason why is the reason we moved out to California in the first place."

Milton raised his arm like a kid at school. The Sam Browne belt rode up over his stomach, exposing the gun holster that he polished with a passion even though the holster had never held a thing more lethal than a box of Milk Duds.

"Milt?" Bud said.

"To get out of the cold?" He adjusted the holster for emphasis.

"No, Milt, I didn't get us all together to discuss warmth."

"That's why I came out here." He patted the patrolman's hat in his lap like it was a puppy.

Edith looked at her brother, and her hand covered her mouth. Not that she cared about her buck teeth in this crowd. She was feeling frisky, and this party under the stars in the pastel lights matched her mood exactly. She touched her family brooch, seeing Bud so serious. She thought about how friends did not need reasons to get together besides love. They were all so frugal and poor, anyway, how else were they going to entertain themselves? Hop tables at the Brown Derby?

"I came out here to make costumes," Roland said softly. "Before I got religion. Reee-lig-ion!" he shouted suddenly, raising his face to the lanai ceiling.

Everybody stared at him. They respected his faith, but they could never seem to get used to his fervor.

"We all appreciate your beliefs, Rollie," Bud said as gently as he knew how.

"Because I was born here," Mr. Wait said.

"Okay, what about you, P.O.?" Bud asked, resigned to let them all have a say.

He bounced his hands under his chest. "For the titties on the beaches."

"Please, P.O.," Roland said, chancing a glance at Cheval, whose breasts, on display in their halter top, were surely more interesting than Jane Russell's, even to a religious man like himself.

Callum officiously touched the end of the ballpoint to his tongue.

"I mean *to dream*," Bud said to a murmur of assent. He re-crossed one leg with the other, executive-style, and lifted his empty coffee cup as a signal to Edith, who came over with the percolator. The other men held out their cups, too. "Let me ask you a question," he continued. "Who is the one person we share in common? Who is the one person we love the most?"

"Jesus Christ," Roland replied.

"Jesus Christ, yes, Jesus Christ," Bud said, not getting the reply he expected. "Him but who else?"

The men looked at one another in silent contemplation, but as hard as they searched their memories, they kept coming back to Jesus Christ. Of course, they all liked Milton Berle. Jack Benny was okay. They enjoyed Vaughn Monroe and Johnny Ray and Patti Page. Some of them liked Ike. But the truth was they couldn't say the real answer, not out loud. They loved and admired each other most.

"Okay, who?" P.O. asked.

"Walt, of course!" Bud replied.

Heads bobbed all around. Callum scribbled "Walt Disney" twice in his spiral binder.

"He's our boy, all right," P.O. agreed.

"When you wish upon a star," Milton said.

"Hi diddle dee dee," Callum said to no one in particular and wrote it down.

"He's the kingfish," said P.O. "He swims through dreams the way a shark swims through the water."

Milton looked at him. "How's that?"

"Day and night, day and night."

"Walt's a dreamer," Bud said, getting them under control again. "We're dreamers. Don't we dream of hooking our fortunes to a shooting star? Walt himself just streaked by, don't you know it, and has shown us the way."

Mr. Wait looked up at the ceiling as though to see the stars. "He just streaked by?"

"I meant that he's dreaming new dreams all the time."

"Yeah, for kids," Roland said.

"Oh? Just for kids? How many times you see *Sleeping Beauty*, Rollie?"

"I don't remember," he said, blushing again, which turned his milky complexion crimson.

"Come on, come on, don't be shy."

"Nine . . . okay, nineteen not counting the one I couldn't see because I had the sty."

"Not just for kids then." Bud held out his arms. "His dreams are meant for everybody."

"I suppose that's true enough," Roland said.

"The next question is, What if Walt has a new dream, and his new dream means he has to find a new line of work?"

"Like hairdressing?" P.O. asked.

"I'm trying to be serious here, P.O." Bud cleared his throat. "What if he built a world people like us could visit for Mickey Mouse and Donald Duck and all their friends to live in?"

"Walt makes cartoons," said Roland. "That's all he'll ever do."

"Maybe not, maybe that's where our dream meets his dream in a funny kind of way."

"You're thinking, like, a fun zone?" Roland asked. "Like whirligigs, that kind of thing?"

"That's it, Rollie," Bud replied.

"A carnival. Walt Disney, a carney operator?" Milton asked.

"Yeah, but different."

"He doesn't know the first thing about carnies."

"He's been in Copenhagen and Brighton, England, to find out."

"Disney is not in the land business," Roland pointed out.

"He's in the business of making his dreams come true," Bud said. "Some people write books. Some people paint pictures. He thinks up a mouse, draws it, then animates it. Mickey is as real as you and me on the movie screen. What's the next step? Make the mouse come alive *off* the movie screen."

Milt squirmed in his seat. "Bud, that sounds goofy."

"Maybe not. If I'm right, Walt is thinking of building an amusement park where Mickey and Goofy and Donald Duck can live, like it's their home. We're going to find out where before he does."

"You mean a kind of movie set the public visits?" Roland said as Bud's concept dawned.

"Well, thank you," Bud said. "That's why he went to Europe, to see how they run amusement parks. The Tivoli Gardens are nice, for families. He already tried once with this Kiddieland."

"A needle in a haystack," said P.O., shaking his dandelion head.

"I don't think so," Bud said. "Milt's reason for moving out here was sunshine. Is Walt going to build a fun zone where it's frozen? Of course not."

"Florida's sunny," Milton said.

"Florida isn't where Walt has his movie studio," Bud pointed out.

"He would need set designers to build the place," said Roland, again catching Bud's drift and thinking how perfectly logical it sounded, once he adjusted his thinking to include imagined characters in a real setting. "Set designers and builders are only in Hollywood."

"Now you're really catching on," Bud said.

"But where?" P.O. asked, standing up to facilitate thinking.

"He'll be wary of land speculators," Bud said. "I can't think of a better place than right here in our own backyard, so to speak. I *feel* it. Here's how we horn in on his dream. We find out where he's going to build his place. We get hold of a small piece of the land and when Walt comes to buy, we own the controlling quarter acre or so."

"Could you explain that again?" Milton asked. "I'm seeing this, Bud, but I'm not seeing it."

"We know what he plans to do. We find out where. It's around here somewhere. It could even be two streets from here. I just know it is close. We speculate. Walt then has to deal with us or he doesn't build his dream. It's that simple."

"I still don't see how we can find it," said Roland, sweeping the lanai with his arm, meaning all of them.

Bud tapped his forehead. "We use what God gave us."

"Remind me what that is," said Roland, laughing a little with the glee he was feeling for their having a solid scheme to work on again.

"Mr. Wait knows land," Bud replied. "P.O. knows stuff about county and city offices, Roland knows Hollywood, Edith and the girls and Gladys know people in town, and Milton . . . well."

"He knows birds," Gladys said with a wan smile.

Everybody laughed without knowing they were laughing not at Milton but for the fun of adventure.

"What about you, Bud?" asked Milton. "What do you have to offer?"

"I know *you*, all of you."

"Doesn't sound like God gave us much."

"You'd be surprised," Bud said.

"In a cavern, in a canyon, excavating for a mine, lived a miner, forty-niner, and his daughter, Clementine. . . ."

A young man wearing a miner's costume who took tickets and watched over the gold-miners' amusement rolled his eyes as if to say these duffers were more a nuisance than the price of admission should ever allow. They had arrived at the mine a couple hours ago gabbing about how warm their bellies felt full of Knott's Berry Farm hot chicken dinners with dumplings and gravy. And unlike most visitors they would not leave, as if they actually believed the California Gold Mine was for real.

The sluice where they were standing was built on the edge of Old Town near the tracks, in a depression of Gunnite walls shaped to look like boulders. The ticket booth stood by the exit to an ersatz mine shaft that was dark and stuffed with dummies meant to look like dead miners. The sluice itself was nothing but a long wooden rectangular box. For fifty cents, visitors got a feel for what life had been like panning gold with a real tin pan. Once they had given up, everyone got a little corked vial of iron pyrite to remember the place by.

Bud looked real enough in jeans and a bright red Pendleton shirt. He was leaning into the sluice swishing sand and congratulating himself on a fleck here and there in the bottom of his pan. "Hey, buster," he called to the young man. He was sweating from the heat of the sun, and his arms felt heavy. "Is there any real gold in here? I mean, we've been panning now for a while. We're showin' squat for color."

"Mr. Knott himself powders the sluice every evening," the young man said.

"Powders it, huh?"

"You didn't expect nuggets?" And he laughed deridingly.

"I expect the luck of the draw," Bud told him.

He fished around in the eddy of sand in Bud's pan with his finger. A single flake came out on his nail. "There's your gold."

"This?"

"It's like the history," he said.

"How's that?"

"The nuggets got all the attention back in the Gold Rush days. From what I've read, dust was the rule."

"Can I tell you something?" The guy nodded. "You shouldn't work here."

"Oh thanks a lot."

"You've worked here too long already."

"Just because I said there were no nuggets—"

"Want to know why?" He was going to tell him anyway. "I have never met a miner. I have not read one book about miners. But I know that no miner ever prospected for dust. You may end up with dust. You may end up with that speck on your finger. But you dream of nuggets."

"What's all the palaver about?" Milton asked from the side of the sluice where he was washing sand for his share of the gold. Unlike P.O. and Roland and Mr. Wait, he had not dressed up Western, not even in a bandana. The young man at first stiffened seeing his uniform and the Sam Browne belt and the chukka boots and his gabardine pants and the hat with the grommet and the burnished black bill.

"You a cop?" he asked.

"Yes and no," Milton told him.

"What's the no?"

"A night watchman."

Bud said to Milton, "I am trying to get this guy to tell me if we're wasting our time."

"Kinda looks like it," Milton said. Hearing the conversation, the others laid down their pans.

Bud had come to Knott's to pan gold. He had not come to be colorful. If there was gold to be mined here, they would mine it to death. If the sluice was an amusement for kids and women, what was the use? The sign said this was an authentic gold mine. It encouraged visitors to Knott's Berry Farm to take a chance just like the forty-niners. A chance meant something worth winning, and Bud wanted to know exactly what that was.

"Whether you're wasting your time depends on what you're looking for," the young man said.

"Ah, gold?"

"Then you're not wasting your time."

"Quantity is what we're after. Nuggets, in a word. You seem to think a speck is El Dorado."

"Then you'd be wasting your time."

"How much dust does Mr. Knott sprinkle in here every night?" The young man pursed his lips. "You'd have to ask him that."

Bud threw the pan in the sluice. "Milt, it's a ruse," he said loud enough for the visitors passing by to hear. "Pack it up, fellas. It's a *scam*."

"I'm sure I can arrange to return your fifty cents," the young man said.

"Good. We'll take it," P.O. told him.

"Where to now?" Bud asked.

He regarded P.O. as an authority on Knott's by dint of his having surveyed the Berry Farm's parking lot. Knott's was a tourist theme park, the first in California. The theme was the Wild West, grown out of a boysenberry roadside stand. To attract customers, Mrs. Knott had set out on a card table a wooden replica of a wagon train just like the forty-niners'. And pretty soon one thing led to another and by now Knott's was as famous as the La Brea Tar Pits.

P.O. rubbed his chin. "I don't suppose you'd want to ride the steam train?"

"It only goes in a circle," Roland observed.

"I thought so. What about Boot Hill?"

"Not yet," said Mr. Wait.

P.O. jangled the coins in his pocket. "We still have our fifty cents. If we pool it we can get our picture taken."

"Now *that's* an idea," Bud said.

They wandered over the tracks and up the far end of Main Street. It looked like a movie version of an Old West town, with a boardwalk and two rows of facing wooden-framed shops and storefronts. In the window of the Chinese laundry hung a sign that said, NO TICKEE, NO LAUNDREE. On the door of the Sheriff's Office a note advised "Gone Fishin' ." Music from a player piano came through the swinging doors of a sasparilla saloon. The sticky smell of anise and horehound and ropes of licorice wafted into the dusty street from the General Store. Every now and then a fellow on a saddled horse or a girl on a buckboard went by for atmosphere.

"This is what I was talkin' about," Bud said, coming to a halt by a hitching post in front of the camera shop, an anachronism that was hard to explain.

The others looked up and down the street, but it was plain to see that they needed help.

"What?" Milton asked.

"Well, just think about it. Look around. What is this?"

"Old Town," Callum said.

"What does it represent?"

"The way things used to be."

"Exactly. Mr. Knott had the idea that people like us would pay to see what the West used to be like. He hoked it up a bit. Who cares? People around here want to know. They feel a part of it. What's this Main Street except a movie set that isn't used for movies? The difference between Mr. Knott and Walt Disney is that Walt Disney has created his own . . . ah, what's the word?"

"Myth?" Mr. Wait offered.

"Myth. There's the myth of the Old West and there's Mickey and Donald Duck myths."

It seemed so real here, it was like being a part of the Wild West. This was no longer Bud's crazy idea. Standing on Main Street watching the buckboard with the pretty girl in the blue bonnet go by, it all made sense.

As they entered the photo shop, Bud started to sing, and pretty soon the others joined in: "It ain't no trick to get rich quick if you dig dig dig with a shovel and a pick—in a mine mine mine where a million diamonds shine . . ." A plain woman in a hoop skirt and a cowgirl hat greeted them with a curtsy.

"What can I do you for, gents?" she asked.

"Take our picture," P.O. told her. "It's a historical moment we've got here."

"Choose your scenery then," she said.

They looked around them at paintings of outdoor scenes of the West on large standing sheets of plywood: one of a buffalo hunt, another of a Conestoga wagon on a prairie, and yet another of a bucking bronco. People posed donning hats appropriate to the scene behind the plywood, fitting their arms and head in the cutouts.

"Gold miners," Bud said.

"You boys seem like you'd know your way around a mine, too," she said, flattering them needlessly.

They picked hats off pegs and stood behind the plywood. Callum climbed up on a bench. Then they stuck their necks and arms in the scenery to blend in. The woman bent behind the wooden box camera. She put her hands on her hips. Something was wrong with the camera, and she told them to relax, she'd be back in a moment.

"Let me ask you a question, Bud," said Mr. Wait, who gave the appearance from the camera's side of the plywood of carrying a Wells Fargo sack.

"Fire away, pardner."

"Let's say we find the place—"

"Let's keep our voices down, huh?" Bud said.

Mr. Wait gave the room a squint. "Let's say we find what we're looking for. According to you we buy an acre or less to get a toehold. What I'd like to know is how? I don't have to remind you, we don't have any money, none of us. I mean, we're poor."

"The man in question," Bud said, "isn't going to buy land that's already developed. He'll be looking for a bargain. So that means orange groves or bean fields, places like that. Beach front? I doubt it. An acre of bean field goes for what?"

"It can get up there. It'd surprise you. Eight hundred dollars?"

Bud whistled through his teeth. "That much?"

"We could be talkin' here about money we just don't have."

"And can't get," Roland added.

They fell silent and watched the woman return with a photographic plate, which she slid in the back of the camera. She draped a black cloth over her head and looked through the lens. "Okay," she said. "Now say eureka!"

The men looked disappointed, even crestfallen. They had not figured on problems, and now it looked like the dream was over before it had begun. As if it were a dirge, the men repeated, "Eureka!" And the flashbulbs popped.

"Perfect," she declared. "I'll have this developed in a jiffy, one for each of you?" No one replied, and she asked again.

"Sure, oh sure," Bud told her.

"This puts a crimp in things," Milton said when she left the room.

"Money," said Roland. "It always comes down to dollars and cents."

"Which we don't have," said Milton.

"It was a good dream, Bud," said Mr. Wait.

"Here you go, pardners," the photo woman said, coming back

into the room. She was holding photos in paper folders with "Knott's" emblazoned across the front. She inspected the photo before handing it to Bud. "You guys look like you just struck the motherlode," she said.

Bud looked at the photo for a long time, thinking. Seconds ago, they had looked happy and sounded full of promise. And now they were in the dumps. He pulled his hands out of the scenery and put them resolutely on his waist. "Let's not give up on it this easily," he told them. "You fellas concentrate on finding the needle in the haystack. I'll take care of the rest."

"What are you going to do, Bud, rob a bank?" asked Milton.

Annoyed by the sound of his voice, Bud replied, "If you get a job as a night watchman at one, Milt, I just might try."

"You must be Mr. Wait."

"I haven't always been," said Mr. Wait, standing in the middle of his orange grove. It was the mid-afternoon, about the time he made his rounds every day, visiting his trees, one by one. The day was another in a long string of beautiful weather; Mr. Wait knew it wouldn't last. The cold snap was due soon.

"Glad to meet you," the stranger told him and stuck out his hand, but he did not offer his name. A man who pitched a nameless hand deserved to be watched, Mr. Wait thought.

"How did you get here?" Mr. Wait asked him.

He looked around. "Walked," he said.

They were a half mile and more from a public road in any direction. The man wasn't a walker, that much was plain. He had pudgy cheeks, short arms and legs, and a belly he maintained, by the looks of him, with loving care. His scalp shone even brighter than his shoes. What remained of his hair, sprouts around his ears, was frazzled and ignored. That, and he wasn't dressed for a stroll in a grove. His polished Oxfords were muddy, and a sharkskin suit with a press hardly identified him as a farmer. His hands were clasped as though he were a salesman closing a deal.

"I assume you're lost," Mr. Wait told him. "Your car run out of gas on the highway?"

"Not exactly. I was just looking around."

"A grove? What's there to see in a grove?"

"Lots, if you know how to look."

"You're not telling me anything. You're trespassing on private property here, you know."

"Oh, now . . . strictly speaking you're right." And he suppressed a yawn.

"I *know* I'm right. You're one of those real estate johnnies. Am I right?"

"Yes," he said, puffing up as though being a real estate agent were a distinction. "I was trying to calculate the acreage."

"The maps in the county tax assessor's office list exactly what I own."

"I also felt like getting out of the office."

"A field report."

"That's correct." He pointed toward the muffled sounds in the distance, and changing the subject, he asked, "Do you know the grower on the other side of the highway?"

"She keeps a fine orchard."

"Then you know her."

"I know who she is."

"I was over there earlier. Mrs. Mary Rodriguez. She's very much like you. She loves her land. Old school. She's not old herself."

Mr. Wait offered the man a thin smile. "Would you like me to tell you why you are trespassing on my land?"

He nodded.

"The state is planning to run a freeway through here. It needs my land to complete the job. So it's not going to be a free way for me. Am I getting warm?"

"My lips are sealed."

"Why not come out and say it?"

"There are considerations."

"Such as if the state was identified, I'd panic. You act on its behalf. That way, the state thinks I don't know."

"Let's say for the sake of argument that I know where this new freeway is going. Let's say I buy your land cheap and sell it to the state at a profit."

"But you're not doing that, are you? You are not what you say you are."

He shrugged his shoulders. "What does it matter? You will make out no matter what I am."

Mr. Wait stared at him. "Making out isn't making out if I lose my grove. What's a freeway but a strip of concrete? My grove is a living thing. The state will have to push me off with bulldozers."

"There are less obvious means."

Mr. Wait could not think of one.

"There's eminent domain or there's progress. You can hear its roar from here. Compared to that, the state is a gentle giant. When you have businesses on your borders, your property will be too valuable for oranges. So you will have no other choice. And if you refuse to sell, the state will take your land for defaulting on taxes."

Mr. Wait was beginning to understand how alone he was. "Why are you telling me all of this?" he asked.

"I wanted you to know your options. I would have gone to your house but I was told you don't greet all comers. I was told you wander your grove. I hoped I'd meet up with you eventually. You are famous. You and your jackass are as well known as anything in the Historical Museum over on Prasker. What do you do, Mr. Wait, when you are wandering your grove?"

"You wouldn't understand."

"I'm serious. I'd like to know."

"I suggest you ask at the museum."

The man turned and walked away. A piece of white paper fluttered from his hands, which Mr. Wait picked up—a business card, probably dropped on purpose. It was how people like him worked.

It said, RICKY CONSTANTINOPLE, REALTOR.

It was so hot the smell of road tar suffused the air. Every living soul had run for shade except Bud, who kept a wary eye out for a familiar face as he crossed the street about a block in back of Rankin's department store. He was out of breath when he reached the other side, and pretended to be interested in the front window of a stationery store until his heart stopped racing.

Even without the address he would have known the place on sight. How could you miss three brass balls? A husband and father like himself *needed* that many to do what he was about to do. Bud felt like a geek in Tijuana hawking Spanish fly and French ticklers with pastel feathers on their tips. Deep in his heart he knew the risk, but like a drunk with a jigger of gin, he could not help himself.

He pretended to walk past the shop, and he veered at the last instant into the seclusion of the glassed-in alcove. The display windows held the treasures of folks fallen on hard times. Bud didn't need to look to know what they were—electric guitars, radios and TVs, wedding rings and war medals, rifles and pistols, bows and arrows, bongo drums and Hawaiian steel guitars like Don Ho's. Windows in pawn shops were the graveyards of dreams. Did the young man ever imagine that the guitar that he dreamed would rocket him to fame would end up here? Did the woman young no more imagine that the wedding ring that once held the hope of bliss would be offered for sale alongside a used Gurkha knife?

A bell tinkled a greeting as he opened the door. The noise in his head sounded like a gong. He closed the door behind him like a man slipping out of the cold.

It dawned on him as he found his bearings that dreams, not value, gave common objects their worth. What was the archer's bow on the shelf but a shaft of wood until touched by an imagination that saw in its grain Indians and buffaloes and heard in the twang of its string sharp excited cries on the wind? The whole world and everyone in it dulled without dreams. What was love but a dream with a little friction? No one touched by love ever doubted how its light turned the plainest Jane into a beauty capable of cracking a brave man's heart. Even potentates and princes couldn't say where dreams came from. But Bud thought he knew. He was a dream merchant, and now he was about to sell one to give life to another.

He walked to the back of the shop, where a man was sitting in a cage of iron mesh, like a captive bird. His sleeves were rolled up, and he smelled vinegary with nervous sweat. He had a black eye-shade on his forehead and a jeweler's loupe over one eye. Seeing Bud, he put down a ruby ring he had been examining for flaws. With a look of indifference, he asked, "How can I help you?"

Bud's mouth felt parched. And when he tried to speak he croaked. The man was patient with him. After all, why wouldn't he be? The most pathetic side of human behavior was his stock in trade. He was the embalmer of dreams. And he seemed to recognize in Bud someone who was on the brink of the kind of extinction he knew well. He believed the dying had certain rights. Time and dignity were among them.

"You want to go out and think about it?" he asked.

"I already have."

"Then you'll have to show me."

Bud opened his hand. In his palm was Edith's family brooch.

The man snapped the loupe down over his eye. He made satisfied sounds in his throat and after a moment's inspection said, "This is a nice item."

Bud winced. The brooch was no item. He knew it was nice without being told. Edith marked each star point with their children's names, then touched her lips to its gold center as tenderly as she kissed Callum or Cloud or Blue good night on their foreheads. Bud had given her the brooch ten years ago. It had cost him the money he had inherited when his mother died. This was all they owned as a family that was worth anything—that *meant* anything. As sure as he was standing in this pawn shop, Edith would leave him if she discovered his thieving.

But what was he thinking? Negativism, was all. Without risks like this one, there was no gain. Only pikers expected to hit the jackpot betting pennies. And what kind of a risk was pawning Edith's brooch? He would be back in a matter of weeks, and he would have the money to buy Edith a pearl necklace to boot.

Look on the bright side, he told himself. *There's a diamond waiting out there.*

"I have to tell you—" the man said.

Bud's dream collided with the more powerful hope that he would be sent away.

"—I don't usually handle anything this nice. People who come in here are bottom feeders. They don't know quality. All they care about are knives and guns, Cuban bongos, and shitty fraternity rings."

"Then you're not interested?" He sounded both delighted and dejected.

"Normally I wouldn't be. You don't look like the kind of guy I get in here either." The man raised the loupe. "I can give you eighteen hundred," he said.

"It cost more."

He blew his cheeks. "That's my offer," he said.

Nobody will be the wiser, Bud told himself.

"I came out here from New England," he started to explain.

"Did you now?"

"I wanted to make things better—" and he stopped himself. Why was he explaining to a man he did not know? "Okay, now it's yours," he told him with resolve.

The man slipped the brooch into a drawer, which he locked with a key.

"Take good care of it," Bud said. "It's not a lark, this."

"If it doesn't sell, you can always buy it back. That's how the system works." He wrote out a pawn ticket.

"Do you think it will?"

"I can't say." He counted out the money. "I wish you luck," he said.

"I need luck less than I need calculation."

"A hot tip on a horse?"

"A horse of a different color, you might say."

3

Woe Be to the Orphan

Cloud and Blue had arranged themselves on the living room sofa, in mourning over a fallen idol.

"Yes, it is tragic," Edith told them, watching them through eyes that questioned the true depth of their grief. She was trying to recall who this idol was—an actor, a crooner? If not by death than by worse-than-death, they came and were forgotten, it seemed to her, so soon.

The girls tried to find positions on the divan that mirrored their feelings of loss. Cloud sobbed in her throat and wiped her nose furtively across her sleeve. Blue was nearly prostrate on the cushions, gazing at a deep middle distance. She was searching her memory for the idol's career highlights.

"Is this a bad time for you?" Edith asked.

"For what?" Blue hiccuped with sorrow.

"A talk."

"What's—"

Edith held up a powder blue envelope addressed in royal blue ink.

"The invitation!" the girls screamed in unison. They were off the divan in a hop, dancing in each other's arms.

The invitation to join Job's Daughters had come in the mail that morning. Edith had hugged it to her breast like a lost child found. "This is *my* dream," she had told Bud.

Edith read the invitation. "I hardly have time to make the gowns," she said, nearly out of breath with joy.

The initiation gowns meant as much to her as the Job's Daughters' lofty goals. The gowns were made of pure white satin and crafted with goffered shoulders, a demure front, and a waist that bunched and draped to the tips of covered-to-match pumps. They symbolized a part of life Edith felt she had missed. She wanted to be included, it didn't matter in what, so long as it mattered to others. Job's was the most exalted sorority in Garden Grove. It had a national charter and pretensions that satisfied her social ambitions. Edith could not have imagined anything better.

"There's so much to do," she said, exhilarated and overwhelmed at once. "*Hmm.*" She read the invitation one more time. "There's a grand prize of fifty dollars this year."

Bud appeared in the doorway carrying an empty restaurant-sized mayonnaise jar in his hands. "Did someone say fifty dollars?"

"Prize for what?" Cloud asked.

"The talent contest, you know, like I told you. They have them every year at the initiation night."

Bud jangled the few pennies he had deposited in the mayonnaise-jar bank.

"Mom, the money could go toward Dad's dream-scheme," Cloud said, as usual currying Bud's favor. Cloud knew with an uncanny accuracy that Bud's favorite child was Callum and Edith's was Blue, which left her in a wilderness where no child ever wanted to be.

"The gang would be awfully proud of you if you did," said Bud. "Fifty dollars sure would help."

"Imagine," Edith said.

Bud asked Edith with more than idle curiosity, "What do they have to do?"

"Win."

He looked doubtfully at the girls. "Is there a second prize?"

Edith laughed as if he'd been trying to be funny. "Oh Bud."

"But *what* can they do?"

Edith put her finger to her cheek. "Let's see. Cloud can play the scales on the clarinet." She paused to consider. "No." She looked at Blue. "She can recite poetry." She paused again. "No."

"Anything?"

"We can *dance!*" Blue shouted, revealing her most cherished image of herself. She had taken ballet lessons, but the hard work never matched the image of a swan-necked ballerina in a pastel tutu and toe shoes. The lessons had stopped. The vision had stayed.

"We can make it a real family affair," Bud said.

"We can try," said Cloud, giving Blue her best sidelong glance.

Edith took the girls to Mrs. Hamel's that afternoon.

Mrs. Dora Hamel ran Garden Grove's ballet studio, and quite a studio it was, too. It had a machine-polished wooden floor and mirrors behind the barre. Photographs of Anna Pavlova and Léonide Massine and other dancers decorated the walls. One photograph showed a pretty young woman with long, thin legs and willowy arms. By looking at Mrs. Hamel's water-swelled ankles and doughy hips you would hardly credit her with being the same person now.

"Dora, I want them to dance," Edith told her.

With her hand on her chin, Mrs. Hamel sized up Cloud and Blue in faded-blue school gym uniforms. They were squeaking their white gym sneakers on the waxed floor.

"What else can they do?"

Without thinking, Edith answered, "Why, Blue can read. Cloud can play on the clarinet."

"Then let them."

Edith laughed but she saw that Mrs. Hamel was serious. "It's not what I have in mind, Dora."

"I suppose they could do the *Minuet Waltz*. But you know, Edith, all the girls I get here are lazy slugs. Cloud and Blue are no exception. They only want the tutus and the toe shoes. They don't give a tinker's damn about ballet."

"Please, Dora?"

Mrs. Hamel nodded solemnly. "I guarantee they will do it correctly, Edith, even if they can't do it well. We might as well start right now."

She walked to the middle of the floor and spread her arms. "Now, Cloud," she said, "the young man holds the young lady—Blue, get over there—gently by the waist as she turns once, Blue. . . . Now do it! That's right, around . . . then stops."

Cloud glared at Mrs. Hamel as she slowly lowered her hands from Blue's waist. "*What* young man?" she asked, looking around the studio.

"Why, in the *Minuet*."

"I don't see a young man here. We're girls. I'm a girl, Mrs. Hamel."

"Remember how proud your father will be," Edith said. "*Fifty* dollars."

Cloud was screaming. "Does the young man wear the tutu and the toe shoes?"

"Ask your mother," Mrs. Hamel said, retreating to the barre.

"I'm sorry, sweetheart, but you are taller than Blue, and darker. You have to be the young man."

"What's the costume?"

"What do you imagine the young man would wear?"

"Not a tutu and toe shoes."

"We'll fix you up in something nice." Edith's face contorted with the effort to control her laughter.

"I'm asking, Mom, what's the costume?"

"Mom, don't do it," Blue shouted as if Edith were about to commit an irrevocable act.

Edith blurted out, "Black high-top sneakers and dyed-brown long johns," and leaned over laughing.

Cloud ran from the studio in tears.

Edith looked at where Cloud had been a second ago, then at Mrs. Hamel. "What difference does it make?" she asked.

What difference? Had she not seen the hotrods stop at the house? Had she not heard the horns calling out to the girls? It was a ritual as old as time made new by flames, louvered hoods, and neckers' knobs. Edith had forgotten the agonies of that age. The horns did not blow for Cloud. Dreaming they were calling to her, she went out to meet them, somehow aware that she was like the fat friend you always saw keeping the pretty girl company. Cloud knew. Oh, she knew.

.   .   .

Edith stopped at Wonder Bread's Day-Old Annex, where she stood in line to buy twenty loaves of partly stale white bread that she stored in the deep freeze. Everybody Edith knew bought the same. Day-old was a sign of the times, that and hand-me-downs, retread tires, reclaimed oil, and Parcheesi and Ouija when a first-run picture was at the Gem. Edith didn't think of herself as poor. Poor was a person without children, according to her thinking. Instead she considered herself frugal. And she never bothered to take time away from baking and sewing and hoeing the vegetable garden to reflect on the difference between the two.

Left to themselves Cloud and Blue dawdled down Main Street, gazing in the windows of the five-and-dime until they were bored, then dallying past the feed store to the Gem, where they checked coming attractions (*Rebel Without a Cause* was on the lobby card, and *Torpedo Run*). Cloud crossed the street and looked in a shop window where a brood of cocker puppies played on yellowed newspapers. Blue stood by her shoulder.

"Aren't they cute?" she asked.

Cloud knew that Blue was seeing something besides puppies. She would be weighing a chance to right a terrible wrong. Pets had formed a food chain under her care. Mittens had eaten Tweedie after Tweedie ate the chameleon that Blue had bought as living jewelry to pin on her powder-blue angora sweater. Mittens had upchucked Tweedie's green feathers and then hounded several white mice, a baby crocodile, a lacquered turtle, four hamsters—all dead now.

Blue had not yet owned a dog.

"I wonder if Mom'd let us?" Blue asked.

"Probably not."

"We could call it . . . yes, we could call it Scooter."

"We could ask."

Edith was a bit surprised that her daughters would want anything that required upkeep. She took their interest as a sign of maturity. "I don't see any harm looking," she told them as they were driving home.

"We already did," Blue said. "It's at the pet shop."

"The pet shop? Did you notice what it cost?"

"Twelve dollars," Cloud replied.

"And how much have you saved?"

"But we thought . . ."

"Where do you think money comes from? In case you've forgotten, we're frugal. The sooner you accept that, the happier you'll be. Besides, we're saving to help your father. You want to look for a dog? What about those poor things at the pound? If someone doesn't adopt them they get gassed."

"Please don't use that word," Blue said, turning a light shade of pale.

"Wouldn't it be nicer to *save* a dog?"

"A pound dog? Mom, pound dogs are used," Blue said. "Why can't we get something new for once?"

"It doesn't matter to me," Cloud said.

"How can I call a used dog Scooter?"

"Scooter? Where did that come from?"

"It's a *real* dog's name."

Edith, never one to procrastinate, drove right past their house along Hasker until they reached a grove of eucalyptus trees that hid a nondescript cinder-block building with no windows, one door, and a flat tarpaper roof.

Blue sniffed the air. She had watched Mr. Furrel cruise the neighborhood in his pickup with the windowless box in the back. She thought of him as a farmer who harvested dogs. He greeted them now, happy to have visitors. Blue stared at his hands as he opened the door to the kennel. The smell of urine and dog feces and wet fur roared at them with a din of yowling and whining and barking. Dogs threw themselves against their wire cages in the hope of being noticed. Blue looked around and stared at a door recessed in the cinder-block wall with no lock, no handle, no bar, painted colorless gray. She shuddered at the thought of where the door led.

"I wish I could find them all homes," Mr. Furrel told Edith, folding his arms over a butcher's apron.

"A shame," Edith said, shaking her head.

They strolled up and down the aisles looking in the cages. A few dogs lay on the concrete, not even lifting their eyelids. The newer pound arrivals leaped and licked the air with hope. And those in transition flipped from high to low with the merest glance of a visitor.

"This one likes me," Blue said, bending down to a puppy that nuzzled her hand.

"They all seem to, Blue," Cloud said encouragingly.

"Well, have you decided?" Edith asked as they toured the last cages.

Blue pursed her lips.

"Maybe we should come back another time."

"Wow." Blue screamed sharply and the barking stopped. A tense silence followed as she went to a cage in the corner. "Scooter," she said.

"Well, thank God you found him," said Edith, glancing up at the ceiling.

It was a brown dog, liverish brown, with meat brown spotted lips, a cocoa brown nose, pink-brown eyes, and red-brown short hair. It was shaped thin at the head and fat at the rear. It licked its chops and hugged its tail in its groin. Worst of all, it shivered and it wasn't cold.

The very first thing, the girls and Callum squired the new member of their family around the neighborhood, starting with Lionel Wimbledon next door, who slid down from the garage to have a look. Lionel had limp blond hair and what his English mother called "spots." His ribs showed through his bare chest, and his upper lip was chapped from snot that leaked from his nose all year long. His gangling arms and legs moved with a spidery grace that suited his latest image of himself. Lionel lived on the garage roof, inching along its spine with an arm and one leg raised imitating the jerky movements of the praying mantis he dreamed of being.

Scooter licked his chops and looked at him. Lionel told the girls, "Keep him off our property," and went back to his rooftop.

They next stopped at Maria Suitchek's, down the street. As usual she was draped on her front porch waiting for boys to drive by. She was known for letting all comers squeeze her bazooms for a quarter. They were impossible not to want, and business was brisk. She displayed them in tight sweaters and blouses with deep décolletages. She had once offered Callum a charity squeeze while they were hiding up an avocado tree in the throes of Capture the Flag. His hands had been inches away at the instant the enemy had pounced. Now every time he touched a quarter in his jeans his knees trembled with lust.

Maria kissed Blue and Cloud on both cheeks and looked at Callum as if she could read his thoughts. Her nipples peeked through her sweater when she bent over to pet Scooter, and Callum's mouth went dry. Jack, her older brother, looked at Scooter with loathing. Jack owned white mice. Their population had declined tragically the day he put out newborns to sun in a fruit crate. The next thing, their hairless pink bodies were hanging from the muzzle of Nar, their next-door neighbor's Doberman pinscher.

"He's a fairy dog," Jack said and pulled a mouse from his pocket. Scooter shivered down to his paws.

"Dogs aren't fairies," said Callum.

"Put him in the yard with Nar and you'll see."

"He's not that kind."

"See? A poof."

Maria slipped her brother's mouse under her sweater and giggled as it climbed between her breasts without a clue where it was. Callum would have paid a quarter on the spot, but Cloud and Blue were watching, hoping for the chance to call him a pervert.

"*Fiiive* minutes to dinner!" Edith yelled across three backyards.

On the way home they paused a moment at the Marxes', who lived behind a chain-link fence with Nar patrolling the lawn. Cloud pushed the bell on the fence post. Nar trotted down the path growling with his head low. A slat of venetian blind went up, then down in the window. A solitary light went out. The Marxes had moved into the neighborhood a few months after the war ended in Europe. Bud said that explained everything. He never explained why.

Walking on, Cloud said, "I just had a really neat idea, Blue."

"Does it include me?"

"If you want it to."

"Well, what is it?"

"I was thinking maybe we could teach Scooter to dance."

Blue laughed. "Like this, you mean?" She twirled him in a circle in the middle of the street holding him by his front paws.

"Yeah, like that but different," Cloud said, casting Callum one of her patented sidelong glances.

"A Job's Daughter does not sweat—"

Cloud and Blue shot each other looks of girlish delight that Edith squelched with a frown before returning her undivided attention to Mrs. Bashford, the Invitation Committee chairman of the Job's.

"—She glistens. And, girls, Job's Daughters do not allow their legs to fall akimbo, either, while seated." She glanced across the room at Callum in an overstuffed wing chair. "They do as I am doing now."

Mrs. Hilary Bashford locked her knees with a force that would crack a Brazil nut. With one hand she straightened her woolen tweed skirt, and in the other she balanced a cup and saucer. Home-baked brownies and a cupcake with vanilla frosting crowded a plate on her lap. With this to occupy her and her monologue on decorum, too, she listed in the armchair like a barge at low tide.

Edith crossed her ankles just so, mimicking Mrs. Bashford. She smoothed the fingers of her white tea gloves and tugged at the waist of a pea-green suit. A red silk poppy on her pillbox hat hovered almost magically in the air at the end of a long wire stem. And when Mrs. Bashford told the girls how to use a toothpick in public and pick round vegetables like peas off a plate, Edith's poppy circled her head like a whip antenna.

Edith would have agreed with about anything Mrs. Bashford said that afternoon, no matter how absurd. This tea was Bethel Thirteen of Job's Daughters' way of getting acquainted, and Edith wanted to get cozy. It was how Mrs. Bashford formed opinions about the girls and their mothers. This informal gathering, which had an underlying formality that was making Edith sweat, was an obstacle that she was determined to clear by being as invisible as the stem of her poppy.

On the edge of the parlor, Callum fought back boredom. It was said that boredom was a hopeful state of mind. Bored people waited in anticipation for something to engage their minds. But he did not feel hopeful. A moment ago he had spilled lemonade in his lap in an instant of acute drowsiness. The women's proceedings, the wafts of their cloying perfumes, their gentle voices, and the soft-cushioned wing chair all together had hugged him in the embrace of Morpheus. He had pinched himself, breathed deeply, and scanned the titles on Mrs. Bashford's bookshelf. But the books—*Little Women, Rebecca of Sunnybrook Farm, Beowulf*—made him yawn. He could conjure images of battleships and war planes and such out of thin air, but the floral prints, chintzes, still lifes, and dizzying wallpaper of the decor suffocated his imagination to a blankness as white as a polar night.

He chanced a look over at one of the girls, who had caught his eye. Her long black hair was tied in perfect braids with tortoiseshell clips. Her eyes were as round and dark as any he ever knew. When she smiled he thought of the Crown. But for all that, just a simple glance in her direction and he started feeling odd. She was no different in shape and form from Blue and Cloud, but all the same, she left him with a mysterious feeling that he enjoyed as much as he disliked.

She returned his look, catching him off guard. And he averted his gaze. Suddenly, as though he had no control over them, his eyes darted back, and their eyes met in a blur of excited confusion. When he glanced up again, she was smiling that sea-day smile, looking away but *at* him, as if he didn't know.

Then, as the conversation changed, she turned to a woman seated beside her who had started to tell the group about herself.

Mary Rodriguez told the tea she was a Californio—that was the word she used—descended from the Mexicans who first settled California long before the Spanish or Americans arrived. She owned an orange grove that had been in her family for a hundred and fifty years. She was a farmer—not the wife of one, but a farmer herself. Such a thing was not easily imagined by looking at her. She was thin and fine-boned, with hands with long, thin fingers and nails painted bright crimson.

Mrs. Bashford's expression changed from feigned interest to

thin-lipped tolerance as she listened to Mrs. Rodriguez's description of herself. "You're a Mexican, I take it?" she interrupted her. "I thought you knew that the Job's admit only Americans."

Edith, who was seated next to Mrs. Rodriguez, felt the heat of Mrs. Bashford's question. Sweat trickled down her back. She had chosen her seat because she had admired Mrs. Rodriguez from the start, though she had not known her before today. The silver around her throat, her wrist, and a silver-trimmed comb looked as creative and plainly beautiful as Mrs. Rodriguez herself. It had formed in Edith's mind an image of her as an independent, confident woman and mother—a farming mother. Edith guessed she would know her own mind, but she would also be sensitive enough to feel embarrassed as much for the stupidity of Mrs. Bashford's question as by the awkwardness of any reply.

"Mrs. Bashford?" Edith spoke up in a small voice, dissolving her invisibility. "I believe Mrs. Rodriguez said she was *descended* from Mexicans, like I'm descended from the English and Scots."

"A Californio is not quite the same as being a *Mayflower* pilgrim. Wouldn't you say so?"

Edith stared at her gloves. She knew that Mrs. Bashford was asking her. "To someone who just moved out here?" She looked up. "It darned well should be the same."

"How long *have* you been out here, may I ask?"

"Not long," Edith replied, adding, "by comparison."

"My late husband was a third-generation Californian. What about your husband?"

Again, the question was aimed at Edith. "The same, not long," she replied.

"And what does he do for a living?"

"Drives a soda truck." And she felt compelled to add, "Hires. Squirt. Nesbitt's."

Mrs. Bashford's mouth formed a blunt, zippered line of rejection.

Bud's entering the room created a distraction, and the interrogation ended. Edith smiled with relief at seeing him. Bud was dressed to impress in his red Pendleton shirt and pressed cords, with his hair washed and combed. He waved to the girls and leaned against the wall by the door.

Mrs. Bashford thanked them, and the women and their daughters who filed uneasily out of the room looked relieved to be leaving. Bud came over and kissed Edith and held her hand like they were sweethearts. She introduced him to Mrs. Bashford, and Bud, on the social offensive, praised her decor.

"You like it?" she asked, every bit as houseproud as Bud had gauged her to be. She led him around her living room pointing out an original charcoal drawing she had bought at auction and a fringed divan from Budapest.

"Are you Hungarian?" he asked her.

She looked at the divan and then into his face, and Bud knew the truth.

"English, actually," she said. "I've always had an admiration for the furniture of middle Europeans, however." And with that she excused herself.

Bud was standing near enough to Mrs. Rodriguez to either introduce himself or appear to be rude, and he tried to be polite when he could with people he did not know. She seemed almost grateful when he spoke to her.

"You must know Mr. Wait," he said after a short round of small talk brought them to the subject of Mrs. Rodriguez's grove. "He's just across the highway from you."

"The old man with the jackass?" She shook her head. "I've seen him on the road."

"You'd like him. You and he have a lot in common."

"I know about his grove. I was going to buy it when it was originally for sale, after the war."

Bud looked across the room at Mrs. Bashford. "It looks like we'll be going through this ordeal together."

"Your daughters will make fine Job's Daughters," Mrs. Rodriguez said.

"Edith wants it for them." He was still looking at Mrs. Bashford. "Sometimes I wonder why."

"I do, too, sometimes." She paused a moment, thinking. "A chance. That's why, I guess. There isn't much chance to reach for something better."

"The question is, is this it?"

She laughed, liking him. "You learn to take what you can get."

. . .

The girls were putting on their coats and Callum was slipping toward the door when a voice behind him said, "Hi."

"Hi," he said, spinning around. The girl he had admired from across the room was standing so close he could reach out and touch her. He slipped his hands in his pockets.

"Are you going to be a Job's Daughter, too?" the girl asked, and she laughed, seeing his discomfort.

"My mom wanted to show off," he tried to explain.

"You?"

"She thinks it's important to be proud of your family. She says it's a virtue."

"My mom says stuff like that, too. My name's Serena."

"Oh." He looked in her eyes and the same thrill as before returned this time with a jolt.

Just as a silence between them was starting to rob the room of air, she said, "Bye."

That simple word had never held such promise.

On the drive home, Bud told Edith, "She isn't like the others— and I don't mean Mexican, either."

"The poor soul," Edith said, clucking her tongue.

"She doesn't need our sympathy, Edith."

"She doesn't understand the rules."

"Maybe she's testing them. Maybe she thinks Garden Grove is a better place than it is. Maybe her world *is* a better place."

"Now who's being mushy? I wish Mrs. Bashford showed more understanding though. Mrs. Rodriguez could buy and sell her any day where breeding is concerned."

"A yobbo in a pinafore, Edith, a yobbo in a pinafore." He laughed out loud. "She told me a Tartar king sat on that sofa in her living room. Edith, it was junk."

"Thank you for being so sweet," she told him and scooched over on the seat. "Do you know how lucky we are, all of us?"

"For having nothing, you mean?"

"Oh, Bud." She kissed him on the cheek.

He stared at the white line on the road, feeling like a heel.

•　•　•

Callum was on the living room floor at home reading about Bull Run when he rolled over to get comfortable and something on the rug caught his eye. The book made the war seem dull and distant, and the ache of boredom prepared him for any distraction. This one was an annelid—what fishermen call a worm.

Callum knew worms. Buffalo worms—night crawlers with red blood pounding in their veins—had thundered across the plains of coffee grounds in the darkness of the closet where Bud had farmed them. The world was full of worms Callum could recognize on sight—sluggish fruit worms, wriggling tent worms, common earthworms. He thought he knew them all. But he had never seen this one on the shag.

It was short and luminous with fine burgundy veins. It writhed when he held it close to the light. He thought little of its style and flicked it across the room off the point of his pencil. He would have forgotten all about it if he had not wandered into the girls' room a few pages of history later to find the same type of worm wriggling on Blue's bedspread.

"What's this doing here?" he asked, holding it between his fingers.

Blue stepped back and screamed. Cloud, less skitterish, said she did not know. "It's only a worm," she said.

"*Only* a worm?" Blue shrieked. "On *my* bed?"

Scooter was attracted by the noise. He sat on the rug in the doorway and looked himself over.

Callum glanced meaningfully down at him. "Has he been up on the bedspread?" he asked.

"We let him if he's good," said Blue.

"It's not what you think," Cloud said. "It probably rode in on your sneaker."

Callum would have left it at that and nothing more would have been said about worms if he hadn't been watering the front lawn that evening around dusk. He coiled the garden hose and was carrying it on his shoulder around the corner of the house when a strange movement by the orange trees in the backyard caught his eye. It was Scooter back there with his ears looking as though he were facing a stiff breeze. He was whizzing across the lawn like an ice-skater.

Callum dropped the hose. He had seen dogs do disgusting things, but what Scooter was doing was a new branch of evolutionary development for a dog. He was skimming the slicked wet grass, cutting figure eights around the ivy bases of two orange trees. He was deranged with what looked like relief. And he couldn't stop himself.

Lionel called down out of the gloaming, "I think it's his asshole."

Indeed, Scooter was doing an asshole glide.

Callum whistled, and Scooter, locked in a private ecstasy, changed course and skidded toward the sound. At Callum's feet he raised himself up on all fours with an effort, then sank back down again and spun like a whirling dervish.

"Your dog is the pits," said Lionel.

"It's his training," Callum said, trying to salvage some dignity. "He's been trained especially to do it."

"Unh-huh," Lionel said, unconvinced.

Callum dragged Scooter by the collar into the garage away from prying eyes. He turned on the light and got down on his hands and knees. Cautiously, like someone setting a trap for a rat, he lifted his tail. "Holy cow," he said, retreating as fast as his knees would carry him across the floor.

What he had witnessed reminded him of ground round churning from a meat grinder. The worms were tumbling out in a profusion that suggested they might have invented Scooter as a warm, sunless resort to frolic and multiply in. Callum stood in the driveway and hollered to Edith, who was in the kitchen pounding an abalone steak with a ball-peen hammer. "Mom, shouldn't Scooter sleep outdoors like a real dog?"

Edith whacked the mollusk with a final thud. "If you think so."

"I'll make him a bed in the garage."

"You do that then," she shouted.

Scooter circled in a pile of dirty rags that Callum put down for him. And soon he fell into a troubled sleep.

Right after breakfast the next morning, Callum rode his bicycle into town. The owner of the feed store, who reeked of alfalfa, met him by the gaping doors by the sacks of rabbit food and other animal-feed grains. There was no better aroma on earth than that of the feed store. The man asked him what he needed, and after he explained, they searched the shelves of animal drugs as diverse as dip for sheep and licks for cows and fur-ball laxatives for felines. The owner's beefy arm reached out for a box that he rattled, stirring up a fond memory.

"A customer once used these on one of those camels from Peru," he said, smiling at the recollection. "He said he wanted to get things moving. How was I to know? That camel went berserk whenever it saw a worm after that. Yes, indeed, this'll work just fine."

"I have a dog, mister," Callum pointed out.

"Whatever," he said and showed Callum pills the size and shape of almonds.

When he got home he folded the medication in a slice of day-old Wonder Bread, which Scooter ate without a hitch. He dosed him double what the instructions on the box advised. And after each slice of bread, he lifted his tail. If the pills even discomforted the worms, they gave no sign.

Around the middle of the afternoon, Callum positioned Scooter in the garage on a newspaper. He crouched under him and switched on Bud's bright mechanic's light. The worms' cascade, he was relieved to see, had slowed to a mere torrent, which needed a remedy nevertheless. He quietly drew his squirt gun from his belt, checked the level of the ammonia he had filled it with, aimed pointblank at the bull's-eye of Scooter's anus, and squeezed the trigger.

Cloud lowered the Jockey shorts into the boiling water on the tine of a dinner fork. She placed a lid on the pot and adjusted the gas on the range. Now and then she glanced up at the kitchen clock with the Aunt Jemima arms pointing out the time. When twenty minutes had passed, she cut the flame, lifted the lid, and with a long-handled wooden spoon plucked the underpants out of the scalding water. The Jockeys were dyed approximately the same brown as Scooter's fur.

Scooter was stretched out in a patch of dirt behind the garage watching Blue whack the tetherball. Callum was carving his initials in a railroad tie with a penknife and looked up as Cloud rounded the corner of the garage. She snapped her fingers at Scooter and guided his rear legs through the holes in the damp Jockeys and slipped his tail through the fly. She raised her arms like a tamer of lions. Scooter knew the sign. He rose up on his back legs. His tongue lolled out of his mouth. His eyes focused inwardly as he scratched the air with his paws. Even with the drooping shorts, he gavotted for as long as Cloud could have hoped.

"What a good dog," she praised him.

"Isn't he cute?" asked Blue, hugging the tetherball.

Cloud placed her hand on her chin. "You know, Blue, I really think we could win that grand prize for Dad."

"What prize?"

Callum stared at Blue, and his jaw slackened in amazement. In her self-absorption she could not see what Cloud was making her an accomplice to.

4

Roland at the Last Supper

A machine filled the display window of Roland's Buster Brown shoe store where Tide once stood gazing up at his friend Buster. It was a big shiny thing that looked like a Wurlitzer, but what a jukebox was doing in the window of a shoe store, only Roland could say.

He was admiring the machine from inside the window, and when Bud poked his head in the door, he looked up as if he were expecting him and asked, "Are you looking for the future, Bud?"

Bud wore an impatient look. He had not expected to chat about the future or the past. He had stopped by to pick Roland up to take him down to Laguna. "Well, it sure raises questions," he admitted grudgingly, keeping the door open.

"About what?" Roland asked, hoping Bud would offer an admiring word about his new attraction.

"About what it *is*. Another gimmick, I suppose."

Roland looked offended. "No gimmick. It's a diagnostic machine, Bud. You know how machines are starting to think for people? It's getting so that people don't trust other people anymore. Well, this is a machine." And he stared at it like it was an enigma.

Bud looked at his wristwatch. "I can see that," he said. "Roland, do the Pageant folks care if you show up late?"

"It'd look funny with an empty place at the big table," he said, still assessing the window display.

"Okay, you want me to ask. I will. What is it?"

He replied readily. "It's a Vi-Bee-Beam. It X-rays the metatarsals, cuneiforms, naviculars and phalanges—you know, it shows feet as they would appear in the glow of an A-bomb. It's an attention-getter. A guy the other day came in here and staggered out, I swear, muttering."

Bud took one step inside the door. "It's that good?"

"A woman in this morning got caught up in the depth of her inner beauty. A Mexican scanned her kid's hand before I caught her doing it. Heck, a lady wedged her schnauzer in there. They know."

Callum joined Bud at the door. He had seen the machine from the parking space and couldn't resist a closer look. He slipped past Bud and stepped up into the window. The Vi-Bee-Beam reminded him of the cockpit console of a spaceship. Ribbed chrome wings flared at the sides. A seductive periscopelike eye cup, a stainless-steel pointer, and two arrowed slots near the bottom of the chest-height box were all designed to give the impression of the Vi-Bee-Beam as a piece of futuristic furniture.

"What does your generation think?" Roland asked him, seriously interested.

"Neat."

"That's it? *Neat?* Why not try it?"

"We'll pass," Bud answered for him and stepped inside the store.

"You'll pass? You can't let your own son pass on the future. He *is* the future."

"It looks risky."

"The future always is."

"Besides, Edith would kill me."

"You're afraid of her, not the future, correct?"

Afraid of her, no. Respectful, yes. Letting Callum test the Vi-Bee-Beam was not in the same league with stealing your wife's favorite piece of jewelry. But now that he had taken the Big One, he could not take even a small risk. "Afraid of her, don't be silly," he said.

Roland shrugged, knowing better. "Watch the register for me," he said, "while I get my ditty bag," and he disappeared through a beaded curtain that led to the storeroom.

Callum wandered over to a display shelf and picked up a shoe with a sliding tongue. He wanted to own a pair of Bonerubs like these more than anything he knew, but he also knew better than to ask. Judging by their behavior, Edith and Bud liked to keep him in a perpetual state of anticipation—next year, they'd said, he'd be old enough for this, or the year after for that. His age never seemed to be in sync with his wishes. By the time he was old enough to get what he wanted, either he wouldn't want it anymore or it would be out of fashion.

"These the ones you were telling me about?" Bud asked. He took the shoe and slid the tongue back and forth. "Knapps are made better."

Callum wondered what Knapps had to do with anything. Bud had given him a pair a year ago with a big fanfare, like he was joining an exclusive club. He had worn them once, back and forth across his bedroom floor. They had slapped the carpet like slabs of meat. Knapps were men's shoes, mature-decision shoes, grown-up shoes. Men toiled in them. But at home they slipped on Bonerubs, the shoes they dreamed in, laughed in.

"You should have a pair, don't you think?" Bud asked, handing him the Bonerubs.

Callum beamed. "But I thought—"

"You deserve them," he told him. "You don't ask for much. Besides, you work hard delivering papers. It's good for the soul to wear something silly once in awhile."

"They're not silly."

"That depends on your point of view. I'll ask Roland to find a pair your size." He turned and went through the beaded curtain.

Callum heard them talking in the storeroom. He felt so happy that without thinking he climbed into the display window. He flipped on the switch on the Vi-Bee-Beam and listened as it warmed up with a moan like a church organ. He slipped his feet in two separate holes at the base of the machine. A green light went on, and he lowered his eyes over the rubber viewing cups.

At first he saw a bright blue light. Then an outline came into view. He wiggled his toes and saw a corresponding wiggle in the light. He was seeing through his own skin, looking at the thin white sticks of his own bones. It was better than neat. He raised his eyes from the viewing cup at the sound of Bud's voice and stepped out of the window, thinking how wonderful it was to see something that should have been invisible, like a dream.

A half-hour later Bud was whistling a chanty over the sound of the wind that whipped in the car windows as he, Roland, and Callum drove down Route 101. From the passenger's-side window Callum watched the surfers on their boards bobbing on a flat, iridescent sea. Scanning the surface beyond the shallow swells for a glimpse of the seals, he wondered why dreams always seemed to come true on quirky schedules—sometimes late, sometimes early, but never when you wanted them to. Nothing could ever turn a dream into a layaway plan. He knew that. The trick was to resist all doubts and something would come true. If he needed proof he only had to open the shoe box on his lap.

They drove past a family of Mexicans who had festooned a clothesline with colored serapes and piñatas blowing in the breeze. There was a big sign advertising Mexican jumping beans. Past Corona del Mar, on an open stretch of road, there were stands selling pomegranates, gunny sacks of oranges, hot dogs, tacos, pottery, old inner tubes, inflatable rafts, fresh-squeezed guavas, and Clementine tangerines.

Something about driving the open road along the Pacific Coast on a sunny afternoon always made life worth living.

Bud turned to Roland, sitting in the middle seat. In a voice that was man-to-man, he said, "What can you tell us on the q.t. about Hollywood, Roland?"

"What's there to say?"

"Well, like who did you work for up there?"

"All the big ones—Fox, Disney, United Artists, Columbia—you name it. They all needed costume designers."

"Meet any stars?"

"Ronald Colman, Errol Flynn, you know, Barbara Stanwyck, Carole Lombard. Meeting them was like shaking hands with cardboard cutouts. I made their costumes. Sure I met them. It was less than you'd think."

"Why'd you quit? I mean, it was a job."

He fanned the air as though he smelled a dead fish. "You couldn't begin to understand."

"Try me."

"It was the people. You hold a mirror up to them, Bud, and nothing reflects."

"Like vampires," Callum said, getting in stride with the conversation.

"Vampires can't help what they are," said Roland.

"How can stars be that different from you and me?" asked Bud.

"Their names are in bright lights," Callum said.

"They still go to the bathroom like you and me, don't they?" Bud asked.

"*They* need diapers," Roland said, giving the thought a vicious smile. "The bigger the star the bigger their didees. They have no real self-esteem. They have no values. Right and wrong are directions to them. Then they get to be famous and they take the high road to make amends for what they had to do to get there."

"What made you decide your future was in shoes?" Bud asked. "I mean, why not dresses or suits?"

"They were the part of the job that interested me, so I said what the heck."

Bud licked his lips. "Tell us about Disney then."

"The company or the man?"

"You met him?"

Roland shook his head. "I used to see him around the studio, of course. Meet him? Unfortunately, no."

"The company then. Is it like the others?"

"Naw. Not at all. A nicer bunch of joes you couldn't find, and talented, too. The difference is, they're not actors. They're animators, artists. They're dreamers."

"Being in the movie business must be great," said Callum.

Roland shook his head. "I guess you aren't hearing what I've been saying."

"Did you always want to be a costume designer?" Callum asked.

Roland looked at him tenderly. "You ever play dress-up?" he asked.

"A long time ago."

"It was fun, wasn't it, the dresses and funny hats and your mother's high heels?"

"I guess so," Callum said, trying to remember.

"Some people outgrow dressing up. I never did. When I didn't dress up for myself anymore, I did it for actors. And what a crowd to do anything for."

"Pretty neat?" Callum asked, stubbornly holding to his view of stars as pretty much what they saw themselves as.

"Pretty nuts." Roland laughed. "You've seen the Dracula movie, the one with Bela Lugosi? Remember the guy in the bug house?"

"The one who eats the fly?"

" 'Master, you promised me eternal life'? Well, he's all actors. What I mean is, actors will do anything for attention—eat flies even. They worry about eternal life and seek it in the shape of fame. Take my word for it, they belong in a bug house."

"Doesn't sound great," Bud said.

"I got out of the business because of them, tell you the truth. But I also have to thank them. They led me to God."

Bud glanced at him. "How did that happen, your conversion and all, Rollie?" He was curious about the roots of Roland's beliefs. Among the gang, Roland was the only one to carry a Bible in his back pocket and spout scripture like a Baptist minister. He believed like no one they had ever known.

"It's a long story," Roland said.

Bud got the message and shut up. They continued along the coast road until they reached Laguna Beach, where they slowed down by the oceanfront. The volleyball regulars as usual were displaying their prowess and old people were bicycling three-wheelers and vendors were pushing trunks of dry ice with refreshments. Nobody even acknowledged the presence of the most beautiful ocean on earth. People in Laguna preferred to jostle each other on the hot concrete sidewalks, back and forth, back and forth, drooling in the heat over girls in Catalinas. Bud said Laguna and every other public beach south of San Luis Obispo would be deserted as the Gobi desert—except for kids who didn't know different—if not for the unrivaled chance to ogle girls nearly naked for free.

Bud asked Roland as they slowed down looking for a parking spot, "Do you keep in touch up there in Hollywood anymore?"

He looked at Bud. "Don't even think about it."

"What?"

"I won't do it."

"What?" Bud was smiling.

"I won't do it. I haven't been back in years, and I won't go back now. The apostles themselves couldn't get me to go."

"We'll see," said Bud.

Everybody waiting at the picnic tables under the stunted Australian pine waved at everybody else with an exuberance that only an annual event as special as Christmas and Easter could possibly induce. Milton and Gladys were there, of course, and the girls and Edith, who had driven down with them, as were P.O. and his girlfriend Cheval, who looked spectacular in a polka-dot halter top and short-shorts, and Mr. Wait, sitting to one side, aloof and thoughtful.

As they checked their watches, fearing to be late for the Pageant, they entered the knotty pine foyer of the restaurant. The walls were covered with framed photographs of the oddballs that the restaurant's proprietor, Harry Moon, had known. He recognized Bud and the group right away with a wave; Harry Moon's was their venue for Easter lunch, the pre-Pageant dinner each year, and the times in between when they had an occasion to celebrate. He showed them to a table himself with the phony flourish of a French waiter.

Harry was moon-faced and round with short hairy arms and a bassoon voice with which he talked to his customers often more than they liked being talked to by the owner. He harped on about how Laguna wasn't what it used to be. What was anymore? He railed against the rich bitches, his term for the wealthy home owners who had moved to Laguna after the war. From their mansions on the oceanfront they romped on the beaches in the buff in the holy name of art. And they were giving a town, which Harry had almost settled, a name for kookiness that he thought was undeserved. Laguna, he told them, was a colony of true artists, but true artists attracted fakes wherever they settled, and the fakes drove out the true, leaving the place a desert of the soul.

While Harry sawed on, Edith advised the kids what to order from menus the size of wall calendars that Harry stopped talking long enough to hand around. Edith blushed from one ear to another when Roland turned to her with a flattery—how pretty she looked, he said. She was in a cotton dress with a buttercup-yellow floral print. She touched the hair behind her ear. It was easy to see that Roland loved women in spite of being a bachelor himself. He could find something nice about them to compliment—no matter the reality of their waistlines or problem hair or teeth. Women suspected he was flattering them, and yet they could never be sure he might be telling a truth that no one else, much less themselves, had ever noticed. Few men—and husbands never—thought to give compliments of this order. They were easy and so well received, it was a shame.

"What's your perfume, Edith?" Roland asked, bending closer.

"An Evening in Paris," she replied, lifting her chin.

"Vanilla," Milton said. "It smells like vanilla."

"Ice cream," said Mr. Wait.

"I'm glad you all like it," Edith said. "The girls gave it to me last Christmas."

"Penny's?" Gladys asked.

"Monkey Ward," Cloud answered.

"Doughnuts," said P.O. belatedly, as though he were having a separate conversation.

Milton looked startled. "I thought we agreed not to mention them again," he said.

"I'm sorry," P.O. said. "I mean it." Then he laughed. "My neighbors complained about the doughnut again the other day. They asked what I planned to do with it. They said it's an eyesore."

"You never know," said Mr. Wait. "It may come in handy one of these days."

"It's not an eyesore," said Milton. "It's a raised-glazed."

The doughnut had been their last dream together, a wild idea for a roadside shop that sold fresh New York doughnuts. Not that such a thing existed. The label meant *best*, like there was Paris fashion. No matter how sunny the sun, how sandy the beaches and whistle-clean the streets in California, New England shone as a beacon of greatness to those who did not live there anymore. Nobody in southern California wanted to live there, or anywhere near it, ever again. But, like speaking well of the dead, they never said a bad word about the place they had left behind. They restricted their contact to long-distance conversations on the telephone, winter weather reports on the radio, and—what Bud and the gang had bet their old dream on—New York doughnuts, too.

The dream had been certain to succeed right from the start. Edith and the other women found out how to make doughnuts from the Baptist's cookbook. Raised-glazed and coconut-covered, powdered and sugared and New York plain, it took no genius to deep-fry a ring of batter that a crank machine plopped on waxed paper. They experimented in Edith's kitchen, and before a single Sunday morning went by, they were New York ready to go.

Bud and P.O. took charge of designing the roadside stand. This they did with enthusiasm and even some flair. The chairmanship of the Subcommittee on Site Selection went to Milton, which in retrospect had been a mistake. Bud knew enough to communicate with prospective customers on a gut level. He bet they would not be able to read the letters *D-O-N-U-T*. And thus was created the giant raised-glazed. It was dimpled, toasted a light brown and glazed with a fresh coat of shellac. It measured eighteen feet in diameter, with a hole a stunt midget could have shot his motorcycle through. Mouths would water from afar.

Construction had begun on rented property Milton had selected on the edge of a beanfield a mile from the coast. Like Amish at a barn raising they had hoisted the doughnut onto the roof. Bud had surveyed what they had wrought and decided the doughnut itself wasn't going to be enough. Two weeks later they crowded through the hole a plywood replica of the Empire State Building. The world's tallest building and the world's biggest doughnut overpowered the puny stand below, but it sent out their message in a language even an Okie could understand. Then, in fresh aprons, they had waited. In any of the twelve hours of natural sunlight no more than three cars passed by. One day all three cars were the same car.

They turned to Milton for an explanation. How could he have chosen such an out-of-the-way place? He was just as confused. He admitted that his approach to site selection had not been exactly scientific. Neither had it been anecdotal.

"What do you mean, the Word?" Bud had asked in a confrontation that counted all of them against Milton.

Without a single expression of having missed the point of the doughnut stand, Milton tried to explain. He went to the trunk of his car, and when he came back he was holding an eight ball.

"I asked the oracle," he explained, shaking the ball. He turned it over, and the words that appeared in a little plastic window were "Not Today."

Before the rent was due at the end of the month they dismantled the stand and mothballed the doughnut in P.O.'s backyard and made a bonfire of the Empire State Building on the beach one moonlit night while the grunion were running.

"I bet you're proud to be a part of the Pageant again this year," Edith told Roland, returning his compliment in her own gentle way. By now Harry Moon had served their food, the fried clams and hamburgers with fries heaped on their plates. "I don't know how you do it, not moving a single muscle and all."

That seemed to arouse a question in Roland's mind. "It used to be there was zing, you know, Edith, not moving and all," he said. "It was what made it possible. It was a challenge. But, to tell you the truth, the zing has gone out. I can't explain it better than that. I used to feel a warm glow like what the saints feel when they pray. But now . . . well, nothing."

Edith gave him a worried look. "Maybe it's just you're feeling the jitters."

He glanced at his wristwatch and excused himself, snatching his ditty bag from under the seat. He brushed past Harry Moon, who was bringing them glasses of iced water, on his way to the men's room.

Mr. Wait turned to Callum and the girls. "You know what Roland is going to be this year?"

"At the table again, I guess," said Cloud without enthusiasm.

"Tell me what you'd choose to be in." He looked at Callum first.

He could not recall a single painting. "Currier and Ives," he said.

"*The Dancers*," Blue said.

That reminded Bud, who asked the girls, "How's your act for the talent contest coming?"

"Okay, I guess," Blue replied. "We're practicing the steps."

"We'll win," Cloud told him confidently.

"I can count on the fifty, then?"

"You can count on it, Dad."

"Maybe you shouldn't be so sure, sweetheart," Edith put in. "I wouldn't want you to be disappointed."

"Trust me," Cloud replied. "I've got it all worked out."

Mr. Wait said, "You didn't say, Cloud, which painting you'd be in?"

She had no preferences. "I guess that girl on the dolphin from last year."

"She was riding that dolphin in the nude," Blue pointed out. It had been the men's favorite. "How could you go nude in front of so many people?"

"What's the big deal? It's a hypothetical question."

Blue looked strickened, as she always did when Cloud used a word she did not know.

"Now, girls. That's enough." Edith dabbed her lips and put her napkin down. "Come with me, please," she told them, and they trooped off, pocketbooks in hand, to the powder room. Cheval and Gladys followed a moment later.

Roland passed them in the middle of the restaurant. He had changed into a long sackcloth burnoose belted with a hemp cord. He had raised the cowl over his head and slipped his hands in the abundant sleeves, which made him look like the Grim Reaper minus a scythe.

"Moses?" Bud ventured.

"Later," Roland replied. "But you are on the right track."

"Saint Peter?"

"*Very* warm."

Harry Moon interrupted, clearing their dishes. Roland checked his watch. Bud continued to look at the burnoose. "I give up," he said.

"Saint Luke."

"Do you know what we're talking about?" Bud asked Callum.

"The one we saw at Forest Lawn?"

"That's it."

"It is brilliant, the real *Last Supper*," said Roland. "Like most things, the more you know about it, the better it becomes."

Bud looked over his shoulder, wondering what was keeping the girls.

"When Leonardo was painting *The Last Supper*, he wrote in his diary that he was trying to describe man's soul," said Roland. "In the painting Christ just finished saying, 'One of you shall betray me,' and the apostles are asking, 'Lord, is it I?' Each apostle is showing what in his nature he wants to hide. Christ's statement—'One of you shall betray me'—has startled them."

"He knows who the traitor is," said Milton.

"His palm is upturned as if to say that he's already submitted to the will of God," said Roland. "Yes, he knows."

"What's it like being an apostle?" Callum asked him.

"Nice. A real religious experience. Things come to you. You're not just dressed up pretending. You are who you play. It's humbling." He stirred sugar in his coffee. "Which apostle would you be, Callum?"

"Judas Iscariot," he replied without hesitation.

Bud stared at him in surprise. "Nobody wants to be him," he said.

"Why, why Judas?" Roland asked.

Callum glanced at Bud. "I don't know," he said.

"Of course you do," Bud said harshly. "You said it."

The men stared at him as if he were Judas for saying that he would choose to be Judas. It wasn't exactly what he had meant. He didn't want to be a traitor. Yet there was something he thought he could see, like looking in the Vi-Bee-Beam at his bones.

Roland rested his hand on Bud's arm. "How many of the apostles can you name, Bud?"

He gazed up at Harry Moon's ceiling. "All of them."

"Okay, let's hear you."

"Well, there was Judas of course. Then there was Luke, Matthew, Mark and John and . . . Peter. Let's see, that's six. Peter and Paul and . . ." He pursed his lips and squinted his eyes. "The others slip my mind."

"Everyone remembers Judas first," Roland said.

"It's true," Milton agreed. "I wonder why."

"Because Christ and Judas are one person—one light, the other dark," Roland replied.

The way Callum had been taught, Christ kept himself in the company of bluebirds and lambs and adoring children. Compared with Judas, who wasn't what you expected him to be, Christ was boring. "In Sunday school they teach us more about Christ's death than about his life," he said.

"I can't believe that," Roland said.

"They make his death seem more important. Christ died for us. That's what they say. Christ might have died of old age, in bed, if not for Judas. Where would he be today if he had died in bed?"

Roland gave him one of those from-the-mouths-of-babes looks.

"Jesus Christ," Bud muttered.

"I never saw a famous painting myself," Edith said to Roland. They were at the turnstiles, waiting for Bud to buy the Pageant tickets, after hiking up the road from the beach into the canyon where the Pageant was held each year.

"I've seen a slew," Roland told her. "They were beautiful and important but they didn't have the life these do."

"Tableaux vivants, you said they were called?"

He nodded. "A long time ago poor people had no chance to see art except as living canvases. They weren't the real thing but they were better than never seeing great art at all."

Cloud, one step behind and cranky from the walk, asked him, "Why don't they hold the Pageant on the beach?"

"They did at first. But people came in droves and the Irvine Company loaned them this place. It's a natural amphitheater, you know, carved out of the rock by water and the wind. It didn't cost a dime to build except for the seats."

Bud arrived with the tickets, and they filed through the turnstiles and headed toward the open tents where local artists exhibited their paintings. It was cool in the seared hills this time of evening. Edith told the kids to put on their sweaters.

"See you later," Roland said, then ducked out of the tent and was gone.

P.O. was arguing with a local artist who was sitting on a canvas chair amid framed portraits of females in the buff. He was skinny with a long, thin beard, glasses with rose-colored lenses, and a knit cap.

"You ask just *anybody?*" P.O.'s voice was raised.

"Your wife's a looker. Why not?" the artist asked, casting an appreciating eye over Cheval.

"She's not my wife," said P.O. "She's my girlfriend." He turned to her. "What did he ask you?"

Cheval laughed. "If I'd like to be stooped."

"Shtupped," the artist corrected her.

P.O. did not know what he was referring to, but he didn't like it. "She does not pose, period," he said.

"That's only the half of it," the artist said, holding out a calling card to Cheval. "If you ever feel in the mood, here's where you can reach me."

Cheval slipped the card in her décolletage as she bent over to look closer at a painting on velvet of a girl draped on a rock with sea spray bursting around her. "You get real girls to pose or you just copy from nudist magazines?" she asked.

"They ask *me,*" he replied.

Cheval looked at him, shaking her head sadly.

Mindful of the time, they now hurried toward the amphitheater, stopping long enough to buy bags of popcorn and rent binoculars. The amphitheater was a darkened hillside with a gentle upward slope lined with rows of wooden benches. A hundred or so reserved seats faced the stage in the orchestra, but most people bought places on ironwood planks like a ballpark's bleachers. Bud pointed to an empty row in the middle. As the amphitheater filled up, a plank snapped now and then, and the audience laughed as a team of Laguna High School athletes ran to the spot with hammers and fresh boards and nails. The fate of a hapless man in the reserved section brought the loudest laughter when his canvas-bottomed chair blew out with a dull thud and he disappeared with a groan.

The public-address system, its speakers like mutant morning glories, complained with a squeak and a whine as the master of ceremonies switched it on and cleared his throat. A moment later the lights went down, plunging the canyon into darkness. The stars were a comforting presence, so clear and low in the sky. The moon was bright enough to cast shadows on the ground.

Suddenly the stage curtain parted. The breath of a thousand people drew in at the sight of a shark, its mouth serrated with teeth, attacking a half-naked man floating on a wide sea in a frail wooden boat.

"This painting was done by John Singleton Copley, called *Watson and the Shark*," the master of ceremonies said. "It's a model of romantic imagery. The shark—which in real life didn't kill Watson, by the way—embodies evil. The man holding the harpoon in the bow of the boat is who you might call the Archangel Michael. Watson, in the water, flounders between the forces of good, Michael; and evil, the shark. And if you don't see it like that, then it's just a darned good scary picture."

"The guy with the harpoon moved!" Blue announced, her binoculars up to her eyes.

"He did not," Cloud replied.

"His hand with the harpoon. Look!" Her voice was raised higher. "It moved again."

"Squelch it!" Bud leaned over Callum and whispered.

The Death of Socrates followed *The Potato Eaters*, *A Glass of Absinthe*, and *Whistler's Mother*, an annual crowd-pleaser. *Pinkie* and *Blueboy* drew loud applause.

"And now for the girls we have Edgar Degas's *The Prima Ballerina* rendered in pastels," the master of ceremonies said.

Blue and Cloud rose from their seats as if in a spell.

"The dancer floats in a colored world like a moth drawn to flame," said the announcer, "or as though we were watching her perform at an oblique view from our box near the wings of the stage."

"*The Dancers*," Blue whispered.

"He said *Prima Ballerina*," Cloud said.

"A moth to flame."

"Why do you girls need to talk us through this?" Bud whispered to them. "Your eyes, girls. Use your *eyes*."

"Bud—" Edith reproached him, lightly touching his arm.

The curtain closed and the lights came on and the audience stood up and stretched. Bud, always anxious to make new friends, chatted with an Armenian from Chicago who said he was passing through on a visit to his dying mother in San Diego. Edith gabbed with a woman who held a teacup poodle in a brown paper shopping bag. The lights blinked and the ironwood planks groaned. Beethoven's

Emperor squeezed through the morning glories. The lights went down. The curtain parted. The girls snapped the binoculars up to their eyes. Bud cleared a lump in his throat. Edith wrapped her arms around herself.

It was *The Last Supper*.

"One of you shall betray me," Callum whispered and raised his binoculars.

The apostle at Christ's right seemed to be saying, "It sure isn't me."

Callum could almost hear the one on Christ's left saying, "Such a thing to say after all I've done for you."

Another apostle could have been thinking, *After all we've been through, you end it like this?*

It was odd how obvious the painter made the apostles' thoughts once you knew how to look, just like Roland had said.

Judas was stabbing his finger at his own chest in mock disbelief. He seemed to be telling Christ to mind his own business. *I'll make you a star.*

"Roland blinked," Blue reported.

Roland was holding up well, as steady as a rock. Edith felt so proud of him. Bud whispered to the Armenian that Roland—Saint Luke, the fourth from the right—was a friend.

"The right eye twitched," Cloud confirmed.

"Again. Left eye. Next to him. Lips moved."

Indeed, Roland seemed to be suffering from an attack of nerves. But that was not the worst of it. Something that was not scheduled to happen was happening for all to see, and the audience groaned in collective amazement. Roland lost his concentration. He was not just moving an eyelash or a nostril. He was *moving*. Blue and Cloud and Callum put down their binoculars and stared as he rose from the *Last Supper* table. The other apostles, even Christ himself, turned their heads. Roland looked around as if he did not know where he was and leaned his hands on the *Last Supper* table trying to see through the lights.

"Bud," he called into the shocked quiet of the canyon.

"Jesus H. Christ," said Bud.

"Bud, the zing's back," Roland shouted out and tipped over the

Last Supper table, revealing the knobby knees and hairy legs of thirteen men sitting on folding chairs in Bermuda shorts and cut-off jeans. Roland stepped over the table onto the stage apron proper. He was behind the lights now, shading his eyes. He walked down the orchestra steps and up the aisle looking for Bud, who was signaling him with his arm.

"Bud, put your hand down," Edith hissed.

"He needs me," Bud said.

People on their bench stood up as Roland passed by. They stared at him both out of respect for his character and in awe of his burnoose, fake eyebrows, and troweled-on makeup. His presence this close made them uncomfortable. An apostle was a thing to be revered on a stage. But in their midst, he was a nuisance.

Roland grasped Bud's arm. "Just now—Bud, a voice," he said, his voice filled with wonder. "I can't believe it myself. I'm sorry, but it couldn't wait."

"Calm down," Bud said, pulling him down on the seat that the Armenian had vacated in a fright. "You said you heard a voice?"

Roland swallowed and bobbed his head. "I was concentrating hard on not blinking. It's not easy to do, not blinking. Out of the blue a voice spoke to me as clear as if the apostle next to me whispered in my ear."

"Did it say who it was, the voice?"

He shook his head. "It was resonant, you know, like you'd expect. It said, 'Many prophets and kings have desired to see those things which ye see, and have not seen them; and to hear those things which ye hear, and have not heard them.' "

"The Bible?"

"I don't remember reading it there."

"You know the Bible—"

"By heart."

"Then what does it mean?"

"That something great is going to happen."

P.O., like the others, had been silent, not knowing what to say but wanting to hear what had inspired Roland. The lights came on and the master of ceremonies was offering apologies along with an explanation that the show was over anyway and, no, they would not refund people's money. "Sometimes the strain on our actors is great," he announced. "You can appreciate after tonight what they go through."

"Tell us again what the voice said," Bud asked. Roland, he knew, wasn't one to make a spectacle of himself. He respected the Pageant and would never do anything to embarrass its organizers. Therefore, what had inspired him to break up *The Last Supper*, Bud thought, must be significant.

"That prophets and kings desire to see what we have seen," Roland replied. "What have we seen? We have seen that Walt is going to build an amusement park, maybe in our own backyard. Kings and prophets have not heard what we have heard, you know—what we have dreamed. How would *you* interpret it?"

P.O. rubbed his chin. "You may be right," he said.

"Did the voice indicate anything else?" asked Bud.

"Yes. It said, 'In those days there was no king in Israel: Every man did that which was right in his own eyes.'"

"King, what, no king? I think your voice is telling us to go to the source. There's a new king coming."

"Walt?" P.O. asked.

"Who else?" Bud replied.

5

Milton and
the Green Block

"Budgies are going to be big," Milton had forecast,
an insight that had brought gladness to Gladys's heart.

He and Gladys were sitting in the shade of the live oak, sunk in
their webbed lawn chairs, watching the offspring of their original
budgies, Adam and Eve. Gazing in the cage like this, Milton said,
made his investment worthwhile even if he had not sold a single
pair. He loved the birds' colors, which taken en masse had changed
over the long months since that day when the first breeding pair had
arrived by mail from Mexico. It had darkened from a pale winter
green to deep bruised emerald. The cage had changed, too.

Called the Ark and built with a plywood floor, a two-by-four
frame, and screening, and decorated by Gladys with oak branches
and twigs, feeders, waterers, hooks for cuttlebone, and—on the
advice of the parakeet-breeder's starter booklet—teacups padded
with cotton wool to nest tiny eggs, it had declined to a bird slum
with feathers stuck to the wire and green-gray droppings piled up
like baby volcanoes on want ads from the *Santa Ana Register*.

In the early days Milton had invited Bud to be his partner in the
bird scheme. Bud had declined with the observation, "They don't
do anything."

"Worms do?"

"Worms burrow."

"Parakeets talk."

"Like what?"

"Little things come out—'Come to Mama,' wolf whistles, 'Polly wanna . . . cracker.' "

"Some of them do, some of them don't. Most of 'em don't."

"They're like people in that respect—some are quiet and some are like you, Bud."

"Whistle and shit, whistle and shit," Bud concluded. "That's all they're good for, Milt. Mark my words."

The birds had bred until overcrowding slowed them to a crawl. Now they skipped flying altogether for a kind of six-toed shuffle that Bud said looked like old men on the way to the bathroom.

At the clatter of nervous wings, Milton turned in his chair and threw up an arm in greeting. Bud's Ford rolled up the driveway with the clap of a loose tailpipe. Levering himself up with a groan, Milton ambled across the patch of dirt that once was dichondra, adjusting his Sam Browne belt. He pushed down his highway patrolman's hat and shot his cuffs.

"Howdee doin'?" he shouted.

"Okay, Milt," Bud said, getting out of the car. He pointed to the Ark. "How's the flock?"

"Gladys and I were just admiring them."

"Hi, Gladys," Bud said, giving her an uncertain smile.

She was crocheting a brown coaster in the shape of a butterfly. She dipped her sunglasses. Her thin-line penciled eyebrows went up to signify that what Milton had said was wrong. She wasn't admiring the birds. She'd had it with the filthy things.

Callum, tagging along, was reminded of something Bud had once told Edith: "The thing about your brother, he's never learned the universe isn't his oyster." Looking at Milton now, Callum knew what Bud had meant. The universe was not Milton's oyster, because Bud thought all the oysters belonged to him. He went over to the kitchen steps and sat apart, ignored for the moment, staring at the cage.

"You wouldn't have a pitcher of tea in the icebox, would you?" Bud asked Gladys.

She put down her brown butterfly and pressed herself out of the chair, smoothing the back of her pineapple muumuu. For a brief moment she pondered the birds, staring philosophically into the cage. When she turned around she fixed Milton with a look. "With God as my witness, Milt, I want you to know, this is cruelty." She looked at Bud. "What, do I look like a waitress?"

Bud jumped to, following her up the kitchen steps.

Milton asked Callum if he wanted to join him in the workshop, and together they crossed the yard. The shop was attached to the garage. It was a comfortable room with an overstuffed armchair, a long wooden workbench, several junked television sets, a pegboard on which hung tools, and outdated Texaco pinup calendars. A model Spitfire and the black-and-white pinwheel that he had used in his hypnosis experiments hung from the ceiling joists along with the bamboo tubes for a human-carrying kite that never got off the ground.

"You know what a crystal set is?" he asked.

"No, sir," Callum replied.

"It's a radio, a basic radio. I'm making one."

He began turning the end of copper wire around a wooden dowel in a steady motion. It was a painstaking process requiring an *extreme* degree of concentration. He continued to wrap the dowel but soon parked himself in the armchair with a sigh.

"This is the tuner," he explained in a thickening voice. "Don't ask me why. You change stations with it." He wound the wire around and around the dowel in a motion that was itself hypnotic. After a few minutes his eyes got heavy and he drifted off to sleep.

Callum leaned against the workbench browsing the pages of a *Mechanics Illustrated*. When he was finished, the black-and-white hypnosis wheel hanging overhead reminded him of the evening Milton had put himself in a trance as a party trick. Nobody had been able to bring him out of it. He had blabbered on and on about someone named Torquemada who was after him for building a windmill. Gladys had put him in bed. She put his feet in a pan of warm water hoping he'd come out of it by morning. He spent the whole night confessing things she never knew he did, which gave her ammunition she had used on him ever since without Milton knowing where it came from.

"Bud!" he shouted from his chair.

Callum turned around so fast he slammed his elbow on the workbench.

Milton leaped out of his chair, dropping the dowel on the floor, and bolted past Callum across the yard. "Bud!" he yelled, out of breath.

When he reached the kitchen, Bud was perched on the counter chatting with Gladys, his hand around a glass of tea. Milton swung open the door, his eyes wild with excitement.

"You ever watch Criswell on TV?" he asked him.

Bud put the glass down on the counter, keeping his eye on him. "Sometimes," he replied with studied calm.

"He talks to Mars."

Gladys said, "He's a kook, Milt, and everybody knows it."

"I wouldn't be so certain," Milton replied.

Criswell was a visionary with a flattop, a boyish face, and blue eyes, and everybody in southern California knew who he was. He predicted events like earthquakes, recessions, and pennant winners, and sometimes he repeated whole conversations he claimed to have had with Martians. Martians took an avid interest in Orange County, California, according to Criswell's accounts. Those Martians ignored famines in Africa and uprisings in Algeria, but they knew weeks in advance when a frost might kill the crops within TV range of Criswell's voice. Each Friday evening when Bud would say, "Here comes the kook, Edith," Callum knew it was time for *Criswell Predicts*.

Gladys asked Milton, "What on earth are you talking about?"

He shrugged. "I don't know," as though he had lost his train of thought.

"You don't *know*?"

"I was thinking. . . . Okay, tell me this. Is there a difference between a car and a dog?"

"I *knew* it," Gladys said with a fatal finality.

"Let him explain," said Bud.

"A dog is a dog and a car is a car only because of the arrangement of molecules. The molecules are the same. Therefore, the dog and the car are the same."

"Except for the arrangement of the molecules," said Bud. Milton's logic was hard to deny.

"What about the immortal soul?" Gladys asked. When she lowered her sunglasses, her eyes looked worried.

"That's religion. This is science. We're making UNIVACs now because our bodies will be obsolete. We're going to become UNIVAC's ancestors. They're going to carry around our knowledge when we're gone. It's the next step, from man to machine."

"I don't feel obsolete, do you, Gladys?" Bud asked, trying to keep Gladys from exploding. It didn't work.

"You're a *kook*, Milt," she said. "A kook just like Criswell."

Milton seemed not to hear her, and if he did, he didn't seem to care what she said. "We get diseased and die, don't we? What would you call death if not obsolete? And what about space travel?"

"What about it?" she asked, sounding disheartened now.

"Our bodies can't withstand the pressures of space and the heat and the poisonous gases. If we're to travel through space, we'll have to send machines."

"Did Criswell tell you that?" she asked.

Callum, who had come into the kitchen behind Milton, could see now how Criswell sucked you in, and before you knew it, you were Them.

"Most of it I thought up myself—just now out in the workshop."

"Well I wouldn't be proud of it," she said.

Milton walked out of the kitchen with his shoulders hunched. He put himself down heavily in the lawn chair under the oak. Callum went with him, and after a brief silence contemplating the parakeets, he asked, "Do me a favor?"

"Anything," Callum said, feeling bad for him. It wasn't nice for a wife to call her husband a kook.

"I need toilet-paper tubes. Thousands of them."

The thought dawned on Callum at that moment how events caromed like billiard balls. The fun of being around adults was seeing which ball would go where. Adults were like kids without the restrictions. The consequences of their actions were more dramatic, which made them more fun to be around.

"Toilet-paper tubes?"

"That's right. Do you think you can help me?"

"Sure," Callum replied. "When would you need them by?"

"As soon as you can. Okay?"

"I'll try."

"Not a word about it to anyone, promise?"

"Sure," Callum said.

At the sound of the screen door squeaking, Milton set up a folding chair for Bud. He looked up at the porch where Gladys was standing with her hands on her hips, glaring at him through her sunglasses.

"What do you want?" he asked.

"A *kook*, Milt," she said and went back into the house.

"Oh, don't mind her," Bud said a moment later, joining them under the oak.

Milton was thinking about the birds, his feet resting on the center column of their cage. "You know, not one of these damn things talks. Squawk and shit, squawk and shit. That's all they ever do. You ever met anybody who wants to buy a bird that does nothing but squawk and shit?"

"You can't say I didn't warn you," Bud said.

"No, I can't," Milton said. "And I can't begin to tell you how I appreciate your pointing it out to me. Besides that, is there another reason you stopped by?"

"We were wondering what you thought you could contribute to the dream-scheme."

"We?"

"P.O. wanted to know."

"Oh he did, did he?"

"Now don't get defensive, Milt. He was just asking."

"I suppose he sent you over to keep an eye on me."

Those had been P.O.'s exact words. After the failure of Milton's chairmanship of the Subcommittee on Site Selection for the doughnut stand and his failure to sell even one of his budgies, there was reason to keep abreast of Milton's efforts.

"What *have* you been doing?" Bud asked.

"I don't think I'm obligated to tell you."

"But you have been—doing something, I mean?"

The tone of Milton's voice was dismissive. "I can only hint at my contribution."

"It's a secret," Callum told Bud.

Milton said, "You can tell P.O. for me, if you think you need to, that it is of a scientific nature involving radio beams."

"Fine, fine," Bud said, glad the conversation was over. He couldn't wait to tell P.O.

After Bud and Callum had gone, Milton stared into the cage. Those at the top of the feathery heap stared back at him with sullen contempt. Like an army marking time, they rocked from one slender leg to the other with a malevolence that was surprising from feathered green creatures of such diminutive size and usually harmless demeanor.

"You're like rats," he told them.

Without conviction or enthusiasm he searched for the key on the ring of his belt. Mumbling to himself, he said, "I could never tell you apart, to be honest. I don't know Adam from Eve. You probably don't understand. We tried to teach you. 'Come to Mama, Come to Mama.' Not one of you learned."

He inserted the key in the padlock, then swung the cage door open.

"Shoo," he said, flapping his arms.

The birds pressed against the screen, like shoppers against the doors on a sale day.

"Shoo, now." He whipped his holster in a circle. "You're too dumb to understand," he told them. "I'm letting you go. *Vaya con Dio, amigos.*"

A hundred wings stirred with the sound of shuffling cards. One pair of birds departed through the open door, then, inching across the plywood, more found their freedom. They formed a winged plume in the sky, a thin column of green feathered smoke heading south. Milton waved his cap. In less than a minute the whole corps of the Ark had spilled into the air. Flying over the house they were like an emerald banner. Milton rocked back on his heels and howled.

"Hey, Gladys. Lookit what just happened out here!"

6

Frost Bite

Walking his grove was what Mr. Wait did every day of the week in the silent company of Bob. By the end of the week, he had passed every tree in his bushy kingdom, each of which he inspected, nursed, trimmed, fussed over, and often talked to. Some people would think this was a lonely routine, but they would be wrong. The reason was the trees. He was in his grove now, walking in stride with Callum, whom he told, "Trees are as good as being around simple people."

"Or Bob," Callum said.

"Or Bob."

At the double mention of his name, Bob, who sauntered behind them with his muzzle to the ground, did nothing.

"This one here," Mr. Wait said, indicating a tree that was thinner than its neighbors, "caught a chill when it was just a shoot. It's always been sickly. They come from Spain, you know, orange trees. Thin branches. They're used to the Andalusian sun."

Callum liked hearing Mr. Wait say things like that. The comment wasn't meant to make a point, unlike Bud's. His statements were sharp swords. Bud's friends scored one another on points made in an endless verbal game that Callum could not always follow. The things Mr. Wait said, by contrast, weren't intended as anything. Often they weren't even meant to be understood.

"How long ago was it a shoot?" Callum asked. Orange trees did not give him the same sense of longevity as giant sequoias, but the question was worth posing. Questions always were worth asking no matter how stupid they seemed. Bud said it was a good way to learn. The only thing you ever discovered sitting on your hands, he liked to say, was that your ass was fat.

"Eight years ago, or so," said Mr. Wait, running his hand along the end of a spindly branch. "I put in a whole section of new trees after the freeze that came just after I bought this land."

"Trees freeze?"

"The same as you and me. They have water in their veins like our blood. The only difference is trees can't keep warm without our help."

He walked over to a smudge pot, one of hundreds in his grove, which was sitting on a raised circle of earth between the trees. He unscrewed the cap on its fuel reservoir, and seeing it needed filling, he lifted a jerrican of kerosene from Bob's saddle rack.

"This is how we help the trees stay warm when there's a chill on," said Mr. Wait.

"Is that why the fogs are bad, because of the pots?"

"If they are working right they are supposed to make clouds, and the clouds hug the ground. The fog serves as proof that the trees are warm. It's like a blanket over you when you sleep at night. Some of the younger growers are setting up these new propeller blades to whip the air. Circulating air keeps the frost out too. I prefer the old way. It makes sense. You fire up the pots like a wood fire in the hearth at home and you feel warm just watching."

"It was foggy last night," Callum pointed out.

Mr. Wait screwed the cap back on the reservoir and returned the jerrican to Bob's rack. "Nature never meant for citrus to grow here," he said in his storyteller voice. "The climate isn't right. It's like everything else. People don't know when to stop."

"But why should they?" Callum asked.

"Because they push nature like she had no feelings. Then they have to rely on science to get them out of the jam. The smudge pots keep my trees alive. I shouldn't complain." He put his mouth close to Callum's ear. "I'll tell you a secret, sonny. Science isn't all it's cracked up to be."

"Roland says it's the future."

"It is the future. And it should be, too."

Callum did not understand. "But you just said—"

"Sometimes we don't use common sense. That's all I'm saying. Take atoms."

"Yeah," Callum said. Atoms were awesome even if nobody had ever seen one.

"Atoms were going to benefit mankind. But the first use they were put to was a bomb." He tapped his temple with his forefinger. "Stupid, too much knowledge is."

"We have air-raid drills at school."

"You'd never make it," he said, and then, as if he had said more than he wanted, he looked up at the sky. "As for the grove here, it doesn't matter."

"What doesn't matter?"

"Whether the trees keep warm."

"You love your trees."

"The groves are disappearing. Young families with boys like you, that's the next crop."

"People aren't a crop," Callum said.

"Depends on who you are and how you look at 'em," Mr. Wait said.

They continued down a row between trees, and a short time later they came out along the highway. They followed a dirt path Bob and Mr. Wait's treading had packed hard as clay. Every few yards Callum bent over and picked up empty soda bottles that had been thrown out the windows of passing cars.

"Pigs," Mr. Wait remarked.

"I'm glad," Callum said. Each reclaimed empty paid two cents, five for the quart bottles. And over the summers he had saved more than fifty dollars, deposited at the Dime Savings Bank. He was proud of what his passbook meant. He had saved enough to leave home any time he chose.

"It means that people don't care about their neighbors. Like your father says, it's all getting too impersonal. It's the newcomers."

Everyone Callum knew was a newcomer. A family was historical if it had lived in the same house for five years. "What's an old-comer?" he asked.

Mr. Wait pointed his finger across the highway. Following its direction Callum saw another grove.

"The lady over there," he said.

"We met her and her daughter—Serena," he said brightly and described the Job's Daughters' tea.

"I've seen a young woman riding a tractor along the irrigation row. Knows how to operate it like a real farmer, too."

"A tractor?" He couldn't imagine it.

"Her mother's property has a lineage that goes back to when the Mexicans gave away land like it was dirt. It's part of history. Those land grants are broken up now. Irvine is left. Flood, down San Diego way, is, too. I doubt anybody cares anymore."

An amber bottle flew over their heads, thrown from a passing car. It landed with a thud. Callum walked into the grove and picked it up. He could still feel the warmth of the hand that had thrown it. "When will we know if the dream is a success?" he asked. It was a question he had wanted to know the answer to ever since their general powwow on the lanai. He thought he might have missed the answer while he was taking notes, but when he went back through his minutes, he knew that no one had bothered to ask.

"These things take time," said Mr. Wait.

"Bud says, 'What good is a dream if you aren't going to be around to enjoy it?' "

"I understand his impatience. He needs a success," Mr. Wait said.

"Why is it so important?"

"Because it validates his being here."

"Shouldn't you make him see that it's okay if he doesn't suc-ceed?"

"Bud's a grown man."

"Isn't that what friends are for?"

"Yes and no, yes and no. Friends are meant to listen. The listen-ing helps. That's all they're good for. Friends can't run your life for you. It's a hard lesson for some people to learn. Take if you are bored. You say, 'I'm bored.' Only you can do something about it.

Boredom is a state of mind. Pick up a book. Paint a picture. Write a song. Dig a hole. Think a thought. Dream."

"What if you can't?"

"Then go shoot yourself," he replied, impatiently. "At least it won't be boring." Mr. Wait sucked in his breath. "Oh my oh my," he muttered as if he were stricken, and he lurched off the path pulling hard on Bob's rope. He plunged into the grove, finally stopping by a fallen smudge pot in a circle of trees with leaves that had turned a sickly brown. The trees seemed to shiver in their moribund bareness.

"I was afraid of this," Mr. Wait said, kneeling down. He picked up the pot and strapped it on Bob's back, then set off through the grove at a pace that was hard to follow.

Callum kept him in sight, feeling sad for how he invested his emotions in chlorophyll. It wasn't like the dead trees were human or there weren't more where they came from. Mr. Wait had made the trees his friends, and he mourned their frosty passing. It wasn't natural, anyone would tell you.

Back at the clearing Mr. Wait dropped Bob's rope and slapped his butt, shooing him in his corral. Bob, sensing trouble, moved faster than Callum had ever seen him, watching Mr. Wait from over the wall of the corral. His ears stood straight up scanning the air for danger.

"I'll wait out here," Callum shouted across the yard.

"You do that, sonny," Mr. Wait said and slammed the screen door behind him.

7

Here Be Dragons

Cheval had chosen tight pedal pushers and a loose blouse unbuttoned halfway down. A mirror behind the diner's counter reflected her cleavage in all its abundance when she hunched over to dig into her ice-cream float. Men from nearby city offices eating lunch to her left and right goggled at her reflection as though she were the blue plate special. Callum could see why sometimes on summer evenings the neighborhood dads would set up their folding chairs in her front yard to watch her pull weeds. At those times her front garden could get so crowded it would turn into a lawn party.

"P.O.'s a new man," she was telling him between spoonfuls of float, "like when he was panning gold in Alaska. Did I ever tell you about that?" She leaned forward laughing, and the men at the counter loaded their hungry eyes. "He was camped at the bottom of a mountain up to his ass in mosquitoes. It was dark as a cave. He was asleep and a single itty-bitty stone bounced down thousands of feet right off my honey's head. He never found the lump of gold he went for. But he came home with one on his head. Now with your dad's dream he's feeling lucky again. He thinks he can't lose."

"I think so, too," Callum said.

"I tell you, your father is a smart one. *He* doesn't need to go all the way to Alaska to find gold. He just saw all these itty-bitty pieces of a puzzle and put them together in his head. I like your father." She wiped her mouth on a paper napkin. "Is he a college graduate?"

"He wasn't able to attend because of money," Callum replied, echoing Bud's standard explanation of why a man of his learning did not have a degree.

"Not because of brains, that's good. He *could* be a college man. I tell you, your mother's a lucky gal. One of these days, Bud is going places. And you know what? You are going to live in a house with a swimming pool."

"You think so?" he asked, hardly convinced.

At that moment P.O. sneaked up behind Cheval and wrapped his arms around her waist. Cheval shrieked, and while they hugged, Callum admired the skull tattoo on P.O.'s arm. He was just like Randolph Scott except for his dandelion hair, which served as a reminder of his status as war hero. Even persistent rumors of a Section Eight had not shaken Callum's belief in him as the bravest man he knew.

The men at the counter returned their eyes to their lunches.

"Ready to go?" P.O. asked.

Cheval dabbed her lips on the napkin and slid like oil off the stool. With her stiletto heels clacking, she walked arm-in-arm with Callum and P.O. down the street to the county building. Callum felt like he owned the world walking beside two such handsome and confident people. Their optimism and their pleasure in each other's company warmed him like the sun.

Through the doors and up a wide staircase they followed a polished corridor around a rotunda to an office that smelled of old papers. The man in charge was standing behind a waist-high counter. He pushed back a black eyeshade and smiled at Cheval, who hardly noticed. She was lucky enough to be ignorant of how life worked for the majority. She didn't know, for instance, that men didn't smile at every woman. She didn't know that the world offered the ugly ones the questionable compliment of invisibility.

When the man adjusted his glasses, the lenses magnified his eyes. His smile faded, and without a word of explanation, he opened a gate, saying to P.O., "You know how it works."

A moment later they entered a room of wooden storage cabinets with wide drawers. There must have been ten of them lined up side by side along the windows.

"These contain maps," P.O. explained. "Now what we're going to do is look at each map and, well, see what we can see."

"Oh, *that's* helpful," Cheval said. "What are we looking for?"

"The needle in a haystack. You're going to have to interpret what you see. It's not going to be easy. And we'll probably make mistakes. You can see what we're looking for as easily as you can miss it."

Cheval folded her arms across her chest. "Come on, P.O. We have better things to do," she said.

He shook his head. "If Walt is building his fun zone around here, the property will show up on these maps. One pair of eyes is as good as another. Besides, there are too many maps for me to do this alone. You'll get the hang of it. You wait and see."

"Hang of what?" Callum asked.

"You pull a map out of the drawer. Spread it out on the cabinet. Look it over. Try to find properties of more than a hundred acres near main roads. Okay? If a property is near a main road and larger than a hundred acres, I want to know about it. But if a property is more than a hundred acres and near a main road and is an airport or a military installation or if it is owned by the government, go on to the next one. Get my drift?"

"Isn't military land good enough for Walt?" Cheval asked.

"The army doesn't sell no matter what. Now let's get cracking."

The first map he pulled from his drawer confused Callum, but once he accustomed his eyes to the matter of scale, he found his bearings. He spotted a few likely properties—the U.S. Government owned the largest tract near the coast, an ammunition dump left over from World War II. It gave him pleasure to see on the maps places he had passed by. Bud said mapmakers in the Dark Ages wrote in the blank spaces of unexplored continents, "Here be dragons." To dream of places that he could touch on maps with the tip of his finger—places like the Congo or the Hindu Kush—was almost like going there. "Here be dragons," he said to himself, looking at a map of Orange County.

"What's that?" P.O. asked.

"Dragons."

He ran his finger along Ball Road, pinpointing Mr. Wait's grove. He was surprised to see how many acres he owned. His grove spread west from the highway nearly to the foothills. He brought his face down close and followed the thin line of highway that separated Mr. Wait's from Mary Rodriguez's. Both Mr. Wait's and Mrs. Rodriguez's had more than a hundred acres. And both bordered the most traveled highway between Los Angeles and San Diego. Those two groves were what P.O. was looking for. Yet, Callum asked himself, why should he say anything? P.O. knew Mr. Wait's property, if not Mrs. Rodriguez's, as well as he knew his own back yard. Mr. Wait would not sell his land even to Walt Disney. And Callum did not want to think of Mrs. Rodriguez selling hers. She and Serena would have to move, maybe out of the county, and he would not see them again. He glanced up at Cheval, who was gazing out the window, and he secretively slid the map back in the drawer.

"What have you found?" P.O. asked him.

"La Mirada," he told him, stuttering at first. "It has eight thousand acres. The Willowcreek Country Club has more than a hundred acres."

"Nothing else?"

Callum almost felt guilty replying, "No, sir."

P.O. rubbed his chin. "The La Mirada won't subdivide. Eight thousand acres, you said? No. That's not what we're looking for."

"Why not a thousand acres or ten thousand?" Cheval asked. "How do you know Walt is looking for only a hundred?"

"An educated guess."

"What's the educated part?"

"I calculated the acreage of the Pike and quadrupled it. Walt'll be thinking he'll need to expand with the success of his place. He's not the kind to make an estimate based on failure. Besides, he has done nothing you'd call small up till now. He'll be making a splash, which means big—a hundred acres or so."

"Why not more, was my question."

"One expense he can control is the cost of the land," he said, sounding impatient with her questions. "Besides, he won't *need* more. Did you find anything?"

"The Santiago Canyon Road property," she told him. "The map didn't say who owns it."

"The Catholic Church," said P.O. automatically. "That's the *only* one you found?"

"Don't blame me, P.O."

He held up a piece of paper. "My only prospect is near the coast."

"The Pike is near the coast, too," Callum said.

"*On* the coast, not near it," P.O. corrected him. "Walt wouldn't want comparisons made between his fun zone and a carney like that. And oceanfront property is darned expensive. This plot I found here is agricultural. It's in from the coast by a mile or so. It's where that geezer Mr. Tucker has his trading post."

"Do you think that's it then?" Cheval asked.

"Who knows? There's a lot more work to do. I know Tucker's land. Not much there but beans and dirt and clouds."

"So it isn't a prospect, or it is?" Cheval asked, confused.

"A prospect, yes, and maybe no more than that. I said it was going to be a needle in a haystack."

Cheval looked glum. "Well there sure are a lot of haystacks, P.O."

"And only one needle," he said. "It's a puzzle, Cheval. It's exciting!"

"Are you saying it may not even be in the county?" she asked, covering a yawn with her hand.

"That's a question I think we should ask Answer Man."

The calaboose where Answer Man lived was on a narrow dead-end alley off Main Street.

With space for one prisoner, a bunk, a chair, and a table, the single jail cell was no larger than a decent-size outhouse. The jail was a feature of Old Town, and to reach it they had to pass Knott's chicken-and-dumpling restaurant, the gold miners' sluice, the mine shaft, and the railroad tracks. They hurried along Main Street with the cowboys and young women in hooped skirts and calico bonnets who were helping visitors make believe.

Callum went up to the jail door and peered through the wooden bars at the convict everybody called Answer Man. He had visited him many times before, partly because he felt sorry for him and partly because he represented a danger that was safe as long as the cell's bars separated him from his guests. No one seemed to know his real name or, for that matter, his crime or even the length of his term, but his black-striped prison suit was dusty with age. He was hunched over a table reading a yellowed newspaper by candlelight. His black beard, which grew longer each year, lay across the table like a neglected tablecloth. His cheeks were sunken, and his eyes had the gaunt look of someone who had been deprived of the sun for too long.

"Afternoon, P.O.," Answer Man said in a hoarse, tired voice, with his back to the door.

"You *know* him?" Callum asked P.O.

"P.O. knows *everyone*, honey," said Cheval, rolling her eyes.

"Better than that," P.O. said. "I know his alter ego. Come on out, Ernie," he called. "I know you can see me."

A moment later a door opened behind them. Callum looked around, confused. He had never noticed that door before. He could see now that it was concealed in the bare siding of a building on one side of the alley. An obese man in denim coveralls and a bright blue plaid shirt stepped out, blinking in the sunlight. The sound of his laughter as he stood there watching them was so deep it might have echoed from the bottom of a well. His eyes were dark and his face was hard to read through all of its spare flesh.

"Answer Man," P.O. announced.

The man looked at Cheval approvingly. "*You* can call me Ernie," he told her.

"But—" Callum pointed to the jail cell.

"A dummy, that's a dummy in there, kid," Ernie said matter-of-factly.

Callum felt disappointed, or worse, as if a friend had died. He wanted to complain that this slob Ernie did not know what he was talking about, but he looked at him, then P.O., and he said nothing.

"Come on inside," Ernie told them and closed the door behind them. They were standing in an office crowded with papers stacked on shelves alongside dictionaries, encyclopedias, *Who's Who*s, almanacs, maps, directories, and books on biology and chemistry and anatomy. A wooden swivel chair shrieked when Ernie deposited himself in it.

"It works like this, kid," Ernie explained. Callum did not know if he wanted to hear, but he listened. "That jail out there is rigged with a microphone right by the bars. I hear the questions people ask in the speaker here"—he pointed to a speaker on a shelf—"and I look up the answer if I don't know it."

"But what about the names Answer Man calls people by?" Callum asked. The man in the cell called out the names of his visitors like he was glad to see them. It shocked some of them into running right back down the alley, and always made people laugh.

"See that there?" Ernie pointed to a hole in the wall the size of a quarter. "People in the know, like parents, tell me the name and age of the person they want the dummy to say hi to. Like P.O. would whisper your name and how old you are through the hole. I say hi to you in the microphone here when you look in the jail cell. There's a speaker in the dummy's chest so it seems like he's doing the talking. Scares the living shit out of kids and old folks. I swear to God."

Callum looked at the floor thinking how he liked Answer Man as a gloomy presence in a jail cell who never failed to cheer him up. But as a complicated system of microphones and speakers connected to a fat man in a book-filled room, he was only a cheap trick. Bud said knowledge was a good thing. But sometimes it robbed people of the mystery that made them feel better about themselves. It was hard to know what to believe in anymore. Ernie—fat, mean, and armed with facts—was nothing compared with a prisoner who had reassured Callum, until a few minutes ago, that at least one grown-up, even if he was a crook, knew the answers to everything.

"What brings you by?" Ernie asked, leaning back in his swivel chair and folding his hands behind his head.

"We were just over at the county offices," P.O. said, "trying to get to the bottom of a deduction. I don't want to give it away, Ernie. It's a secret. But I knew you would help us with some answers."

"I owe you, P.O.," he said, referring to a dispute with a neighbor P.O. had settled with a survey of Ernie's backyard. "The questions I get, you know, aren't stumpers—how fast's the speed of light, how old's the oldest man, what's the biggest ocean, who killed President Lincoln? They're from kids."

"I understand."

"Skeeter, age twelve," a voice whispered through the hole in the wall.

Ernie leaned forward. "Hi! Skeeter aged twelve!" he shouted and pointed to a convex mirror over the window above the door. The reflection showed a boy fleeing down the alley.

"Works like a charm," Ernie said.

"Do you like scaring kids?" Cheval asked him.

"Sure do. They like it, too." He saw that he needed to explain. "Being scared is a lot more fun than *not* being scared, isn't that true?" he asked Callum.

Callum had to admit he was right. He nodded.

"Now back to you, P.O."

"What's the speed of light, Answer Man?" asked a sibilant voice through the speaker.

Ernie threw up his arms. "Give me a minute's rest, will you?" He leaned into the microphone. "A hundred eighty-six thousand miles a second. Goodbye!" With a humorless smile, he told Cheval, "And I thought it was going to be a slow day. Now, fire away."

"Just in general," asked P.O., "what would you say the biggest change has been around here lately—I mean in the county?"

He thought about that a minute. "No question about it. The way it's growing."

"Exactly," said P.O., as if he couldn't have said it better himself.

"The infrastructure can't keep up. You drive the roads. You know. The beaches. Aren't they just getting a bit too crowded?"

"My thoughts exactly. Would you call it a trend?"

"Interesting question," Ernie replied. "What you are asking is, is it a permanent growth or just a fad?" He scratched behind his ear. "Back in the forties, right after the war, people settled in the San Fernando Valley. That was the promotional work of the family that owns the *Los Angeles Times*. They and some others bought up a lot of arid land and diverted water from the Owens Valley to the east and made it habitable, and they sold the land for a big profit. That pattern changed a few years ago. Now, because of vets like you, P.O., Orange County is taking off."

P.O. knew this was true, but he liked hearing it. His next questions had to do with conditions that would make an area attractive to anyone who wanted to build an open-air amusement park. Weather was the key. "What can you tell us about rainfall?"

"Here in Orange County? We get an average of twelve inches a year."

"What about further up north around Los Angeles?"

"Pasadena gets twenty."

"What about temperatures?"

"Summers, seventy-six degrees around here on average. Winter temperatures, sixty-seven degrees on average. Ninety on average in Pomona. Cold as winter, summers are in San Francisco. So this county has the best temperatures in the state for creature comfort."

"Now here's a tough one. What about humidity?"

That did stump him. But Ernie found a report on a shelf. In a short time he was stabbing his finger on a page. "Orange County has sixty-five percent humidity, almost perfect."

"Do you see what I'm driving at here?" P.O. asked him.

He sat back in his chair. "I can't say I do."

"What do these facts tell you, Ernie? Put them together and what have you got?"

"That Orange County is a great place to live. We all know that. We don't need statistics."

"No, but a person we may be dealing with does."

"A businessman?"

"Something like that. Now, let me ask you the big question. If Orange County is a great place to live, wouldn't it also be a great place to visit?"

"Would be? It already is. Why do you think all these kids are asking me questions? They come out here from back East with their parents on vacation. Knott's and Sea World are the only attractions unless you count Forest Lawn and the beaches."

"An amusement park could stay open year-round, nights, too, couldn't it, in Orange County?"

"Knott's does."

A voice whispered through the hole in the wall, "Amy Louise, age seven."

A girl giggled and tried to ask a question and giggled more. Finally she got herself under control and asked, "Answer Man, what's the capital of North Dakota?"

Ernie scowled. "Aw shit, not that one again," he said.

. . .

P.O. was in his backyard with his shirt off and his muscles bunched under the weight of a dumbbell in each hand. Watching his exertions, Cheval was on the grass in white spiked heels and a purple orchid-print bikini, leaning back on her arms as though she were posing for a suntan ad. Her voice was as bright as ever when she said hello to Callum, who entered the yard from the driveway.

P.O. dropped the dumbbells on the grass and wiped his brow. He did a couple of cool-down squats. "I swear," he said, taking the towel that Cheval handed up to him. "I used to be able to lift weights all day long."

"You look fine to me, honey," she told him, crossing her legs.

Callum was clutching his paper-route booklet and his zippered canvas change purse. "Collecting," he said.

Cheval started to get up, but she changed her mind, looking across the yard at Mr. Buffum. He had set up his recliner on the edge of his back lawn facing P.O. and Cheval's. From time to time he glanced up from pages of the *Saturday Evening Post* to see what Cheval was doing.

"He's waiting for me to get up," she told P.O. "Is there no privacy?"

P.O. glanced at Mr. Buffum and waved cursorily. "Give him a thrill, Cheval. It doesn't cost anything and you know what it means to him, what with his wife and all."

Mrs. Buffum weighed a quarter of a ton, and Mr. Buffum didn't look heavier than a wet towel.

"Mr. Buffum," Cheval shouted at him, getting to her feet, "isn't it time for your dinner?"

He leaned forward in his chair and stared. "Nope," he said.

Cheval marched in the house and a minute later came out with Callum's paper money and a Labatt's for herself and P.O. Mr. Buffum looked at her with a hurt expression, as if she'd forgotten to ask him what he wanted to drink. He watched as she reached into her bikini top for a piece of mimeographed paper, which she held out to Callum.

"What's this about?" she asked.

"Oh that," Callum said, recognizing the piece of paper as his own creation, the flyer he had delivered to every customer on his news-paper route.

"I honestly never heard such a thing."

Neither had Callum but he nodded agreeably. "Edith got me started on it," he said, repeating the lie he had made up. "The Boys' Club is behind it. I don't know much about it otherwise."

Cheval handed the paper to P.O.

SAVE THE CHINESE CHILDREN!
Toilet-paper Tube Famine Relief
The starving children of China need your toilet-paper tubes
to survive. Please help them. Just put the tubes aside and
your paperboy will pick them up on collection day.

THE GARDEN GROVE TOILET-PAPER TUBE
FAMINE RELIEF COMMITTEE

"Oh, sure," P.O. said, giving the same skeptical voice to the solicitation that Callum had heard from other customers. "The Chinese are the kings of weird, but not this weird."

Callum shrugged, trying to act casual.

"I know those Chinese children are starving, honey," Cheval told him. "But I doubt if toilet-paper tubes are going to help them."

Callum stared in the distance. "That's what I was told," he said.

"Maybe you were told wrong," Cheval said.

Callum was fast finding out how protective people felt toward their used toilet-paper tubes. They chucked them in the garbage or burned them in the incinerators, but give them away? Not on a Chinaman's life. Most of his customers had told him they did not save the tubes; Lionel's mother next door said she didn't use toilet paper at all. But she was English.

Edith had asked him when he gave her the flyer, "Tell me why again?"

"For Milton's parakeets," he had told her.

"Toilet-paper tubes?"

"That's what he said."

"He is for the birds then."

A while later, when he had told them, Cloud and Blue were embarrassed. "You're almost as weird as he is," Cloud told him, referring to Milton.

"It's sick, is what," said Blue.

Callum knew then that he had to disguise his intent. He noted that Edith went on like a missionary if they left one speck of food on their dinner plates. With the Chinese as an excuse, he had figured that anything was believable. He was finding, however, that the Chinese were not far enough away or strange enough to pull off his toilet-paper tube subterfuge with enough customers to satisfy Milton's request. But it would have to do.

"Maybe he should hear the story about what happened to me on Rat Island?" P.O. asked Cheval.

"It's a good object lesson, honey," she agreed, giving him a warm smile.

He cleared his throat and put on his best storytelling voice. "In the war, as you may know, I was a pom-pomer. We patrolled the Aleutians on a navy cruiser."

Callum got comfortable on the grass. "The Aleutians," he repeated, liking the sound of the word.

"We'd been out for months defending a rock called Rat Island, and we put into Hawaii one time for a refit and shore leave. We were popping our buttons with excitement. We figured we could get away with anything. What did we have to lose if we were only going to be killed the next time out? One night I decided to crash a formal military dance purely for the hell of it. I put on my dress-white uniform. I looked spiffy as hell. I was wind-burned and full of piss and vinegar after three months of rosy palm and pom-poming the Japs. When I got to the dance I never saw so many officers in one place. Well, it *was* the Officers' Club."

"I thought you were a seaman," said Callum.

"That's what I'm saying. The ballroom was full of bird colonels and admirals and captains and except for them there was me and about a hundred Filipino waiters. In short, this was not my crowd." He wiped his face with the towel. "There was this girl there almost as pretty as Cheval. She's what made me stay. She had pouty lips and thick honey-colored hair that fell to her shoulders. Her eyes were brown and wide and moist. Her ankles were thin. Every part of her was willowy except for up here"—and he cupped his hands under his chest—"which were, well, full."

"Get on with it, P.O.," Cheval growled.

"She was standing on the dance floor alone, this girl was. A minute after I saw her, a full-bird colonel, a Marine—and boy, was he sharp, his flattop was standing at attention and his dress blues had creases you could draw blood with—came up to her. The way he behaved, I could tell she was his daughter.

"The Marine band struck up a waltz and I danced over to the cash bar. I slugged down a bourbon and watched the girl and her full-bird father. After awhile, I started feeling like I was cool. You know, real cool, like I could do anything. The girl danced with her father and some older officers and every now and then a lieutenant or captain had the guts to break in. Everybody was watching her. I mean—excuse me, Cheval—this was a goddess we're talking about here.

"A few foxtrots came and went—'Mountain Greenery,' that kind of beat. I shifted into maximum cool, thanks to Mister Beam. I walked on the dance floor. Little dots of light speckled the ceiling like they do at proms. I tapped the girl's partner on the shoulder. He was too surprised not to give her up to me, and besides, he was an officer and a gentleman. And with her finally in my arms, we glided across the floor. Her hair smelled like honey. She smiled at me and her teeth sparkled. She said her name was Rebecca. Rebecca, Rebecca, I thought, I will take your name with me to a watery grave. We were the gob and the goddess."

Cheval nodded, policing a story she knew by heart.

"Are you following so far?" P.O. asked Callum.

"Yes, sir," Callum replied, wondering when he would get to the pom-pom guns.

"Well, about then I applied a little pressure in the small of Rebecca's back. She danced in closer. I could feel her warm breath. I kept the pressure on. I should have led her back to her father and said good night then and there. But those long days around Rat Island staring in the spider's-web sight made me crazy. I felt her under the taffeta, and I ran my other hand through the hairs on her neck. She lowered her arm and we slowed the tempo. I remembered thinking, Oh jeez. I bent over. But she pulled me into her. She knew

I was carrying loaded ammo. There was no one else, no one on Hawaii, no one in the ballroom, no war, no Rat Island—just the two of us, the goddess and the gob.

"I was cocked on a hair trigger by then, and if you don't know what that means, someday you will. A light zephyr would have set me off. Rebecca under all that taffeta gripped me tighter, not wanting to miss out. I whispered in her ear, "Darling, *je vous aime beaucoup*," you know, like in that song. My knees wobbled and I let go right in my whites. I held her away from me and she smiled weakly. All we needed at that point was to share a cigarette. The full birds and admirals were watching with smiles fixed on their faces like wax dummies. I thought I was home free.

"Rebecca looked like she was in love and we were on our wedding night. I took her over to her father's table—as many full birds and admirals as you would see at a peace conference. Their chests sagged with medals. Their eyes went from her to me. I thought we were Romeo and Juliet. They looked at me like I was a Jap with a sword.

"Rebecca's full-bird father hustled me out of there by the arm. I didn't even have time to say goodbye. My feet hardly touched the floor.

" 'Look at yourself, sailor, just look at yourself!'

"Those were his exact words." P.O. laughed out loud at the recollection. "He demanded my C.O.'s name.

" 'You have vio . . .' The word stuck in his throat 'You have vio . . . lated my Rebecca.'

" 'Maybe, sir, you could tell me . . .' I said to him, ready to deny everything. I never got the chance.

" 'Look at yourself,' and he pointed at my crotch.

"A yellow stain like the map of Chile, I mean it was a jagged cutlass of a stain, ran from my crotch down to my knee. It was as decipherable an expression of all my lonely months at sea as the medals on the admirals' chests were expressions of their bravery. I mean, it was the Cumgressional Medal of Honor."

"Wow!"

"Easy, P.O.," Cheval warned him.

"I'm sorry." And he laughed again.

Callum couldn't see what there was to laugh about. P.O. had been in serious trouble.

P.O. took a deep breath. "After that, Rebecca's father reported me to my C.O. He said I was a pervert. And when our ship set sail again for Rat Island, I was told in no uncertain terms to watch my step.

"About then the Japs started swarming. It was hell. Have you ever seen a pom-pom gunner in action?" he asked.

Callum sat up straight. "No, not really, not in person."

"Well, let me show you," he said. He unfolded his arms and crouched by the mudguard of his motorcycle, which rested over an oil spot in the driveway. He tucked his shoulders under the handlebars and looked up. "It was like this. *Pom pom pom pom,*" he made a popping sound. "Jesus, it was merciless, just forever *pom pom pom pom pom.* This was the only sound the world had ever known, *pom pom pom pom pom.* And those little bastards in their Zeros came in so close I could see their faces."

"P.O.?" Cheval said.

"I can't stop now, Cheval," he said, waving her off. "Do you know the worst of it?" he asked Callum. "The helmet. Because it was like this"—he held his hands beside his ears. "It wasn't like an infantry helmet. It had a walkie-talkie inside and weighed more than a bucket of water. Just look." He pointed to his powerful neck. "This was a chicken gizzard before the pom-poms. The helmet had a chin strap made of rubber. I suppose it originally was made of leather, but progress, you know. If it wasn't rubber in those days, it wasn't worth a damn. Rubber was the future. We had to keep the helmets on because they helped us shoot down the Jap kazooties. We had to shout in the mike and listen up in the earphones. It was awful."

He paused again for a well-earned breath. "So there we were, the pom-pom would recoil, and the helmet would lift off my head. The rubber chin strap snapped it down again with a bang. The helmet was knocking me silly."

"Wow!"

"At first I put up with it, you know? But after a couple weeks, I started going nuts."

Callum clenched his fists.

"My aim went off. I couldn't sleep. I was seeing snowflakes. I couldn't see the Zeros through the blizzard in my head. I asked my battery ensign, the little shit, if I could take the helmet off. He said no, and if I kept complaining, he'd put me in the brig. He went to Villanova. I appealed his order to the C.O., the friend of Rebecca's father. He listened and thought I was a malingerer. Back to the pom-pom I went. *Whap whap whap whap.* Down came the snowflakes."

Cheval started laughing, and Mr. Buffum looked up from his magazine.

"The next time the ship put in for a refit, I bought a box of Kotex at the drugstore."

"What's that?" Callum asked.

"They're for girls to wear," Cheval explained.

"Like shoulder pads," P.O. said. "And when we put to sea again I just lined my helmet with them. Suddenly I wasn't seeing snowflakes anymore. My shooting got so good they gave me a commendation for twelve Zeros confirmed and five maybes. No one else did as well. They started looking up to me like I was a hero. Mr. Villanova talked to me like I was his equal. Even the C.O. began doubting the story about me and Rebecca."

"Did they give you a medal?" Callum asked, having trouble getting P.O.'s drift, whether this was a hero's story or wasn't.

P.O. shook his head. "That's the point."

Callum felt his heart sink.

"One day, that little turd from Villanova made an inspection of our living quarters. He sniffed around and said, 'Seaman, what is this?' He marched me by the collar right up to the bridge with that Kotex box. The captain asked me what I was doing with a box of ladies' you-know on his ship. I denied it and the next thing I knew, blam! He slapped me with a Section Eight mental discharge."

Callum winced.

P.O. threw his hands over his head. "I was out. I was on a boat home. No more Rat Island, no more pom-poms, no more navy. You get the point I'm making?"

Callum wanted to say yes. "Not really," he said.

"Things don't always end up the way you think."

"But you have to try."

P.O. laughed. "Don't say I didn't warn you."

Cheval got to her feet. "This boy sure knows his own mind," she said. A moment later she came out of the house. "God bless you, honey," she told him, handing him a single cardboard toilet-paper tube. "It's a start."

"Ah so," he said with a slight bow.

8

Sonja Henie's
Glide Salon

The Santa Ana winds blew hot off the San Gabriels with no relief except what a dip in a swimming pool or a sprint through a backyard sprinkler could provide. Bud, the last to arrive in Mr. Wait's grove, stripped off his Knapps and socks. With a sigh he dunked his feet in six inches of tepid, stagnant water that once had been Sonja Henie's Glide Salon.

"I'm surprised you can't hear them sizzle," he told the gang— Roland, Mr. Wait, P.O., Callum, and Milton. They were seated on the concrete curb, dowsing their feet in the same shallow pond.

They took pleasure in the coolness of the water, the breeze in the grove, the washed-out sky. It was an afternoon for being a boy again, for not thinking about a single important thing, for dreaming, and for yarns—as if Sonja Henie's puddle were a campfire in a shadowy forest.

"I'm surprised the mosquito eradication folks haven't been around here," Milton said. Mosquitoes bred by the billions in the still water of the artificial pond. The high-pitched whine of their exertions was easy to hear.

"Nothing wrong with mosquitoes," Mr. Wait said, fanning the air.

Bud started laughing. The men looked at him, wanting to share the joke. A minute went by and they looked at him like he was nuts, and after another moment, they looked at him worriedly.

Mr. Wait wandered over to a tree ladened with ripe fruit and picked them each a fresh navel, which they peeled and ate without a word, waiting for Bud to stop laughing. He was happy, that was all. He wasn't laughing at a joke. He was laughing because he felt the tide of fate shifting in his direction.

"Do you know how it makes me feel that we've got a rock-solid dream at last?" he asked them. "Shooting stars have been passing us by for years and finally we are hitching a ride."

"Well, Bud, I wouldn't—" Milton started to say.

"Wouldn't what, Milt? Wouldn't propose another open-air ice-skating rink?"

Milton bolted straight up, and by the color of his face he was mad. "I might remind you, we agreed not to discuss that," he said.

"We did," said Roland, bobbing his head. "Rules are rules."

"Discuss it, Milt?" said P.O. "We're cooling our heels in it."

Now they all laughed. It's what people did who had hold of a shooting star. They laughed like people do on the first drop on a roller coaster. After awhile, Bud got off the curb and walked across the dirt to a line of thirty or forty junk refrigerators resting at different angles in the sun. Some of them were rusted, others dented, some were missing doors. They were a uniform porcelain white, and about the same size. To anyone who happened on the clearing in the grove, the refrigerators would have inspired thoughts of totems, as if this were a shrine to the goddess of refrigeration.

"This was the first," Bud said, patting one of the appliances fondly. "And I'm glad they are all being preserved. In a millennium, these'll be like Stonehenge. People from all over the world will come to visit and take pictures of their kids beside these monuments."

"Like an exhibit in a Museum of Persistence," said P.O.

"You think people will write about our origins?" Roland asked.

"Nothing succeeds like success," said P.O. with a confident nod.

"They'll study us in schools," said Mr. Wait.

"Maybe then someone will give the rink the chance it deserves," Milton said in a voice that they would not have heard if what he said hadn't sounded so outrageous. They stopped talking and looked at him in silence, wondering what went on in his mind.

Months before, the sight of abandoned refrigerators rusting in the heat had inspired Milton to shout out to a flock of seagulls, "Eureka!" He had not been seeing junk. He had been recalling fond memories of cold afternoons back in New England when he and Gladys had warmed their hands by an open fire on the edge of an ice-covered pond, watching other couples glide by arm-in-arm, humming waltzes. New love was a necessary feature of outdoor ice-skating on a village pond. It made the cold tolerable if not altogether a joy. Who else but lovers would spend the day by a frozen lake, except for boys, for whom the chance to ram one another on ice skates was a dream come true?

Looking at those scrap refrigerators, Milton had entertained a vision, a dream, and the Sonja Henie Glide Salon was born.

He asked Gladys to get Bud's permission. And she in turn had asked Bud for a moment alone on the lanai. She had hiked up her muumuu and sat down on a lawn chair. Raising her sunglasses, she had said, "You know how Milt is, shy and all?"

"Milton?" Bud had asked, wondering whom she was talking about.

"Sensitive."

"If you say so, Gladys."

"He has a dream."

"Well, what is it?" Bud had asked.

She shook her head. "He asked if he could handle it by himself."

"In secret?"

"Yes."

Gladys had dropped her sunglasses over her eyes, smoothed her muumuu, and left the lanai as quietly as a spy in the cold.

A week later, Roland had come by to ask Bud for a conference, which they conducted on the lanai.

"Have you seen his sign?" Roland had asked him. "He wanted me to help him forge his advertising campaign. That was his exact word, Bud. I told him to appeal to kiddies and old folks and see how it went. Then the other day I was going down the highway past Mr. Wait's property. There was this sign you couldn't miss painted in huge letters with an asterisk. 'Come See Sonja Henie in Person.' I nearly drove off the road. Sonja Henie is a big personality, Bud. She fools around with Gary Cooper and Ernest Hemingway and . . . and you know. She doesn't come to places like this. She drives through, if anything, as fast as her car will take her. Then I realized the sign must be Milt's handiwork. I slammed on the brakes and walked back. Do you know what the asterisk meant?"

Bud sighed. "I can't imagine."

"In letters so small you'd find them in a mortgage agreement he wrote, 'asterisk—Look-a-like.' He can get in trouble for that, Bud. The FCC will eat him up."

"He wants to be an impresario."

"The next thing, he'll be advertising the Ice Capades."

"I'll have a word with him."

A day or two later, Mr. Wait had come by to ask Bud for a conference, also on the lanai.

"You know how frugal I am," Mr. Wait had said to him. He reached his in shirt pocket and handed Bud a receipt for a bill.

"Wow!" Bud had exclaimed and tossed it back in Mr. Wait's lap.

"I called the Light and Power. Sure enough, it's my account. Then I remembered that Milton asked if he could use a bit of my juice. I said sure. What was he going to do, light a light, maybe power a saw?" He slapped the bill with the back of his hand. "It looks like he's bent on draining Hoover Dam."

"I'll have a word with him," Bud had said.

As it turned out, he never had that word. He didn't know why, except that he wanted to believe in Milton against the odds. Along with everybody else, he attended the Grand Opening on an afternoon with the Santa Ana winds blowing down off the San Gabriels. Milton appeared out of the grove in Speedo bathing trunks. Even Gladys looked amazed at the sight of his thin, hairless legs and white torso. It was a shame, all that sun and no tan. He was instructing a girl who looked around Cloud's age. It *was* Cloud, wearing ice skates and a tank suit with a white silk sash stitched in iridescent-blue sequins with the words SONJA HENIE.

"Can the FCC sue her, too?" Bud had asked Roland as they had walked over to the edge of the skating rink.

"No, but Sonja Henie can."

"Doesn't she look lovely," Edith had said, wishing she had brought the Brownie.

The clearing looked like the Sear's department for large appliances. The junked refrigerators hummed in the heat. And when the time came, Milton waded into the middle of the pool and held up his arms for silence.

"We've got a glitch," he announced. "If you'll be patient we'll have our ice show under way in a moment." He splashed out of the pool and went over to a bunch of extension cords knotted together under an orange tree.

When P.O. saw him he shouted, "Get out! Get out of the pool!" to kids who were playing in the water of the rink. He unplugged the cords like a man defusing a bomb. He said later that wiring the refrigerators together didn't exactly compare with throwing a plugged-in toaster into a bathtub, but it was close enough to give him the willies.

Now, all these months later, Milton still wanted to give the Glide Salon another try.

"We never did ask ourselves why we need a dream-scheme to come true," Bud said, changing the subject for Milton's sake.

"It seems self-evident," said P.O.

"Ha!" said Mr. Wait.

"As for me," said Roland, "it's a test of faith. You may smile behind your hands at what happened at the Pageant—"

"We wouldn't do that, Rollie," said Milton.

"It was the most important event in my life," Roland said. "I know this dream-scheme of ours will come true. It's a done deal. I don't even care that much. I've had *my* moment. I was spoken to. And you can all laugh. I received the Word."

"Why didn't the Word make more sense?" P.O. wondered.

"Because that's how the Word is. Some things don't conform to what you want to hear. I happen to choose to believe. That's faith. I heard a voice. That voice showed us the way. I imagine God is jealous of dreams. That's why His messages about them are so hard to understand."

"Why would God be jealous of a dream?" Bud asked.

"Because people sometimes worship them."

Callum raised his hand. "Can I ask a question?"

They all looked at him. They had forgotten he was there.

"What's the difference between a dream and a prayer?"

"*Huuummm,*" said Milton in a long exhalation.

"Good answer, Milt," said P.O. "I don't have a better one. Do you, Roland?"

"One is based on greed, the other on faith."

"I prayed we would make a lot of money with the doughnut stand, and that didn't happen," said Callum.

"You don't ask God for a neon sign," said Roland. "You don't ask him for tickets to a Rams game. You don't ask him for a fox fur. You ask for love. You ask for forgiveness. You ask for salvation. Things like that."

"Stuff that doesn't cost, in other words," said Milton.

"Things that are beyond worldly value."

"Then I prayed wrong," said Callum, searching the surface of the pool for mosquito eggs.

"I just want money," said P.O., to nobody's surprise. "That's what this dream means to me. And I'm not embarrassed to say it either."

"Good golly, why should you be?" asked Bud.

"Because it's crass," said Mr. Wait. "At least you could say you wanted to build a new house or buy a new car, something else besides just wanting the money."

"That's what I meant. I don't want money to put in a bank. I want money to spend. I can't make it plainer. Getting a load of money without having to work or steal, that's the American dream."

"But you *are* working," said Bud. "It takes hard work to make a dream come true."

"This is more of a lark than work."

"I see," said Bud, a bit disappointed in him. He looked at Callum. "What about you?"

"Because it's fun, I guess."

"That's all, fun?" P.O. asked.

Callum thought he had said something wrong.

"Milt?" asked Bud.

"A chance for vindication."

"We can get behind that," Bud said. "You mean it won't change your life?"

"Why would it?" Milton looked worried.

"Money changes people," Mr. Wait pointed out.

"You read that somewhere," Milton said. "That may be true in books. And it may be true for young people. It may even be true for older people who think money reflects their worth. They think rich means smart, that rich means cosmopolitan. At my age I know better. Money? What's the charm?"

"You wouldn't stop working for the Wire and Cable?" Bud asked him.

"I've got the best job in the world."

"But you wouldn't *need* a job, Milt," Bud explained.

"You think I work for money?"

"Most people do."

"I happen to like what I do."

"Your co-workers, for instance?"

That made them laugh once more. Milton, as a night watchman, had no co-workers.

"I take something from it. I don't know what to call it."

"Next," said Bud. "How about you, Mr. Wait?"

"I'm with Milton. What do we want to get rich for?" he asked.

Bud stared at him. "*Excuse* me?"

"Getting rich is why California exists," said P.O.

"What's wrong with rich?" asked Roland.

P.O. stamped his feet. "Greed greed greed," he chanted.

"Babes!"

They all went suddenly silent. "Who said that?" P.O. asked, looking left and right.

Milton shyly raised his arm.

Roland asked Mr. Wait, "Tell me, what's wrong with rich?"

"For one thing, it's predictable. Any one of you is smart enough to get rich if that's what you wanted."

"We're poor, Mr. Wait, and I don't think we want to be," said Bud.

"Wrong. You like the idea of money, but rich, no, you don't want to be rich. Aren't you happy as you are?"

"Well, sort of . . ." Bud answered without conviction.

"The Disney song says when your heart is in your *dream*. It doesn't say anything about in your outstretched hand."

"It's a measure, Mr. Wait, money is, a yardstick," Bud said. "It measures how the dream succeeds. That's all. A dream and money are separate. But they go together. Don't you see? We don't have a pot to piss in. And I for one don't see anything wrong with getting rich off our ability to do what nobody else has thought of. It's called entrepreneurship."

"Do we need money to be friends?" Mr. Wait asked.

"Now that you mention it, no."

"Let's do whatever this is, Bud, for ourselves."

They stared at him. "And no money?" Roland asked.

"The original dreamers out here came for the gold fields," Bud said.

"They dreamed of adventure, not gold," Mr. Wait said.

"Did you ever ask them?"

"Of course not. I don't need anything except my grove—for now, anyway."

"For now?" Bud asked.

"Things are changing."

"Your grove isn't."

He looked at the trees with a wistful expression. "A real estate agent came snooping around the other day, about a hundred yards in that direction." And he pointed.

"Did he offer you a deal?" P.O. asked.

"He didn't have to. I know this property is doomed. The land wants to be a parking lot, or a concrete plant, or a shopping center. It wants to change, and I'm too old to let it go."

"Land can't change by itself," Callum pointed out.

"Let me tell you, sonny, about seventy years ago all this was sheep farms. And the land decided it was time for a change. Some fella brought an orange tree from Brazil. And that tree did so well that this land decided the tree was better than the sheep. And now all you see are orchards. Pretty soon all you'll see are sheds and signs and roads and buildings and paved-over places. I wish I was young again. I'd move on."

"The money can help you," said P.O.

"It won't help this property."

"That's sad," said Callum.

"No, that's tragic," Mr. Wait corrected him. "Young people will never have the chance to pick lunch off a tree."

Bud was tired of listening to Mr. Wait. He loved him, but he loved him as one of a vanishing breed. Mr. Wait was old southern California. Bud considered himself the new. To him, Orange County meant vitality and growth, a place where people welcomed new ideas no matter how strange. He rolled up his trousers and waded around the rink, sliding his bare feet on the mossy bottom. The others soon joined him without a word, splashing through the webs of mosquitoes. They stretched out their arms for balance and dipped with bent knees and turned in tight and graceful spirals. To look at them from the edge of the grove, you would almost think they were ice-skating.

9

Milton and
the Amazing Crystal

"What'd you say?" Milton asked Gladys, breaking a silence that had lasted the length of Whittier Avenue as they drove with Callum in the direction of the coast, between bean fields that were so vast they appeared to grow clouds.

"Nothing," Gladys replied from the backseat, where she rode for safety's sake. In spite of her artistic streak, she spent her whole life watching the ground while Milton gazed at what he hoped were stars.

"Good," he told her, creating a kind of dialogue.

"I was just wondering like I sometimes do," she went on after a long sigh. "I was wondering what'll ever become of us when we slide into our Golden Years."

"The damned DynaFlo's acting up again," he said, jiggling the shift lever.

"Good," she said.

Milton fiddled with the gearshift until he was satisfied that the DynaFlo would take them to a bean field where a billboard rocked in the gusting wind: TUCKER'S TRADING POST—SURPLUS.

He parked on bean plants, and they walked across rows of matted beans over to the shady side of the billboard where a man sat on a kitchen chair with his boots up on a raised plywood desk observing customers browse an acre of dusty field.

Milton waved, but the man did not wave back. There was no reason for him to. They had not met, though Milton thought that the celebrity of the man's name on a billboard gave rights of familiarity. With a dismissive push of her hand Gladys headed for the open field, and Milton, with Callum tagging along, made straight for the Quonset hut with the half-circular corrugated metal roof where army and navy surplus objects with a known value were kept. The hut had one door and two windows, and the light inside was dim. As their eyes adjusted to the shade, a shape bore down on them. The whole length of the Quonset, about fifty feet from stem to stern, was occupied by a battleship, the *Missouri,* on sawhorses, a model that had been the creation of naval architects in World War II.

"Boom boom," Milton said, squeezing past the miniature midship gun batteries.

Callum stared. Just looking at the great ship's lines thrilled him. He could not explain why models like this one excited his imagination the way they did. He ran his hand down the smooth gray hull, and the touch alone stirred images of perilous waters and a superior Japanese navy.

"Isn't she beautiful," he said to Milton.

"Sure, sure," he replied.

Milton had no appreciation for an old war bucket. Flat feet had excused him from service. He never apologized either. He would say proudly to anyone who asked that he had not been able to serve his country, as though he thought of his feet as badges of courage. "Keep your eyes peeled for a headset," he told Callum. "You know, like pilots wear."

Callum meandered beside bins along the wall that spilled over with Plexiglas, stripped radio parts, electrical cables, switches and resistors, bulbs, cathode tubes, prop blades, and screens. Now that the war was history, these objects had been cast aside by an ungrateful nation. Callum alone saw in each item of surplus junk a thread in the fabric of victory.

"Here they are," he called out, bending over a box.

Milton clamped them over his ears. They made him look like a mouse. An electrical connection with a plug hung in a V down his front. Any other man in earphones, P.O. for instance, might have stirred in Callum visions of a pilot in Bomber Command's debriefing room. On Milton they looked like rotting grapefruit halves.

Outside the Quonset hut, in the sun again, Milton mumbled, "High-frequency current emits radio waves that travel through space at the speed of light. A wire captures those radio waves and sends them to a diode. The diode shaves off the bottom half of the alternating current, and the headset transforms the electrical impulses into sound."

"What?" Callum asked him.

"Technical stuff," he replied.

Under the billboard, the owner of the trading post, Mr. Almore Tucker, scratched a stubble beard and cast Milton a sour look that said not to ask, it didn't matter what. Tucker hated questions. He had been asked at least a hundred times whether the glass beads in the boxes in the bean field were electrical resistors. Of course they were. And even if they were not, what difference would it have made? Tucker discovered years ago that people did not ask questions in hope of the answers. They asked to show off their own knowledge or to enlarge on some personal experience that, more often than not, could petrify a rock.

"Tucker," Milton asked, "I'm in the market for a large diode."

That interested him. He abandoned his seat in the shadow of the billboard for the first time that afternoon. "I got just what you're looking for," he said, with a smile that exposed teeth the color of oolong tea.

In a shadowed corner of the Quonset that Milton would never have explored by himself, Tucker stooped down over a wooden box, which he opened with a slight hesitation. "I don't understand why the navy wanted one this big in the first place," he told them. "It was experimental, one of their China Lake boondoggles."

Even in the muted light the crystal reflected sharp, darting shafts of brilliant light as though it were illuminated from within. Like some hungry presence, it absorbed the available light and transformed it miraculously into a spectrum of blues and reds and greens. The crystal was clear. That was the odd part. But those spectral colors pulsated along its smooth surface like it was painted that way.

"It's germanium," said Tucker, handing Milton the box.

"I imagine," said Milton, trying to sound in-the-know.

"What does this have to do with . . . you know?" Callum asked, sounding a discordant note.

"That's for me to know and you to find out," Milton replied sharply, feeling about Callum's question just the way he sounded.

Callum did not press the issue. He knew that Milton approached invention from oblique angles. Yet no matter how hard he tried, he could not make a connection between the germanium, the earphones, *and* the dream-scheme. Bud said that Milton was contributing as much as any of them. Callum believed that was true, but he still wondered what a glittery stone could tell them about a needle in a haystack.

"How much?" Milton asked, getting right to the point.

"I always feel reluctant to sell a thing of such beauty," Mr. Tucker replied. "Take it outside. Show it to your wife—that is your wife, isn't it, in the muumuu?"

"Just say so if you don't want to sell it."

"It is for sale," Mr. Tucker assured him. "Everything is." With his chin in his hand, he observed Milton's Sam Browne belt and the empty holster. "You look like a lawman to me. I'll give you a public servant's discount. It's yours for a hundred bucks, no haggling."

Milton handed him back the box. "You might as well have said a million." He turned to walk away.

"What isn't over your head?"

"Probably nothing you'd be willing to consider," Milton replied.

"How does eighty sound?"

"Do you believe ten?" Milton asked.

Mr. Tucker stuck his neck out. "You're begging," he said in a squeaky voice. "A cop like you. Look at you. You're groveling. Your hand's out. You're asking something for nothing. That's like robbery. Your sworn duty is to arrest people like you. You said ten? Could you go fifteen if we worked out a deal?"

"With a break on heavy-gauge wire and the headset, yes."

Mr. Tucker smiled. "If you're using this for what I think you are, you won't need it for long."

Milton nodded. "Have you ever tried to use it, you know, like that yourself?"

Tucker shook his head. "Not interested. Strictly not interested."

"You're selling it for fifteen, right?" Milton asked, wanting to get the terms straight.

"*Leasing* it," Tucker corrected him. "Three months for fifteen dollars with a fifty-cent-a-day charge over ninety days, just like overdue books at the library. If you decide to buy it, the price will be eighty less half the fifteen and any daily surcharges you run up."

"Deal," Milton said. He held out his hand, but Tucker did not seem to know what to do with it.

Outside, Milton surveyed the field of Tucker's junk. Spying Gladys, he shouted to her, but she was off in her own dreams. They watched as she lifted her muumuu and squatted by a box of glass electrical-resistor beads, which she let run through her fingers.

Milton lowered himself to the ground by Tucker's desk. With his legs splayed and the box with the germanium between his knees, he rubbed the crystal.

"I wonder if rocks have memories," he said as much to himself as to Callum, who had sat in the dirt beside him.

"I never heard they did," he said.

"Imagine all that rocks have seen—the wonders of the ages. Imagine what they could tell us if they could talk. I bet they'd have little whispery voices. They'd know less than ten words. What would they be?" He turned to Callum.

"The words?"

"*Mommy, poo-poo, night-night, bah-bah.*" He thought about that for a second. "Not much when you consider," he went on. "Most people think rocks are just rocks. Do you?"

"Yes and no," Callum replied.

"If you ask me, rocks live. They're like us but slow. They probably breathe, oh, once in a hundred years."

Mr. Tucker scuffled across the dirt and handed Milton a sales receipt and said with a conspiratorial wink, "Happy listening, now."

Callum put down the cardboard box that contained the toilet-paper-tube donations. He pulled a cord for the attic ladder and, picking up the box, climbed the steps into the musty space that Milton and Gladys used to store Christmas-tree decorations and old lampshades. Around and above him a hundred tubes wrapped in copper wire shone in the dim light, like a golden hive of gigantic bees. Surprised and a bit frightened, he dropped the box, and the tubes spilled down the ladder. "Bees!" he screamed.

He ran downstairs, crushing several of the toilet-paper tubes underfoot in his haste to get out of there before the queen bee returned with her deadly escort of workers. He rounded the corner of the dining room and slid to a stop in the kitchen, where at that moment Gladys was making lunch.

"Bees!"

"I'm baking egg pies for lunch," she said, pushing up her sunglasses.

"Bees," he said with a bit less intensity now, seeing how calm she was.

She squinted at him. "What about them?"

"They're in the attic."

She dismissed the idea with a wave of her arm. "Oh, pay no attention," she said. "Go tell Milton lunch is about ready."

Outside, Milton was in the backyard lifting a spool of heavy-gauge wire out of the trunk of the car.

"There's a hive in your attic," he told him, assuming he would want to know.

Milton dropped the spool on the ground. "Oh, that," he said. "That's my new command center." He bent down over the spool. "Give me a hand," he said.

They hauled the spool over to the telephone pole by the fence at the boundary of the yard. Milton sized up Callum and made a stirrup of his hands and boosted him up to the pole's rungs that linemen climbed on. Callum rested his whole weight on one foot like a trapeze artist and breathed in the intoxicating creosote that sweated on the pole. Milton handed him the end of the stout wire and told him to loop it around the pole. He walked with it across the yard, up the driveway, and around the pole on the sidewalk in front, then back down the driveway. He did this twenty times. Dark rings stained his armpits before he was through.

"Is this part of finding Walt's place, too?" Callum asked.

"Now that the birds are gone, my every waking moment is

devoted to that. Trust me. Now, nail those wires to the pole so they don't slide down."

Callum set his feet on the steel rungs, and cinching Milton's belt around his waist and the pole, he leaned back and swung from side to side, gazing at the empty sky.

"You're making me nervous," Milton said, looking up at him.

"Egg pie's ready," Gladys shouted from the porch.

Callum slid down the pole, and Milton carried the box with the germanium crystal into the kitchen with the reverence of a priest with a chalice.

"What were you boys up to out there?" Gladys asked, sounding cheerful as she served slices of the egg pie.

"Nothin'," Milton said.

She looked out the back window. "Stringing up a perch for the birds to sit on?"

"That's it, Gladys, a perch," he told her.

10

Woe Be to the Orphan II

"You leave me no choice," Mrs. Hamel scolded Cloud, addressing her with her hands on her hips in front of the studio's wall-length mirror and ballet barre. "I'm going to have to tell Edith that you're a recalcitrant."

"You would be, too," Cloud told her right back. "Whatever it is."

"See what I mean?"

Trying a different tack, Cloud asked, "Mrs. Hamel, were you ever a boy?"

Mrs. Hamel searched her face for a sign of sarcasm. Seeing none, she said, "No, to be truthful, no."

Cloud came over to the barre. "I never imagined myself as a boy either. I can't see it. It's something I can't see myself as."

Mrs. Hamel reverted to her greatest weakness as a teacher—softness. "Dear, dear," she muttered. "Yes, I understand. But what can we do?"

"You could talk to Edith. I *do* play the clarinet, you know."

"So I heard. But I'm afraid Edith has her heart set." Her face brightened. "Maybe Callum could stand in."

"He can't be a Job's Daughter. They won't let boys in. But it was a good thought anyway."

"Then maybe Blue will dance the boy's part. Have you asked her?"

Cloud shook her head with little hope.

Blue was admiring herself at that moment in the floor-to-ceiling wall mirror, turning this way and that, trying different expressions, oblivious of Mrs. Hamel, Cloud, or Callum, who was sitting in a corner with a book open in his lap.

"Blue, can we interrupt you a moment?" Mrs. Hamel asked. "Blue!"

She tore herself away from herself with a long sigh. Walking across the polished floor, she turned her toes outward like a real ballerina.

"I don't suppose you'd want to be the boy?" asked Mrs. Hamel.

Blue gagged on a high-pitched whine.

"Yes, I thought that would be the case," Mrs. Hamel said and turned to Cloud. "Well, young lady, you'll have to overcome your prejudices."

"I guess I don't mind," Cloud said in a sudden reversal.

Mrs. Hamel looked at her suspiciously. "You don't?"

"Edith has her heart set on it."

"Yes she does."

A knock at the studio door, and Mrs. Hamel told the girls, "Excuse me a minute."

Mrs. Bashford came in wearing a knit suit with ornate brass buttons and an oval pin. Her hairspray smelled like the Tustin phosphamidon plant. In contrast to the hostess of the other afternoon's tea, she now looked worried and out of control.

"Dora, I must talk to you," she told Mrs. Hamel in an urgent voice.

Mrs. Hamel clapped her hands. "Take a break, girls," she said, and the girls fell to the floor. Mrs. Hamel steered Mrs. Bashford over to the corner of the studio, beneath the photograph of herself as a slim young Giselle.

"I just don't know what the world's coming to," Mrs. Bashford told her, close to tears.

"It can't be so bad," Mrs. Hamel said, patting her shoulder consolingly.

"They leave everything to me, everything. I'm taken advantage of, Dora. And I'm sick of it, sick."

"Now, now, Edna."

"How would you like it if you got dumped with the whole initiation?"

"You have your committees, Edna."

"They're a bunch of old hens."

"You're doing a wonderful job."

"Thank you, Dora," she said, taking a deep, cleansing breath. She then lighted a Pall Mall with a gold lighter and inhaled and puffed all at once in an amazing display of human air-duct plumbing. "The women have failed me, Dora. The refreshment woman, Alice Bosworth, you know, has done nothing. The decorations woman, Betty What's-her-name, hasn't the first idea of what to do. And the membership committee chairwoman has created a serious problem I don't know *how* to deal with."

"What's that?"

She glanced around her over the top of Callum's head. "I don't like to say it." She paused a second. "It's the Rodriguez woman and her daughter, Serena. How do I say it?" She rested one hand on her hip and stared into space. "She just isn't *us*."

"Now, now."

"Now it's all up to me." For the first time she noticed Blue and Cloud on the floor by the barre. "How're they doing?" she asked Mrs. Hamel with a sniff.

"Blue could turn out to be a fine dancer."

She laughed bitterly. "And Cloud, I suppose, could be her manager."

Blue plunged to the floor in a *plié*. Encouraged, Cloud flung herself into an arabesque.

"Girls, girls, girls," said Mrs. Hamel, once Mrs. Bashford was gone. She walked across the polished floor with her arms out. "Let's finish this afternoon by exploring the eight directions of the body and the five basic positions at the barre. Let's emphasize *ports de bras*, *grands battements*, and *pliés*."

Cloud lowered her leg from the barre and asked, "Did you ever hear of *Le Baiser de la Fée*, Mrs. Hamel?"

"Why yes," she replied brightly.

Cloud walked over to her gym bag and came back with a book that she held up to Mrs. Hamel. She opened it to a page she had marked and started to read. "In the midst of a tempest a fairy kissed a baby boy who grew into a handsome young man. On the eve of his wedding, a gypsy, who becomes the fairy, seduces him in the bridal chamber. And they lived happily ever after."

"Seduction in a bridal chamber!" Blue said, clutching her breast with rapture.

"Good for you, Cloud," Mrs. Hamel told her. "Where did you find the book?"

"At the library."

"What initiative," said Mrs. Hamel. "I remember when I was your age I fell in love with the Fairy's Kiss, too. It was one of the very first dances I learned. Would you like to see me do it?"

Cloud said, "I'd love for you to."

Mrs. Hamel set her swollen ankles and spread her saggy arms and began to dance the introductory movements of the ballet from memory. "Would you like to try it now?" she asked the girls.

"I'd love to," Cloud said.

"Go out to the middle of the floor there," Mrs. Hamel told Blue. She led them through the paces with special attention to the harmony and movement of their arms. "Now the hands, simple and graceful— not flowery. That's it. Now the gateway. That's good. Fifth position, *battement tendu*. Good, that's good. Now, Cloud, you come around, over here by me. Demure, please. And you wait. Now, Blue. Do you see?" The dance required *glissades*, *jetés*, and *enchaînements*. "See, girls, it's the interpretation. The *artiste* transforms a simple tale into a world of dreams. You *do* understand."

"So where does the handsome young man come in?" Cloud asked.

Mrs. Hamel exaggerated the point of her toes as she crossed the floor. "We are in the bridal chamber, yes? The handsome young man is in the recess, here, behind the two women—you, Cloud, and you, Blue. Let's pretend for a moment that I am the young man."

Mrs. Hamel covered the floor, caught up in her own fond memories of youth, and before long she was lost in the Fairy's Kiss, swinging her arms, kicking, hopping.

The funny thing was, to Callum she looked just like Scooter when he was dancing behind the garage.

As he stood in line out in the rain, Callum read the prohibitions stuck on the glass of the Gem's ticket booth: no cherry bombs, no pea shooters, no squirt guns, no whoopee cushions, no slingshots, no admission to the balcony without a parent, no making out, no exceptions. He inched forward in line, pulling his jacket closed tighter against the steady drizzle. He read every word of the lobby card for *Ten Seconds to Hell,* which showed a torpedo running toward its Jap target. The movie was going to be great! But even if it wasn't, it didn't matter. By the time the Movietone News, the previews, and the serials (Buster Crabbe in *Flash Gordon*) were over and it was time for the feature to begin, the theater would be bedlam. The manager would stop the projector, turn on the over-heads, and threaten to call the cops. When the lights went out again and the screen lit up, the air thickened with *stuff*. The manager, a harrassed man with a bad toupee and no discernible humor, was the only one who did not understand that the joy of rainy Saturday matinees wasn't the movies. It was the chaos.

Selling him a ticket now, the manager looked Callum over as if to say he'd remember him when the cops came.

In the carpeted lobby Callum entered the refreshment line. The delicious aroma of fresh popcorn and the colored boxes of Goobers, Milk Duds, Ju-Jubes, Red Hots, and Abbazabbas stacked in rows in the glass case made his mouth water. There were red-skinned hot dogs on a rotisserie and four-gallon cartons of three flavors of ice cream in a dry-ice bin. A kid against a wall was pouring popcorn in his shirt, flattening the cardboard box into a glider. Another kid with a maniacal grin was balancing an opened can of Libby's creamed corn in his hand as he headed up the balcony stairs. A boy's cheeks bulged like a chipmunk's with ammo for a pea shooter that he carried behind his ear. Kids poured in and out of the bathrooms, surreptitiously loading up water balloons, water guns, water bags, canteens, and bottles.

A girl two or three people in front of Callum bought a box of Milk Duds and turned away from the counter. Recognizing her, Callum slipped out of line, stepped up behind her, and touched her shoulder. Startled, she dropped her Milk Duds, and they both bent down, bumping foreheads. He blushed, she blushed, and they straightened up in speechless embarrassment. In that moment she looked prettier than he remembered. She was dressed in jeans, with a flannel shirt and silver combs in her hair. He liked girls better without party-dress frills.

"You like war movies?" he asked for something to say.

"It's raining," she explained.

He looked around the crowded lobby. "Is your mother here?"

"She dropped me off. She's busy with the Job's dresses and all." She made a face.

"My mom, too," Callum said. "My sisters are at ballet class. They think they are going to win the talent contest. My dad needs the money."

"I'm going to play the piano," Serena said shyly.

"Who's your favorite player?"

"José Iturbi," she replied.

Callum could not believe they had this much in common. "Mine, too," he said. "My dad's is Carmen Caballero."

"Who's she?"

"It's a man, dummy," and he laughed. "He plays for Esther Williams."

She looked more confused than ever. "I thought she was a movie swimmer."

"She is," he said as if that cleared up her question. "She's married to Harry James."

"Oh," she said, trying hard to keep up.

"Cloud and Blue aren't wild about being Job's. Edith is. My sisters are only wild about winning the fifty dollars. Do you really want to be a Job's Daughter?"

She thought about the question. Her reply was not automatic, as he had thought it might be. "My mother says I should take advantage of the opportunities that are given to me," she said.

"What opportunity?"

As if she had not thought about that, she replied, "I don't know. It'll help me later on?"

"I wouldn't join if I were you," he said, trying hard to give her a hint. "You should tell your mother I told you."

She laughed. "Why on earth should I tell her that?"

"The Job's don't like people who aren't like themselves."

She looked in his face, trying to find a hidden meaning. "You know something you aren't telling me, don't you?"

He stared at his feet. "Mrs. Bashford doesn't like us very much either," he said softly.

Tears welled up in her eyes and poured down her cheeks. She stared at him through the tears. As if she blamed him for Mrs. Bashford's prejudices, she said, "You should keep your opinions to yourself, you know."

"I'm sorry," he said.

She turned and ran out of the lobby, her hand over her mouth, her sobs loud enough to make him wince.

He went after her, but she would not look at him, much less talk to him, the whole way home. They were soaked through to the skin and his teeth were chattering when she marched up the steps and disappeared in her house with a slam of the front door.

Even in his misery he was awed by the house she lived in. He had thought places like it existed only in fairy tales. It was a Victorian house with gingerbread on the eaves, four gables, and a wide wrap-around porch with a railing and brightly painted posts. A house that old was rare. Even in the rain he could not recall ever seeing one this antique. White lace curtains hung at the shuttered windows. He was trying to see in one on the second floor when the curtains parted and Mrs. Rodriguez looked out. She saw him but did not wave, and then the curtain closed.

He felt bad for hurting Serena. He had intended the opposite. And now he had wrecked their friendship, he bet for good. He wiped the rain off his forehead and turned to leave. It was going to be a long walk home. As he was nearing the end of the driveway, Mrs. Rodriguez called out to him from the porch. He turned around and, seeing her motion to him with her arm, he started running, his sneakers squishing with each stride.

He did not climb the porch, but rather stayed on the gravel path waiting to see what she would say.

"I know Edith taught you to come in out of the rain," she told him with a warm smile. "Don't be shy."

She took off a kitchen apron she had tied over a pair of khaki trousers. Her dark hair was pulled back in a ponytail. A turquoise and silver bracelet the width of a man's belt circled her slim wrist. She wore cowboy boots that were so scruffed there was no evidence anymore of their original shade. She was so original that, looking at her, Callum wished his own mother wasn't so plain.

As he climbed the porch steps, a portly man unexpectedly stepped forward out of the front door and stood behind Mrs. Rodriguez. He was short and round and wore a suit and carried a briefcase in one hand and formally stuck out his other hand for Mrs. Rodriguez to shake. "I won't keep you any longer," he told her. "May I call you Mary?"

"Mrs. Rodriguez is fine," she told him in a polite and yet firm manner.

"Yes, yes, you are right. Keep it on a business level. It's okay to stop by at the end of the week then?"

"Yes, with the papers, please, Mr. Constantinople," she told him. She did not want to continue the conversation, that much was clear. But Mr. Constantinople did not know enough to leave. When she said nothing further to him, he closed his raincoat and stepped down from the porch. At the door of his car, he waved. But by then, Mrs. Rodriguez had turned to Callum.

"You know what I've done?" she asked him, bending down to his level, looking him straight in the eye. "I lit a fire in the fireplace because I knew Serena was going to be cold when she got home. It is a little chilly, wouldn't you say?"

He nodded and followed her in the house. The front room was smaller than his own living room, but it had the first fireplace he had ever seen. He extended his arms near a grate that threw off a welcoming warmth. Mrs. Rodriguez pointed him to a stool beside the hearth and pulled over a rocking chair. "I'll call your mother," she said. "I'm sure she'll come for you. If she can't, I'll drive you home myself."

"I can walk," he said.

"I know you can."

Callum looked out the window at the sound of Mr. Constantinople's tires crunching in the gravel of the driveway. From upstairs he could hear sobbing, not loud or varied in pitch like Cloud's or

Blue's when they were making a statement that had nothing to do with sorrow or pain. This was real. Each cry hurt him as much as he imagined Serena's broken feelings hurt her.

"I'll ask Serena to come down in a moment," Mrs. Rodriguez told him, folding her hands in her lap. "Serena was telling me a little bit about what you told her at the Gem. Maybe you will tell me what you said?"

"I didn't mean to make her cry."

"I know you didn't. Yes, that much I do surely know. You're a good boy, Callum. I know that, too. What was it you said to her?"

"I was repeating what I heard Mrs. Bashford say at the ballet class. She said, 'Mrs. Rodriguez and Serena aren't *us*.' I don't think she likes my mom and Cloud and Blue much either."

Mrs. Rodriguez smiled sadly. "So you told Serena she shouldn't join the Job's?"

"I think that's what Mrs. Bashford was saying."

Her lips formed a thin line. "That would be Mrs. Bashford, all right," she said.

"I thought Serena should know."

"You are right, Callum. And the reason she should know is one reason why I want her to join the Job's."

He cocked his head, trying to understand. "You want her to join, knowing how Mrs. Bashford feels?"

"You're darn right. Serena's an American just like you. She is also Latina—that's how we call ourselves, Latinos."

The word, the way she pronounced it, sounded musical and altogether lovely, like Mrs. Rodriguez herself.

"Her being an American isn't something you see," she continued in a strong voice. "Her being Latina is. That is where the trouble starts. People around here don't think much of Latinos."

"Mexicans, you mean."

"No, Latinos. How would you like it if everybody called you a Scot?"

"I'm not. My grandfather was."

"Exactly what I am saying. We can't see your Scottishness like you can see Serena's Latinness. I want her to understand how people like Mrs. Bashford react to her Latina side. She will have to live with that her whole life."

"I don't understand."

"It's not easy. The point is, I want her to join the Job's because I *love* her."

"But you said nobody likes Mexicans."

She laughed now. "Mexicans want the same for their kids as everybody else. The only differences are they speak Spanish and the color of their skin is different. That sets them apart. And they are poor."

"I think we are, too," he said.

She smiled, but her eyes showed a sadness and her voice took on an edge when she said, "Mrs. Bashford can't keep us out. We *do* have the distinction of our family name. The Job's like distinctions, some of them, even if we aren't *them*."

"I should have kept my mouth shut."

"Oh, no." She leaned forward and caressed his hair. "You meant to be kind. You meant to protect her. That was a loving thing to do."

"I wish Serena thought so."

"She will. Yes, she will."

The roar of a tractor engine made him stand up and look out the parlor window. Serena was perched in the tractor seat in the rain with her hands on the tractor wheel and her head turned toward the house. Callum looked at Mrs. Rodriguez as if for permission to go outside.

"I guess she got over it," she told him with a wink.

He ran from the room into the foyer and out onto the porch, letting the door slam behind him. Serena gave him a bright smile. "I didn't want to see that awful *Ten Seconds to Hell* anyway," she shouted over the tractor engine. "Come on, jump on back and we'll go for a ride."

He climbed down the porch steps and onto the tractor hitch, and she advanced the throttle and engaged the clutch with a jerk that nearly threw him off. They accelerated down the gravel driveway and turned sharply into a row between orange trees.

Serena's laughter and Callum's shouts of joy brought Mrs. Rodriguez out on the porch. She looked melancholy watching the tractor disappear into the grove, and when it was gone she started to cry.

11

Corner of Goofy
and Mickey Mouse

"The wire isn't a perch for the birds after all?" Roland asked Callum as they drove together through the city traffic in Roland's spiffy English MG with the convertible top down.

"He won't say what it's for," Callum shouted over the rush of warm air. "I don't think it's for the birds, though."

"What would you imagine, then?"

"An antenna of some sort for a crystal-set radio."

"Milton wants very much to show us what he can do," Roland told him seriously now. "Remember Gladys saying he only knew about birds? She was saying he was *for* the birds. We all need to show what we can do this time around."

"I don't see why you need to, Roland."

"I want to see a dream come true, that's why."

He tugged at his tweed snap-brim cap and concentrated on driving his shiny maroon sports car through downtown traffic. There was not much to see even with the top down except buildings and billboards. Humans were a rare sight in Los Angeles, except for those in other cars. Hardly anyone used sidewalks. In one of his pronouncements Bud said Los Angeles was a bean field with a tar pit, and no matter what claims for it the chamber of commerce made, it was still a bean field with a tar pit. He said that folks planned their cities. And so it could be no accident that the civic leaders of Los Angeles were building an art museum over a tar pit. Gilding the lily, he called it.

As they motored past the pink stucco Beverly Hills Hotel, Roland said that movie stars frolicked there. Callum caught a glimpse through the shrubs of white shorts and heard the *thwock* of a tennis ball, and he wondered if Randolph Scott played tennis. They followed a narrow road up into the hills and down the other side, where the seared San Fernando Valley spread out as far as the eye could see. The air blowing in the convertible was chappy hot, and off the MG's fender a river with a concrete bottom ran dry as old bones. They followed the river a few miles along Riverside Drive and around the contour of the hills. At the sign for the Forest Lawn cemetery, they hooked a left.

"Your father is a wonderful man," Roland told him after a long silence, giving voice to his thoughts. "The dream isn't for him. I don't think so anyway. It's for me and Mr. Wait." He looked over at Callum. "We're isolated and we're getting old and lonely."

"But you are all friends."

"We *are* friends if knowing one another makes us so. But we're too crotchety to be friends the way you imagine. That's why Bud included us in his dream. He wants to force us out of our old ways. By getting us out of ourselves, he hopes we'll find what he found for himself."

"What's that?"

He paused before saying, "It's love, I think."

"How can you find love with a dream?"

Roland thought about that a minute. "By being foolish, by laughing, by showing sides of ourselves we normally hide, by being together in something we all want."

"That's what love is?"

"It's whatever you want it to be. Let me tell you, love is the most flexible, tolerant, gentle thing you'll ever know. Some people say it's demanding and rigid and that it makes you ache. But that's not what Bud knows it to be. It's mostly yourself, love is. You don't give love so much as allow others to take it from you."

Callum did not understand that, but like so much else, he imagined that people like Roland who said they understood love really had no more of an idea than he did. Love was what you made of it, Callum would have said. And you made something of it because you felt good in its presence. That much he knew. He wondered what more there needed to be?

Not much later, buildings the size of airplane hangars appeared, painted a khaki color that reminded Callum of a military base. His impression was reinforced when Roland pulled the MG off the main road into a private drive and was forced to stop at a guard house by a uniformed policeman who watched the arriving cars through a sheet of glass. He wore white gloves, and when he came out of his guard house he saluted Roland and stuck a piece of paper on the windshield and pointed his arm to a visitors' parking lot.

In no time they were strolling down a sidewalk shaded by leafy elms and spidery oaks between buildings with big black numbers painted on their doors. Looking around, Callum was reminded of a village in which residents looked animated in a way that struck him as friendly. People walked here. The sidewalks and the center of the main street were not exactly crowded with pedestrians, but enough of them were out to suggest that a few people around Los Angeles knew how to use their legs. Callum and Roland walked until they reached an intersection, where they stopped. Roland pointed to the road sign, and Callum laughed to see that they had arrived at the corner of Goofy Avenue and Mickey Mouse Way.

They sat down on a wooden park bench in the shade of an elm tree and watched electric golf carts with fringe tops buzz by on the main street carrying men in short-sleeve shirts and women in cotton dresses. There wasn't an automobile to be seen on Mickey Mouse Way, or a truck. The quiet made watching all the more interesting.

"Everybody looks happy," Callum said, feeling happy himself.

Roland nodded. "There's more imagination on these sidewalks than anywhere else on the planet," he said. "Imagination is what makes these people happy. It's like a free ticket to anywhere anytime. Everybody has an imagination, you know. All you have to do is turn it on."

"Why did you leave if you were so happy?" Callum asked.

Roland looked at him like one who had been caught in an inconsistency. "It's a long story. But it had nothing to do with these folks." Callum held his eye. "Okay, I'll tell you. But first, let me ask, who's your favorite actress?"

"Mercedes McCambridge," he replied without hesitation.

Roland leaned back against the bench. "Well, okay. Miss McCambridge may be an exception and there are exceptions, to be sure, to my golden rule. It is that actresses are nuts. So are actors, but I wasn't in love with actors."

"What makes them that way?"

"What they do. They come alive when someone tells them to come alive through the end of a megaphone. In one movie role they are princesses, in another they are paupers. In between the roles they are nothing. The harder they try to be famous, the more of themselves they put in the roles they play. When you try so hard to be someone else, you lose yourself and after a while you don't know who you are anymore."

"You quit because of that?"

"The life, too. It's a life that *Good Housekeeping* magazine does not recommend. I fell in love with an actress and was going to marry her. I wanted to have a traditional marriage, you know, like Bud and Edith's. She said her mother already was playing that role in Iowa. She hated me for wanting to make her normal. She was in love with being crazy. I had to get away. I'd have ended up just like her."

"How was that?"

"Oh, the last I heard she was a salesgirl in a department store in San Francisco, selling perfume and telling people she'd been an actress once, holding on to what was left of her dreams. That's another thing. Once you try and fail, you never can go back. You live on the fringes. It's sad. I hear she still thinks she might be discovered selling eau de toilette. Maybe she will. Name's Colette, if you ever see it on a marquee."

Callum had other questions, but at that moment a golf cart stopped right at their feet by the curb. Roland all but jumped up in surprise. He knew the driver of the cart and went around and pumped his hand.

Mr. Selwyn Troute twittered the ends of a graying mustache that swooped up into sharp waxed points. His eyes twinkled. He was bald, and his tanned head glowed in the dappled sunlight with the richness of antique mahogany. He wore a loud black-and-white checked jacket held closed with a sash. Two-tone white-and-brown shoes gave him a certain cosmopolitan air. Dressed as he was for a day on the links, the golf cart suited him well.

With the cart's engine purring, they glided along Goofy Avenue in a style that reminded Callum of a float in a parade. Everyone in the village at this noontime hour was heading toward the same building, and everybody seemed to wave at everybody else. Parking the cart, Mr. Troute held the door to the canteen open for them.

"Does Walt eat here, too?" Callum asked Mr. Troute, taking a tray from the stack at the start of the buffet line.

Mr. Troute pointed over to the windows. "That's his table over there," he said. "He's not here today. He gets terrible headaches and has to stay home."

"Holmby Hills?" Roland asked him.

"Yeah, his new place over there."

They slid their trays along the stainless steel rails past the glass-fronted cabinets and steam tables.

"The food here still awful?" Roland asked Mr. Troute.

"Nothing's changed," he replied, lifting a plate of soggy lettuce off a glass shelf. "To Walt it's just fuel for the imagination. The kitchen staff isn't motivated because he doesn't care. We soldier on."

Callum carried his tray with a peanut butter and jelly sandwich, potato chips, and a carton of chocolate milk over to a vacant table. He listened to the laughter of the men and women seated in the room and was impressed by the camaraderie. They were just like Roland had described them, a nice bunch of joes.

"Do you know Walt yourself?" he asked when Selwyn Troute sat down with his tray.

"Not personally, no. I see him all the time," he said. "He's shy."

"He goes on television," Callum pointed out. "He can't be that shy."

On television Walt laughed with Goofy and Mickey and Donald Duck and the others like they were old friends. Bud's adage that you were judged by your friends—"If you run with midgets, you'll never run far"—meant that Walt was truly a vivid imagination clothed to look like a human. Callum wondered if by meeting him some of Walt might rub off on him. Maybe that fact alone explained his shyness. His imagination rubbed off. Pretty soon, if he kept meeting strangers, his imagination would be gone.

Mr. Troute leaned over to Callum. "Roland told me all about you," he said and took a crayon out of his pocket. He started drawing on the paper tablecloth with speed and dexterity, as if a circuit connected his imagination with his hand, as he outlined a profile of Goofy.

"What do you do here?" Callum asked him, watching him draw his own profile now beside Goofy's.

"Do you know what animation is?"

"I guess not," but he wasn't certain.

Mr. Troute took a notebook from his pocket. Drawings of Mickey Mouse and Minnie were on each page. He flipped the pages with his thumb. The characters moved—Minnie leaned over and kissed Mickey. The kiss seemed real.

"Where does that come from?" Callum asked, pointing to the drawing of Goofy on the tablecloth.

Mr. Troute tapped his temple with his forefinger. "From up here." He cut out the drawing with a penknife. Turning to Roland he asked, "How's it going down there in Santa Ana?"

"Some of the old zing is missing. It comes and it goes."

"I was surprised to hear you were selling shoes."

"Not very glamorous, huh?"

"Not what I would have expected. You probably don't appreciate how good you were as a costume designer."

"Sel, it was fake."

"Your career, Roland, wasn't fake."

"I know, I know. But this place, you know, isn't real."

"This place, as you call it, is as real as I'm sitting here," Mr. Troute said, flushing with anger.

"Yes, of course it is. What you produce isn't."

"Create, you mean."

"Create, produce—none of it has the least bit of substance. It's shadows on a wall."

As they argued Callum pushed back his chair and went over to Walt's table by the windows. He pulled out a chair and sat down on its edge. Bud said the way things were going, California would dry up as a place for dreams in a short time. That's what would happen if too many people moved here. People searching for dreams would extinguish the spark that created them. Trying to see what Walt saw, Callum peered through slatted venetian blinds on to a blacktop parking lot. He had expected different—a garden maybe, a view of mountains, anything but this strip of tar. He wondered if Walt filled that blank with creatures from his imagination. Callum blinked, and suddenly, the whole gang was in the parking lot playing baseball—Mickey and Minnie, Goofy and Pluto and Donald. He could hear their laughter. He knew it wasn't real, what he was seeing, but when he shook his head and closed his eyes, then opened them again, they were still there. He sat at Walt's table watching the game, losing all thought of time, until he heard his name being called. He slid off the chair and glanced back over his shoulder. The game went on.

When he reached the table, Roland and Mr. Troute were still bickering. Callum took his seat and kept his eyes off the windows, not wanting to know if the game had been only his imagination.

"I'd have pegged you for men's clothes. Hats even. Shoes surprise me."

"I needed to get my feet on the ground," Roland explained.

Mr. Troute leaned closer. "We could use a bit of that around here, feet on the ground, I mean," he said.

Roland sat back. "The place looks prosperous to me."

"Looks can deceive."

"At Disney they're meant to."

Mr. Troute was shaking his head. "That's true enough. But things aren't great around here, no matter what you see."

"Television is killing the industry, I hear."

"It's that, it's foreign markets, it's production costs, you name it. Between you and me, Roland, Walt had to hock his place in Palm Springs the other day to raise money."

"No!"

Mr. Troute nodded hard enough to sway his mustache. "Another rumor is he cashed in his life insurance."

"That's just crazy, Sel."

"You're telling me."

"What is it, a movie project?"

"We'd be relieved around here if it was. We know how to make movies." His eyes darted around the crowded lunch room. He had said too much already.

"Reminds me," Roland said. It didn't remind him at all. "Sel, I've been hearing a rumor. . . . It concerns an investment Walt may be making."

"His brother Roy handles that end of the business."

"No, this would be Walt himself. It is an investment in land."

Mr. Troute sat up straight. "The Disney Company is *not* a land company," he said, like he was reciting from memory.

"Sounds canned to me, Sel."

Mr. Troute stared at his plate. "If anyone knew I was talking about this, I'd lose my job. Seriously, this stuff is top secret."

"Can I tell you what I heard?"

Mr. Troute stroked his mustache. His eyes said yes.

"Walt's got an idea to build an amusement park that the banks won't finance. They think he's a genius making animated movies, but what does he know from yesterday about amusement parks? So he has to raise the money himself. He hocked the house in Palm Springs and cashed in his life insurance to get the idea started so that he can show potential investors drawings and stuff like that."

"Crimine," Mr. Troute said. "Where did you hear all that?"

"I made it up, just now."

Mr. Troute looked relieved.

"A favor?" Roland asked.

"Almost anything."

"The idea just now, smile if I'm right."

Mr. Troute looked like a man with a sudden acute pain. His lips quivered and his eyes watered. His shoulders shook. His cheeks paled and puffed out and in. He looked at his plate, then out the windows. He stuck his hand in his mouth. He tweaked one end of his mustache. But finally, it happened. A big, toothy smile spread from one side of his face to the other.

An old man with baggy knees in Bermuda shorts shaded himself under a beach umbrella by the side of Sunset Boulevard. A sign leaning against his folding chair advertised maps to movie stars' homes.

"Shouldn't we get one?" asked Callum as they drove past in the MG.

"You never find anything with maps," Roland said. "You use this." And he tapped his nose.

"Bud says Walt owns his own private railroad."

"It's what he does. He sits on the coal car behind the steam engine. *Lilly Belle*, he calls it. He wears a striped engineer's cap. And he sits there and dreams up stuff with each turn."

"To make people happy," Callum said, as if he knew.

Sunset Boulevard snaked westward through Beverly Hills, and at the end of a stretch of the road with a grassy esplanade, Roland turned the MG into a lane of mansions that sat back from the road behind walls, iron fences, and hedges. The streets in the neighborhood were washed clean, and the lawns cared for. There wasn't a single car parked by the curb. Power lawn mowers operated by Japanese and Mexican gardeners droned from all directions at once.

"Are we allowed in here?" Callum asked, sensing the threat of exclusivity.

"It's a free country," Roland replied.

The lane narrowed further under tall maples. Branches formed a dark, leafy tunnel, and the temperature dropped in the welcome shade.

"That the one, you think?" Roland asked, pointing to a Spanish-style house with a red tile roof.

Callum did not expect to find signs or statues, anything like that, but this house, besides its size, had no character. That was also true of its neighbors. Rich people, it seemed to him, worked so hard to afford their houses that they did not have the time to understand what a real house with character should be. He shook his head no. It wasn't the one. Not in this neighborhood.

Several turns later and the mansions began to take on a uniformity that could have been bought cheaper in a housing tract like the one Callum lived in. A moment later they turned into an avenue named Carolwood.

"Over there!" Callum shouted, pointing with his arm.

Beds of early summer flowers, dafs and red hot sallys, janie flames and janie golds, brightened the boundary of a lawn that rose up in gentle little hills and dales. There was a brick path that was meant to amuse visitors. Its twists delayed their arrival at the front door, as if to make them appreciate the sky and the flowers, the clouds, and the fragrance of blossoms in the air. Beds of blooming roses surrounded the English Tudor house, solid and homey with curtained windows, gables, a slate roof, and a weathervane with a rooster crowing above the tallest of four chimneys.

A brick wall cut off a view of the backyard. But it couldn't contain the sound of an engine that almost certainly wasn't a lawn mower. This sound huffed and puffed, and metal rattled against metal, and a high-pitched toot whistled through the branches of the trees. With a shock of recognition Callum heard a deep-throated laugh that he would have recognized anywhere. And for most of the next hour, he and Roland sat in the parked car, and to the sound of *Lilly Belle* and laughter imagined themselves on the ride of their lives.

12

The Scepter
and the Tube

"You remember the time you called Gladys an Aire-dale?" Milton asked Bud, turning in the car seat, expecting Bud to say no.

"I do remember it well," Bud replied, his eyes misting with glee. "Yes I do."

"I was trying to give you my impressions of her in so many words," Milton said, his sincerity evident by his tone.

"Milt, that was eighteen years ago," Bud complained.

"I was telling you about her honesty, her willingness to work and save, how artistic she was."

"And you said nothing about what she looked like, if you recall," Bud said, tugging at the tam-o'-shanter he had pulled out of the closet that morning. "You were asking my advice whether you should propose marriage to her. I hadn't met her. I didn't know."

"I told you all her wonderful qualities," Milton said, "and you said, 'What's the snag, Milt? She an Airedale?' "

Bud didn't think Gladys was an Airedale now. Now he would not compare her to any dog. He did not want to argue with Milton, and he fell silent in the hope that Milton would let it pass. He could not understand why, after all this time, he was bringing it up now.

The car windows down, the scent of hot rubber and exhaust

fumes blowing on the wind, a set destination ahead with just the guys, a beautiful, clear sky—Bud could not have imagined anything better. They had driven past the Firestone factory on Rosemead— the one with the Assyrian relief sculptures on its façade with lions charging chariots driven by warriors with square beards and stove-pipe hats. In the far distance the hills of Hollywood shimmered in the haze, and smog covered the city like a lid.

Looking out at the billboards, Bud said to Milton, "So it's the Griffith Observatory?"

"It's a hunch."

"No, no, where we're going, the Griffith Observatory."

"That's correct. On a hunch."

"What's the point?"

"I said hunch, not point," Milton said.

Callum was riding in the backseat with the warm air making him drowsy. Bud had told him the trip was educational. "Does it have to do—" he asked before Milton cut him off.

"Not everything I do has to do with the dream," he said, leaning over the seat. "Besides, who made you the dream policeman?"

"I was only asking."

"If you must know I'm getting an angle on something, if that answers your questions," Milton said.

"An angle . . . ?" Bud asked, unwilling to leave it alone.

"I'm hoping, in fact, to get some perspective."

"On what, perspective?"

"What I read in a book is called a p.o.v."

"A pov?" Bud thought about that.

"Point of view, short for point of view."

"Okay, p.o.v., then. Pov on what?"

Milton shook his head, and his wattle oscillated. "It's bad luck to talk about it. So I won't. I will go this far. I am conducting an experiment at home. There's a man at the Griffith Observatory named King who is an expert on this kind of experiment, and I want to solicit his advice."

"Good," Bud said.

In the next half hour they went through towns—Downey, Ana-heim, Norwalk—that nothing, not even a foul odor, distinguished. Not a single building was older than a decade. That suited Bud fine.

He said he didn't miss the antique saltbox and cape houses and quaint covered bridges in New England. Tract houses made him feel young, he said. Callum thought he knew what he meant. Part of being young was feeling bored, and these towns they went past were nothing if not boring.

"You got a bug up your ass?" Bud asked Milton after a silence that lasted too long for his comfort.

"Bud, let me ask you a question. Do you believe there's life on other planets?"

Bud's Adam's apple went up and down, and he cleared his throat. "Maybe there is. Maybe there isn't. And I don't care just so long as they keep their hands to themselves."

"Dr. King, the man I want to visit, has written that Earth is a grain of sand on the beach of the universe. It stands to reason that another planet in another galaxy in the universe supports life like ours."

"Who's Dr. King?"

"George King, DD—doctor of divinity. He's in charge. He was in a book I read at the library."

"Sounds like a doozie to me."

"These other-planetary people are far in advance of us, Dr. King says. They have been sighted over a hundred times. I've seen the photos of them myself. I know you're going to say that they're a hoax. But Bud, I looked and I couldn't spot the hoax. I also read accounts of eyewitnesses from as far away as Mother Russia, England, and New Mexico. They saw the same shapes, sounds, colors, and lights. Isn't that odd? That far away from each other and they report the exact same details. The Extras, they call them."

"Unhuh," Bud said, listening with half an ear.

"They don't just show up on Earth. They scout it out without making a fuss." Milton put his arm over the seat-back again and looked at Callum. "The U.S. Air Force knows more than it admits," he said. "It doesn't want people screaming in the streets. The Extras keep their hands in their laps, so to speak. They're out there, all eyes, but they agree with the air force about not wanting to start a riot."

"Cobwebs!" Bud said all of a sudden.

"Here comes Mr. I.Q. Skeptic," Milton said.

"I'm not kidding. They are cobwebs."

"The Extras move across the sky. Cobwebs don't move across the sky."

"Has anyone talked to one of them?"

"Let's go beyond that. For a minute let's assume they exist."

"Okay, let's."

"Where do they come from? Why are they here? What are they telling us? These are the most important questions facing mankind today."

"Let's start at the beginning. How did they get here?" Bud asked.

"In mother ships shaped like cigars five thousand miles long."

"Right now, Milt, answer a question, which may be the most important question facing mankind today. If these Extras are as smart as you say, smart enough to reach Earth, why would they build their spaceships in the shape of a cigar?"

"Laugh all you want," Milton said and stared moodily out the window.

"I'm sorry," Bud said after a moment. "I apologize. But have you thought about that aspect of it?"

"Yes, and I'll answer if you'll just shut your mouth. The mother ships carry scout vessels. These are propelled by magnetic devices. I can't tell you exactly how they work. They are made of an organic metal that reproduces itself. The metal reacts to the thought waves of the pilots. That makes them maneuverable. You've heard of people describing how the ships stop on a dime, then go left and right? That's the pilot's thought control. The ships are protected by a force field that refracts light and makes our photographs of them fuzzy."

"Where'd you learn all this?"

"At the library. You wouldn't believe how much stuff there is written about extraterrestrials."

"Shouldn't the mother ships be called flying cigars and not flying saucers?"

"The scout vessels—not the mother ships—are round with a dome and a little ball on top. Like saucers. They are your flying saucers, the scout ships. They have a crew of five. They're invisible, but if you could see them they would have a diameter of thirty-five feet and six inches. They rotate streams of photons around the spacecraft in three-hundred-sixty-degree arcs."

"No kidding," Bud said, losing interest.

With the men's voices comforting him, Callum reflected on a newspaper article he had read that morning. An airliner had crashed in the mountains near Laramie, Wyoming—a United Airlines DC-4. It had carried sixty-six passengers. The paper said it was the worst aviation disaster in history. Searchers were looking for the wreckage in a mountain blizzard in the hope that some passengers had survived. Callum had just heard Milton tell Bud that the existence of Extras was the most important question facing mankind. Callum thought death was.

"Men and women from Mars operate the saucers," Milton was saying. "They're doing training stints, like missionaries, helping mankind. You can tell when you see them by their smiles and the words they use. They have a gentle wisdom."

"Would I be able to see them?" Bud asked.

"Oh, sure. They wear seamless one-piece suits like mechanics' coveralls, only tighter and made better to keep bacteria out. They have sandals on their feet. You'd be interested in that. You like sandals. Nothing they wear is made from animal by-products. Not even wool. They respect animals. Oh, and they don't eat. Their energy comes from breathing."

"And they look like us?"

"Yeah, but nicer."

"Have *you* ever had a word with them?" Bud asked cautiously.

"That's an interesting question. Very interesting. A while ago they beamed a message from outer space to a mountain in England."

"What did they have to say?"

" 'Radiation.' Like that, 'Radiation'! "

"Did their voices sound like baby chickens under water?" Bud asked, and it was clear by his question that he was starting to get silly.

"I wasn't there and you know I wasn't."

"Then you haven't talked to them."

"Not yet."

Bud hunched over the wheel. "What's a photon, Milt?"

"It has something to do with light, I think."

Callum tore his thoughts away from the ill-fated DC-4. "What are the toilet-paper tubes for?" he asked now that Milton was on the subject, or close to it.

"That's top secret," he replied too quickly and winked at Bud. "For the birds, you know."

"The birds escaped," Bud reminded him.

"They stay around. You'd be surprised." He leaned forward, holding onto the padded dash. "Go straight, go straight!" he shouted. "Don't pay attention to that sign."

Bud pulled the car over to the curb. "We're going where we're going," he said and found a Texaco road map in the glove compartment. Unable to refold the map or find where they were on it, he balled it up and threw it over the seat, then accelerated into traffic.

"You have a third type of ship," Milton said, weaving his conversation as seamlessly as the Extras' jumpsuits. "This ship is flown by the Ancient Ones. They control all humanoid life in the solar system. The Ancient Ones visit Earth in vehicles of light. The star of Bethlehem was a vehicle of light."

"I must tell you," Bud said while Milton organized his thoughts. "The idea that God positioned a star over Bethlehem to guide the Three Wise Men makes me feel warm all over. If what you say is true, these spacemen are God."

"The Ancient Ones drove their vehicle of light close to Earth so they could impregnate Mary."

"Do what?" Bud asked, swerving the car over the center stripe.

"Impregnate her, get her pregnant . . ."

"You mean"—Bud made an in-and-out motion with his forefinger.

"Exactly. Jesus was half Venusian."

"I know you don't mean to shock me, Milt. I know you believe this stuff." He glanced over the seat-back to see whether Callum was listening and nearly missed the turnoff at Los Feliz. He went right, then stopped by a brass marker with the history of Griffith Park set in a boulder by the side of the road.

"This isn't it," Bud said to Milton. "From now on I wish you'd leave the navigation to me."

They entered the park a few minutes later. Griffith Park wasn't the park that Callum had imagined. It was a hangout for geeks and freaks. A man in shorts on a bench was stroking his own bare leg as though he loved it. An elderly woman in a black lace dress strolled under an unaccountably opened black umbrella. Families picnicked on the litter-strewn lawns and kids swatted badminton birdies and chucked soft balls in the smoke of barbecue fires.

"You notice anything different about P.O. lately?" Bud asked Milton as they took the only road possible through the park, passing a sign for the observatory.

"No."

"He's working hard. He's a real go-getter."

"Now that you mention it, isn't he taking the dream too seriously?"

"Like how, too seriously?"

"Like missing work?"

"He feels the same as I do about it," said Bud. "This is it, as far as I'm concerned. There may not be another shot as good as this one. You heard what Roland had to report. The guy smiled. Isn't that enough proof that we're on the right track?"

"Yes, but . . ."

"*But* nothing, Milt," he said, surprising even himself with the strength of his feelings. "If we blow it this time we have only ourselves to blame. I know you are doing what you can to help. The others are, too. But the way you asked the question just now, I wonder if the scheme means anything to you." The words were no sooner out of his mouth than Bud thought about Edith's brooch. Usually he thought about it when he awoke in the mornings. Each time the brooch came to mind, he worried. Once he had braked the car with thoughts of how Edith and the kids and the house were a refuge that he might lose over the brooch. He wished the others could appreciate how serious this dream was for him and what he had put at risk.

"It does mean a lot and it doesn't," Milton said, confirming Bud's worst suspicions.

"I don't see why a few of us should carry the rest of you. If we're going to share the spoils, we should share the effort."

Milton did not say much after that. "I'm afraid I don't *have* much to give," he said after a while in a pitiful, whiny voice.

"What? You don't have that much to give? Of course you do! And I appreciate it," Bud said, sounding like a pep-squad leader. "We're driving up here to the Griffith Observatory, aren't we? You have a hunch. You're one of our stalwarts, Milt."

"You think so?" he asked brightly.

"I said so, didn't I?"

"Well, thanks, Bud." He sat up straight, trying to find the right direction as if his credibility depended on it.

Bud slowed down and told Callum to get in the front seat. Through the branches of a sycamore, the Hollywood sign loomed large on the hillside. Callum had never seen it up this close. Bud said that next to the La Brea Tar Pits, the sign was Los Angeles's greatest cultural landmark, "a billboard without the bill."

"Oh, baby baby baby," Milton exclaimed and pointed out the window at three white domes that shone through the branches of the trees in the late-morning sun. "The architect was almost certainly an Extra," he said, apropos of nothing. "He designed these to attract the attention of the scout ships, like a radio beacon at an airport."

"Is that what this is, then, a flying-saucer port?" Bud asked, humoring him again.

"I expect so."

"Well, keep your heads down."

Moments later they walked from the observatory's parking lot to a view site from where they looked south over Los Angeles. Maybe because of the haze, the sight was actually pleasing to their eyes, which burned from the smog. Bud tried to point out the Los Angeles pueblo on Olivera Street where the sprawl began back in the last century. Callum shaded his eyes to see the Disney studios, but one building looked like all the others. Milton stared up at the observatory's domes.

As they walked along the narrow path from the view site to the observatory's front doors, they paused long enough to admire a statue on a pedestal in the center of a lawn. The statue was dedicated to Sir Isaac Newton and Johannes Kepler, the German astronomer.

"Who was Kepler?" Callum asked Bud.

"A scientist," he said with finality.

The Griffith's heavy doors swung open into a foyer that was dim and cool as a cavern. Gilded stars representing the constellations dotted the vaulted ceiling. The heels of their shoes made hollow sounds on the polished marble floors as they approached a uniformed guard to ask the schedule of the observatory's shows. Callum and Bud went over to a steel pendulum that described the earth's invisible rotation while Milton bought the tickets.

Milton held up the front cover of a magazine he had brought along, *UFO*, for the woman in the ticket booth to see. "I read about you in here," he told her. "Where can I find Dr. King?"

She smiled sweetly. "There's nobody here by that name, sir," she told him.

Milton just shrugged and caught up with Bud and Callum entering the planetarium. They chose seats by the narrator's podium, rested their heads on the seat-backs, and stared up at the domed ceiling. The planetarium was circular, nothing more than a fancy movie theater, with the screen on the dome. The seats faced a machine with huge bulbs that reminded Callum of a mutant ant.

"There's your projector," said Milton, pointing his chin. "It's the most complicated projector anywhere on Earth. Made in Germany."

"How do you know all that?" Bud asked.

"*National Geographic.*"

"I forgot you were a member."

Bud read the *Geographic* every month. It was his bible. But he refused to subscribe because the *Geographic* was a society. The president of the *Geographic*, Mr. Grosvenor, allowed in a few kooks like Milton. Bud was glad Mr. Grosvenor had taken Milton in. He borrowed each issue, sometimes minutes after it arrived, and parroted what he read. Bud liked the illusion of knowledge as much as the next man.

"What are we looking for?" Bud asked.

"You'll know when you see it," Milton replied more enigmatically than ever. He wanted to speak to Dr. King. This planetarium stuff was a sideshow, unless Dr. King himself appeared on the dome. Such things were not unheard of, according to *UFO*.

The lights dimmed as the ceiling lit up with stars. Even camping out at night, the sky never blazed like this with stellar life. Callum was alert both to what he had never been able to see with his bare eyes and for what Milton had come here for. It wouldn't be normal, that was for sure. It would be weird, or merely different and no trouble to spot. Milton could find out about the constellations at the library, but for information about the Extras' airport, he had to come to the source. Callum guessed the Extras would appear on the ceiling, and he waited for a first glimpse of their giant cigars.

The narrator, whom Callum guessed doubled as the Extras' air-traffic controller, started out telling them how the mutant ant was the most sophisticated projector in the world. (Milton was way ahead of him.) What the camera threw on the ceiling was not real, he said. In fact, only about two thirds of the stars shown were visible anymore in the real night sky. With a flashlight he pointed out the zodiacal constellations and then Mars, the North Star, the Southern Cross, and the Dippers—the *Pinkies* and *Blueboys* and *Last Suppers* of the heavens.

"Where are we?" the narrator asked.

Callum fixed his stare on the ant as it swung its pocked head in a lazy arc, expecting it to advance on the audience in search of a human snack. Milton said it was built in Germany, and Germany was a place that was known to have snacked on humans a few years ago, in the war. He had seen the pictures. He knew it was true.

Under glittering though false starlight, Milton started snoring.

"So, where are we?" the narrator asked one more time for drama, as if he didn't know.

With the help of a movie projected on the dome, the audience was rocketed into outer space at an incredible speed. In only seconds they were looking back through a porthole of the spaceship as they flew through the Earth's atmosphere into the solar system and the Milky Way beyond. Before long the rocket reached the universe of universes—the Edge.

"That," the narrator said, "is where we fit in."

The house lights came on bright enough to make them blink. The ant retreated into its hole. Milton wiped the sleep out of his eyes and smacked his lips. "What's for lunch, Gladys?" he asked.

· · ·

Out in the sunlight by the Kepler and Newton statue again, Bud turned to Milton. "Did you find what you came for?"

"What?"

"You said you had a hunch."

"Funny thing about that. No, I didn't."

Bud was a little annoyed with him for wasting their time. "You wanted to visit the Griffith Observatory," he said. "Now you've done that. So? What can you tell us?"

"I was supposed to meet Dr. King. He was supposed to be here."

"*I* didn't see cigars," Callum said.

"You didn't see crabs or bears either," Milton said, turning on Callum as if he had touched a nerve.

What he said was true. Callum had wondered why the old astronomers had named constellations after bears and dogs and horses. Try as he might, he could never quite make them out in books or in planetariums. What in the sky at night looked anything like a candy bar? And Ursa Major looked just as much like a large mattress as it did a bear.

"You were looking for *cigars?*" Bud asked Milton, looking between him and Callum.

"Yes and no." He took the copy of *UFO* out of his back pocket. "I'm sure it says . . ." He paged to the article that had mentioned the Griffith. "*Lower* Griffith, Bud. By golly, we got the wrong one."

They rushed back to the car and drove out of the parking lot in silence. Bud was fuming. Milton was trying to figure out how he could have missed the lower part of the Griffith Observatory. Signs along the road down the hill from the observatory warned of deer, though they did not see any. Hawks flared on thermals in the smoggy air. Farther down they picked up signs for the Greek Theatre. A billboard announced upcoming appearances live onstage of Frank Sinatra and George Shearing and his combo. The Greek was the original theater in Los Angeles, which did not have the money at the time to build a real one. It was a natural amphitheater just like the Laguna Pageant's. They rolled past the Greek's ticket booth, and Bud made a U-turn, then another, more or less going around in a circle. He often told Edith that one of the most important decisions in a man's life was whether to stop to ask for directions. As a general rule, wives wanted to. Bud didn't know why this was. He did not think of himself as an explorer, but he liked to press deeper into the wilds. The unknown attracted him, and this asking repelled him. Lost, he could only be found. Being lost broke up the monotony of a long trip. It confirmed for him that he was as out of control of his life as he thought himself to be.

"Maybe we should ask," Milton said just as Bud was pondering the subject.

"Milt, I *know* where it is."

Milton started shouting, and Bud pulled over and stormed out of the car, leaving the door open.

The head and torso of a young woman with vacant eyes was framed in the window of the Greek's ticket booth. Her hair was blond and shoulder length, and her eyes were unnaturally green. A yellow sweater was stretched over her considerable breasts. Bud smiled at them, giving them all he had. "I wonder, can you help us?" he asked, looking her in the eyes.

"Sure," she said and leaned on her elbows, her chin in her hands. "You an actor?"

"Why would you think that?"

"*I'm* an actress."

"That's nice," Bud said.

"Well really I'm at acting school—the Meisner method," she went on, with Bud staring at her wondering why she would think that he cared. It wasn't as if he didn't have his own life, or that he was soliciting this blonde for a date. "I get bit parts," she continued unfazed. "I get second callbacks. My agent says I have a good chance if I keep at it, not that there's any question of going home, not to that dump. You sorta look familiar. You sure you're not somebody?"

"Positive," Bud replied and straightened his shoulders. "Do you know where we can find the Lower Griffith?"

She gave him a look of mock surprise. "*Vroom, vroom,* huh?"

"I don't know what you are talking about, young lady."

"Don't be embarrassed." She leaned out of the ticket window. "Eight or ten blocks out of the park gates on the right side. You can't miss it."

Back in the car, Milton asked him, "What was she like?"

"A doozie," Bud said and drove on.

In a few minutes they passed through the park gates, then across Los Feliz into a residential neighborhood of homes with tile roofs and big lawns. Los Angeles seemed to be a place where nobody ever knew where they were. One place looked the same as all the others, though some houses had greener lawns. A few blocks down the hill, they came across a commercial district of barbershops, beauty parlors, pizza joints, and burger stands.

Bud pulled over to the curb to confer with Milton. "You were stiffed," he told him.

Milton was reading *UFO*. He looked up, around, and shouted, "Hey! Over there!" and shot his arm out the window.

"Yup, you were stiffed," Bud repeated.

In the center of a dusty and otherwise vacant lot sat a worn-out house trailer, its axles resting on cinder blocks, its wheels and tires missing. The vacant lot was wedged between a three-story house on one side and a Mexican upholstery shop on the other. Junk littered a field that weeds in profuse varieties had overrun. A window was cut in the trailer's plywood side. A counter was built in the hole. A hand-lettered sign on the trailer roof advertised chili dogs, cream sodas, hamburgers on buns with tomato and lettuce, shakes. Beneath the menu, a sign announced, THE LOWER GRIFFITH OBSERVATORY AND AETHERIUS SOCIETY.

For several minutes they sat in silence.

"You can't judge a book by its cover," Milton said.

He was the first out of the car and crossed the lot and stood by the trailer window whacking the dust out of his pants with his patrolman's cap. A short, paunchy man in an apron appeared in the window of the trailer wearing an uneven smile. "What can I do for you, officer?" he asked, wiping the counter industriously with a filthy rag.

"I'm looking for Dr. King, doctor of divinity."

The man slapped the flat of his hand on the countertop with a loud bang. The napkin dispenser, sugar and creamer, and Heinz ketchup bottle rose and fell with a clatter. "This is the place," he said. With a shy look he added, "Well, this is the refreshment area, anyway. I know it's confusing. I myself urge George to dress up the stand here with rocket ships and flying saucers so visitors like yourself will know without having to ask. But he won't hear of it.

He says it would debase the American headquarters of the Ae-therius Society. George is a purist, you know. He doesn't dare offend those for whom the observatory exists, if you catch my drift. I wasn't suggesting anything radical, decoration-wise. What's wrong with calling what we sell here Space Boogers and Saucer Dogs? I can't see how that would offend them, can you?"

"Well, no," Milton said, looking disappointed in spite of himself. Yet, hadn't the man just said "offend *them*"?

"George isn't sure what offends them, to be honest," the man said.

He had referred to *them* twice now in as many sentences. *Them* had to be what he was looking for. He cocked an ear and listened for their names.

"For all we know they'd be flattered to have a hot dog named after them," the man went on. "We just don't know that much about them. He just says no when I ask. Some days he gives automatic yeses and some days automatic nos." He waved at Bud sitting in the car. "Invite your friends up here. I'll tell George. It's more respectful of those he represents if visitors are announced, if you get my drift." He winked. "They scare the pee out of him. Back in a jiffy." And he left by the trailer's back door and disappeared through a gate leading to the three-story house.

"What's he doing?" Bud asked, walking up to Milton.

"Telling George King we're here."

"Then what?"

"How would I know?"

The man returned muttering to himself. "It'll take a few min-utes," he said, climbing back in the trailer. He wiped the counter again with the rag. "Can I sell you fellas a cold drink while we're waiting?" He looked startled and passed his hand over the counter. "I should introduce myself. Richmond, Richmond Emerson." He looked Bud up and down. "Yeah, we've been here in this same spot half a decade now. Five years ago George got the command to become the voice of the interplanetary parliament. He was doing health food at the time. He was sitting over there"—he pointed to the three-story house—"when Master Saint Goo-Ling of the Great White Brotherhood appeared in a vision. George calls him Ae-therius. And that's how it began. From that time on, George received messages, like the Twelve Blessings from Aetherius and other intelligences like Master Jesus and Mars Sector Six. A lot of people got excited about it. How'd *you* hear about us?"

"An article," Milton replied, holding up *UFO*.

"Big supporters."

"Do you mind if I ask you a question?" Milton asked. "You mentioned before that they scare him . . . ?"

"The pee out of him. I've seen it happen. George denies it, of course. He says, 'Emerson, you're full of shit.' When he puts a foot wrong, that's when it happens. They threaten him and he pees. He says something they don't like and *blam!*" He slapped the counter-top again. "George is cosmic garbage. It keeps him on his toes." He glanced at his watch. "I think we can go see him now."

He folded his apron with care, then left the trailer and with a rolling gait led them across the lot. The yard next door was un-kempt, with shrubs and bushes growing wild and tires, a baby buggy, and hubcaps strewn across what once was lawn. A load of timber rotted under a tarp. Paint peeled off the house in strips like eucalyptus bark. The window screens had holes in them cats could have climbed through.

Richmond pulled back the cellar door, and from a well of dark-ness he beckoned them to follow. In the cellar a bare bulb cast a light on a stack of snow tires, a clothes washer with rollers and a sink, cardboard storage boxes, a push lawn mower, and a rusty bike. A toilet ran in the corner. They ducked their heads under a stair-case, and there against the wall was a dais festooned with Christmas tinsel and colored lights. A spotlight was aimed on the face of a man who stared straight ahead as if he were in a trance. One of his arms hung stiff by his side, the other one was crooked out in front of him, making him look like the kind of iron slave sculpture that rich people put on their driveways. He was wearing a worn Ike jacket, army surplus, an open-necked dress shirt, and faded khaki pants. By his gentle smile he looked like a man who had found content-ment. A second spotlight aimed at the wall behind him created the illusion that he was floating on air. Two pendular chrome micro-phones hung by his temples. Draped over his crooked right forearm was the flabby inner tube of an Italian racing bicycle.

Emerson put a recording of mournful organ music on the record player.

"Let me tell you the most wonderful news of modern time," George King said—for it was he—in a resonant tone that complemented the organ music. "The news is that you are not alone. You have never been alone. Every one step you take toward the Great Masters, they will take two steps toward you. When Aetherius made this profound statement, he gave his gospel and guarantee, as did that other Venusian who chose to be born the son of a village carpenter nearly two thousand years ago—'Came I not to Kings and Princes but to ordinary Man who has faith.' This is the inspiring message, the personal offer, extended to each of you with an unconditional money-back guarantee from the depths of the great heart of that saintly Venusian we call Jesus of Nazareth."

Milton removed his patrolman's cap and Bud his tam-o'-shanter with a reverential grace. Milton whispered to Bud, "That's what came to Roland at the Last Supper."

With awe in his voice, Bud whispered back, "I know."

"Dr. King, is it you?" Milton asked in a pious tone, taking a step forward.

Dr. King stared straight ahead. "What more do we need?" he asked as if he were alone. "What more can we ask? The future of the Earth is in our hands, for every thought and every action we take today is the foundation of tomorrow. Take your hands from the pockets of isolation and join them together in cooperation and soon such a line will be formed as to span the whole world, a line of brothers who together will influence today's action and thus mold tomorrow's outcome."

Milton took Bud's hand.

"Those of you in this line that will span the world will have not just conviction but the courage of those convictions."

Milton took hold of Callum's hand, too.

"You can change the outlook of the world and succeed where science and politics have failed. This is the power which will guarantee that the young children of today will grow, learn, and live in peace, that the coming generations will not be born as misshapen mutants, devoid of that balance which is sanity. Look at any helpless baby—look deep into its trusting eyes—and you must agree that you owe it the chance for a good and peaceful life. The Masters who are now coming to Earth in flying saucers have told you what to do. The responsibility is . . . yours."

"Well, I'll be," Bud whispered, overwhelmed by George King's messages.

Richmond took the needle off the organ-music record and snapped off the stage lights. Gently he removed the bicycle inner tube from Dr. King's forearm.

"Can I ask him something?" Milton asked Richmond.

"Sure, but I can't guarantee he'll answer," he replied. "Sometimes he gets wiped out after a session like this."

"Can you tell me why the Masters need Christ? I'll understand if you're too tired."

Dr. King opened his eyes. They were a startling robin's-egg blue. "The Masters need Christ because that's the way it is," he said, as if everybody knew.

"Well, for what reason?"

"Christ or Buddha or Mohammed conveyed the Masters' message to Terra. The Masters can't speak for themselves, so they appoint sales reps."

"What's the point?"

"Ascension. When you ascend you speak in a thousand tongues and travel through space for all eternity." George King smiled. "You stop, have a swim and a hot meal, maybe a lime rickey, Magic Fingers on the bed, then off you go again. It's a good life."

"And how do we get to this Ascension?"

"You'll know it when you see it." He closed his eyes, and his smile, if possible, seemed to widen.

Callum liked Dr. King. The words he was saying didn't matter. He bet he didn't give a hoot who believed him either. He wouldn't care who visited, or listened, or asked questions. He wouldn't care what he ate, how he dressed, whether he owned a late model car, or a twelve-inch TV. He was so far gone, all he cared about was staying out there.

"Ask him about Walt, for Christ's sake," Bud stage-whispered to Milton.

Milton took no notice. "What about talking to them direct, like you do?"

George King crossed his arms. "What about it?"

"How's it done?"

"You pass through stages. If there are shortcuts, I don't know them. What do you have in mind?"

"Nothing," Milton replied a beat too fast; of course he had something in mind. That was why he had wanted to visit Dr. King. Yet, he couldn't bring himself to describe his giant crystal and the toilet-paper tubes, the copper wiring, and the antenna that Gladys thought was a perch for birds. "I don't understand one thing," he said.

"Only one?" asked Dr. King. He gave Richmond a comical know-it-all stare.

"If the Masters are what you say, I mean benevolent and all, why are they nasty to you?"

"They aren't."

"Why do they scare you?"

"Who gave you that idea?" He glared at Richmond.

"You look scared right now," Milton said.

"Well, I'm not."

Richmond stamped his foot. "You are, too, George. You know what they do. I don't know why you won't admit it. These people'll understand." He turned to Milton. "It's just messy and real embarrassing when he stains his chinos down the front. Huh, George? Everybody knows, George."

"They do not!" He looked petulant with his lips pursed and his chin stuck out.

"What causes him to pee, exactly?" Bud asked Richmond.

"Messages of a scary nature. He gets them anywhere, anytime. *Blam!* He pees himself. It means they're talking to him."

"Does this happen to everyone who talks to them?" Milton wanted to know.

"I can't say. They don't talk to me."

"I am incontinent," Dr. King said, defending his honor. "And that's the last word I'll say on that subject."

"My friend came here to ask you a question, Dr. King," Bud said, slapping Milton on the shoulder.

Dr. King looked relieved to leave the subject of his bladder. "Ask. Ask."

"It has to do with dreams," said Milton.

"We could use more of them around here ourselves."

Bud sensed that Milton would never get around to asking. "What my friend wants to know, can the Masters or Extras or whatever you call them read Walt Disney's mind?"

Dr. King thought about that a second. "Not only his mind."

"Mickey and Donald's, too?" Callum asked.

"No problem."

Callum inferred that Walt's creatures—the ones he had seen playing baseball in the studio parking lot—were as real as he had hoped. The inference would confirm that Walt was building a home for Mickey and Donald. Only if they were real would they need a real place to live.

"We'd like to find out where Walt Disney is buying some land," Bud said.

Dr. King looked over at Richmond. "Is this in our brief?" he asked.

"How should I know?"

"We can have a look, can't we?"

Richmond shook his head doubtfully, but he reached into a storage closet under the staircase and came out with what looked like a stovepipe on a wooden tripod. He blew dust off it, then looked down into a box for parts. He wiped the lens of the telescope with his shirttail and lifted the tripod on his shoulder.

"There's your *Lower* Griffith," Bud whispered to Milton.

"The uniform doesn't make the team," Milton said.

Richmond and Dr. King argued all the way up the cellar steps over where to set up the telescope for the best view of the truth they were seeking.

"It's better over in the lot," said Richmond.

"I say on top of the trailer," said Dr. King.

"You always leave this part to me," said Richmond. "And I say in *back* of the trailer."

"You better be right, buster," said Dr. King.

Callum said nothing, though he wanted to point out to them that it was daylight. He looked for confirmation of this fact into a dull gray sky tinged a sulphurous yellow. It was the middle of the afternoon.

Richmond started to set up the telescope on a flat spot behind the trailer. "Dr. King has not engaged in this kind of extracurricular inquiry in some time," he told them. "What I mean is, don't get your hopes up."

"Don't complain and never explain," said Dr. King, who spread his legs and clasped his hands behind his back as he lowered his eye over the sight of the telescope. He fiddled with the focusing screws and aimed the tube into the midday sky. He asked, "Property, huh?"

"About a hundred acres," Bud said.

"I got something here. Don't hold me to it. It's a field. I can see the ocean. It's not *on* the ocean but close. There's a billboard. People are wandering around a round-roofed house." He looked up. "Does that strike a chord?"

Bud shook his head. "You see anything else?"

Dr. King tried again. "That's it," he said and bounced on the balls of his feet. "Damn, it feels good getting in harness again. I should do more of this." He looked down at Callum. "You wanna peek, son?"

Callum glanced at the crotch of Dr. King's khakis, half expecting to see a stain. "Do you know about the airplane that crashed yesterday?" he asked him.

Dr. King looked doubtful. "Did one?"

"In a blizzard in the Rockies," Richmond told him quietly.

"Why didn't you tell me?"

"I gave you the paper. Do I have to read it for you, too?"

Callum asked, "Would the Masters know what happened to those people? It was United Airlines flight four-oh-nine. Sixty-six people."

Dr. King bent down to his level and held his hand. "You mean, ask what happened to them?"

"Can you?"

"I can sure try," he said and leaned into the telescope, scanning the bright, hazy sky. "*Hmm,*" he said.

"What are you looking for?" Bud asked.

"A sighting. Strange. It should show up here. But it's all fuzzy."

"Maybe it's the blizzard," said Callum.

"Not that kind of fuzzy. More like fuzzy-wuzzy." He raised his head. "Look for yourself."

Callum did. It wasn't fuzzy or wavy or wuzzy. It was *nothing*, just as he had feared.

"I was patching in. Strange." Dr. King spread his legs again and lowered his eye to the telescope, adjusting the focus knobs.

"Don't strain yourself, now," warned Richmond.

Callum's heart sank. He felt terrible for those passengers, all dead for sure. And he was thinking how their families were going to feel when they found out what had happened. He felt like crying all of a sudden and he might have, if a faint familiar odor had not reached his nose. He looked at Richmond, who pressed his forefinger to his lips and pointed at Dr. King's khakis.

Dr. King was still looking in the telescope. "Fuzzy-wuzzy is all I'm getting here."

"Oh, George, look at your pants!" Richmond scolded him. "You did too see something and you're not telling."

Dr. King looked down. "Oh, dear me," he said and covered his crotch with both hands. "You can understand my embarrassment." He shook his leg and said to Richmond, "I said I saw nothing and I meant nothing. They got in touch just now, I admit. Okay? But they had nothing to say about the crash."

"They never say *nothing*," Richmond told him. "You complain about their jabbering away like baboons. You say they fill up the airwaves. And now it's nothing? Not even humming?"

"Nothing."

"This is remarkable," Richmond told them. "You are witnesses to a remarkable event."

"*Nothing* is remarkable?" asked Bud.

"You've got to understand. They're chatty kathies."

The airline passengers were dead for sure, Callum thought, and he wondered why Dr. King could not see that. The Masters had broken the news without his knowing. He had missed the one thing that holy men had sought a glimpse of for epochs. He had committed the perfectly human error of mistaking the hereafter for fuzzy-wuzzy.

Dr. King shot Richmond a hostile look over his shoulder as he waddled across the lot, pee squishing in his shoes.

"Nice folks," Milton said when they were in the car again and driving through the afternoon traffic of Los Angeles.

"What about that inner tube?" Bud asked him.

"Everybody has their own thing—the Pope his crook, Mohammed his rug, the Jews their beanies, Catholics their beads. Dr. King has his inner tube."

"Well—"

Milton turned to him. "Well *what*?"

"Did you get what you came for?"

"I came to find out where Walt is buying the land."

"Did you find out?"

"A bean field near the water but not *on* the water, and a billboard and people wandering around a shed with a sloped roof."

"A round-roofed house," Callum corrected him.

"That's your answer, pure and simple," Milton told Bud. "What more do you need, the address?"

Bud looked skeptical. "I'll take it under advisement, Milt. It's a piece in the puzzle. Hey, it's a good piece, too. Don't get me wrong."

"You don't believe him."

"Sure I do."

"No you don't. I can see it in your face. You thought Dr. King was a doozie."

Edith's brooch popped into Bud's mind. "I wouldn't bet my life on what he said, no," he told Milton.

"He's telling you what he sees, and he sees the future. It's a piece of the puzzle," and Milton's mouth set with resolve.

All of a sudden, Callum knew what the toilet-paper tubes were for. Bees, he had thought. The enormity of the concept overwhelmed him in a manner that went beyond imagination. Milton was making a huge radio right out of *Popular Mechanics*, but it wasn't a rock-'n'-roll station in Watts that he was hoping to listen to.

At the bottom of Vermont Avenue, Bud asked Milton, "You know where we're heading?"

"Home," he replied hopefully. Milton was tired and he had work to do in the command center.

"That's where you're wrong."

"The Tar Pits?"

"More along the lines of a taco," Bud said.

Callum sat back, relieved to hear that. He would rather go any-where than the La Brea Tar Pits. Bud said the pits were proof that something in Los Angeles had stirred before the movies. People drove hundreds of miles to say they had visited the site where sabre-toothed tigers and woolly mammoths had lumbered in the tar and never lumbered out. On his one visit he had looked down into a pool of black goo waiting for a bubble. That was the event at the pits, a bubble that went *blub*. One had formed, large and round, out of the tar and burst as predicted. The air of a million years ago came from the burst bubble, and the amazing thing was, it had smelled the same as a modern fart.

Finding a parking space near Alvera Street was no cinch, and Bud drove around bickering with Milton about what constituted a legal space. Alvera was the main drag of El Pueblo, where Los Angeles had started out as a town. Now it was a tourist trap, a long arcade of shops with a narrow promenade closed off to traffic. The shops on the arcade sold piñatas and *caracas* and strings of *huerachas* draped on striped awnings. Mexican vendors sold jumping beans, vegetables, fruit and juices, and tacos, and a mariachi band did all in its musical power to lend the street a festive Spanish air.

Bud ordered tacos at a stand, and while he was shaking on Tabasco sauce, an old woman with a red headband signaled to him from across the arcade. She was sitting behind a wooden plank under a string of garish lights. As Bud walked over to her, she raised a penciled eyebrow and gave him a broken-toothed smile.

Bud asked her about herself, and she said she hailed from near Kiev and had reached America via Spain and Mexico. Her name was Madame Murcielago and she read the future. "I've seen things," she told him, narrowing her eyes.

"Like for instance?" Bud asked her.

"Things one pair of eyes should never see."

Bud turned to Milton. "Ever had your fortune read?" he asked him.

"I don't hold with clairvoyance."

"That sounds final," Madame Murcielago said. She looked at Callum. "What about you, loverboy?"

"His future, tell him about that," said Milton.

Madame Murcielago held his opened palm in her leathery hand. "There's an *M* written here," she whispered. "Memento mori. It stands for 'I will remember death.' It's a reminder, see. Everybody has one. It means we are all going to die. Now, let me look here," she said and winked at Bud. "Why don't you come over here beside him so you can hear, too?" She smoothed Callum's palm. "You will marry a girl who knows you better than you know yourself. Now this *is* interesting. I see places and things that few people see. These things *you* will see. By the time you are old, your eyes will be full." Seeing something in his palm that surprised her, she said, "Well, I'll be," and pushed his hand away like an unwanted gift.

"That's all?" Bud asked. He laughed, thinking she was a doozie. He stuck out his palm and rolled up his sleeve like a man preparing for a polio shot.

She tickled his palm with her hoary fingernails. "You've had a good life," she said. "You have a loving wife, this boy here, and two girls. You have not always been satisfied with how things are. You wish you had traveled, but you will not."

"Right so far," Bud said, smiling over at Milton.

She brushed his palm. "You have an artist's hands. You aren't an artist. You aren't a farmer either. You are a dreamer."

"Got that one right," Milton told her, suddenly interested.

"Tell me, will my dream come true?" Bud asked her in a voice that conveyed such need that Madame Murcielago looked him straight in the eyes.

"Your dream *has* come true," she told him and turned his hand over flat on the wooden plank.

"My dream-*scheme* is what I meant," he told her, almost pleading with her. "What about my dream-*scheme*?"

"That's different. That? You will miss it," she told him and indicated with a turn of her frail shoulders that that was that.

"Let's get out of here," Milton said, disgusted.

They hurried down Alvera feeling tired, thanks not only to the long day but also to Madame Murcielago's depressing fortunes.

They didn't believe in palm readings, but they didn't *not* believe either. If her prognostication had called for riches, they would have proclaimed her prescience. As it was, they just felt down. Madame Murcielago had ruined what had otherwise been an instructive day.

"I don't think she played by the rules," Bud said when they reached the car.

"There are no rules in her game," Milton pointed out to him. "They don't license clairvoyants that I know of."

" 'You will miss it,' was what she said. How would you interpret that?"

"The same as you."

"If you miss something, you are dead or asleep. What a stupid thing to say."

From the backseat of the car, Callum asked in a tired voice, "Dad, have you ever flown in an airliner?"

"No, but I'm going to one of these days."

"I wish you wouldn't," he said.

"Gypsies aren't supposed to say stuff like that," Bud said.

"I wouldn't get worked up," Milton reasoned with him. "You go back to her tomorrow, she'll have you living as long as Croesus."

"Methuselah, Milt. Croesus is the one I'm going to be."

Edith twirled.

"Hey Blue, Edith is twirling!" Cloud shouted down the hall toward her bedroom.

Bud poked his head out of the kitchen and stared at her. Callum, who had been Simonizing his Schwinn on the back porch, came in with Scooter and watched. Milton and Gladys, who were licking S&H Green Stamps and putting them in the books on the living-room sofa, looked up in amazement.

And still Edith twirled on the living-room carpet. Her Job's dress, hot off the Singer, ballooned as she spun in circles. She looked just beautiful as she tiptoed with her arms out to her sides, her head back with a smile of such joy she could have been a dervish queen. She kept at it, too, twirling and twirling, not caring who watched or what comments they made. She felt prettier than she thought she would feel, and if twirling froze the feeling, she would twirl until dizziness dropped her to her knees.

"Mom, that's enough, Mom," Blue said, starting to feel scared for her. Edith was her pillar, the one who was always reliably in control, and now this. . . . "Come on, Mom. Stop it!" she shouted.

"You're going to make yourself sick," Bud said, wanting her to stop, too. One twirl was fine. Two was okay. But this was a side of Edith he did not know and had never suspected. "How about a glass of iced water?"

As Edith laughed, her face and neck colored from the ecstasy of the twirl. She would not stop. The people in the living room exchanged worried glances, and finally Milton rose from the sofa and, timing it perfectly, jumped into the zone of her twirling to get her to stop but was caught up and the two of them, like Astaire and Rogers, twirled on.

Bud started laughing at the centrifugal force swinging Milton's pistol holster out from his Sam Browne belt. Milton managed to get one arm free of Edith's grasp, which he threw in the air like a Greek hanky dancer. Bud jumped in and snatched Milton's hand, taking Edith's in his other, and they formed a ring-around-the-rosey circle that the others soon joined. Scooter hopped on his back legs, scratching the air with his front paws, searching for a partner. Gladys lifted her muumuu and flipped up her shades and entered the spin, humming the Jewish national anthem, she said later, because that was the song people sang when they twirled. Then came Callum and, with as much enthusiasm, Blue and Cloud. Bud whooped, and Milton made a noise in his throat, and the girls and women laughed as they spun around and around until they were out of breath and close to falling-down dizzy.

"We should do that more often," Bud said, flopping in the recliner out of breath.

"Have you got a cold beer?" Milton gasped.

"Even if nothing else happens with these Job's," Edith declared, fanning herself with her hand, "this twirl has made it all worthwhile."

"What do you mean, if nothing else happens?" Cloud asked her, her face darkening. "We're going to *win*."

Bud said of course they were going to win. "How about giving us a preview of the act?" he asked.

Blue was ready to dance just as Mrs. Hamel had taught them, but

Cloud restrained her with her hand. "It'd be bad luck," she told Bud. "And we're not in costume. Are we, Blue?"

Blue seemed confused by the different signals. What with the original *Minuet Waltz* and now *Le Baiser de la Fée* and not knowing who was dancing what or where, she had forgotten about the costumes. "The costumes will make a difference," she agreed.

Gladys squatted down in front of Edith to smooth the hem of her Job's dress. She tugged the fabric here and there, then, lowering her sunglasses, she made an overall appraisal, crawling two steps backward for perspective. With her finger on her lip she said, "It needs a touch of . . . jewelry."

Bud looked up through startled eyes. "How about some lemonade, Gladys?" he asked a bit too fast. Even Edith noticed.

"What's the matter, Bud?" she asked.

"The twirling. It made me thirsty. I was just being polite, Edith."

"Thanks anyway," Gladys told him, and to Edith she said, "Pearls. Yes, a simple string of pearls would be just the thing to finish off the look."

Bud relaxed visibly.

"Come with me," Edith told Gladys, and the two of them disappeared down the hall.

Bud pulled himself out of the chair. "I've got to get myself some fresh air," he said.

He normally did not announce such needs as fresh air, and everybody in the living room looked at him strangely, as if he might be having a heart attack but didn't want to come right out and bother anybody by saying so.

"We'll go with you," Milton told him.

They got as far as the kitchen when they heard a piercing cry. Bud knew right away who it came from and even why, and he felt his heart break. All he could do was stare out the window with his fists clenched, wishing what was about to happen wouldn't.

Edith was sobbing, and when she saw Bud, the sight of him made her sob louder. "The brooch," she cried. "Bud, the family . . ."

Gladys helped her to a chair in the kitchen, and Bud poured her a glass of orange juice from the refrigerator. She stopped crying long enough to take a sip. "It's gone," she said. "Oh dear, it's gone."

"Misplaced," Gladys said, trying to be helpful.

"I can't find it," Edith said as if she blamed herself. "I always keep it in my jewelry box—you know that, Bud!—and it's not there. Bud, do you know what could have happened to it?"

He could not look at her. "Maybe it fell behind the dresser, Edith." He started to go down the hall to look for it, a charade he hated himself for.

"I already looked, under the dresser, under the bed, under the carpet," Edith said. "I looked on the dresses I've worn in the closet and it's not on them either."

Callum, Blue, and Cloud were close to tears. This was the first real adult emotional crisis of their lives, and they were not prepared for its intensity. Edith seemed so different all of a sudden. She seemed helpless and weak, like she was giving up. They weren't used to seeing her like this. They needed Edith. She was the one who told them what they did not want to hear. She was the strong one; she was the one they always turned to when they were in need. Seeing Edith wring her hands, Blue started to cry, and Cloud joined in.

"You'll find it, Mom, I know you will," Blue said and hung on Edith's shoulders sobbing.

"Oh dear oh dear," said Gladys, sobbing herself now.

"It makes no sense," Milton said and hiked up his Sam Browne belt with an air of authority. "Unless it was stolen."

"Wait a minute!" Bud shouted to get Edith and the girls to stop crying. "We're hysterical now. That's not going to do any good."

"I think we should call the crime squad," Milton proposed.

Bud waved at him to shut up. "That's going overboard," he said.

"They could dust for fingerprints."

"Let's settle down first."

"She's my sister," Milton pointed out.

"She's my wife. I bought her the brooch. I'll help her find it. You're making a federal case out of what may be nothing. My sense is that it'll turn up sooner or later. It's lost. But it will be found."

"Oh Bud, you think so?"

Now he looked her straight in the eye. "I *know* so."

As he passed the shops in downtown Santa Ana, Bud couldn't get Edith out of his mind. He had put her in bed with the hot-water bottle and covered her with a blanket, watching her until she had fallen into a troubled sleep. He had thought he knew what the brooch meant to her, but he had been wrong, underestimating its value by half. He patted his billfold as he walked by the stationery store. When he looked in the windowed alcove of the shop next door, he felt sick. Amid the debris of knives and bongo drums and guitars, a small velvet island of serenity stood out. It was a blue velvet pillow on which Edith's family brooch sat for the world to see. It was like Edith was lying on that pillow, naked as a jaybird.

He pushed open the door to the pawnshop. The owner was sitting in his regular place wearing his eyeshade and a dress shirt with a bow tie and suspenders. He remembered Bud and nodded to him. "That horse, did it come in?" he asked.

"The race is still on," Bud told him.

"We've had a couple of inquiries about your brooch but no offers yet."

"That's the reason I came in. What's the idea of putting it in the window?"

"It's advertising. A nice item like that brings in customers for the bongos and the shitty stuff."

"I didn't know you could just put anything in the window."

He raised his eyeshade and in a resigned voice said, "Mister, you knew. The day you came in here you stared in that window. I watched you. Did you think your brooch would be an exception?"

Bud felt afraid. Edith could have walked past and seen his crime laid out like a corpse. "Would you mind taking it out of there?"

"I would." He didn't even look up.

"Look, it's important to me."

"To me, too."

"Do you want me to plead?" he asked. "Okay, I'm pleading."

"Sorry," the man told him.

"I didn't pawn it for the reason you might think."

"Most of my customers say the same," said the man.

"I told you we came from New England."

"You mentioned it."

Bud hoped to explain but it was hard. "New England was old and dried up and cold. My mother and dad lived there. And who wants to follow in footsteps that are shuffling with old age? I'd lie awake nights dreaming of California. We came all across the country by car. But you know? All I've seen of a better life so far is the weather." He hated to say these things, but what choice did he have? "This brooch belongs to my wife. So please, will you take it out of the window?"

"No can do. You want it out of the window, you'll have to buy it back."

"I've been thinking about doing that."

"Either way is fine by me."

Bud knew what would make him feel happy again—the words "Here's your brooch, Edith." Yet the horse was in the stretch and it was leading the field and unless he had the money to bet with, he could not win. He would be like a tinhorn picking a horse without placing a bet. He had done that all his life. "This is my one shot," he told himself.

"What say?"

"My one shot."

"We get a lot of one-shots in," the owner told him. "We are a house of one-shots. People come in, think they know a winning number, and they don't come back."

"You sure do inspire confidence," Bud told him.

"For that you want a preacher."

Bud reached for his wallet. "I think I'd better buy it back, then," he told him, feeling better just saying the words.

The owner took off his eyeshade and a moment later came from behind the cage. Bud was surprised to see that he was confined to a wheelchair. With an effort he reached inside the window for the brooch and then wheeled back. The speed of the effort reminded Bud of just how fast a life could change.

He wanted to feel the brooch again in his palm. He wanted to caress its smooth surface knowing that he would never do anything this stupid again. He put the bills on the counter, the original notes in the same order as he had received them. The owner counted them and looked at Bud inquiringly.

"Ahh, you're a bit short here, mister," he said.

Bud snatched up the bills and counted them, one by one. He

could hear his own voice counting, and when he was finished the total was the same. He had not spent a single dollar. "No, it's all here," he told him.

"I guess you didn't read the pawn ticket. You owe me the eighteen hundred I paid you *plus* a fifty-dollar commission for my effort."

"But you didn't sell it!"

"I am now."

"You don't understand. My wife. My family."

"You don't have the fifty?"

"You might as well ask for a thousand."

"You took my money," the owner pointed out. "I *own* the brooch, mister. If you want to buy it back, you will have to pay the price I am asking. What do you think I run here, a charity?"

Bud read the back of the pawn ticket with the terms in black and white, not understanding how he could have been this wrong.

13

Hail Caesar!

Draped in a white bedsheet, Bud lounged on a cushion on the backyard lanai, a garland of bay leaves ringing his head and a sandaled foot crossing his hairy knee. He slapped a baton against his palm again and again as though he were pondering a troop movement over the Alps. Earlier he had jutted his chin as though his exulted make-believe status made him proud. He had cared about his toga's folds and wondered out loud whether Edith should have gilded the leaves. Now, as though he were a parody of late Roman history, he slouched and dawdled and yawned, and his toga was a mess.

"You look senatorial with your white hair and all," said a thin man with a small mustache, offering obvious flatteries to keep Bud alert. Bud blinked, unimpressed. The man, a photographer friend named Ab, fiddled with the lens of a Rolleiflex while he stared at nothing.

"Isn't that about it, Ab?" he asked.

"One more."

"It was one more eight ago."

"This time I mean it."

Callum was leaning against the barbecue, winding the string

around a wooden top. He had entered the lanai a moment earlier. "What's the picture for, Ab?" he asked.

"Night-school class."

"They teach that for credit?" Bud asked.

"It all adds up."

Bud looked interested. "Not taking away from it, Ab, but what have we come to here? You get a degree nowadays for taking pictures of friends?"

"It's art, Bud."

Callum threw the top and spiked the concrete floor within an inch of where he aimed it. Friends his age impaled bugs and such with their tops. Callum had outgrown that, but he still loved the top simply for the pleasure of his mastery of the thing. He did not consider it a toy, not anymore. He had lavished on it too much time and concentration for that. Toys were things that demanded no payment in frustration. Toys worked from the start, without effort or the need for patience.

At the sound of a revving motor in the driveway, Bud tossed the end of the toga over his shoulder and got off the cushion. P.O. braked his motorcycle by the lanai and lowered the kickstand. He dismounted with an agile swing of his leg over the postilion. He did not wear a helmet, but goggles left a mark around his eyes.

"Hail Caesar!" he said, extending his arm in a Roman salute.

"At ease, centurion," Bud told him.

"Reminds me of a woman I once knew who wasn't strong on history or geography, or anything else," said P.O., tapping his temple. "I introduced her to a friend who told her he had just come back from a visit to Palestine. He was a Jew. Her eyes got big, and she said, 'Oh, and to think, I just saw *The Bible.*'"

"You know some doozies," Bud said.

"I know you. And speaking of doozies, I just passed Mr. Wait on the road. He was walking Bob. Doesn't he own a car?"

"A pickup," Bud said.

"He likes to walk," Callum said, defending him. He rewound the string on the top. "He knows shortcuts that he couldn't take in a car."

"He's on his way over here. He wanted me to tell you." P.O. reached into the saddlebag on his motorcycle. He had borrowed an armful of maps from the county offices. "We got business to discuss," he said.

"Ready when you are, C.B.," Ab called from the lanai. He handed Bud a beachball that Edith had painted silver. Ab showed him how he wanted him to pose with the ball, like a lawn sculpture.

"What's the ball for, Ab?" P.O. asked.

"Romans always posed with balls."

"Posed for what?"

"Whatever they posed for."

"Did they have cameras in Roman times?"

"Of course not."

"Portrait painters?"

"Not that I know of."

"Then what did they pose for if they posed with silver balls? I'm trying to get to the bottom of this, Ab."

Ab concentrated on his camera, twisting the focus knob, pretending P.O. wasn't there.

"Have you ever shot a beaver?" P.O. asked, having a little fun.

Ab looked up. "I don't do nature work," he replied.

"The other kind of beaver," P.O. said. "I thought guys became photo buffs to shoot girls in the buff. You know what I'm talking about, Ab?"

"No," Ab said.

"But you're hoping to find out?"

Ab shook his head sadly. Satisfied at last with the composition of the shot, he pushed the shutter button and four flashbulbs popped at once. Quickly he changed bulbs.

"Ab," P.O. went on, teasing. "Cheval said she'd pose for you one of these days. Would you be interested?"

"Sure, P.O. Damn straight I would," said Ab.

P.O. looked at Bud. "See what I mean?"

Having polished off Ab, P.O. spread the maps on the concrete. "I was at the tax assessor's," he told Bud. He got down on his hands and knees. "I thought maybe zoning could tell us something."

"And?" Bud said, still in profile, the silver beach ball in his upraised hand.

"And I discovered something strange."

"Please, Bud, don't move," Ab said.

"After I finished at the assessor's, I went down the hall to Water and Power. Walt's not going to buy land without its own water wells. So I was shooting the breeze with this guy and I mentioned our requirements—"

"You called them that?" Bud asked, impressed.

"Yeah, about the acreage, the roads, back from the oceanfront, with its own water." P.O. grinned. "So the guy in Water and Power says to me, 'Gee, what a coincidence. Two guys came in a couple weeks ago asking the exact same things.' "

Ab's flashbulbs popped.

"State people?" Bud asked.

"He didn't know and didn't ask. They came from some place called Menlo Park."

"That's near San Francisco. Did they say why they were asking?"

P.O. shook his head. "Their company is called SRI, the Water and Power guy told me."

"Meaning what?"

"I don't know and neither did he. It's useful, though. When we find the land we think is the needle in the haystack, we ask the owner if he has talked to anybody. If he says yes, that he's talked to a company called SRI, we know we're right."

"That's awfully risky."

"The *exact* same things? They were looking for what we're looking for. They may be doing the same as we are. And companies don't gamble on hunches. In a sense it's like using the items George King told you and Milton about—near the ocean but not on the ocean, a sign—"

"Yeah yeah," Bud said and dropped the ball. "Are we done yet?" he asked Ab.

"If you can't possibly go on," Ab said in a peevish tone.

"Well, I can't." Bud stripped down to his underpants, casting aside the Roman toga. He sat on the chair looking over P.O.'s shoulder.

"One more pose, Bud?" Ab pleaded.

Bud waved him off and leaned closer to the map. "So what are these?"

"I think I've narrowed down our options," P.O. said, pointing to a map. "I know where I'd build it, anyway."

"That's hardly the point."

P.O. raised an eyebrow. "Who put the bug up your ass?" he asked Bud.

"You did, just now. We're not looking for where *you'd* build the fun zone. We're looking for where Walt's going to. If you say you're on to something, fine. Far be it for me to rain on your parade. Roland proved that Walt's going to build a fun zone when he went up to the studio. We *think* it's around this area."

"Well, gee, the whole point, I thought—" P.O. said, sounding less than upbeat.

"You *thought*."

With those words Bud robbed the afternoon of its fun. Under his chairmanship the dream was taking on the characteristics of a business deal. Everybody was beginning to feel it. Leadership changed people who weren't used to it and made them conservative and afraid, and their followers soon hated them. As their leader, Bud was losing the devil-may-care approach to dreams that had got him elected.

"The point is to get it right," he told P.O. "What did you think it was?"

P.O. hastily rolled up the maps. "I thought it was to imagine. You know? If we are wrong, no big deal. I thought we were supposed to be having fun. I guess I was getting carried away. I won't make the mistake again." He snapped the rubber band around the map.

Mr. Wait had entered the backyard and hitched Bob to the lanai post while they had been arguing. He had stood listening to Bud make P.O. apologize. "You have no reason to say you're sorry," he told P.O. from the lanai entrance, and both men turned to him in surprise. "You can believe what you want to, P.O." His anger shone through the control he held himself in. "We are in this together, as friends, and if that has changed, I would like to know about it now."

Bud toppled the garland from his head. "What's wrong with taking our best shot?"

"Maybe your best shot and P.O.'s best shot are not the same shots."

"All my life, *all my life*, I never took a thing like this seriously," Bud said. "If you don't take things seriously, they don't have a serious chance. This *once* I thought we should give ourselves the chance to have a chance. If we goof off, we goof up."

"You're overlooking one thing—other people," Mr. Wait retorted. "What does it matter what P.O. does as long as he's happy? If it doesn't make you happy, Bud, do it yourself the way you'd choose to."

Bud turned away, disgusted.

"Well, why not?" asked Mr. Wait. "Are you in this for the money only?"

"What money?" Bud asked, turning around.

"There'll be a bundle if we're right."

"Why can't I be in for the reason I want, even for a bundle?" Bud asked.

"I'm not saying you can't be. Just don't force your reasons on others."

Callum was mad at Bud for letting him down. Bud wanted the dream to work, and the prospect of success kept him keen. On the way to Hollywood, Roland had told him that Bud was showing them how to love. Maybe that was true, but he was going about it by showing them how to *win*. As far as Callum knew, winning wasn't loving by a long shot.

"You came here for something?" Bud asked Mr. Wait.

"Yes I did, but it's not important now."

Callum left the house with Mr. Wait and Bob—under the circumstances, he considered them better company than Bud and P.O. As they walked down the street, the clip-clop of Bob's hooves was altogether comforting after the harshness of the men's voices.

"You told me he would disappoint me," Callum told Mr. Wait. "That's what I feel right now."

Mr. Wait clapped his hand on his shoulder. "That's not disappointment," he said. "You'll know that when it hoves into view. That back there was a problem of focus. Bud will see where he's gone wrong once he's mulled it over."

"He's turning the dream into a job."

"Oh, you're bigger than that. I think we should leave Bud alone from now on. I told you before, you can only encourage and watch friends. You can't live their lives for them."

"But I want him to succeed."

"And you *don't* want him to succeed the way he is going about it. You do and you don't."

"He's forgotten that it started out as a dream. It's supposed to be fun."

"And it still is. The reason you don't think so anymore is the nature of *this* dream. This one has a good chance of success, and that changes it. You take from it what you will. Don't impose your judgments, and I mean on Bud, too. Don't be so harsh on him."

A little later downtown a few cars were parked by the curb and fewer people were on the sidewalks. For the most part, people came into Garden Grove for the bank and the day-old bread at Wonder, and the five-and-dime and the feed store, but they conducted their business and left. Garden Grove did not have a pool hall or a bar and grill to hang out in.

"Why do places have to change?" Callum asked Mr. Wait when they stopped to watch construction workers in an open ditch that would soon be a new supermarket across from the Gem.

"Because they must."

"If it was up to me, I'd keep them the way they are."

"And so would those men down there in that ditch. But their livelihoods depend on building new things. Nobody really likes changes, most of all people your age. Change makes things happen."

"I hate it."

"And you will be a part of it."

"No I won't."

"You'll see." He stopped in front of an office and compared the number above the door with the printing on a business card he took from his wallet. "I think it's time I found out what's going on, speaking of change," he said and tied Bob's rope to a parking meter.

He smiled at a secretary who monitored visitors at the door. He held up his hand for her to stay seated and walked right past her to a man who was at a desk under a wall clock with his feet up reading a color brochure for automatic washing machines. Callum recognized him as the same man who had been leaving Mrs. Rodriguez's in the rain.

Mr. Wait kicked the corner of the desk to get his attention. The feet and the brochure came down at once.

"Why, Mr. Wait," he said. "What an unexpected surprise."

"Ever heard of an *expected* surprise?" Mr. Wait asked Callum as he handed the man the card. "You dropped this in my grove. You said to get in touch anytime. Callum, this is Mr. Ricky Constantinople, a Turk, I imagine."

"Greek, actually. Thrace."

He shook Callum's hand, then rounded up chairs. Most of the desks in the office were occupied by men in business suits. Their shoulders were rounded over adding machines and the pages of thick bound ledgers. For this reason the office had an atmosphere of silent torture. The walls were painted a battleship gray with nothing decorating them except clocks and maps. The workers looked deprived of humor. The only sound was the click of tabulator keys, the flop of turning pages, and an occasional heavy sigh.

Mr. Constantinople sat on his leg. He raised a finger in the air at the sound of his telephone ringing. "Long distance," he explained and then went, "Har har, har har. Mr. Bellasco, you are a card. It's no trouble. I'll do it myself. No trouble." And he hung up. "No trouble," he repeated. He raised his head and fixed the same smile as before. "Now, how can I help you?"

"You're the proprietor here, are you not?"

"I have partners, but yes, I am the managing partner."

"You deal with the principals yourself directly?"

"Or their attorneys," he said. The subject clearly made him uncomfortable. He folded his hands on the desk in front of him.

"And when you act through the attorneys of your principals, Mr. Constantinople, you are always informed of the principals the attorneys are representing?"

"Yes, otherwise we could be representing just anybody without knowing. But why—"

"I'm on a fishing expedition," Mr. Wait told him.

He looked relieved. "And I'll help you out as far as I am able."

"The other day when I found you in my grove, you remember?"

He smiled sheepishly. "Trespassing."

"You implied you represented buyers."

He looked at his manicure. "I see what you're getting at. Principals do not always wish to be known."

"You told me they had looked at my property. That gives me rights."

"It was a manner of speaking. They have not seen your grove themselves. They have not walked in it or visited it as I have done, Mr. Wait. They know it from survey maps."

"What did I tell you then, Mr. Constantinople, about giving up my land? Do you remember?"

"You said the government would have to push you off. You would never sell."

"Do you represent agents of eminent domain, Mr. Constantinople?"

He puckered and mimed turning a key to lock his mouth. "My lips are sealed."

"Do you represent the State of California, Mr. Constantinople?" When he did not respond, Mr. Wait asked, "Why would anyone want to use you as a front man? Why wouldn't they stand up for themselves?"

"There are many reasons."

"Give me one."

"The Internal Revenue Service. Some of my clients do not wish to have that agency of the government know what they are doing. They are private people who may not want to be known, especially to the owners of the land they hope to buy. In that instance they would hope to pay the fair market price for land and not a penny more. Some sellers would add on premiums if they knew that the buyers were wealthy."

"Hide behind you, you mean."

"Exactly what I am here for."

Mr. Wait rested his elbows on the desk. "Well, then let me tell you, the people you represent may be vandalizing my grove. If it's the State of California, you tell them again for me, I won't sell."

Mr. Constantinople sat up in his chair. "I can guarantee my clients would do no such thing."

"I wish I could believe you."

With a look of genuine distress, he said, "Tell me exactly what happened."

"Someone knocked over a smudge pot. A quarter acre of citrus trees died in the frost because of it."

Mr. Constantinople looked lugubrious. "I am sorry. I am equally sorry that you blame my clients. They would do no such thing. Believe me, they are not vandals."

"The trees froze. The frost killed them." He turned to Callum. "The boy here saw the damage. Your clients want my land. I won't sell. They know I won't sell, and therefore they are trying to force me off the land by laying waste to the trees."

"What assurances can I give you?"

"You can give me their names."

A deliberation went on behind Mr. Constantinople's eyes. He looked from Mr. Wait to his own folded hands as though the truth would reveal itself there.

"Will you give me their names?"

"Oh . . ." He looked up. "I will have to check with them first, of course."

14

Woe Be to
the Orphan III

The Red Shoes was wedged between the Deep Six
Scuba Diving Center and a store that sold unglazed lawn elves and
birdbaths shaped like man-eating clams. Before getting out of the
car, Edith touched up her lipstick in the rearview. "Now," she told
the girls, blotting with a Kleenex, "behave."

The Red Shoes, as the name implied, sold ballet tutus, tights, toe
shoes—the works. The owner, with dyed black hair and a lithe
figure, had an obvious investment in ballet that went beyond the
products she retailed. On a phonograph the music from *Peer Gynt*
played just loud enough to penetrate the consciousness. Posters
advertising famous ballets from Paris and Rome to New York
covered the walls. There was a sign-up sheet for a bus trip to a ballet
in Pasadena and another list asking for volunteers for a bake sale to
raise money for poor students of dance. Down the center of the
store, tutus according to size hung on circular racks. In the back,
two dressing rooms had floor-length mirrors.

"Pick out a sensible one and a pair of tights, too," Edith told the
girls, who stampeded the racks.

The owner of the shop stood beside Edith, watching the girls with
a bemused smile. "I still don't understand the mystery after all
these years," she said.

"It's hard to remember back that far," Edith told her.

"Did you study dance?"

Edith did a double take. "I meant back when dreams were like they are at that age. Everything back then was a dream."

"Some folks never outgrow them."

"And some folks never grow up."

The woman looked at Edith, surprised by the nature of her comment. The two women silently watched the girls graze the racks of tutus, trying to remember.

Blue was almost certain about her choice of tutu. She held it up to herself and pirouetted before the mirror, admiring the dynamic effects of the starched ruffled netting that stuck out like the bristles on a chimney brush.

"What about the toe shoes?" she shouted down the length of the store at Edith.

"We'll see about them later," Edith replied.

The owner asked, "Are they taking lessons?"

"Why, yes, at Mrs. Hamel's," Edith answered, keeping an eye on Cloud. She had agreed to buy her a tutu and tights and toe shoes the same as Blue if for no other practical reason than to keep the peace. Cloud promised in turn to wear the longjohns and black high-cuts without complaining. It was a deal.

The store owner asked Edith, "Are they learning Classical or Romantic ballet?"

Edith shrugged. The woman was making a nuisance of herself.

"Are their shoes exercise or toe?" she asked.

"I didn't know it was so complicated," Edith told her.

"I'll show you what I mean."

A moment later she reappeared with a floor-length tutu. "A Romantic tutu," she said, and held it up against Edith.

"Oh, Mom, that looks nothing like you," said Blue from twenty feet away.

"Be quiet," Edith scolded her and took the dress away.

Callum wandered into the store after lingering outside the scuba center gazing at the tanks and regulators and weight belts in the window. He had no desire to breathe underwater or go eye-to-eye with a tuna, but the equipment fascinated him. Now he looked at the tutus and felt dumbstruck. Every item Edith bought for the

girls meant more than their very existence to them at the time.
Hours went by before they consigned whatever it was—skates, hula
hoops, bicycles, dolls, baby carriages—to the attic or the trash. He
did not get tutus on any level, including trash. Nor could he remember
ever seeing anything that looked so dumb.

In the living room Edith kneeled over the girls' initiation dresses
laid out on the carpet, her lips bristling with straight pins. "I was
just about to call you," she mumbled to the girls, who wandered in
from their bedroom. "Do you know what time it is?"

Cloud squinted at Blue, who said, "Mom . . ."

"What, honey?"

"Can we help you?" Cloud asked Edith.

Edith looked up with such suspicion she pricked her finger on a
pin. She surveyed the girls for a hint of deception. She didn't have
any reason to believe they were playing games with her, but for
Cloud to volunteer for anything raised warnings. "Okay, what's
going on?" she asked them. "If either one of you does anything to
embarrass me this afternoon, I swear there will be hell to pay. Do
you understand? *Do* you?"

Bud entered the living room at that moment dressed in a suit
with a white shirt and a necktie. He looked so different, the whole
family stared. Edith rested on her heels. "You're a darned handsome man," she told him.

Bud seemed as uncomfortable with her compliment as he was
with the necktie.

"I haven't felt this nervous since our wedding," she told him as
the girls stood idly by. She snapped at them, "Put a fire under your
tails," and she folded the finished dresses over Bud's outstretched
arms. "Careful," she warned him. "Lay them over the backseat
now." And Callum went with him carrying the milk-glass plate of
homebaked peanut-butter cookies.

The Garden Grove Grange Hall was a basketball court with a
stage at one end. It smelled faintly—even with the windows wide
open in a breeze—of gym socks. Depending on the season, the court
was used for dancing classes, roller-skating, Scouts' assemblies,
roughhousing on gym mats, plays, graduations, and of course, Job's

Daughters' initiation ceremonies. For this the hoop and backboard were raised to the ceiling on a pulley. Folding chairs were arranged in neat rows on the lacquered, lined floor. The punch bowls and the platters of cookies and cakes baked by the ladies were set out on two long folding tables covered with white cloths. Vases of cut begonias and nasturtiums and bird-of-paradises rested on the wings of the stage. Paper streamers in a riot of pastels hung down from the tall windows. The maroon velvet curtain was closed and the stage apron was bare except for a microphone on a stand and a satin yellow-and-orange banner that proclaimed,

BETHEL #13
JOB'S DAUGHTERS
GARDEN GROVE
CALIF.

Callum felt conspicuous in his jacket, white shirt, and tie as he kneeled in the stage wings beside the upright piano. He snapped his fingers and Scooter sat on a stack of tumbling mats, and together they watched the girls and their mothers arrive with their talent-display paraphernalia—musical instrument cases, books, costumes, and magic-act stands. Above their nervous chatter, the scraping of the folding chairs, some uneasy laughter, and sharp commands from mothers with nerves on edge came from the other side of the curtain. The amplifying speakers whined as the girls limbered up, tuned up, rehearsed splits in sequined gowns, fixed and licked reeds, pirouetted, and warmed mouthpieces. Their mothers repaired ripped hems, brushed down wisps of wayward hair, smoothed baggy knees and drooping drawers until they could do no more.

Scooter stood up and barked once by way of alerting Callum to the call of nature. Callum led him by the leash out the back fire exit to the parking lot behind the hall. Cars were entering in a steady line, cruising the lot for empty spaces, which were disappearing fast. Scooter lifted his leg on a fat whitewall tire, leaving a yellow stain. He kicked imaginary gravel with his rear legs, and when he was through and Callum was leading him back to the fire exit, the sound of Edith's voice stopped them both in midstride.

"What's *he* doing here?" she yelled across half the length of the lot.

Her evening gown luffed and billowed as she sailed toward him shimmering like a million tiny mirrors in the sunlight. Her hair formed a gleaming busby of fixative. Her makeup, particularly the magenta eyeliner, made her hardly recognizable as the mother Callum knew and loved.

"He followed me," he told her.

"Take him home right now," she commanded.

"Edith, we should hurry, don't you think?" Bud told her, shooting his cuff and glancing at his wristwatch.

She shook her head. "Tie him up somewhere outside, then," she told Callum.

"Ah, Mom, Callum will watch him," said Cloud. "He'll be all right backstage with us, I promise."

A strand of Blue's hair distracted Edith, who primped it. "Stand in front of me," she told Blue, expertly resnapping a rubber band on her hair. She looked Cloud over and smoothed out a wrinkle in her costume with the flat of her hand.

Blue, in her blue pastel tutu with the white tights and the blue silk bodice, was a vision. Cloud, on the other hand, looked like a denuded crow in her brown longjohns and black high-tops. On her head she wore a black French beret that made her look like a sourdough frightened out of a mountain cabin in the middle of a storm.

"Stand up straight," Edith ordered the girls. By now she had completely forgotten the Scooter problem. "Look like Job's," she told them. "Make me proud. Remember, I love you." She kissed them on the tops of their heads.

"You look beautiful, Mom," Callum told her, finding her transformation as hard to believe as those of Blue and Cloud.

"From a handsome young man, that is a fine compliment," Edith told him. She caught herself touching the gown over her heart, where she would have pinned the family brooch. The effect on her was like a cloud passing overhead. She clutched Bud's arm, and with a sigh she pointed him toward the front doors of the Grange Hall. Cloud, Blue, and Callum shooed Scooter in the fire exit. Backstage they found a place in the shadow of the upright piano and sat in a small circle and whispered, as a woman from one of the Job's committees hissed loudly.

"Now, girls," she said, crossing her lips with her finger. "You know your order of appearance. If you forget, I'll call out names in the microphone before I introduce you. Good luck!"

"Okay, here we go," Cloud whispered.

"What do you mean, 'here we go'?" asked Blue.

"There's been a change in the program," Cloud said.

"Oh," she responded with arched eyebrows.

Cloud unzipped the ditty bag she had brought along. "I'll give you the details when I get back," she said and, standing up, disappeared into the confusion at the opposite end of the stage.

Callum held Scooter around the chest and slipped the dyed Jockey shorts on him, which he fixed around his waist with rubber bands. He snapped a sequined dunce hat over his ears at a jaunty angle. Scooter looked good, and what was more, he seemed to feel comfortable in the costume. He sat down and waited like a trouper for his cue.

The lights blinked, then dimmed.

Cloud returned, changed out of her longjohns and beret into the pink pastel tutu and tights that Edith had bought for her, as transformed in her own way as Edith in her Job's dress. Callum would never have thought that Cloud could match Blue for prettiness, but here was proof. Cloud had been miscast in life as the gawky, spindly sister who was never given a chance to show her stuff. She had taken the chance herself, and the risk paid off.

"Mom will kill you, Cloud," Blue said with a look of real fear.

"Blue, did you really think I was going to go out there on a stage looking like a scarecrow?" She was not asking for an answer either. "Let's go over the change in the program." She was all business now, and God help Blue if she refused. "Blue, do you remember the dance *Le Baiser de la Fée* that Mrs. Hamel taught us?"

"Sure, the *Fairy Princess*."

"Do you think you can dance it now?"

"What happened to the *Minuet*?"

"It ran out of time."

"Oh."

"Callum, you're going to hold Scooter over there." She pointed to the wings. "I'll signal with my hand like this"—she fluttered her hand—"when the time comes."

"I know the drill," Callum said, meaning he had intuited Cloud's deception almost from the start.

Blue looked at Cloud. "Mom will just kill you," she repeated.

"When we walk out of here tonight with fifty dollars, Dad won't let her kill anybody," she said, but her face showed the strain.

Blue stood apart, oblivious now, fluffing the netting of her tutu and pointing her toes with such self-absorption she could have been anywhere.

Callum asked Cloud to watch Scooter while he peeked out at the audience from behind the closed curtain. He spied Edith four rows back near the center of the gym with Bud beside her, holding her gloved hand. She looked relaxed and happy. And why shouldn't she? These Job's Daughters were Edith's new milieu—as she said, her "crowd."

Edith's tea gloves were damp from nerves. She could see all she needed to staring straight ahead over a small sea of maroon fezzes and poofed shoulders. Bud's tam-o'-shanter was parked in his lap. "Why did you bring that?" she whispered to him.

He looked at it. "To throw in the air," he replied.

"Don't be so sure. I suppose that's why you wore the suit, too?"

"When do they cough up the fifty?" he asked her.

"How would I know?"

"Is it a bank check or what? Do I go up on the stage? Will a speech be necessary?"

"*You*, Bud, won't be the winner."

"Nope, just the beneficiary."

"You are putting a terrible burden on the girls," Edith told him. "You don't know what they can do. This is Cloud and Blue we're talking about. They are going to dance. It's a simple thing called the *Minuet*. If they get through it a miracle will have happened. I wouldn't count your chickens."

Mr. Wait leaned over. "What about chickens?" he asked. "Did you say chickens?"

"Edith was engaging in a figure of speech," Bud told him.

"Oh," he said and leaned back in his chair.

"Don't be nervous," Roland told Edith, patting her other hand. His nerves were causing his face to blotch. He had a stake in the contest. He had altered the girls' basic ballet costumes, transforming them into works of art with black sequins on Cloud's longjohns and black sparkles on her sneakers. For Blue he had devised little wings of wire and cellophane.

An odd quiet came over the room.

"Oh, Bud, look," Edith said with genuine delight.

It was Mrs. Rodriguez, walking up the side aisle looking for a place to sit. She had not conformed one bit. She announced her status as a proud Californio in a pleated floor-length black skirt with shiny black boots, a silver conch belt studded with turquoise, a white shirt, and silver jewelry up her arms and shining combs in her hair. She was a picture of elegance. But the contrast of her blackness with the white of the Job's goffered gowns aroused a chorus of murmured dissent.

"Now *that's* class," Bud said, waving to get her attention. He stood up to make way for her and told Roland, P.O., and Cheval to scoot down so that she could sit beside Edith. With a dignified nod, she slipped into their row. When she sat down, Edith whispered to her, "You look great," and clutched her hand.

"I just couldn't bring myself to wear the dress," Mrs. Rodriguez explained. "It made me look like a bride and that was a betrayal."

"I understand," Edith said.

"At least I'll be able to live with myself."

"I hope I can say the same. Where's Serena?"

"Backstage."

"Dance?"

"Piano."

At that moment the blare of a trumpet from the back of the gym startled them. Everyone turned around to see a little man with a black smudge of a mustache being enveloped by a gown of astonishing proportions. In the gown was Mrs. Bashford. She wore a tiara of rhinestones. Medals as impressive as an army general's sagged on a velvet sash across her abundant chest. She stared straight ahead knowing the impact she made. Her escort struggled in the dress's folds. He was wearing canary yellow pieces-o'-eight satin pants, a

Moroccan fez, a short tunic festooned with fake gold dubloons, a silver ceremonial cutlass, and felt brothel creepers with turned-up toes and brass bells that tinkled when he walked.

"Yobbo in a bolero," Bud whispered to Edith.

"Whew, what a fairy," said P.O.

The man was a Shriner, there could be no doubt, a fraternal sect that sometimes dressed in Upper Nile, Egypt, finery. The Shriners worshipped the pharoahs, though their bylaws and ceremonies were kept a secret. Bud said they mumbled mumbo jumbo and drank themselves goggle-eyed, terrorizing whole towns at their annual conventions in places like Milwaukee and Pittsburgh. The Job's, as far as he knew, were the Shriners' sister organization. The whole fandango reminded him of social climbers in pinafores, yobbos in boleros, and worse.

With Mrs. Bashford on his arm, the man in the jingle-bell shoes stepped down the center aisle, and they proceeded like a couple in a wedding processional. Mrs. Bashford glimpsed left and right, nodding to friends and supporters on both sides of the aisle. Before taking her seat in the front row, she bestowed on the audience her blessing with a wave of her white-gloved hand.

Edith reached into her clutch bag for a hanky and dabbed her eyes. The dampness of her gloves no longer bothered her. She had hung them out to dry on the rung of her folding chair.

The mistress of ceremonies found the opening in the curtain and lifted her face into the spotlight. Her white satin dress reflected the light, and for a moment she seemed to be on fire. She introduced herself and welcomed the audience, then without further ado, she uttered a platitude about Mrs. Bashford, to muffled applause.

"We Job's believe in the arts," she told them in a speech she read from a piece of paper. "An appreciation of the finer things in life is why we exist. We encourage our young members to take their role in our community as the future sponsors of its cultural life. Culture lifts us up. It makes us better as individuals. And so we sponsor an annual talent contest for our younger members. We believe talent and hard work deserve remuneration and that is why this year the grand prize will be fifty dollars paid in cash to the winner. I know you in the audience are looking forward to the contest this year as much as our younger members are looking forward to performing for you.

"Let the show begin!"

She announced the first contestant and the curtain parted. A Job's initiate was standing in the middle of the stage beside a black music stand. She raised a clarinet to her lips and blew. Her reed needed moistening throughout her recital, but the audience applauded as though they had just heard Benny Goodman. Other girls who followed the clarinetist performed acts that were ill-practiced and plain lame. Three sisters sang a song off-key and without rhythm but with the mistaken impression that they were accomplished merely for standing on the stage. Theirs wasn't ability or talent; it was moxie.

Callum held Scooter to his chest, and he could feel the rapid beat of his little heart. He massaged his thighs and tested the rubber bands around his Jockey shorts. At the sound of Serena's name, he turned his attention to her.

She walked from the opposite wing and stopped at the lip of the apron, bowing with her arms folded at her waist. A bright red skirt with white crinolines, a ruffled blouse, and black patent leather shoes set her apart, like her mother. She went to the upright piano and paused by the keyboard before sliding onto the stool. She poised her hands over the keyboard and in a fury began to play a classical tune that sounded like a recording, and from memory, too!

By the audience's applause when she had finished, Serena had already won the fifty dollars. She bowed and exited the stage, and the curtain closed.

The mistress of ceremonies next announced Cloud and Blue.

Cloud stage-whispered to Blue, "Whatever you do, whatever happens, do *not* stop dancing!"

The curtain parted, and Cloud floated out onto the stage in her tutu and toeshoes. She approached the microphone and told the audience how she and Blue had changed their program at the last moment. She read from a piece of notepaper, "In the midst of a tempest, a lovely young woman, carrying a baby boy in her arms, struggles along a lonely country road vainly trying to reach the happy village where she was born. Who this lovely young woman was, or why she found herself in distress, without shelter, abandoned and burdened, none can say. . . ."

The pleated dresses in the audience rustled, and the dubloons jangled.

"Then with no strength left, the unfortunate traveler sank to the ground, utterly exhausted, sighed softly once or twice and died there where she had fallen."

She went to the back of the stage and placed a needle on a record player. When the music started she toe-walked in circles to the center of the stage. She dipped her arms, left first, then right. She bent her knees and skimmed the floor. Blue entered from the wing and fluttered her arms, a beauty all her own.

Cloud signaled with her hand as she fretted past Callum.

"Go get 'em," he said and pushed Scooter forward into the lights.

Scooter whizzed onto the stage with the earnestness of a has-been on the comeback trail. He didn't know where he was; the stage was alien and not at all like the backyard where he had learned to dance. And the spotlights blinded him. He could not recognize Blue and Cloud in their tutus. His mouth was clamped shut and his ears lay flat on his head. He was not having fun, but he danced tight figure eights behind Cloud and Blue. The cone on his head, which tilted at a reckless angle, did not distract him a bit.

Cloud fretted up to him. "Atta boy," she said. And the sound of her voice settled him into a kind of bouncy routine.

A collective gasp came from the audience at the sight of a dog on the stage. The silence that followed changed to muffled applause. The men in fezzes and their wives were enjoying the novelty of watching survival as art. There was even a unity to the movements of girls and dog. In a manner that was hard to describe, Cloud and Blue and Scooter were telling a coherent story.

They would have been the contest winners, too, if Scooter's underpants had not started to slip by degrees, an inch now— Scooter hopped himself in a frenzy—another inch then. The rubber bands were loosening with his heated exertions, and Scooter's rigid tail made the lone difference between his dancing, surviving self and disaster.

The *Fairy's Kiss* wobbled out of control.

Scooter was moving around the stage by now like an old man with dropsy. The girls, caught up in their own selves, fretted without noticing how Scooter's ears shot up and his eyes appealed to Callum with a haunted look. He staggered over to Cloud and whined for help. She shooed him away. Thinking he was all right if she had not scolded him, he started a tricky leg-crossing samba. And only two minutes had gone by.

The treacherous underpants only partly accounted for Scooter's increasingly odd behavior.

With an expression of guilt and self-hatred he lowered himself to the stage and stopped dancing. Hardly noticeable at first he got down in his asshole glide. He soon lost all control and, forgetting where he was, dragged his butt across the boards. White worms, which had reemerged, littered the boards in his wake as he glided in circles, in figure eights, in diagonals. It was the shade that caused the worms' return. They had been there all along, in hiding, and in the dim light of his jockey shorts they had come out to play.

"I think you can kiss your fifty goodbye," P.O. leaned across Cheval to whisper to Bud.

Mrs. Bashford was on her feet, and with a look not unlike Scooter's own, she raised her hand to her throat, threw back her head, and screamed until the lights in the hall went on and off and on and off. Her escort tried to rescue her and, manfully pushing aside his cutlass, clutched her around her waist, like a lineman humping a telephone pole. She cuddled her cheeks with her hands and keened like a bedouin at a funeral. Mercifully, a moment later she slumped to the floor in a faint. The muffled tinkle of her escort's shoe-bells was all that could be heard.

"The girls certainly showed imagination," said Roland, hardly noticing the fracas.

"The best!" exclaimed Mrs. Rodriguez with a throaty laugh.

Cloud heard the bloodcurdling scream from the audience and looked into the wings at Callum, who pointed back onto the stage at Scooter. For a moment Cloud stared at him as though she did not understand. In another instant she caught on and came down off point, her hands scoldingly on her hips.

Blue fretted past Scooter. "Stop it!" she shouted.

Cloud rose on her toes, fanning the air with her arms. "Dance, Scooter, just dance," she told him.

At about that moment, Blue spied Scooter's worms. She stopped dancing, dropped off point, and let out a curtain-ripping howl. Her arms windmilled in the air as she ran from the stage and out of sight.

Scooter was moving like a cheap Japanese windup toy. Blue was screaming from backstage, and Cloud was shouting with her hands on her hips. The lights went on and off. Scooter had become a soloist, gliding in an ecstasy of relief until Callum, urged on by the girls' wails, scooped him up in his arms. He raised him over his head and bowed from the waist. The audience did not notice, or if they did, did not care. A crowd circled Mrs. Bashford as other Job's separated themselves from Edith and Mrs. Rodriguez and Bud, like they were pariahs.

"So much for that," Roland said, looking toward the exit.

"Wait till I get my hands on that mutt," said Edith, who wasn't really angry. As she looked around her at the pandemonium her girls had wrought, a laugh of an amazing depth and mirth came over her. The Job's women glared at her for such insolence. It was the final straw. Edith began to raise her hand to cover her mouth but then looked at it as if she had never seen it before. She returned it to her lap, and she laughed even after the music stopped and well after the curtain closed on her dream of becoming a Job's.

"I was hypnotized," Edith told Mrs. Rodriguez the next day, by way of saying hello. She was standing on Mrs. Rodriguez's porch with a straw basket of peanut-butter cookies on her arm.

Mrs. Rodriguez was framed in the door, in her usual khaki trousers. "Good riddance to them, too." She laughed. "Why do we do these things to ourselves, Edith?"

"It's not us, Mary, it's hypnosis." She held an imaginary teacup and extended her pinky. "They revived Mrs. Bashford, you know, with smelling salts. It is our legacy to them."

"Has she said anything to you?"

"Mrs. Bashford? Well, yes."

"Hold it a minute, Edith," said Mrs. Rodriguez. And, expecting a good gossip, she went inside for refreshments. A moment later she came out with a tray of fresh-squeezed lemonade, which she carried across the lawn and put down on a table in the gazebo on the front lawn.

"She thought I'd planned it," Edith told her. "Can you imagine that?"

Mrs. Rodriguez bent over with laughter. "You could have told her it was a surprise to you."

"When I saw Scooter up there, I came to. That's the really strange part. Snap! It was like I had been hypnotized for months, ever since the invitation came in the mail. I'm glad you were there with me, Mary. When I saw you in your black skirt I knew I didn't belong."

"That's sweet of you," she said, then clucked her tongue. "All the work you did, though, the dresses, the cookies, and such."

"The dresses looked silly. Airs is all that is."

"Did Mrs. Bashford leave you a choice?"

"Not that I will ever know of. You?"

"I resigned in a note I wrote this morning."

"You knew they were snobs right from the start, didn't you?"

"It's nothing new, Edith. Mrs. Bashford didn't want your girls to join because of what they did on the stage. She didn't want Serena in because of who we are. We could do everything right and she wouldn't accept us."

"Serena should have won the prize."

"See what I mean? You hope prejudices change for the better, and for the sake of your children you test the climate now and then. I know now that nothing in my lifetime has changed."

"I'm here talking to you," Edith pointed out. "I may not be on the exalted level of Mrs. Bashford but I'm your friend. . . ."

Mrs. Rodriguez got misty-eyed all of a sudden, and Edith thought it was because of what she had said. Mrs. Rodriguez looked out at the grove for a moment, reflecting on its sylvan beauty. Finally, she said, "I don't suppose it matters anymore."

Edith looked at her inquiringly. Such a statement sounded odd coming from her. "Of course it matters," she told her.

"We may be leaving here soon," she said.

Edith was taken aback, but what could she say? Mrs. Rodriguez had phrased it to sound conditional, as if she might not, but her voice told a different story. "I'm sorry to hear that," she said. "I truly am."

Mrs. Rodriguez continued to look at the grove. "The land is getting to be a burden."

"But you've owned it forever."

"We were never zoned agricultural-residential before now. We got the notice of the zoning change two months ago. The acreage is worth more for other uses than farming with the change. The property taxes are going to be sky-high."

"You could pay it if you wanted to, couldn't you?"

"I own land, not money, Edith. I am not well off. I could sell off bits and pieces, but the end result will be the same."

"This much land must be a handful, anyway," Edith said, trying to make her feel better.

"Three children are more to handle, I'd imagine."

"You don't mean that. These trees *are* your family."

Mrs. Rodriguez nodded sadly. "I have tried to imagine what I will feel like without this place. All I can say is that the grove is so much a part of me I don't notice it most of the time. It is like so many other things in life that we don't notice until they are gone. My husband, Serena's father, perhaps I have mentioned him to you? No, maybe not. Well, he showed me what the land meant. When he was a boy, his parents lived in a shack with a dirt lot for a yard and nothing green in sight. When we were married he thought our grove was paradise. He called it that. Would you stroll with me, Edith?"

"Pleased to," Edith said, getting up from the gazebo.

At a leisurely pace the two women entered the grove at the side of Mrs. Rodriguez's house. Quiet and a peacefulness that were hard to find anymore surrounded them. Edith did not think she had ever visited an orange grove, even to pick an illicit orange. She had passed by hundreds of them in the car, but not once had she had a reason to lose herself in their bushy wonder. She liked how cozy she felt with the scent of citrus and blossoms around her. Off in the distance a tractor growled, then the sound of its engine faded. Again there was silence.

"I think we might have a romance budding, don't you?" Edith asked Mrs. Rodriguez, walking beside her.

"You've noticed. He's an awfully nice boy, your Callum."

"Thank you."

"He spends a lot of time with the men, doesn't he?"

Edith had not thought about that, but saw nothing wrong with it now. "He's been serious since he was a little boy. He watches and he listens, and sometimes I look at him and I don't know where he came from. I don't think Bud and the others appreciate what he understands about them. I swear he seems older than they do sometimes. He hangs around with them, if you ask me, because he's afraid things are going to change. He worries about what is going to happen. All kids do, I guess. They want to grow up but they want to stay the way they are. Callum, I think, feels that he can control what happens if he hangs around grown-ups. He can influence their decisions and keep changes at bay."

"He showed himself to be true-blue when he tried to tell Serena about the Job's."

"Oh?"

Mrs. Rodriguez explained. "He wanted to spare her feelings."

"Well I'll be," Edith remarked.

"I'm very fond of him because of that, Edith. Serena is, too. We don't have a man around the place to look out for us. Sometimes the protection of a man feels right even if it isn't necessary. It lets you know you aren't alone. Callum tried to protect her from humiliation. It was an act, well, almost of love. He risked her anger in order to protect her. Yes," she said in a serious tone, "I'm very fond of that boy."

They had walked a distance that was impossible for Edith to measure. At first their direction had seemed pointless, but the further into the grove they went, the deeper Edith's impression was that Mrs. Rodriguez was heading for a specific place.

"How did your ancestors get all this land?" asked Edith, curious to know more about Mrs. Rodriguez.

She laughed lightly. "It's an odd story but it's true. My great-grandfather arrived along the coast of California by boat from the Bay of Topolobampa. Don't ask where that is. He was a sailor. Well, he worked for a Spanish landowner who grew fond of him. Before he died, he made him a proposition. He would give him all the land he could drag a rowboat around in a single day." She laughed again.

"People were odd in those days. He hitched a boat to a team of mules. The landowner stood by his offer. It's the same land now that it was then."

The story transported Edith to another time, as they continued their walk. She imagined grandees and conquistadors and spirited horses. She could easily imagine Mrs. Rodriguez in that fanciful setting, a lovely, strong woman. A bit further on they came on a clearing with a carpet of lawn that was Mrs. Rodriguez's obvious private refuge, an oasis in the middle of the grove.

"How perfectly beautiful," Edith remarked.

"My Orlando passed away seven years ago," Mrs. Rodriguez explained. "We used to come here in the evenings, he and I." She pointed to a wooden bench set out in the middle of the clearing. "We would sit there and talk and dream," and she recalled those times with a wistful look. "He said he lived in paradise and he knew the paradise where he was going wasn't the paradise this was."

"He was a young man?" Edith asked.

"Not yet in his prime. He hated to see what was happening to the land. He died of a failed heart. When he was in his last days we carried him out here. We carried him all over the grove before we stopped here. We had a picnic, the three of us. He kept staring up trying to find the hole in the sky that he would leave the earth through. He looked and he looked. 'I see it now,' he said in a voice that did not sound like him. And then he was gone."

Edith wiped a tear with the back of her hand. "How can you leave here?" she asked.

"How? With no choice."

The growl of a tractor grew louder, and a John Deere appeared through the rows of trees. Serena straddled its hitch behind the driver. She did not see them in the clearing. The driver, an old Mexican, clamped a hand over his straw hat as he turned under overhanging branches. The tractor was gone almost as soon as it had appeared, leaving behind a cloud of dust.

Edith waved at the trembling branches of the trees. She waved again at where Serena had appeared, but by then even the dust had disappeared.

.   .   .

Scooter chased his tail in a tight circle on the living-room rug.

"Stop that this instant," Blue scolded him, still mad at him for his performance at the Job's.

He was not chasing his tail out of playfulness, as Blue thought. He was trying to look up his own butt. The truth was, after the talent contest, an acute paranoia had swept over him. This running for a peek into the void was its worst manifestation. He checked his rear like clockwork to see if his visitors had been fumigated for good or were hiding in their bunkers deep in his bowels waiting to reemerge like old Nazis to claim the victory that was rightfully theirs.

"He needs help," Blue said to Cloud, counting Scooter's rotations.

"You would, too," Cloud opined.

Blue looked at the coins stacked in front of them on the carpet. They were counting change that they had shaken out of their piggy banks. "How much have you got?" Blue asked.

"Four dollars."

"I've got two and a half," said Blue, indicating stacks of pennies and nickels and dimes.

"Wouldn't it have been great if we had won?" asked Cloud.

"Fifty dollars!"

Bud poked his head around the kitchen door at the mention of money. The girls glanced at him, then away on the assumption that the more attention they paid to their parents, the more at risk they were of being ordered to do something, like work.

Cloud, brown-nosing, told Bud, "We were thinking how nice it would have been if we had won the prize."

Bud stretched on the floor beside them and rested his head on his arm, smiling at the thought of what might have been. "You were wonderful, both of you," he told them.

"Yes, it was a clever idea," Blue said, taking full credit now that Bud had praised their performance.

"I'm just sorry the committee didn't agree," Bud said.

"What do they know?" Cloud asked. "Serena deserved the prize. Did you hear her play? She plays better than Carmen Caballero. Nobody came close to her, did they?"

"Only us, if Scooter hadn't acted up," said Blue.

"You took the prize for imagination and that's what counts," Bud told them. The money on the floor distracted him. "What's this for?"

"You," said Cloud.

"That's your Christmas savings," Bud said. "You can't give that away."

"We will at Christmas. Why not now? Why can't we make Christmas whenever we want to?"

Bud went into the kitchen for his mayonnaise-jar bank, which was a quarter filled with loose change. The jar made a solid clunking sound when he shook it.

"Let's count it all out, okay?" he said, and it was easy to see how excited the prospect made him feel.

Blue took charge of the quarters, and Cloud, the dimes. Bud took the nickels and fifty-cent pieces. It was fun, counting and stacking. It gave them a sense of the worth of money that was hard to find otherwise. When they had finished they had twenty-two dollars and thirty-three cents between them.

"Are you sure you want to put your money in?" Bud asked them as he poured his coins back in the jar.

"We'll have Christmas every day if you and your friends guess right and the dream comes true," said Cloud.

Bud nodded, believing it himself.

They stopped what they were doing to look at Scooter. He chased himself, round and round, as if the worms were there, mocking him.

15

Hello? Milton Here.
Over.

Gladys stuck her head in the oven and fiddled with the gas knob.

"Whatcha bakin'?" asked Milton, who walked up behind her.

"Earrings," she said and pulled her head out with a sour look.

"A new recipe?" he asked, wanting to make conversation.

"Earrings. Jewelry, Milt," she said and dismissed him with a flap of her hand.

"Well, they look almost good enough to eat," he told her.

She ignored him and inspected the odd shapes on the cookie sheet.

"Just thought I'd check in," he said.

"They're not what they should be," she said. She looked at him, as if she were noticing him for the first time. "How've you been, Milt?" she asked.

"Good. Thanks for asking," he told her. "I've been listening to some great stuff."

"That's nice." She tested the temperature of the jewelry with the tip of her finger. "Music or what?"

"Conversations."

"Ike on the radio again, or Adlai?"

"Walt Disney and the Vastness."

She stared at him. "You're eavesdropping on conversations between Walt and *Martians*?"

"You bet."

She scraped an earring off the cookie sheet and examined it front and back.

"I guess I'll go back up to the Command Center now," he told her.

"Shout if you need anything."

The vent fan sliced a shaft of light in thin pieces as he shuffled through the gloaming, hung his Sam Browne on a nail in an attic joist, and lined up his boots by a plastic lawn recliner. He slipped the headset over his ears and laid back on a silk throw pillow. Stacks of copper-coiled toilet-paper tubes bubbled up around him, each tube an obsession. By the time he had settled down, he looked like an intergalactic rocket pilot in a movie that everyone knew was fake.

The attic hatch cracked open.

"Hey," he said and swung his legs off the recliner.

Callum pushed the hatch open all the way. "Gladys told me you were up here," he said.

"Stay awhile," Milton said, peeling off the headset.

Callum crouched on his heels under the eaves, wanting to leave as soon as he could find an excuse. No one liked the company of adults more than he did, but this was going too far. He was intruding on an adult fantasy that was not meant for his eyes. The sight of the tubes and Milton with the earphones reminded him of a photo he had seen in the *National Geographic* of a monk twirling a top that held prayers. These toilet-paper tubes were Milton's top, each coppery turn a thread of hope. Callum stood still, afraid of what a sudden move might do to Milton.

"Well, what do you think?" Milton asked him.

"Wow!" Callum shouted pro forma.

"I bet you were wondering why I wanted the tubes. After I finished the coils I soldered the lead wire of each one to the end wire of the next tube. The entire bank is linked in one network."

"I can see that."

"Next thing was to thread this wire coat hanger through the hole in the ballbearing. I soldered a long piece of copper wire to the coat hanger. That allows me to roll the ball bearing over the tubes. And that is connected to the base of the germanium crystal. It forms a looping circuit. Our antenna is out there on the telephone poles." He sank back with a sigh and closed his eyes.

"What's it sound like?" Callum asked.

Milton took off the headset. "Like hissing, like whispering, like the sigh of shells. Like words, I don't know—in Japanese."

"But not the Extras?"

"You have to believe to receive. You have to know how to listen. Two events are happening here. I am locating the precise frequency at the precise moment when the signal hits the antenna. Radio telescopes in Wales do the same. This one is on the cheap."

"Why Wales?"

"Druids," he replied as if he had given it serious thought. He shook his head. "The concept isn't right yet."

He started wrapping a length of the copper wire around his index finger.

"What will you hear, when you hear, do you think?"

"The Vastness."

"Are you going to talk or just listen?"

"Just listen."

"What would you ask them if you could?"

"A good question," he said and thought it over. "They would get offended if you asked for stock market tips, stuff like that. I can't imagine they are commercially oriented as such. I'd be disappointed in them if they were. I suppose I'd ask two main questions. One, I'd want to know why there are always bugs. It is a profound question. And two, I'd like to know about love. Like for instance, I'd like to know where love goes when it dies."

"Where it goes?"

"Yes. When you look at someone you once loved and you don't see them in the same light as before, where did the love go? It stands to reason it went somewhere because it doesn't exist anymore."

"Does it *have* to go somewhere?"

"Of course it does," he said. "If I were to guess, I'd say it was reduced to an algorithm, compressed like dried fruit waiting for water to bring it back to life. In that state of suspended animation it floats around outside the body looking for an object to attach

itself to. At birth everybody has two feet, two legs, one head—and
one love. It searches in wrong places but eventually it finds a home.
It doesn't even have to be another human. It can be your own self.
But most of the time it is another person of the opposite sex. That'd
be my guess. I'd ask that." He put his finger to his lips. "Oh, and
I'd ask them what our last words before dying mean. People say the
darndest things."

"You mean like *argh*," Callum said.

"Yeah, and other things, too. I wonder if it doesn't indicate
something about the hereafter."

"Maybe it says about where they have been."

"Could be, could be. There was a guy I read about once who said,
'Oh, God, I'm bored,' and then he died, and I wonder if Heaven
isn't boring, you know, because he had had a glimpse of what it
looked like."

Callum had questions of his own, like why the Ancients should
know the answers to Milton's questions about love and death and
why there always have to be bugs. "Are these the Extras, in the
cigars?"

He shook his head no. "These are their superiors, more involved
in the Big Picture, you know—why planets were formed in the Big
Bang, et cetera. Dr. King's people are the ones who orbit earth in
the cigars. I don't think they are reliable. Real Galactics like the
Ancients don't need to prove themselves. They stand back. They let
the others make asses of themselves."

"I see."

"My mistake was that I thought their rep on Terra was Dr. King.
I was wrong. They don't deal on his level. They only deal with
geniuses."

"Like Dr. Einstein?"

Milton fanned the air with his hand. "I've got to tell you I don't
understand a single word that man ever said. Ask anybody in the
street who is a genius and he'll say Einstein without thinking. Can
you mention one thing Einstein did that was genius?"

"Relasivity?"

Milton held his nose. "Rela*tiv*ity. Heck, what's that but this or
that?" he asked.

"Then who?"

"Walt Disney."

"Gee, I never thought of that."

"You better start to," he said, and now that his fingers were wound in copper wire, he started coiling the wire up his hand.

The tailpipe scraped the gutter as Bud gunned the car down Milton's driveway, braking hard in the backyard near the garage. He hit the horn: shave-and-a-haircut.

"Bud, for God's sake," Edith said. "Don't give the girls the idea that a horn is a polite form of address."

Gladys appeared on the back porch. Even with her sunglasses on she shaded her eyes against the bright morning light. "My goodness," she said as she climbed down the steps. "Can I get you some coffee or a doughnut? I do envy you going off to church."

"You can join us, Gladys," said Edith.

"Oh, they wouldn't have me."

"It's church," Bud said. "They accept *everybody*."

"It's been too long since I last went. I wouldn't know the words."

"They want people like you. You're a new catch."

"Maybe some other time," she said.

Edith handed her an angel food cake out the car window.

"Aren't you kind," Gladys said, holding the cake platter in both hands.

It was the kind of gesture Edith often made. She never baked a single cake. She baked a second and a third for a person, like Gladys now, who was on her mind. Edith said that the bounty of sharing made people think of someone besides themselves.

"Where's Milt?" Bud asked Gladys.

She looked over her shoulder at the house. "He's up in the attic."

"Give him a yell, will you?"

Gladys sighed. "That may not be a good idea."

"What's wrong, Gladys?" asked Edith. "You seem worried."

"It's just the bursitis acting up again. It's the cold snap. It's on its way."

Callum, riding in the backseat with the girls, asked Bud if he could go to the bathroom.

"Oh, God!" Bud shouted. "Didn't I tell you to go before we left the house?"

"I didn't have to, then."

"Well make it snappy."

"Don't forget to lift the seat," Gladys told him.

Callum went in the kitchen wondering why Bud thought a pee was elective. He *needed* to pee, he didn't want to. He heard Bud switch off the car engine. As he was lifting the seat, he heard a shout from somewhere in the house that sounded like a cry—between a howl and a whoop. There was no pain involved, more a sense of wonder. He finished and washed his hands and was walking down the porch steps when the door opened behind him.

Milton was smiling as though the bees of bliss had stung him. He was beautiful, like a living sunbeam, wrapped from his neck to his ankles in copper wire that the morning light turned to flame. With his arms extended in front of him he climbed down the steps and shuffled across the yard humming a happy tune.

"They talked to me," he said when he was close to the car.

"Who?" asked Bud, all eyes.

"The Ancients," Milton explained as if everyone should know. "I heard them. I was in my Command Center."

Bud looked over at Callum. "The toilet-paper tubes?"

"I found their frequency," Milton went on. "They beamed right at me."

"What's the suit for?" Bud asked him.

"Until I plugged myself in, they couldn't reach me. I became the frequency. I *am* the radio."

"These are the Dr. King's people you're talking about?" Bud asked.

"They're from Beyond, from a place without a name. We haven't even imagined where these people come from."

"But they speak English, right?"

"Yes, and some other language I've never heard before."

Bud rubbed his chin. "Okay, Milt, let me ask you the big question. What did these people say to you?"

He pressed his finger to his lips. "Well . . . 'Hi,' " he said.

"Say again?"

" 'Hi,' I already told you. 'Hi.' "

"That's it, that's all they said?"

Milton nodded. "Who cares *what*? They reached out to me

through a billion light-years of space from a galaxy beyond the beyond. 'Hi' will never be the same again."

Bud checked his watch. "We've got to go or we'll miss church," he said and started the car and put it in gear. Edith waved to Gladys, looking worried. The girls and Callum waved to Milton, thrilled for him. "Bye," they yelled.

" 'Hi,' " Milton said, waving stiffly goodbye.

A minute later Bud turned the car around in the middle of the street. "Just drop me off and you go on to church," he told Edith.

"I understand," she said. "See what you can do for him, please."

After they dropped him off he went straight in the house, through the kitchen, and up the stairs to the attic Command Center. Milton was lying on his recliner in the golden honeycomb, in the arms of Morpheus.

"Amazing," Bud said to himself, looking around and shaking his head.

Milton sat bolt upright, looking sleepy. He had heard something of interest in his earphones, and he crabbed across the floor pointing to the earphones as his eyes widened. He stuck out his tongue concentrating on the sounds, and holding up his hand, as if to interrupt, he told Bud, "They're giving me a jingle." He bobbed his head, held it steady, and shook it in reluctant disagreement as he listened to the sounds in the earphones. He fine-tuned the ball bearing on the crystal. After several minutes he pulled off the earphones and climbed out of his copper suit, dropping the big Slinky on the floor. "They're chatty this afternoon," he said. "You wouldn't believe the resonance, like a million hums humming. You should listen, Bud. I just can't get over it."

"I thought they only said 'Hi.' "

Milton smiled. "That was all they did say before just a minute ago. Now they're expanding the conversation. They're getting comfortable."

"What more did they tell you?"

" 'Bon chance.' That's what they said. 'Bon chance.' "

"What's that?"

"Their voices sounded just like Maurice Chevalier's when he's singing one of his songs."

"What do you think it means, *bon chance?*" Bud asked, for a moment putting his doubts aside.

"How should I know?"

"What language is *bon chance?*"

"French, I think."

Bud put his chin on his hand. "Let me see what you wrote down," he said and turned the paper this way and that. "I suppose it's plain if you understand it. Do you know anybody who speaks the language of love?"

Milton pointed downstairs. "Gladys listens to Edith Piaf records all the time."

Gladys was puttering at the sink when they clattered down the stairs. She was washing up the pans after baking her signature French egg pie, this one with onions, mushrooms, and dark spinach patches. Without a word, she served slices on plates and, taking the hint, Milton poured himself a glass of milk. He tested her egg pie with a fork. "Tastes as good as when it's warm," he told her, reaching for a compliment.

"Doesn't taste like anything, Gladys," Bud told her after trying a bite.

"It's not supposed to taste like anything," she told him, and he couldn't tell whether she was being sarcastic. "Egg pie is for using your imagination with."

"Could you explain what you mean by that?" Bud asked her.

"Don't you know anything?" she asked. "When Marie Antoinette told the French peasants to eat cake, she was really referring to egg pie. Those peasants would eat it, and because it had no taste, like you said, Bud, they dreamed they were eating tarts and *boef* Wellington and *mousse au chocolat.* That's what Marie had in mind. Egg pie is what you make of it."

"Go ahead and ask her what those words mean" Bud reminded Milton.

"Oh, yeah." He showed her the notepaper. "Are those words French?" he asked.

She raised her sunglasses. "It means 'Good luck,' *n'est pas?*"

Bud wiped his mouth on his sleeve. "Good luck?"

"There's no other translation for it," she told him.

"By God, Milt, they're endorsing us, they're sponsoring us, throwing their hats in our ring."

"You think so?" Milton asked.

"I know you didn't make it up," Bud said, impressed in spite of himself.

Milton looked at Gladys, and it was clear by his expression that he wanted her to believe in him. "You believe me, Gladys?" he asked her.

"Milt, I *always* believe you," she said. As usual with Gladys, knowing her real meaning wasn't easy. "But why would space people speak French?" she asked.

"It's the language of love, is why," Bud replied for Milton.

"It's the international diplomatic language, too," Milton said.

"Maybe they meant 'good luck' the way school kids mean it, like 'good luck' if you say you are going to jump off a house. In other words they're saying you will need all you can get."

"The Ancients aren't kids," Milton told her.

"You mentioned that they deal in past, present, and future but not in specifics," Bud said, trying hard to think. "Could they be giving us directions?"

"They're telling us we're *in* the right direction," Milton said as though he had known all along.

"I think you could be right," Bud said.

They put down their plates of French egg pie and went outside. The sky was overcast. A cold snap was on its way.

16

Dogpatch

"He's going to be trained," Edith told Bud in a determined voice.

Scooter's ears went up and down. He knew by instinct that he was being discussed.

"He's a dog," said Bud, pointing at him. "His brain knows nothing but sleeping and eating and taking a dump. I can't believe we are having this discussion. A dog, Edith. That's a dog laying there."

Scooter looked around him as though he wasn't sure.

"He's going to be obedience-trained and that's that," she said and folded her arms belligerently. She wouldn't come out and say it, but she had noticed his chasing after his own tail and she wanted this defect repaired. There was an element of revenge in her decision, too. She might have been thankful to him for making a mess of the talent display, and yet part of her was angry with him. She felt no confusion about enrolling him in a school where he could learn to obey.

That afternoon she shoved him in the backseat of the car with the girls. Cloud was dreaming about becoming a pom-pom girl in the pep squad; the blue-and-gold pom-poms and the snappy poodle skirts transported her. Blue was dreaming of Don, a sharp dresser with a high-fidelity set that could blow out his neighbor's patio windows if he turned the volume up high. Scooter jumped over the seat and stood in Callum's lap with his head out the window and his ears back, trying to read his fate's direction.

By now nagged by guilt, Edith told the girls, "If you don't like the school, or if you think it won't be good for him, he'll come home with us. I promise."

"He won't know the difference," said Blue. "School will be good for him."

"What do you have to say about it, Cloud?" Edith asked.

"I don't care one way or another."

"Don't care?"

"He's Blue's dog. He's not mine."

"I didn't ask Blue's opinion," Edith said. "I asked yours."

"He never had a chance to learn right from wrong," Cloud said. "It'll do him good. Maybe he'll make new friends. He'll *like* it."

They turned off Euclid into a neighborhood of shingled wood-framed homes with wide front porches and large windows. Each one had a front yard with grass that the sun had baked a turkey brown. Royal palms had grown over the years to giddy heights in the esplanade. Edith pulled in the dot-sized shade of one palm in front of a house. A loud yapping came from the backyard.

The barking reached hysterical levels when they climbed the porch steps and rang the bell. No one answered, and Edith led them around the house to the backyard. She unlatched the gate, and with the yard opened to view, she said, "Will you look at that!" and turned around and told the girls, "Actually, I wish you wouldn't."

"Gross, Mom," Blue said, staring at her feet.

"I think we should leave," said Cloud, backpedaling.

An old woman with baggy flesh was standing stark naked under a palm tree. She was aiming the nozzle of a garden hose at the sky, watering the hot afternoon air as fifty or so dogs yowled at her feet. She giggled and hopped like an Apache. The backyard was littered with dog filth and the remnants of cloth, wood, leather, and rubber left over from the exertions of the dogs' jaws.

Edith was closing the gate trying to get away when the woman shouted, "Hey, you!" and aimed the hose at them.

The woman had wrinkled breasts hanging down like flypaper,

which flapped as she ran toward them. Her skin was a contour map of lines, moles, and slumped flesh, and her gray hair straggled in her face.

"Do you know you're not wearing clothes?" Edith asked her from a few feet away.

She turned the hose behind her and looked down her front. "I'm nudist," she announced.

"Are you Mrs. Constantinople?"

"Elizabeth. Never cared for Constantinople. It was my husband's name, you know. Skin cancer. I buried him in the buff. You never know."

"And do you run a canine obedience school?"

"I restrict my nudism to the backyard these days," she said, still on an earlier thought. "In the old days I recruited an army of men to nudism. I don't have much to parade around anymore. Used to, though. You know nudism?"

"Not formally," said Edith.

"A nice group of folks. Sharp canasta players, too." She shooed the dogs away. "You here about a dog?"

"Well, yes," Edith said, searching for her bearings. "Could you tell me, Elizabeth, what you were doing with the hose just now?"

"That ball up there"—she glanced up at the sun—"I was giving the dogs *and* me an afternoon spray."

"And these dogs are in obedience training?"

"Most of them are." She looked at the girls. "These two yours?"

"Yes," Edith replied and told her their names.

"There's a program for nude preteenagers called Youthful Adventurers—boys and girls together."

"How interesting," Edith said. "We have a dog we're thinking of getting trained."

"Is he your dog?" she asked the girls.

Cloud and Blue were staring at her in speechless horror. Their own bodies, either stripped or dressed, embarrassed them. That a female would flaunt her nakedness was new to them. Cloud later called Mrs. Constantinople's bold nudity "dirty." She claimed she had a different odor from anybody she had ever smelled before. Part of Blue's horror came from an intuition that Mrs. Constantinople wasn't a freak. She was her tomorrow.

"They're in charge of Scooter, yes," Edith replied.

Two big dogs started fighting in back of Mrs. Constantinople while the other dogs scratched and drooled. Mrs. Constantinople turned the hose on the fighters.

"He's somewhat timid," said Edith, meaning Scooter.

"Let's have a look at him, then," Mrs. Constantinople said.

"Mom, I don't think it's a good idea after all," Blue said, stepping backward.

"Let's go get him and let *him* decide," said Edith.

On the path near the street, out of Mrs. Constantinople's hearing, Blue told Edith, "The woman is weird."

"There's nothing weird about nakedness. But in her instance, I agree with you."

Edith bent down to snap on Scooter's leash, but he bolted. He ran twenty yards, turned, and watched to see if they were chasing him.

"Come here, Scooter," Edith coaxed in a gentle voice.

More alert than they had ever seen him, Scooter sat down on the lawn, ready to move not just down the sidewalk but into another neighborhood, another town, a whole other life, if need be.

Callum stayed in the backyard with Mrs. Constantinople. He felt self-conscious standing this close to her. The hours he had spent dreaming of breasts in general had come down to this pair of saddlebags. He permitted his eyes to wander southward over the parched terrain of Mrs. Constantinople's belly and for a fleeting second over her bush, which reminded him of a Chinese bandleader's goatee. He sent his eyes back north, and she was smiling at him as if she could read his thoughts. Stammering with embarrassment, he told her, "I know a man with your name."

She sprayed herself with the hose. "You must mean my boy, Ricky. We're the only Constantinoples in the phone book. Ricky's a big cheese and getting bigger every day. It's going to be he won't have room to fit anywhere pretty soon. My nudism embarrasses him, though."

"I visited his office downtown," said Callum.

"*Il formaggissimo,*" she sang, warming to her subject. "Sees himself as an anglophile. He's never been closer to England than Earl Grey's tea. That's what happens when you're a big cheese. You ignore who you are and the people who helped you get there. You make up your past so it fits with your present. He tells people he went to Oxford. La dee dah! He's working for Walt Disney now, if you can believe that."

Callum stared at her. "Walt Disney from the movies?" he asked.

" 'Whistle while you work.' That one," she replied. "He likes approbation, my Ricky does. That means praise. He likes to impress folks. I could tell you a few stories that would knock him down a peg. He picks his nose. Imagine a man his age doing that."

"What does he do for Walt Disney?" Callum asked her.

"He buys land for him. Ricky's a realtor."

Callum was about to ask another question when Edith came into the yard dragging Scooter. The other dogs greeted him with a chorus of growls. Edith kicked at one of them to keep him back. She was out of breath from chasing Scooter down the sidewalk and mad at herself for bringing him here in the first place. "Will you please tell the dogs to go away?" she asked Mrs. Constantinople.

"They're saying 'hi,' is all," she said and sprayed a dog that was mounting Scooter from behind. "He'll be fine. I can tell he'll fit in once he knows what's what."

Scooter shivered and looked at the opened gate.

"I don't think he's cut out for pecking orders," said Edith and dropped the leash. "Not here, anyway." And she smiled as Scooter bolted out of the yard and jumped through the opened car window.

17

The Vision

"Am I seeing a mirage?" P.O. asked Bud as they drove past fields of beans.

"Probably," Bud replied without looking up.

"Just look and tell me what you see out the window," said P.O.

Bud sat up. "Fields, bean fields," and he yawned.

"Yeah and what else?" P.O. excitedly hammered the steering wheel with the heel of his hand.

"The coast up ahead there, a billboard over there, more bean fields."

"Gee, Bud, what's that building over there?" P.O. pointed to the left of the car by the billboard.

"A Quonset hut," he said. And he blinked hard. "A round-roofed house."

P.O. pulled over on the shoulder of the road. The dust from the tires blew past as they sat listening to the wind.

"What did you just describe to me?" P.O. asked Bud, knowing he had almost but not quite got it.

"What is this, a game?" Bud asked.

"It's Dr. King's vision you're describing, is what it is," he replied.

Bud leaned into the windshield and looked left and right. Starting to laugh, he shaded his eyes, as if the windshield were giving him a false illusion. He got out of the car and threw his tam-o'-shanter in the air, and a puff of wind carried it into a ditch of clear, fast-running water.

"No mirage, P.O.," he said. "This is it." And he danced in a dusty circle. "How far'd you estimate the ocean to be?"

"Two, three miles."

" 'Near but not *on* the water' were Dr. King's exact words," said Bud. "Everything fits. People wandering around. Look at 'em, browsing the crap over at Tucker's, the Quonset hut, the billboard. If this isn't what he was referring to, I'll eat my hat."

P.O. spread his arms. "I never thought a needle in a haystack could look this good."

A few errant seagulls like scraps of paper blowing on the seawind broke the sky's monotony.

"I can't believe we've found it," Bud said and snapped his fingers. "Just like that, too."

"This land topped my list all along," said P.O. "That's what I was trying to tell you that day you were acting like a prize Roman dork."

"I apologize," Bud told him. "In light of my mistake, I beg your forgiveness."

"I *knew* it." P.O. shaded his eyes. "It's a hundred acres, thereabouts, with room to grow."

Bud looked around. "Do you know who owns it?"

"Yeah, Almore Tucker."

Bud knew Tucker, and he laughed at the idea of stealing a diamond from under his hairy nose. "Tucker doesn't own anything he isn't willing to sell," he said.

"Be coy," P.O. warned him as they boarded the car.

"Coy's my middle name," said Bud as they drove toward Tucker's sign.

Tucker was presiding over his cash box in the shade of the billboard. Sizing up Bud and P.O. he scratched his scalp and smelled his fingernails.

"Howdy there," Bud said, acting down-home. "We were just passing by. A nice piece of land you got around here."

"Beans, if you like beans," Tucker said. And at that instant his seat bottom acted as a sounding board for a tattoo of snare-drum flatulence. A zephyr of hair-curling odor wafted up from his pants. Bud and P.O. glanced at each other with the same thought, that Tucker had violated a principal tenet of male decorum that said farting was allowed among friends but never (the odd mistake excluded) in front of strangers.

"We have no interest in beans," Bud said, as the offensive odor reached his nose. "No, none at all. Like I said, your land is nice. We're looking at land."

"You boys farmers?"

Bud seized on this opening. "Kiwis," he said.

"You fellas from New Zealand then?" asked Tucker.

"Fruits," Bud elaborated.

"I wish you were from New Zealand. I never met a man from New Zealand I didn't like. Never met one, period." He laughed deep in his throat at his own wit. "What, fruits?"

"Kiwifruits," said Bud. "It's the fruit of the future—chartreuse with little black seeds, looks like something you'd find growing in outer space."

"Interesting. How do these kiwis grow?"

"Like grapes on vines . . . only bigger."

Tucker rubbed the stubble on his chin. "Huh," he said, impressed. "Isn't there a bird of that same name?"

"A long-billed creature from Down Under."

"Any connection or just coincidence?"

"One eats the other," P.O. said, sounding like an authority.

"We're looking for land to farm kiwifruits on," Bud said.

Tucker lowered his feet and tilted his chair forward. "What gives you the idea my land is for sale?"

"Nothing," Bud replied. "We were driving by and I said to my friend here, 'What a nice piece of land.' I assume from what you say that it isn't for sale."

"Don't be so hasty," Tucker said, rising to his feet. He slapped the seat of his pants and a bubble of captured odor escaped.

"My friend here knows agriculture better than I do," Bud said. "He may have some questions."

Tucker actually smiled. "Fire away," he told P.O.

"Kiwis are an intense crop," said P.O. "Very intense, in fact. Compact is the word we use in the antipodes. We'd be looking at buying, say, an acre . . . or less."

Tucker sat back down. "Did I hear you correctly?"

P.O. went on, "But before we would get into details we would want to know about encumbrances."

"You mean like liens?"

"That's the exact word I was looking for."

"Free and clear. I inherited these acres—a hundred and ten total—from my dearly departed missus. She went to the pearly gates five years ago of goiter. She had the damndest one you ever saw, too. It hung down like an old man's balls." He indicated from his chin. "A big goddamned thing. She referred to it like it was alive. 'Oma' is what she called it. 'My Oma needs a nap,' she would tell me, and I would put her into bed and tuck a little blanket around her Oma." He swept his arm indicating his property. "She inherited these acres from her parents."

P.O. swallowed hard. "No contracts outstanding on the land, then?"

"I own it free and clear."

"Competitors, is what I am asking. Has anyone else inquired to buy it? Has anyone offered a bid, anyone from Palo Alto, for instance?"

Tucker looked like he had been told his land contained uranium. "You mean this land is worth something?"

"He's not saying that," Bud corrected P.O. "It's a nice piece of land but there are lots of nice pieces of land. Our lawyers recommended that we ask these questions, you understand. We wouldn't want to contemplate buying land that was under contract to another party. That's all my associate meant."

"You said you are looking for an acre," Tucker said. "Did I hear that right?"

"Or less . . ."

"Compact. Well, I'll be a son of a bitch," Tucker said.

"What would that kind of holding sell for, would you say?" asked Bud, holding his breath.

Tucker gazed off at the horizon. The slopes of the San Gabriels could be seen through the haze. A dust devil turned in a distant field, and overhead a biplane plodded through the sky, its engine popping. It trailed a crimson banner with a sales message that was too high to read. For Bud and P.O. the earth stood still. Tucker smacked his lips. He shielded his eyes and followed the biplane until the sound of its engine died away.

"I'd have to consult my consultant on that, before I can say," he said finally.

Bud stared at him. "For less than one acre you need a consultant to come up with a price?"

With a cunning smile he replied, "Yup."

When Tucker did not move, Bud asked, "Is this consultant around?"

"It's a she," he explained and looked up at the sky. "And ah, no. She'd be at lunch right now."

They returned to Tucker's later that afternoon in spite of a drizzle that otherwise would have kept them indoors, napping or watching baseball on television. Tucker spied their car from a distance and crabbed across the wallow of his lot to his desk under the billboard, where he pretended to help a customer in a yellow slicker.

Bud and P.O. parked in the lee of the billboard. Unfurling umbrellas, they looked cowed by the inclemency. Rain in southern California was such an unfamiliar occurrence, it affected emotions, which could swing from a cozy welcome of a drizzle like this to feelings of mortality. Bud and P.O. felt betrayed by this onset of leaky weather, as if the heavens themselves had let them down at the exact moment they needed allies.

"Howdy, boys," Tucker said as they walked up.

"Have you had a chance to consult your consultant yet?" asked Bud, all business and determined to keep an upper hand.

Tucker shook his head. "I forgot you boys said you were coming back," he said, testing the waters.

"Did you, now?" said P.O., who looked at Bud. "I think Mr. Tucker isn't interested in an offer for his land after all. That would be my guess. What do you say, Bud, we go by that other piece of nice land we saw? I'm sure the owner over there will remember us."

"Callin' my bluff, hey?" asked Tucker.

"Bluff, bullshit," said P.O. "We come all the way back here, busy men like us, and you say you haven't even consulted with your consultant?"

At that Tucker got to his feet with telling haste. With his hands over his kidneys, he leaned his head back into the rain like a chicken trying to drown itself. "If you'll just follow me, gentlemen, we'll hash this baby over."

Bud kept in stride across the muddy lot. "Who is she, your consultant, a realtor?" he asked Tucker, trying to find an advantage.

Tucker held the hut's door. Glad to be out of the drizzle, they squeezed past the *Mo*'s hull. Under the battleship's miniature fantail, level with her miniature screws, Tucker leaned his palms on a round card table covered with tattered green baize. He pulled out a chair and indicated for Bud and P.O. to do the same, like players settling into a hand of Lamebrain Pete.

Seated in the half dark, the one source of light the Quonset's grimy window, Tucker reached under the table for a fishbowl. As if it gave off warmth, he set it upside down on the table and covered it with his hands. After a few minutes' fondling it, he rested his hands palms down on the table. With a groan deep in his throat like a morning gargle he shut his eyes tight and lolled his tongue out and rested his chin on his breastbone. He reached out for Bud and P.O.'s hands.

"Excuse me a minute here," Bud said. When he turned his head, the *Mo*'s starboard rudder grazed his cheek.

Tucker made another gargle sound. Releasing Bud and P.O.'s hands, he clutched the fishbowl again, and his eyes rolled up in his head, leaving a cobweb of red lines.

"Rose," he said. "Rose . . ." He paused, rolling his head on his shoulders like a blind man. "Okay, I'm sorry I told them about Oma."

Bud mouthed to P.O., "Oh boy."

"I don't know why you won't let it alone," Tucker went on, sounding defensive. "I'm telling you I didn't mean it. Can't you get over it? Are things that boring where you are, Rose, you have to dwell in the past? My God, don't they have shuffleboard or canasta or bingo up there?"

Bud looked at Tucker to see whether he thought this was a ruse. Tucker looked convincing and made the right sounds for someone in a trance. His dialogue with Rose sounded like a conversation a man would have with his wife.

"Rose, these fellas here want to grow kiwifruits on our land. I've got to give them a price for an acre—"

"—Or less," Bud put in.

"An acre or less. Rose, what do you think it's worth from your standpoint?"

The suspense was getting to Bud, and P.O. could hardly take his eyes off the fishbowl.

In a disembodied voice, Tucker asked them, "Rose wants to know which acre you are thinking about?"

Bud shrugged, looking over at P.O. "I suppose it doesn't matter to kiwifruits which one we buy. In the middle, I guess. Yes, in the middle of the field."

"Rose, you hear that? No, he said in the middle if it's all the same to you." He paused, cocking an ear. "She says she can only sell an acre bordering on Salt Road."

"Fine," Bud said, nodding his head. "No problem."

"Rose says an acre by the road is the cheapest."

"That's good news," said P.O., quickly adding, "from a business standpoint. No sense spending the company's money if we don't have to. Heh heh."

Tucker gargled. "Rose says she can't go lower than—"

"Yes?" Bud asked, leaning forward.

"—Than twenty-five hundred."

"Holy shit!" he shouted and the sound of his voice echoed in the Quonset. He bucked back in his chair and banged his head on the *Mo*'s prop. "That's not even in the ballpark," he said, ignoring the pain in his head, pointing a finger at Tucker. "You tell that to Rose, right now, you hear me?"

"He wants to dicker, Rose," said Tucker.

"Don't you have a say in any of this?" P.O. asked him.

"Hold it, hold it," Tucker said, raising his hand for quiet. "She's wavering. She's willing to . . . two thousand dollars, last price, firm." As proof, if that's what it was, his eyes rolled down in their sockets. He focused and wiped his mouth. He asked them, as though he didn't know, "Did Rose bargain or did she hold firm?"

"I think she did both," said Bud.

"Good, because she can be touchy. Leads me to believe Heaven isn't all it's rumored to be."

"You leave all these decisions to Rose?" P.O. asked.

Tucker stared at him as though he had just heard the dumbest question of his life. "She *owns* the land," he said. "I can't go around her. I'm only the caretaker."

"But she's dead."

"And how would *you* know?" he asked indignantly.

"I have to be sure," Bud said to P.O. as they walked up to Glumm's Reconstituted Oil. "That's why."

P.O. did not argue with that.

"It was a vision," Bud explained, "Dr. King's vision. He could be a doozie. And what he said, even if he is an oracle, isn't enough to base the biggest risk of my life on."

"You won't get an argument from me," said P.O. "By the way, where's the money coming from?"

Bud gave him a cold look that said, Don't ask. "I've had it squirreled away. Even Edith doesn't know about it."

"Oh," P.O. said, wondering why Bud hadn't mentioned it; the last time money was discussed, Bud had said he would take care of the problem. Milton had joked about robbing a bank. People and money. You thought you knew your closest friend, your girlfriend, your husband, even your wife, until money came between you. And you discovered a stranger.

They entered a shed with a corrugated iron roof that smelled of solvents. The ground under their feet was soaked with petroleum spilled from bubbling tanks that turned dirty crankcase oil into clean crankcase oil. In the back of the shop was a smudged-glass door that opened onto Fred Glumm's office. Bud had known Fred for years as his oil man, and while they did not know each other well, they had sketched the outlines of their lives in those moments Bud had waited for Fred to fill up his can with clean oil, dropping off the old.

He got up from a chair when Bud knocked on the door. He wore golfer's pastel pants with a Ban-Lon shirt stretched over a belly like a bowling ball in a bag. He smoked Luckies fitted in an amber holder, was thin and bald, and sported a contoured black mustache.

"Hey, Bud. Weren't you here last month?" he asked, mistaking the purpose of his visit. "What? Got a new car?"

"Another agenda, Fred," Bud told him, introducing him to P.O. "I came about your chair."

Bud pointed to the armchair at Glumm's desk. It was a captain's chair made of ebony with a crest.

"My chair?" Glumm asked.

"Your chair. I'm wondering about the scrollwork on the back there."

Glumm studied the chair as if he were seeing it for the first time. "It's a college chair," he said. "When you are a college grad you can buy a chair and sit on it."

"You went to college?" P.O. asked.

"Stanford."

P.O. looked doubtful. He harbored the image of college graduates gathered around conference tables with water pitchers and little cups of sharp yellow pencils. He pictured secretaries in tight skirts writing in spiral binders. He pictured wet bars behind bookshelves and sofas for nooners with girls from the accounting department. Greasy rags and bubbling pots of soured oil did not fit the image. If what he said was true, Glumm was an affront to higher education.

"Class of thirty-seven, the depth of the Depression," Glumm said. "I graduated in engineering, with honors."

P.O. didn't believe him. "And you're reclaiming oil?"

He laughed. "At one of my reunions the wife of a classmate asked what I did. 'You're in oil? From Texas?' I told her no, California. She followed me around the whole weekend thinking I was a tycoon like Getty or John D. Isn't it amazing what people choose to believe?"

"When you graduate from college and you mention you're in oil, people think bigger than this," P.O. said. "That's why you go to places like Stanford."

"It's true," said Glumm, rubbing his chair with an oily hand.

Bud said, "I'm looking for information a Stanford man might have, about Palo Alto."

"I lived there as an undergraduate. I visit often enough even now, three, four times a year."

"Ever hear of a company called SRI?"

"What about it?" he asked, as though he knew.

"What is it, to start with?"

"The Stanford Research Institute. It's called SRI for short."

Bud smiled at P.O. "See, I knew Fred would know."

"It's a think tank," Glumm added helpfully.

"Like what, a think tank?" asked P.O., still suspicious.

"If you want to build a bridge, SRI will write a feasibility study. Sell your goods in Timbuktu? SRI will tell you if there's a market there. The Stanford faculty hires out to SRI for private jobs. It's a clearinghouse for brains."

"Would the State of California hire it, for instance?" asked Bud.

"Anybody with moolah—state, foreign governments, private business, industry. They would work for me if I paid them."

"Even a movie company?" Bud asked.

"Even the commies."

"You seem to know an awful lot about this SRI," P.O. said.

"Four or five of my professors worked for it when I was studying up there. My senior advisor, in fact, went to the Belgian Congo for SRI to figure out how to get their uranium down to Léopoldville. He spent years there. Onga bunga." He pointed to the wall. Three wild-looking African masks hung there. "I asked him to send me some postage stamps. This is what I got."

Bud looked at P.O. "A moment ago when I mentioned about a movie company, Glumm, I was thinking about Disney."

"You're saying that you think SRI is doing some consulting work for Disney?" He pursed his lips, thinking. "I don't see anything unusual in that. Want me to ask for you?"

"You could do that?" Bud sounded surprised.

"Of course, my pleasure."

"We're kind of under pressure," Bud said.

"What is it, a venture?"

"A fling is more like it," Bud said.

"Not another ice-skating rink, I hope." And he smiled knowingly.

"No, we're working on a plan," said Bud, annoyed that Glumm associated the Disney dream with Milton's Sonja Henie Glide Salon.

Glumm edged his Stanford chair up to his desk. Before dialing, he referred to a number in a leather-covered address book beside the telephone. "Hello, Buzz?" he said into the phone. Buzz, it seemed, was Glumm's frat brother—ties that bound. "We're sinking new wells all the time, Buzz," he went on, talking and listening for several minutes. He mentioned Disney's name once.

He hung up. "Are you going to let me in on this?" he asked Bud. "Buzz seemed put off, my asking like I did. He sounded like this Disney thing is hush-hush. He's a nice guy, too. What is it? Defense Department?"

"First tell me what he told you," Bud said.

"No, you tell me first."

Bud shook his head. "I'm under the same constraints as your friend Buzz. If he was hush-hush, I'm hush-hush."

"You drive a soda truck, Bud," Glumm reminded him. "You *can't* have the same constraints."

P.O. was smiling. He loved hearing Glumm whine; he liked to watch him plead. It meant that his buddy Buzz had said some things that had excited Glumm's greed.

"I *can't* let you in on it, Glumm," Bud repeated.

"Okay then, as a friend, Buzz—his name is Buzz Price—says he is the project director for SRI. When I mentioned Disney he said he is working on a job for a private company called W.E.D. Enterprises. He is looking into the purchase of land based on a list of particulars. He wouldn't tell them to me. He said it was hush-hush."

"He didn't happen to tell you what W.E.D. is?"

"A land-developing company."

"That makes sense," said Bud. "He didn't say *where* this land-developing company was developing land?"

"These people never give out details."

"Or who is behind it?"

"I told you, SRI will do anything, even what sounds crazy to the average person."

"Well, that sure sounds like Disney to me," said Bud.

18

A Bitter Display

Bud trailed his fingertips in the water over the gunwale of the gondola. "You either ante up wooden matches or you play with the coin of the realm," he told the others in the boat. "At the next lighted section, P.O., why don't you go over the findings for the fellas?"

"With the maps?" P.O. asked out of the darkness.

"That's right, the maps."

"Blue Moon" was playing through the tinny speakers. Every now and then the shadow of another Venetian gondola floated past them going in the opposite direction, close enough for Callum to imagine girl's dresses up over their heads and guys bouncing on top. Any girl riding a gondola in the Tunnel of Love was by definition hot stuff, he believed. Especially when an empty gondola went past, he imagined furious lovemaking on the boat's bottom boards. Empty gondolas, full gondolas, gondolas with single couples, it didn't matter to him. This was the sexiest place he had ever visited.

They had picked the Pike to pieces while it had still been daylight, from its food concession stands to its honky-tonk games with the fuzzy-wuzzy prizes. Callum had seen nothing to criticize in the double Ferris wheel with the whoops of terror from the heights. Aside from that—no one had braved the roller coaster that roared overhead at steady intervals—nothing about the Pike appealed to their notion of family fun. Callum had kept a wary eye on the denizens, the sailors in their bell-bottom trousers, drunk Marines from Pendleton with vomit on their spit-polished shoes, young men loitering in the shadows dragging on cigarettes French-style. He had seen a dope fiend with a gaunt face and frail figure, and a young whore in spike heels and black fishnet stockings. The Pike was a place that made you shiver if you imagined spending a minute there alone.

Now their gondola floated into a section of grotto lit by hazy blue neon. Hurriedly P.O. unrolled his maps. In the stern end of the boat, Roland and Milton bent down looking at the maps upside down. Bud, Callum, P.O., and Mr. Wait were squeezed on the seat in the bow with the maps right-side up.

P.O. was wearing Levis and a tight white T-shirt that gave definition to his biceps. Earlier he had scowled at a couple of Marines who had laughed at Roland, and seeing P.O. twitch his arms, they had backed off. "In this area I pared down the options to seventy-one possible sites in all," he said, referring to the maps.

Bud shrugged in the darkness, his mind already made up. This floating tour was an exercise in leadership, education, and restraint, but it wasn't going to change his thinking. Tucker's was the needle in the haystack; it jibed with too much not to be the place Walt was going to build his amusement park.

"If a parcel was owned by the military or the government, and if it had no water, or no road nearby, it was rejected," said P.O.

"Educated guessing, then," Roland said.

"Yes and no. The most interesting site has seventeen parcels along Salt Road totaling a hundred ten point nine acres. It's all beans. Tucker's place. The acreage is perfect, flat, open, with plenty of irrigation. The land is sandy loam with good drainage. It is free of dairies and oil leases and that kind of junk. It has three artesian wells." He pointed his finger to the place on the map as the gondola floated into an area of darkness.

"Like I was saying," Bud said, "either wooden matches or real money. I say we decide this issue this evening, once and for all."

"P.O. has maps and water tables and elevations and such," said

Mr. Wait out of the gloaming. "I for one think that is fine. But what about other opinions? Aren't they worth hearing, too?"

"That's what we're here for," said Bud, sounding agreeable. "Let's have everyone get his oar in. Milt, you can start."

"Hey, on specifics, I defer to P.O.," Milton said, his voice echoing off the walls. "The Ancients don't deal in maps and such. Their message was, whatever we decide is going to be the right decision. That's all I have to say."

"Whatever it is we decide?" asked P.O.

"It's right because *we* made the choice," Milton explained. "The Ancients know what choice we are going to make even before we know. They know it's going to be the right one. Therefore, they endorse it."

"Sounds like we can't miss," said Roland.

"Don't forget what Dr. King told you," P.O. told Milton.

"I rate that high, as well," he said.

Roland shuffled his feet on the planks. "I've had my say, and Selwyn Troute won't tell me anything more. He's petrified the upper echelons will hear about his smile. There were people eating lunch in the cafeteria that day who saw him."

Groans of erotic pleasure distracted them, and in the dark they turned to stare at a rhythmical bumping against a passing gondola's wooden floor.

"Can you imagine that sort of thing at Walt's fun zone?" Roland asked. He sounded disgusted.

"He'd throw them out on their necks," said Bud.

"Sounds to me like they're having fun," said Milton. "They aren't hurting anybody."

"It's the Tunnel of Love," P.O. added.

"Okay. Next. Anyone?" asked Bud.

"I guess I haven't been much help to you, and I'm sorry," said Mr. Wait.

"Don't say that," Bud admonished him. "You've been great."

They went over what they knew, each of them individually, in silence. The effect was distorting. To a man they believed in P.O.'s maps. That's how the world turned. Science and maps and machines had won the war. Skeins of atoms and molecules with names and weights and numbers moved mountains. But science played no role among friends and could not account for what bound them together. Reports from the Ancients and epiphanies, surmises, and grumpy common sense, these had created their bond.

"I'd like to talk a minute about wooden matches and coins of the realm," said Mr. Wait. "It dawned on me we never sought a consensus. Why can't we stop now, and leave this whole dream with our guesses?"

"And not take a position?" asked P.O.

"Not with money, no."

"That's how the world works," said P.O. "And you should know at your age, Mr. Wait. Guys who claim they had the idea for this or that years before the inventor who made millions out of it are a dime a dozen. They're even in Russia, where they invented everything under the sun *after* the fact. If you believe in your dream, you have to take risks. That's what great men do. Take Guglielmo Marconi. What if he had piddled around? What about Edison? He risked being called a goofball. You have to put something down. Otherwise you're a blowhard in a bar moaning in your beer about how you could have been somebody."

Bud's feet felt cold. "Tucker's asking price is a lifetime's savings," he pointed out. "That's what Mr. Wait is saying, I think."

Roland spoke in the dark, "I agree with P.O. When I see somebody like Walt Disney, I think of how he dreamed up creatures like mice and ducks that are cute and talk with lisps. He came from nothing just like us and risked everything making the duck and the mouse work. Now he's famous and rich. Would we call him a genius if he was a guy with a few smudged drawings pinned on his bedroom walls? The difference between genius and loudmouths is a throw of the dice. If you don't throw, you live your whole life waiting for something to happen that never will."

P.O. clapped him on the shoulder.

"Can I add something here?" Milton asked. "I just want to ask how well prepared we are. Look at us. Our boasts sound big. But I'd like to point out, we're not Mississippi gamblers."

"Amen," Bud said.

Their sudden silence spoke to the truth of his observation. Roland had fled from the high rollers' life, and none of them had ever put their dreams on the line like this before. Bud joked about how he thought the doughnut stand and the skating rink, the worms or the minks would never have succeeded anyway, as if to tell the world that he had not taken those dreams seriously. In other words, this was their moment, and they did not want to fail. Failure this time meant that the next dream would be a joke, or if not a joke, it wouldn't be anything at all.

The concessionaire, a porky man in a gray Notre Dame sweat-shirt, was leaning on a boat hook watching the gondolas float by. "Having fun, fellas?" he asked as they neared the dock. Off in the distance, the double Ferris wheel turned and the Cyclone roared on its tracks.

Once more covered in darkness, Roland quoted the Bible. " 'But if any provide not for his own, and specially for those of his own house, he hath denied the faith, and is worse than an infidel.' The First Epistle of Paul the Apostle to Timothy five:eight."

Which said it all.

"I get a little put off, Roland, your quoting Scripture to make your points," said P.O. "Maybe for once *you* could say what you believe."

"It's his way," Bud explained.

" 'The love of money is the root of all evil,' Timothy six: seven," P.O. said. "That's the problem. There's something in the Bible for everybody."

"Let's not get personal," Mr. Wait said. "Let me go on the record saying that money and friends don't mix."

"Recorded," said Bud dismissively.

"We're not going to buy swimming pools with the profits from this," said P.O. "We're not moving to Palm Springs. You don't have to worry, Mr. Wait."

"It is profit," he said.

"Profit that's honestly gained," said P.O.

"Aren't we putting the horse before the cart here?" asked Milton.

"Not anymore," Bud told him. "We've finally reached that point where it doesn't matter where the cart is."

They came out of the tunnel into the neons, and Bud signaled for the boat keeper to hook them over to the dock. As the others were getting out, Mr. Wait held Bud back by the arm. "You know you may be right after all about measuring success in dollars and cents," he told him confidentially. "I can think it's a shame but I can't change it." He pointed his chin at Callum. "I only wanted to show him there was another way."

Bud had not asked Callum his opinion. And he had one. He didn't have to guess like the men, but if they weren't going to ask him, he wasn't going to volunteer.

Instead, he told Bud he wanted to ride the Cyclone.

"You don't want to do that," Bud said, thinking that he might have to go along, as a father should. He pondered his options in front of a shooting gallery. "We don't have time for the Cyclone," he told him.

Milton, the group's sharpshooter, seeing the arcade, said to no one in particular, "I think I'll try for a fuzzy for Gladys," and the arcade attendant, a bald man with bright blue eyes, loaded a rifle.

"You sure you don't want to shoot a load instead?" Bud asked Callum. "You always want to shoot. Come on, shoot."

"I'm not asking you to ride with me," Callum told him, and Bud looked relieved. "I *want* to ride it alone."

"What do you think about him riding alone?" Bud asked the men.

Nobody wanted to be the first to bring up that several times each year the local newspapers ran stories linking the Cyclone with coronaries in men about their ages. Mention of the Cyclone's name alone was known to have stained grown men's Skivvies.

"People ride it all the time," Milton remarked as he waited for a second load of bullets.

"Sure they do but those people are different," Roland said, thinking of the Pike's denizens.

"Oh, let him go," Mr. Wait said in a weary kind of way. "He can take care of himself."

"That's not what worries me," said Bud. What worried him was Edith. He wanted to tell Callum no, then and there, and give him a hundred good reasons why. But he realized, the pump-action .22 ringing in his ears, that Callum was challenging him. He was asking if he was brave enough to let him go. Bud didn't know which was worse, watching him ride, riding with him, or telling him no.

The men stood watching with a fascinated curiosity as Callum stepped up to the wooden booth for a single ticket. Milton rocked back on his heels surveying the superstructure that elevated the Cyclone's sinuous track, while in the near distance, the train roared along its path from pants-wetting start to slack-faced finish.

Holding a ticket in his fist, Callum glanced over his shoulder one last time, as though he were leaving the men for good. Milton waved wistfully, while Roland and Mr. Wait watched him go in pensive silence. Bud, joking with P.O., alone appeared not to care.

Callum walked up the cut-back ramp. At the wooden docking station, he looked down at the ticket in his palm, moist with nervous sweat. He felt a chill in the night air and was thinking of turning back when the Cyclone hissed with compressed air and came to a sudden stop in front of him. A single rider got out with the nonchalance of a business commuter leaving a bus. Callum looked around, wishing for the companionship of a stranger, but no one else was in line. A young man with a tattooed forearm in a dirty T-shirt and Levis slung so low they hung off his hips took his ticket and directed him into the front car. He pulled down and locked a restraining bar over Callum's legs, and stepped over to a long lever that sent the train on its twisted course.

The maroon Naugahyde seat felt nice against his bare arm, and the bar that pressed down on his thighs gave him a feeling of security. He realized in a flash that the sumptuous padding was meant to prevent broken bones, and his mind turned to mayhem. His heartbeat quickened, and the train lurched forward with a clunk. With a hiss its locks fell free, and it slid slowly around a narrow bend into darkness.

The train hooked into a heavy chain that made a ratcheting clatter as it jerked the Cyclone up the steep slope. He thought about Bud's failure to ask his opinion, and the more he thought about it, the more a new emotion crowded out his fear. Bud had played him along. But the moment the stakes were real, he had dissolved their partnership.

He was riding the ridge of the Cyclone halfway up the incline, high in the air. He was risking the wrath of this creaky invention to let the men down below know that he was doing what they would not dare. It was his way of telling them that he was no longer *their* equal. He was telling them that he was mad; and he was telling them that from now on, they could go their way, he would go his.

A terrible silence came over the Cyclone, as though it were holding its breath. He could see the running lights of freighters in the Long Beach harbor and, far off, the gas flares of the Signal Hill oil fields and the amber glow of L.A. He sucked in a lung of air and squeezed the restraining bar. With his shoulders hunched and his head pushed out, he stared down a track that was too steep to matter. The train fell through space and he flew weightless into a void with a loud grunt from deep in his chest.

He saw the men for a fraction of a second, and he would have shot over their heads if the Cyclone had left its track. They were not watching him or even *for* him. Bud was still fooling around with P.O. The other men had turned their attention elsewhere. Another curve yanked the train off in the opposite direction, and by the time he had held his breath, it had ridden up a shallow ramp and, with brakes applied, stopped at the bay.

Callum sat stunned, with the feeling that he had missed the ride. He had done it. He had flown in the front car, alone on the train, from start to finish, and yet he claimed no victory. It wasn't enough to get through an experience, he thought. Anybody could hunker down under a restraining bar and hold on for dear life resolving at the end never to try again.

The skinny attendant came over. "Again?"

"I don't have another ticket."

He gave him a what-does-it-matter shrug. "This one's on me, kid," he said and stepped back.

The Cyclone started another run, and around that first curve the chain went *chink chink chink,* and his blood started to pound. At its apogee the Cyclone hung in the same zone of silence as before. Callum gripped the bar between his knees and felt his stomach stretch. He had assumed a survival, get-through-it-at-all-costs tuck position when he thought, *Why should I be afraid? The Cyclone is meant to be fun.*

He pulled his hands from the bar and flung his arms over his head. Realizing he was still alive, he screamed from the pit of his stomach. Even as the Cyclone was reaching its top speed, he waved his arms back and forth like a fan. And he kept them raised as the

Cyclone slammed around that first curve. With the rush of wind and roar of wheels he looked over his shoulder, and for an instant he caught sight of Bud staring up at him through eyes that glowed with fear.

"A waltz, Walter, please," Mrs. Hamel told Walter Shipke, who lumbered onto the polished gym floor and over to a portable record player that sat on a folding card table.

Girls sat in wooden chairs on one side of the gym with their patent-leather Mary Janes in a neat row, fussing with the ruffles of their party dresses. The boys sat along the opposite wall, rough-housing under Coach Shipke's watchful eye.

Not for the first time, Callum sized up Coach, who wore a green tweed sport coat sizes too small for his long-ago athletic frame. Coach Shipke was a moron, which even the kids recognized. The players on his teams only wanted to have fun. Fun meant playing. Callum had fun shagging hardballs with unerring skill in practice, but the minute Coach pressured the team to win at any cost, he muffed even the dribblers. Sometimes the whole team caved in to the coach's need to win, and the fun of playing baseball went out: what took its place then was watching the coach's spastic rage.

The coach showed what he thought of the dancing class part of his job by acting like an oaf. He bounced the needle on a 78-rpm of a foxtrot.

"Waltz, please, Walter," Mrs. Hamel told him. "Look for the word *Strauss*."

Callum counted, one-two-three, one-two-three. Across the way, her hair as black as her Mary Janes and her fluffy-ruffled white dress the prettiest in class, sat Serena. He wanted to ask her to dance, but so far he had balked, and now the class was nearly over. He didn't know which was worse, asking her or not asking her. Blood pounded in his ears either way.

Mrs. Hamel said with a dramatic pause, "Let's make this last dance a *boys'* choice."

The boys stampeded across the floor. The music played and the pumping and one-two-three-one-two-three began, with Mrs. Hamel moving through the couples with tips and instructions. Callum stayed on the folding chair. Over by the phonograph the coach began pounding a fungo bat on his palm. No one was allowed to sit out a dance. To Callum's horror Serena was still in her chair. She was stubbornly waiting for him to make his move.

Callum could not understand why a thing this painful could be something he wanted this bad.

The Coach thwacked the fungo and took one step in his direction. Callum slid off his chair as though he had been shoved. He was now amid the dancing couples. One kid burped and another farted and the girls giggled and Mrs. Hamel pretended she had not heard. The coach zigzagged through the dancers like a player on a fast break. Callum ducked behind a fat girl's crinolines. A second later he was standing on the girls' side of the gym, and what caught his eye was Cloud alone and picking at her party socks pretending she wasn't there. Before he knew it, he was bowing to her. Mrs. Hamel smiled; the coach put down his fungo. Cloud got to her feet, abashed by Callum's offer. The coach asked Serena to dance, jerking her arm like a pump handle. Cloud pushed Callum away to watch her feet, and in no time they were waltzing like Viennese.

Callum felt that Serena could not have been closer if she had been in his arms. In a sense, she *was* in his arms. He was not really dancing with his sister, stiff and spindly and counting in a whisper. He preferred dancing with Serena this way. He thought of something witty to tell her; in his mind he was as suave as Randolph Scott and felt as proud as any man could be with the girl of his dreams in his arms.

Up ahead Mr. Wait emerged from the grove like a wraith, with Bob at the end of a slack rope. Callum pedaled his bike up to him and said, "Good timing," and he looked in the direction Mr. Wait had come from. "How did you cross the highway?" he asked, bewildered.

With a quizzical look Mr. Wait replied, "We waited. How do you think?"

Anybody with eyes knew that the traffic on the highway was incessant and heavy and sped along without a care for what it went past. You could wait for a break for hours, even days. It was murder out there; road-killed rabbits and opossums and flattened dogs and cats said it all.

"At the overpass?" asked Callum.

"No, over there." Mr. Wait pointed through the grove.

Callum went on ahead knowing he wasn't going to get a straight answer. He paused long enough to observe one of Mrs. Rodriguez's workers setting out smudge pots in anticipation of the cold snap. The temperature dropped about this time of year as a harbinger of seasonal change. People from New England said they missed the seasons in California, but they weren't telling the truth. The cold snap *was* a season, cold enough to need sweaters and woolen blankets and pea soup with ham hocks.

Mrs. Rodriguez stepped out on her porch and didn't notice him at first. She was wearing a black pleated skirt decorated with small glass mirrors that shimmered in the sun. As she walked down the porch steps, loose strands of gray shone in her hair, as brilliant as her earrings and the delicate silver coin necklace against her skin. By the swing of her hips she told the world that she enjoyed the company of men. Bud said that for some women flirtation was a natural way of stirring the pot of life. He said that most men thought a flirt should end up in bed, but a flirt in the sheets wasn't a flirt. It was a seduction.

"What a nice surprise," Mrs. Rodriguez said when she noticed him.

A loud honking and Callum turned around. Bob was hee-hawing behind Mr. Wait, who looped his rope over the gazebo railing and waited while Mrs. Rodriguez walked out to greet him.

"We're neighbors, I believe," he told her graciously.

She looked him over with an agreeable grin. "I saw you at the Job's initiation. I meant to tell you then, except for the disruption I would have—your grove is lovely."

"That is music to my ears," Mr. Wait said, smiling. "I've admired yours, too, over the years," and he bowed to her quaintly. "I apologize for just barging in on you like this."

"I don't mind at all."

A tractor rolled out of the grove pulling a wagon rounded with fresh-picked oranges. Serena was sitting on the golden heap. Callum waved, glad to catch her eye, and she jumped off and smoothed her skirt. A bandanna bobbed up and down on her ponytail as she ran toward the gazebo.

"Serena, you know Callum," said her mother.

"Of course," she said.

Callum looked at her, then at his sweaty palms.

Mrs. Rodriguez looked from one to the other, learning little she did not already know. "And this is our neighbor, Mr. Wait."

He held out his hand and Serena curtsied.

"Your daughter sure gets around an orchard," he said.

"We're trying to pick what we can before the cold snap," Serena told him.

"It's early this year," Mr. Wait pointed out.

"I suppose you're picking your oranges, too?" Mrs. Rodriguez asked him.

"Myself, no, I only worry about keeping the trees warm."

The wind chime on the gazebo chirruped, and Bob breathed rhythmically. The silence grew in the space of a few seconds, and the gazebo seemed to shrink. Callum could smell the scent of soap on Serena's skin, and he looked at her elbow thinking he had never seen one lovelier.

"Well for God's sake, Callum," said Mr. Wait irritably. "Get on with what you came for!"

"What is it, Callum?" asked Mrs. Rodriguez.

"About selling land," Mr. Wait prompted him.

"It's no secret," she said. "I just didn't know that anybody cared. I'm afraid I have to. And you, are you selling, too?"

"They're going to run *me* off with their eminent domain," Mr. Wait told her.

"It gets to a point where it's inevitable," she said sadly.

"What do they plan to use your land for?" he asked.

She shrugged. "The new owners can do what they want with it—oranges or tracts or a highway. I'll have no say in their decisions."

Mr. Wait turned to Callum. "Don't you think you should tell Mrs. Rodriguez why you wanted to visit?"

"Your trees," Callum said, feeling less foolish than he thought he might. "I thought I'd like to buy some of them. I didn't know they were already sold."

"They aren't, strictly speaking," she said quickly.

"Would you sell some to me, then?"

She gave him a serious look. "I don't know. You'll have to tell me why you want them."

"It's a secret," he said.

"Whatever your secret is, there's no charity to be found here, Callum. I'd have to sell to you for the same price I am selling to the highest bidder, and even then I don't know if I would be doing the right thing. The last time the real estate man came by he agreed to pay me two hundred dollars an acre."

Zeros whirled in Callum's head as he figured the total. "I had no idea," he told her. But he did have an idea. No matter what price she quoted him, he had known before asking that her land, as it stood, was beyond his reach.

As they were walking home, Callum turned to Mr. Wait. "She's not a farmer anymore," he said. "She's what Bud wants to be."

"In some things."

"Dad calls her a sharp cookie."

"Did you want to buy her land for the reason I think?" Mr. Wait winked at him and the wink made him look silly.

Callum laughed. "Maybe so."

"My lips are sealed."

"When we were in the Tunnel of Love, you said guessing right should be our reward."

"And P.O. barged in about money."

"I think I'm on your side."

"*You* don't have a choice."

Callum was browsing Rankin's notions' department, considering whether his gift should be a scarf or perfume. The saleswoman had piled scarves high on the glass counter—silk, wool, cotton, and rayon in all colors and patterns. She had started off thinking he was cute, but after a dozen scarves, he was growing up fast in her eyes.

"It's hard to know which one," he explained his indecision to her.

"Maybe you should start by telling me who this is for, your mom?"

"A girl."

That perked her up. "A girlfriend, then," she said.

"Yes but not exactly. She's more a person. But you might call her a girlfriend."

"Well thank heavens that's settled." She looked with dismay at the mound of scarves on the countertop. "She's your age, I imagine. Something in an animal print might appeal to her."

She showed him one with a lion staring out of a bush with its mouth open. It wasn't exactly what he had in mind, but he was tiring of the hunt, and he told her to wrap it up. He waited as she slipped his money and the receipt into a shuttle, which she fed into a pneumatic tube. She wrapped the scarf in tissue and a Rankin's box and was tying a gift bow when the shuttle returned with his change. "She'll *love* it," she assured him, watching him leave with a sigh.

He walked his bike across the street and stopped to check out the knives and guns in the pawn shop. He loved to look in that window. Where else could he see brass knuckles, arrows with aluminum shafts, telescopes, and discarded stamp albums in one place? His eyes skipped over the items as something in the back of his brain sent a warning, and his eyes focused on the pillow. He felt relief. And with the Rankin's box under his arm, he burst triumphantly into the shop.

"That brooch in your window was stolen, mister," he told the man in back who was looking through a jeweler's loupe. He glanced up when Callum said, "I think I should probably tell the police about it, too."

"Oh, you think so?"

"It was stolen from my mother's jewelry box at home."

The man sat up straight. "That's a serious charge," he said. Even though he had never seen Callum before, he knew whose son he was by looking at him.

"It's a crime," Callum explained.

"Don't be so hasty," the man said. "Sometimes things aren't what they appear to be."

Callum thought the man would be glad that he had spotted a theft. Instead he was reasoning with him. "I better just tell the police," he said with finality.

"Your father will get mad at you if you do," the man said, reaching for subtlety.

"What does he have to do with . . . ?"

Callum dropped the Rankin's gift box as he ran out the door crying over the realization of how Edith's brooch had landed in the window. People passing by were concerned, and one woman asked him what was wrong. He wrenched himself from her grasp and swung onto his bicycle, horrified at how Bud had sold out their family for a dream. What made the revelation even more painful, beyond learning that his father was a thief, was that Callum now knew Bud had chosen the wrong dream.

Clods of dirt arced through the air at Lionel, who, with one arm and one leg raised, was on the roof next door creeping away at a speed that was unseemly for a praying-mantis wanna-be.

Cloud was throwing, and Blue was breaking up chunks of dirt to fit her hand. Even for a lefty, Cloud could throw. Her face was flushed with anger. "It's disgusting," she said, shaking her head. She exhorted Callum to join in. "You aren't going to help your own sister?" she asked, loud enough to be heard across the yard.

"I didn't say that," he told her.

"Lionel's a pervert," Blue informed him, and she pointed to the clothesline. Hanging by wooden pins was a week's worth of the girls' underpants, Blue's with the days of the week, Cloud's in seven feminine pastels. "We caught him . . . sniffing our panties."

Lionel had misjudged them. As an only child he could not have known how Blue counted the days by her panties and Cloud coordinated clothes by that day's color; he couldn't have known how girls the world over measured their lives in underpants.

"Get him, Callum!" Blue shouted as Lionel moved along the roof's spine.

"I got things to do," he told her.

"That's it, huh?" Cloud said, pursing her lips. "You never help," she shouted at him. "You never do *anything*."

With her lip curled Blue told him, "You're a pervert just like he is if you don't help. You and your disgusting toilet-paper tubes."

"You don't do anything!" Cloud repeated. "You never do. It's like you aren't even part of the family."

She pitched a clod that exploded on the roof just as Lionel raised his head. It caught him on the ear, and he started to bawl. At the sound of crying his mother ran out of the house with her arms in the air.

Cheval was smoking a cigarette at the kitchen table with Edith. She smoked like a man, dangling a cigarette in the corner of her mouth. The ash grew to an improbable length, and at the instant it fell, she stuck out her palm without missing, no matter what else she was doing.

Edith's face was flushed from laughing. Usually it mattered less what Cheval said to put her in a good mood than the words she used. Cheval, as a single woman without kids, often gave her a view of life she felt nostalgic for. She rarely followed her advice, yet she said she felt better hearing options she would never choose than not hearing them at all.

Callum waited to tell Edith about seeing the brooch in the window, but her gaiety made him mad. He leaned against the sink, struck by how women discussed men as if they shared a secret. He didn't know its exact nature, but he would have said that women pretended that men knew all the answers. In private they laughed themselves sick at what men did, and worse, they spoke of them as not entirely responsible.

"Can you tell me why he wears that little cap?" Cheval wanted to know, pretending to push a hat over her ears.

That set Edith off. "He watches Broderick Crawford on TV."

"But Edith, he guards wire."

Edith was nodding, her eyes watering. Though they had not said his name, Milton guarded spools of Anaconda copper wire, which wasn't funny.

"I'm amazed he didn't connect the factory to his radio," Edith said. "Poor Gladys."

Cheval plucked a tobacco speck off her lip. "Oh Lordy. Where do they get their ideas?"

Was it that the women knew that things never changed, that if you were poor, you stayed poor? They professed a belief in dreams, and yet they saw as humor what men saw as hope.

Callum went to his bedroom and sat on his bed looking out through the blinds. Joey Yaw was playing in his front yard with his

screwy dog Snowball. Snowball was as black as coal—the Yaw's one
outing with wit, Bud liked to say. Joey's father was a fighter pilot
and had nothing in common with the neighborhood. In his living
room a scale model of the jet he flew sat on the TV. Every evening
as he passed over the house on his final approach to El Toro, he
pressed a button in his cockpit, and the nose of the scale model lit
up to let his wife, Bunny, know it was time to put in the TV dinners.

Cheval whooped with laughter. Edith said, "He didn't, no, he
didn't, no . . ." and even Cloud screeched.

He lay on the bedspread wishing he could forget the pawn shop.
He got off the bed and walked back in the kitchen. The women
quieted down. As he headed for the door Edith asked him, "And
where do you think you're going?"

"Out," he replied.

"Not without a jacket. It's the cold snap."

The women studied him in silence as he put on his windbreaker.
Edith said, "Dinner in an hour, hear?"

He picked his bike off the drive and pedaled to the end of the
street. A minute later he was on the two-lane road that connected
Garden Grove with Orange. Fog was pouring through the trees. He
pressed the light generator against the front tire and snapped on a
pale beam. He watched the cars going in the opposite direction for
Bud driving home from work, but the fog was so thick he could not
tell one car from another.

He turned off Chapman and found himself in dog-pound lane. At
the sight of Mr. Furrel's truck parked in front, he pumped harder,
with the sound of wind in his ears. Out of breath he skidded onto
a dirt track at the end of the lane that led to Ball Road through a
quarter mile of orange grove. Tractors with wagons of fresh-picked
oranges bound for the storage barns used the dirt road, which was
now empty as a cemetery.

The fog drifted in around him and clotted in the trees.

He felt invisible. The dense air muffled the sounds on the highway and silenced the rattle of his bike. He walked deep into the
grove off the road past the trees. He paused by a smudge pot and
held up his hands to its flue, feeling its intense heat. In his mind's
eye he saw Edith's brooch. He heard Bud boast about the dream.

The vision made him angry, and he raised his foot and kicked over the burning smudge pot, which he straddled, watching kerosene pour from its reservoir and burst into flame.

He told himself they were only trees. He didn't think of himself as a murderer, but he could live with the crime of vegicide if he had to. He shivered as he pedaled out of the grove, not looking back for fear that the sight of death might haunt him.

The flashlight shone out the door. "Who's out there?" Mr. Wait shouted in the direction of Bob's corral. He walked across the yard and stumbled in the fog. "Who's out there?" he shouted, certain that he had heard the rattle of a hubcap he had thrown in the lot for intruders to trip over.

"It's me, Mr. Wait," Callum said in a small, shy voice.

"Where are you, sonny?" Mr. Wait asked.

"Over by Bob's corral."

Mr. Wait aimed the light in his face, knowing immediately that something was wrong. "How long have you been out here?"

Callum's teeth chattered. "A while, I guess," he replied.

Mr. Wait snapped off the light. "Come on inside with me," he told him.

"In your *house*?"

"That's what I said."

On the porch he told him to take off his shoes. A single step in the door explained why. Mr. Wait's house was a world of dreams no one would have imagined, with dark teak floors that glowed under a rich bees wax shine. The walls, made of yellowed stacks of newspapers visible on the outside, inside were lacquered a clear eggshell white, as smooth and creamy as Edith's japan boxes. Woodcuts in whites and hazy blues described seas and mountains. Clean straw mats covered the floors off the hallway, and Oriental vases and bowls decorated tables of burnished rosewood.

Callum thought he had entered a mansion. The precise order of Mr. Wait's things held a meaning that was as private as the house itself.

Mr. Wait pointed him to a room that was larger than the others, lit from above by a false ceiling of rice paper with no apparent seams. The room held an altar of sorts. Silver frames sat on three identical black tables. One held a stark black-and-white photo of a boy with short brown hair, dark eyes, and wide cheekbones. A girl resembled a China doll in a geisha dress. A woman's face smiled out of the middle frame.

On the wall behind the tables hung an ornamental screen. Naked, long-haired demons wielded heavy clubs over their heads herding Japanese toward a bloodred flaming bush. The screen evoked a sense of chaos and terror, as though the men with the clubs were devils over whom there was no control.

Mr. Wait stared at the screen. He sank to his knees and folded his legs under him and poured a cup of tea from a pot on a charcoal brazier. He bowed to the photographs. Callum took his eyes off the screen and sat down. There was so much he wanted to ask, and yet he did not dare. Mr. Wait handed him a cup. The tea tasted like ashes.

"What were you doing out there just now?" Mr. Wait asked him.

It took him an instant to realize he had been spoken to. "Waiting," he replied.

"I understand," he said and raised his eyes to the screen. "Do you like my Hell Scroll?"

No, he did not like it, and said so.

With a wooden match Mr. Wait lit a stick that he stuck in a vase as if it were a flower, and the scent of rose filled the room.

"It's not meant to please," Mr. Wait said.

"I don't know why you would want it," Callum said.

"We read the future in the past. Maybe that's why."

"You read a lot of newspapers, I know that."

"The photographs there and there"—he pointed to the tables—"are of my children. Elizabeth is now eighteen and Robert is two years younger. The woman in the center is Suki, my wife. They live in Japan." He sipped the tea like a bird at a feeder, and his face never changed expression. He cradled the cup in his palm. "We used to live near Tustin. Suki was born in Japan, but she came to America when she was a girl. I sent them back to Japan."

"Is that when you changed your name?" Callum asked.

"I was taken into the desert to a place called Manzanar. After that, I changed my name."

Callum's eyes wandered over the Hell Scroll.

Mr. Wait let out a sigh, as though he had said too much. "You and Bud are my family, too. . . ." he said.

"But what about them?" Callum meant the boy and girl and woman in the photographs.

"I'm waiting for them to come home."

"It's been a long time."

"Suki will get in touch."

Callum thought about what Mr. Wait's house was made of. "In the newspapers?" he asked.

"The personals, that's right. That's how we left it."

19

Bargain Basement

Callum waited with his hands in his pockets, scared that he had not thought his plan through. When thinking through anything, the beginning was easy, the end was easy, too, but the middle part, like now, was hard. He could not know if he had found a way with his equivalent of Milton's bugs.

"Yes, please?" the bank teller asked him.

Callum stepped up to the window and slid the plastic envelope with his passbook across the shelf. "Withdrawal, please," he told the man through the bars. "All of it."

The teller pursed his lips and looked over Callum's head. "You'll have to speak to our manager," he said, handing him back his bankbook. "Next in line please."

Across the thick carpet the manager sat on a platform at a rolltop desk. He had propped his wooden leg, which Edith said he had lost to gangrene in the Great War, on a wire wastebasket as if he were trying to throw it away. Waiting to be noticed, Callum looked at the leg with an inch or two showing between the top of his shoe and his pants. Oddly, the manager had put a Band-Aid over its pink skin.

Callum cleared his throat. "I want to withdraw it all," he said and stared at the manager, who looked up with a smile of recognition.

"Oh, Callum," he said, retrieving his leg from the wastebasket.

"Well, well. Did your mom give you permission to take your money out? It's your Christmas Club, you know." He checked the pages of the passbook.

"She doesn't know anything about it," Callum replied.

He smiled as though they shared a secret. "Tell the teller it's okay. What's it, Edith's birthday?"

"My dad's," Callum said, congratulating himself on his guile.

Outside the bank on the sidewalk, he breathed in the sweet smell of twenty-three greenbacks, fifty dollars in fives rolled in three ones. The wad warmed his pocket like a heater on the way to the library, where he had decided there was something he had been meaning to do.

At the card catalog he looked up a name but found nothing listed. Undaunted he went to a shelf with books bound in dull green covers that cataloged periodicals. Again he searched for the name, this time finding several listings. With a pencil from the librarian's desk, he wrote them down.

Callum used the library often and felt comfortable with its mechanics. It never failed him when he needed to know what no one else seemed to know; as he paged through the bound issues of *Life* in the stacks, he wondered why Bud had not thought of doing this same thing. It seemed natural and even an easy thing to do. But he guessed the library was too obvious for Bud, who respected books but associated libraries with doozies like Milton.

Reading cross-legged on the floor with his back against the stack, Callum discovered two important truths. One described Walt Disney as the child of a woman from Mojacca, Spain, named Consuela Suarez, who had been engaged to marry a local man. He got her pregnant before being killed in a war with Morocco, and a couple in America adopted the baby soon after it was born.

This version sounded full of romance and hooey, offering no hint of the specific truth that Callum sought.

Besides, what kind of a Spanish name was Walt?

Truth two described him as a descendant of the French d'Isignys, who had anglicized their name when they reached England after 1066. About six hundred years later, the d'Isignys—now called the Disneys—made the mistake of supporting the duke of Monmouth's aborted rebellion against King James II and fled to safety in Ireland, where they remained for the next two hundred years. In the 1830s they came to America.

Walt's grandfather was a dreamer who took his sons to California in the 1840s in search of gold. Along the way one of them decided to stop in Kansas and married a woman named Flora Call. Later, he moved to Kissimmee in Florida, where he farmed an orange grove. During the freeze of 1888, the trees died and he moved his family to Chicago, where Walt was born, the fourth of five children, on December 5, 1901.

Callum closed the *Life*, amazed at simple solutions. He wrote down the truth he had come for.

It was Walter Elias Disney—W.E.D.

Serena was shucking peas when he rode his bike up to her front porch. He wanted to tell her how much he had enjoyed their foxtrot together at dancing school, but he did not think she would understand. Besides, she seemed cool, even distant, and he credited her mood to loneliness. Cloud and Blue liked Serena, but being a Latina made her different, and different was hard for the girls. Callum had overheard Edith telling Bud that conformity meant everything to them at their age. They conformed to prejudices easily. It was a shame, she had told him. They were better than that.

"Are you sure?" Bud had asked her.

"They will be," she had replied.

"There was some awful fog last night," Callum told her now.

She glanced over her shoulder as if she was expecting her mother to come out. Wrapping her arms around herself, she said, "Yes, it was cold."

"Was there any damage in the grove?"

She looked in her lap. "Quite a bit," she told him in a soft, sad voice. "The cold snap killed some of 'em."

"Can I see what they look like dead?" he asked.

"If you want to," she said.

She took the colander of peas in the house. When she came out again, she pulled herself up on the tractor seat. Riding on the hitch behind her he smelled jasmine in her hair, and feeling intoxicated by her nearness, he lost track of where they were going until she stomped the brake and he was nearly wrenched off, catching himself by the seat rim. He looked up at her and back again in a slow double take. As bad as he thought it might be, he would not have imagined this.

"This was where we found the pot," she told him, bending down under the limbs of a tree. "Our worker found it this morning."

"You mean someone meant to do this?"

"Somebody tipped it over." She looked him in the eye. "On purpose." She climbed back up on the tractor. "It's kinda sad."

Driving back to the house, he saw a grove that looked like a fire had burned through it. The bark and the branches of the dead trees looked naked and cold. It wasn't that he did not want the trees to die. What a lighted pool of kerosene and a flue meant to the trees amazed him. He would not have imagined such frailty. Orchids, maybe. But not thick-limbed trees.

He hopped off the tractor in front of the house. When she joined him on the porch, he asked if her mother was home. She looked almost relieved as she went inside to get her. Mrs. Rodriguez came out of the house and wiped her hands on her apron. She looked at his bicycle and asked, "What brings you by, Callum?"

He had believed himself capable of lying, but now he wanted to run. "I'm sorry about your trees," he told her.

Mrs. Rodriguez looked tired. "Serena said you had something to tell me. Is that it?"

"The freeze, Mrs. Rodriguez. Does the cold snap change anything for you and Serena?"

"How do you mean?"

"The trees being dead."

"It may, Callum. I hope not, but it may."

Jimmy O'Doyle, the owner of O'Doyle's Donut Shop, refilled their mugs. Bud poured in sugar without measuring from the dispenser.

"Another glazed?" O'Doyle asked him, dusting white flour off his forearms. He was a big man, with heavy arms and shoulders from stirring the doughnut batter with a wooden paddle the size of a canoe's.

Bud sipped the coffee. "I'll explode if I do," he told O'Doyle.

"What about you, mister?" O'Doyle asked Almore Tucker, across from Bud.

"Sure," Tucker replied and wiped his stubble with the back of his hand. "Business makes me famished. It was a jelly."

Bud was reading a standard contract he had bought that morning. Every line was a blank. He unclipped a ballpoint and clicked it nervously. "So," he said by way of calling to order this most important meeting of his life.

"I spoke with Rose after you left," Tucker told him. Bud looked at him hopefully. "She budged again after you said you couldn't go more than eighteen hundred. That Rose is one tough cookie but she is understanding."

Bud leaned back. "Tucker, between you and me, was that séance with your wife real the other day?"

He looked offended. "Of course," he said. "You're a married man. You know how wives can be."

"How's that?" Bud asked.

"Pains in the ass." He sipped his coffee and his eyes brightened with a recollection. "When Rose was alive I looked like a baboon, I had such a red ass with her nagging," he said. "She was a whiner from the moment I said 'I do.' For ten years I thought whining was a deformity of her nasal passages. She could say 'Good morning' and it would sound like a mosquito was in the room." He glanced up at the ceiling. "Her goiter Oma was not a pretty sight. One day she died of it and a week later I found a book on séances in the junk. From that day on our marriage improved. It is now what I'd call blissful. Imagine, a little thing like that?" He reflected, tugging the hairs in his nose.

Bud stared at him. "A little thing like death?"

"Right."

"It's good you each have your own interests now," said Bud.

Tucker bobbed his head in total agreement. "Heaven and earth, heaven and earth."

"Tell me, Tucker. You seem like a man of the world. Did you ever sneak anything behind your wife's back?"

"You mean cheat?"

"Yeah."

Now his head bobbed so fast he looked like a feeding turkey.

"There was a gal once, before Oma dragged Rose down. Her name was Gustine. What a doozie." He paused dreamily, recalling her. "She was a horse jockey until she got kicked in her head and quit. She drove a tractor on a bean field near here. We got friendly, you know, a feel here, a feel there, which led to doing it in the Quonset hut. She'd tell me, 'Mount up!' when I had my pants down, and she'd lay back under the *Mo*'s fantail and I'd get aboard and she'd say, 'Treat me gentle, Almore, like I was a filly the first time in tack.' After awhile she'd get galloping, you know how it is. She'd head around the four-furlong pole and in the stretch she'd scream out so loud my ears rang, 'Go to the whip! Almore, honey, *gooo* to the whip!'"

Bud found the heart to tell him that this was not what he had meant. "Lies, I meant lies."

"Oh, no. I never had the occasion."

Bud raised his eyebrows and decided conversation with Tucker would never flow in straight lines. He concentrated on filling in the contract with the names of the gang. It might be his money, but it was their dream.

"How do I describe the parcel?" he asked Tucker.

"I went out and measured after you called." He showed Bud a scrap of paper on which he had written four distances from two telephone poles on Salt Road.

Bud put all that in the contract. "Here's the cash," he said, handing Tucker an envelope that he couldn't let go, as if it were glued to his hand. Tucker tugged on one end of it, and Bud held on to the other with a helpless grin. "My hand won't let me let it go," he complained.

"Your hand makes your business decisions?" Tucker said, leaning back.

Bud stared at the envelope, conscious of what letting go meant. This was the moment in his life he had waited for, the moment when he was about to become somebody. Yet he felt afraid, knowing that once he let go he could not look back. He had dreamed for the dream to become a reality with such fervor it had brought him all the way across the country. On that trip, with the kids screaming in the backseat, he remembered the thrill of seeing real Indians for the first time, and broad skies and blue rivers. He had sat on a stuffed bucking bronco in Flagstaff raising a cowboy hat in the air, and he had thought, This is life! But when he had reached California, the dream settled into a routine. He had traveled the width of America to transform himself and nothing had happened. Now he had reached the end of the road, where real hope loomed up in front of him like a billboard advertising a better life. Why shouldn't he do what he was about to do? He had paid for his dream in miles and years. What was an envelope thick with money compared to that?

It slid out of his hand and landed on the table with a thud.

"That's better," said Tucker, scooping it up.

They shook hands over the coffee cups and signed the contract. "Glad to do business with you," Tucker said.

"I hope you're right," Bud said.

He looked surprised. "With kiwifruits, what could go wrong?"

"We're not Down Under now," Bud said.

O'Doyle delivered Tucker's jelly doughnut on a paper plate. He looked over Bud's shoulder, reading the contract.

"You mind putting your John Hancock on here?" Bud asked him. "We'll make you the witness to this transaction."

"Sure, Bud," Jimmy said, wiping his hands on his apron. "What's the deal?"

Bud fixed Tucker with a stare. "I just bought the blocking acre to Walt Disney's new fun zone. In other words, Jimmy, the deal is, I'm going to be rich."

Tucker looked at the ceiling. "Jesus," he said with a nervous twitter. "What's Rose going to say?"

"What now?" Milton asked, looking around with the gaze of an explorer upon first spying a new land.

"Nothin'," Bud replied, in a better mood than he sounded.

"It looks friggin' great to me," said P.O.

"Beans?" asked Roland, stepping daintily over an irrigation furrow running with clear water.

"Use your imagination," Bud said. "Try to picture whirligigs and this and that all in bright colors and the face of Mickey Mouse on the telephone poles."

Milton squinted his eyes. "I can't," he said.

The men continued circumambulating their new domain, and

though their banter sounded cranky, they were proud of themselves, remembering how they had nurtured the original germ of an idea to this final fruition. They showed their pride by discussing vastness.

"Ain't it grand?" Bud rocked back on his heels and looked as proprietary of his acreage as a shopkeeper with clean windows.

"Yes indeedy, grand as a ponderosa," P.O. agreed, hands on his hips.

"It needs trees," Mr. Wait said.

"Trees smees," Bud told him. "Pretty soon mice and ducks and fairy princesses will run all over this place."

"I can anticipate one problem." P.O. looked from Salt Road to the access path that ran beside an irrigation dike.

"Nobody asked you to," Bud told him, determined not to let his partners ruin this moment.

"Right of access."

"Tucker told me Rose gave us permission to cut through her property any time we wanted to."

Milton raised his hand.

"Yes, Milton," Bud said.

"I asked you a moment ago. What now? I mean, do we do anything or just wait or what?"

"Like I said, we do nothin'," Bud told him.

For a whole moment, they listened to the wind blowing off the Pacific.

"For how long?" Milton asked.

"Milt, the essence of waiting is not knowing how long."

"But how will we *know*?"

"If nobody contacts us, or if Walt announces the opening of a fun zone in Pomona or Needles or Pismo Beach, we guessed wrong. Okay? We'll know when we know."

"He's looking for assurances," said Roland.

"I understand that. I'd like some, too. This is the tough part, the waiting. It separates the sheep from the wool. This is where the nerves of steel come in. It's testing time."

"What are we talking, a week, a month, a year?" Milton asked, still wanting to know.

"Days. But I could be wrong. Days, because that fellow from

Palo Alto, Buzz Whoever, seemed upset that we knew something, and that must mean he's closing in."

"While we're waiting, we might take care of these bean plants," said Mr. Wait, bending over a dead stalk.

"We're not in the agribusiness," P.O. said rather offhandedly. "I don't see how it matters one way or the other what happens to a field of beans."

"It does to me," said Mr. Wait.

"Be our guest," Bud told him and he sat down in the dirt. "If you gentlemen feel so inclined we might discuss a real issue." They all looked at him. Their concerns were not serious until now, but if Bud mentioned one, it had to be real. "We've got a decision to make," he told them.

They sat in a semicircle facing him.

"Decision like what?" asked Milton.

"Milt, am I going to have to teach you how to suck an egg here?"

"What does that mean?" Milton asked. When the other men smiled at him, he said, "I've always wanted to know what that means."

"Sucking an egg is something that even a dog knows how to do," said P.O. "In other words, you don't need brains to suck an egg."

"I never sucked an egg," said Roland.

"It'd be like eating snot," said Milton.

"Hold it!" Bud shouted. "Can we get back to where we were?" He lost the thought. "Where were we?"

"A decision," P.O. reminded him.

"Yes, thank you, P.O. The decision is, what price should we sell our land to Walt for?"

"Shouldn't we wait until he gets in touch?" Milton asked, echoing what he thought Bud had just said.

"Negative nelly, Milt. If we wait, he might catch us off guard. It's always better to be prepared."

"Millionaire has a ring," Milton said, smacking his lips.

"Are we agreed that is our goal?"

They all thought about that.

"Yes, a million sounds fine," Roland said as if he dealt in those figures every day.

"Okay by me," said P.O. And he stood up and danced a jig on a bean plant.

"Mr. Wait?" Bud asked.

"I'll give my share to Callum."

Bud frowned at him. "Sure, whatever you want." He turned to the others. "So we hold out for a million?"

"Puttin' on the Ritz," P.O. shouted, loud enough to frighten a bird flying overhead into changing direction.

20

A Human Dream

Mr. Wait placed the heavy cast-iron pot on the grate with a sigh. He squatted on the floor by the lacquered table and raised a handleless cup to Callum. With a polite bow he uttered a few words of Japanese and drank a sip of tea that hardly moistened his lips.

"Is there anything," Callum asked him, "between a dream being a dream and not being a dream?"

"You are still thinking about that? It's a good question. I could tell you the answer I have found, but it wouldn't mean a thing to you, sonny."

"But what if *Bud's* dream comes true for *me*?"

"I can't answer that either."

"But there is a difference."

"And what would that be?"

"The end of one dream and the beginning of another."

Mr. Wait looked up at the Hell Scroll with its naked demons. His dark eyes were as hard to read as Gladys's behind her shades. Callum did not know why, but the private meaning of the Hell Scroll dawned on him at that moment. The painting was the story of Mr. Wait's life for anyone with enough sense to see. The Hell

Scroll had frightened him at first, but he had not bothered to look beneath the scab of paint for meaning until now.

Once he knew how to look, he could understand why money meant nothing to Mr. Wait and why such things as plants and trees and animals like Bob meant the world to him. Mr. Wait had traveled beyond things. A fire as bright as the bush in the Hell Scroll had consumed his things years ago and far away. Mr. Wait was the one person of all the people he knew who could advise him without letting money interfere, but first he had to record the truth.

"Bud told me that your newspapers represented a lot of something," he said, still looking at the Hell Scroll.

"They get me through the day," he said.

"And that's it, nothing more?"

Mr. Wait looked sharply at him as if he had crossed a line of privacy that no one had ever been allowed to before.

"How can Suki get in touch with you, Mr. Wait?" Callum asked him.

"Through the newspapers, sonny," he said with a burst of anger. "That's what they are for, didn't I tell you?"

"She can't know you changed your name." He thought Mr. Wait would hear only what he wanted to. But he was wrong.

"You read the Hell Scroll good for a youngster," he told him. "*I* call it the Hell Scroll. Do you know what the artist who painted it calls it?"

"I have an idea."

"What?" And he looked Callum straight in the eye.

"Atom bomb?"

"Close enough." And Mr. Wait actually shuddered.

Callum's thoughts unaccountably turned to Bud at that moment. He had tried so hard to hate him, he had forgotten how much he loved him for all that he was and all that he could never be. Bud was not perfect as a father. More than that, he had committed a crime. But Callum had committed one, too, and he did not feel less lovable.

"You could read every paper on earth until the end of time and Suki would not get in touch, Mr. Wait," telling him what must have been obvious.

A tear dropped from his eye onto his hand. "I made them go back," he said.

"But what happened to them is not your fault."

"You and your father talk all the time about dreams," he said, so sadly that Callum wished he would stop. "You say you know dreams, and I guess you do. My dream is different. That's why I give Bud a hard time. He is right when he says that I don't have my heart in his dream. That's because my own dream is older. My dream is to learn what happened to Suki and my children."

"But you already do know."

He held up his finger. "No! I don't! No! I may never know. That is better than *knowing*."

Mr. Wait lived in a terrible waking dream. "If I did a bad thing to make Bud's dream come true, is that bad, Mr. Wait?"

He put his arm around Callum, hugging him in a way Callum had only seen him hug Bob. "Do what you think you can live with," he told him. "That's the best you can do. You are old enough. You know right from wrong. There's a Latin phrase you should learn— *Quid ad aeternum*. It means 'What is it in the light of eternity?' Understand, sonny?"

"I think so, sir."

Milton entered Rankin's like a scion and stood with his hands on his hips and his lips pursed peering over the cosmetics kiosks. With his bearings set he marched toward the up escalator past goggle-eyed cosmeticians. He took the moving stairs two at a time.

That the department store was all but empty had less to do with the time of day or the season of year than with people's pocketbooks. Normal people visited the store now and then to view what they could not afford, like minks and chinchillas and vicuñas. Visits to Rankin's were like wandering through a rich man's house, uninvited. The store's four floors were laid wall-to-wall with spongy carpeting. Shoes from Switzerland sat on baize tables, and designer dresses from Paris and New York hung on racks that seemed to go on forever. It was a foregone conclusion that Rankin's did not have a toy department or for that matter sports or hardware departments even in the basement. It had a lunch room with smoked mirrors where the air was suffused with the scent of lilac and the sandwiches contained avocados, tomatoes, and cucumbers sliced thin enough to see through.

A salesgirl on the fourth floor sat at an ormolu writing table, her long legs crossed, doing her nails with an emery board. She wore a red dress that split across her knee and exposed a length of thigh. She kicked her leg up and down absently, her slip-on shoe off her heel. Her blond hair was set in a permanent wave, and she had painted her face with rouge and powder, and her eyes with mascara. She smiled as though she were glad for the company, and she asked Milton how she could help.

"Furs," he told her, looking around to be sure he was where he wanted to be.

Milton had once said that he had trouble staying awake in department stores. Something in the air, he claimed, put him to sleep faster than a lullaby. While Gladys would be trying on this or that in the changing room and he would be cushioned in the husbands' waiting chair, he would doze off just like that, and later he would say that he wasn't even tired. Milton said snooty people shopped at Rankin's. He even said he would like to blow the store to kingdom come for what it represented. But now he was walking around saying "Furs!" as though he owned the place, proving what a difference a day could make.

"I'd like to buy my wife something nice," he told the saleswoman.

"In?"

He looked suddenly fatigued. "I don't know," he replied.

"Rabbit, otter, raccoon . . . something pricier?"

"A stole."

She pointed a pretty fingernail. "Why don't you take that chair over there, sir, and I'll show you a few items." She disappeared into a fur vault that argued for the high value of the goods being sold. Milton gave no sign of intimidation.

This shopping spree was only the latest in a series. P.O. had bought a new Buick on time payments that he couldn't afford, and Roland was tearing out the interior of his store in a remodeling that was way over his head. He was even talking about a cruise to the Holy Land. Mr. Wait was staying in bounds, but even he had new subscriptions to a couple of out-of-town newspapers. Bud had bought a new water softener that the girls said they needed for their hair. He was talking in terms of a brand-new Nash Rambler for himself.

The men were buying like they were rich, but nothing had changed.

P.O. had asked the bank manager with the wooden leg to float him a thousand-dollar loan because he was "about to become a millionaire." The manager had not lost his leg to gangrene in the Great War for being a fool. That, and the bank's own habits, were all that stood between the men and a binge.

The saleswoman cleared her throat. Milton was asleep in the chair, and she nudged him gently. He sat upright, and she twirled in a dark fur stole with a clasp of a dead fox head biting itself on the ass. Milton did not need to be told how women loved furs. They would wear anything furry, even a fox biting itself on the ass.

"No," he opined thickly. "I think white'd be better."

"Rabbit?"

"Maybe rabbit."

The woman smiled, not at all minding. She returned to the vault promising to be right out. A family went past on the aisle. They moved like spectators at a tragedy, afraid of being separated from each other. They said nothing as they ogled the furs with a shyness that reminded Milton of his former self. They shuffled in the direction of the lingerie department as though, if they stopped moving for an instant, an employee might ask them that most terrifying of department store questions, May I help you?

The saleswoman burst into the room, this time hugging a bright white stole that got Milton's attention. She pirouetted before the ottoman. The stole moved in a manner that made Milton stare. A hundred severed rabbits' feet were stitched in rows on the stole.

"Sold!" he said like a man at an auction.

"Let me get this straight," Mrs. Rodriguez said to Callum. "You mean you want the *dead* trees?"

"Fifty dollars' worth," Callum replied, all seriousness.

When she shook her head, he did not know what she meant, and he dug into his pocket for the bankroll. She held out her hand to stop him. "I believe you," she said and turned to Mr. Wait. "Have you discussed this with him?"

"It's news to me," he said. "But I think I know what he's driving at."

"Then maybe you can tell me."

"He's grown-up enough to ask to buy some of your trees, so he's grown-up enough to tell you himself."

Callum looked up at the sky deciding how much he should tell her. He knew he could trust Mrs. Rodriguez with a secret, but the information was worth millions by his count, and as he already knew, money did strange things to grown-ups. He wrestled with the choice as the wind rustled in the trees.

"I have something to prove," he replied, avoiding the question as artfully as he knew how. "That's why I want the trees."

"That may be a reason. It's not *the* reason, Callum," she told him.

Then, all in a rush, he explained. "Mr. Constantinople, the real estate man, is working on behalf of Walt Disney." And he waited for her reaction.

She thought about what he said. "Mr. Wait, what do you know about this?"

He was looking at Callum. "Mr. Constantinople also works for the State of California."

Callum looked surprised. "Did *he* tell you that?"

"Yes. Remember when we went to his office? He got back to me, finally. He represents the state highway commission."

Mrs. Rodriguez clasped her hands thoughtfully. "I told you the price he is willing to pay me for an acre of my land, Callum. You told me it was more than you can afford."

"What did Mr. Constantinople say your land was going to be used for?" asked Mr. Wait.

"Citrus," she replied with a doubtful shake of her head. "But like I told you, it doesn't matter."

"The *dead* trees," Callum repeated. "I want dead trees." When she did not say no, he held out the bills.

"You don't understand," she told him.

"It's all I've got."

"No it's not," said Mr. Wait in a moment of utter clarity. "You may not realize it, sonny, but you hold the key to what may be a fortune."

Mrs. Rodriguez looked confused, but she was interested.

"Mr. Constantinople is offering you two hundred dollars an acre," Mr. Wait told her. "It's not a fair price."

"It's the price I was offered," she said, suddenly self-conscious talking about her business with a boy and an old man she hardly knew. "And since I have to sell, the price I am offered is the price I have to accept."

"But Mr. Constantinople is cheating you, Mrs. Rodriguez," Callum told her. "Your land is worth more."

"It's worth what he is willing to pay."

Mr. Wait held up his hand, and they waited for him to speak, knowing what he said would be wise. "Callum is doing you a favor, Mrs. Rodriguez," he said. "He has reason to believe that Mr. Constantinople is representing Walt Disney. Walt Disney does not want to pay more than he needs to. That's being smart. He hired Mr. Constantinople to negotiate the sale of the land on his behalf. I'd estimate its worth, under these circumstances, as at least four thousand dollars an acre."

"*Thousand?*"

"That's right."

"And he's offering me two hundred?" She looked away. "What do you think I should do?"

"Demand the higher price. If he walks away, Callum was wrong. You can get two hundred an acre from another buyer. And you haven't lost a thing. If he *doesn't* walk away, Callum was right. You become a millionaire many times over instead of a farmer who sold out and had to go to work in a factory to make ends meet."

"In other words Callum may be giving me three thousand eight hundred dollars for every acre I own?"

"No, not giving you," said Mr. Wait. He looked at Callum. "I didn't hear him say that he was giving his information away. He is *trading* in return for what he wants. It is a shrewd deal. You should accept it."

"And he wants dead trees?"

"For fifty dollars."

"In that case the trees are yours," she said, and she shook his hand with a firm grip.

Mrs. Hermione Zion took pride in the sculpted spectacles she wore like a string of pearls around her neck. With rhinestones the colors of the rainbow and frets and filigrees that swooped and soared where the frame met the earpiece, the glasses looked like a piece of thoroughly modern art.

"This is quite an unexpected surprise," she said, getting up from her office chair.

As manager of the Citrus Escrow and Title Company, she rarely attended to clients herself. But Mary Rodriguez, as the longest continuous landholder in the county and the owner of one of its most valuable tracts, was a notable exception. She was destined to become a millionairess some day, and Mrs. Zion respected her past, present, and future for that reason alone.

"I want to make the sale official," Mrs. Rodriguez said after explaining what she wanted from Mrs. Zion. "I don't want to make a fuss."

Mrs. Zion sat down. "May I see the surveyor's report?"

Mrs. Rodriguez scraped a chair up to the desk and folded her hands in her lap. "I don't have a report but I can show you on the wall map."

She discouraged her with a look. "I would advise you to get a surveyor's report."

"Yes, I heard what you said," she said, getting off the chair. She indicated a spot on the map with her finger.

"The bank will need—" said Mrs. Zion.

"We'll have *no* need for banks."

Mrs. Zion studied Mrs. Rodriguez. "So you want to do this your way."

"With your help, yes."

"Why not simply shake hands?"

Mrs. Rodriguez pressed her lips together and sighed. "Now you are being rude," she said. "I want the sale to be legal and official so that the buyer can do exactly what he wants with his land no matter what people try to force him to do. It's to be *his* land."

Mrs. Zion shook her head, troubled by Mrs. Rodriguez's approach to such a serious transaction. But she knew she couldn't change her mind, and pulled out a cabinet drawer beside her desk for a document the size of a nation's flag, with borders printed a dark blue with cross-hatching and a shank of red ribbon and a golden seal. She swept her desk clear and filled in the certificate. "You'll have to get it surveyed eventually," she said. "But for now a general description will do. This isn't the change of deeds," she said, straining for the momentous. "It's the march of history."

"It's a quarter acre," she was told.

"Oh," she replied, fingering her glasses nervously.

"For fifty dollars," Mrs. Rodriguez said and asked Callum, standing beside her, to surrender his money.

Mrs. Zion looked at Callum as though she were recalling an ancient memory. She thought she understood now what was happening, and her voice softened. "I always wanted a real tree house, too," she confided in him. "I wanted one with a rope ladder I could pull up, to be all by myself. I used to imagine how I'd fix it up with curtains. It'd be all mine. I wanted that tree house so bad, I wouldn't mind having it even at my age." She turned the document around for them to sign, and with a device that looked official, she embossed the paper with the seal of the State of California.

"Congratulations, young man," she said, reaching across the desk to shake his hand. "The world can now call you esquire."

"It's yours," Mrs. Rodriguez told him. "You'll have to keep it up. It'll give you a sense of something."

"What's that?" Callum asked, interested to know what change ownership would bring.

"Responsibility."

21

The Wild
Blue Yonder

Alone with his dead trees, Callum thought he heard them moan. He imagined the spidery branches reaching out to strangle him. He had come to the grove to discover the feeling of ownership. But now all he wanted to do was leave the dead in peace. He was turning to go when he saw two men walking in his direction, one of them short, the other one tall. The short one stepped gingerly over the irrigation furrows, and when he came closer, Callum recognized his three-button suit and the small pale hands hanging from his jacket sleeves.

"Morning," Callum said.

"Nice to see you again, son," said Ricky, searching for a level patch between furrows on which to stand.

"Yes, sir."

"Mrs. Rodriguez said we'd find you here," he said and looked at the trees. "So this is yours now, all signed, sealed, and delivered?" When Callum made no attempt to answer, he said, "Like I said, Mrs. Rodriguez told us. A lovely woman, wouldn't you agree?"

"Yes, sir." He was cautious of Mr. Constantinople. To tell the truth, he was afraid of his lies and how he would have cheated Mrs. Rodriguez. He watched his every move and listened to each word he spoke like someone who was trying to suss out a magician's trick.

"We've spent the morning with her, you know. We closed the sale of her land."

Callum clenched his fists in triumph.

Mr. Constantinople looked at the tall man with him. "She sold all one hundred twenty acres, less your land, Callum."

"She signed the contract?" Callum asked.

"Signed and blotted." He patted his coat pocket. "You should be happy."

"Yes, sir," Callum said. "I am."

"Mrs. Rodriguez is not the kind of person to give anything away."

Callum observed the man who had walked up with Mr. Constantinople. His graying hair was cut in a flattop with the sides trimmed close. He was around Bud's age, but he kept himself in shape. He wore city clothes, but he looked like he was used to jeans or khakis. His suntanned face looked strong and honest, and his bright blue eyes surveyed Callum without giving away much of what he was thinking.

"I'm not telling you anything new, am I, if I tell you that Mrs. Rodriguez's acreage has a hole in it," the man spoke for the first time.

"No, sir," Callum replied.

"I'm not telling you anything new either if I tell you that as the new owners of Mrs. Rodriguez's property we've got you surrounded."

"No, sir."

"We'd like to fill in that hole."

"Yes, sir."

"I think I know why you bought the hole."

"Yes, sir."

"What would you say if I offered you what we just agreed to pay Mrs. Rodriguez?"

"Or in that neighborhood," said Mr. Constantinople.

Callum felt afraid all of a sudden. He understood the issues and he knew he had a choice. He decided now was the time to test his luck. "Money isn't what I want, if that's what you think," he told them.

"Yes?" the tall man asked anxiously.

"I'd like to know who you are."

"I'm Buzz Price, from W.E.D. Enterprises," he replied levelly. "W.E.D. is a group of investors who intend to buy your land. We did not like one bit that Mrs. Rodriguez sold a small parcel to you at the last moment. Integrity means everything with land. It means control and she handed control over to you."

"You shouldn't have lied to her," Callum said.

"Oh?" Buzz Price asked, his expression changed suddenly.

"You said you were going to keep the land for citrus."

"Maybe we are." He shrugged. "I am dealing with you right now, not Mrs. Rodriguez. I know why *you* bought the land."

"Why did you lie to her?" he persisted.

"To stop people from doing what you are doing, son," Mr. Price said.

Callum pointed his finger at him. "You're from the Stanford Research Institute. You hired Mr. Constantinople to buy this land."

"You did your homework." He looked worried now.

"Why was the Stanford Research Institute needed to find land that you don't plan to change? It's all over the place, land. Cheap land, too."

Abruptly Mr. Price said to Mr. Constantinople, "Are you ready to leave?" And he walked past Callum, telling him, "My offer stands, son. Mr. Constantinople knows where to find me."

Blue and Cloud were teaching Scooter to shake hands on their bedroom floor, listening to Patti Page ask the price of a doggy in the window. Callum sat cross-legged on Blue's bed watching Bud at the barbecue through the window. He had come in the girls' bedroom looking for company, but as usual they looked through him as though he wasn't there.

He was remembering back when the dream was a game, before anyone mentioned millionaires. It had seemed easy then and uncomplicated. Nobody had secrets and nobody had told lies. Now it was a little like he was learning life to be, and he was having trouble keeping his eye on what counted.

Edith appeared in the door. "You have a visitor," she told him. She never said that before; she never announced their friends. Her quiet statement galvanized Blue and Cloud. "I said *Callum* has a visitor," she told them sternly, blocking the door with her body.

Callum walked down the hall half expecting to see a tree ghost. Nobody and nothing, neither animal nor vegetable, greeted him in the living room. He looked out the picture window. His visitor was waiting for him outside.

Serena was wearing a white dress and a white sweater. Her dark eyes made him uneasy, they seemed so serious. "Can I talk to you, Callum?" she asked when he came out on the front porch under the light. She sounded sad.

Well, of course she could talk to him, but what was there to talk *about*? "Maybe we should go down the street," he told her, looking back at Cloud and Blue pressing their faces against the window.

He had never walked a long distance alone with a girl. He said nothing until the end of the street, where he stopped. She looked at him, and in a quiet voice she asked, "Why did you kill them?"

Callum did not hear her question in his relief that she had spoken.

"Why did you kill the trees?" she asked again.

She was asking as if the question mystified her. "So they'd be dead," he replied.

"I told my mother," she said, staring at her hands. "Oh, don't worry. She doesn't believe me. She thinks I am imagining things."

"Maybe you are."

She squinted at him. "I saw you, Callum."

"I couldn't see my hand in front of my face that night."

She crossed her arms over her chest. "I went back the next morning. You left bike tracks in the dirt, and your sneaker tracks, too. I covered them over. I hid the smudge pot."

"Why?"

"Because my mother would have called the police. I knew it was you for certain when you asked to see the dead trees. I saw your face. I wasn't imagining."

"Why don't you tell my father and mother, then?"

"Because . . . it wouldn't change anything."

He could not figure out why she had told him. "What are you going to do about it?" he asked, expecting the worst.

"No, not me, Callum. What are *you* going to do?"

"I haven't thought."

She said, "You should try."

He was wandering around by the town park, that was all, wandering, when a car braked and made a quick U-turn. It was a cream-colored convertible with whitewalls and a slick Simonize job, the kind of car a movie star might own, with initials painted in gold on the door.

"Wanna ride?" asked a man from under a snap-brim hat.

It was Mr. Constantinople, hardly recognizable in dark glasses and a sport shirt with short sleeves. As Callum settled in the exotic leather upholstery and perched his arm on the window ledge thinking how it didn't take but minutes to get accustomed to things out of reach, Mr. Constantinople shifted through the gears. He drove the car with surprising skill for someone who looked as he did. A while later, he turned the car on to a gravel road where a housing tract was under construction. He headed toward a single tree that bulldozers had left alive and standing, and stopped in its small circle of shade.

"This is the future," he said with a sweep of his arm.

Callum saw the foundations of houses, utility poles, drainage conduits, newly laid concrete drives, and the skeletal frames of a couple of new tract houses, and, beyond, the denuded land that graders and bulldozers were sculpting to an architect's design.

"I wanted you to see it in its raw state," Mr. Constantinople told him. "Pretty soon the whole county is going to look like this. It's going to be *great*! Do you know we live in the fastest growing county in America? There's just no end in sight."

Callum looked at the sentinel orange tree. He was used to seeing trees. When they were no longer there, they were noticeable. This one stood out like an exhibit in a museum.

"You're a clever young man," Mr. Constantinople told him. "You know what progress is?"

"It's new."

"It's *change*. Until a few hundred years ago, people just went along doing what they had always done. What fun was that, I ask, year after year?"

"Maybe it depended on who they were doing it with," Callum said.

"Just my point. With progress you don't need other people. Progress keeps you busy. You don't need anybody."

"I don't see what's so good about that," Callum said.

"Money. Change generates money."

"But what about people?"

"They keep up or they get left behind."

"What's the money for, then?"

"To buy cars like this one." Mr. Constantinople patted a medallion on the dashboard that bore the trademark of Jaguar.

"But you aren't a race-car driver."

"I can *dream* I am." He rubbed the cherry steering wheel.

Callum felt sorry for him. "You don't need money to dream, Mr. Constantinople."

"No, of course not," he said, and he slipped the sleek car into gear.

They drove to an intersection built up with shops near Anaheim. Mr. Constantinople swerved into a drive-in hamburger stand and chose a slot. A moment later a young woman in a short skirt and a tiny apron with a ruffled edge skated up for their order and, admiring her reflection in the car's paint job, skated off.

"You know what's going on, don't you, son?" asked Mr. Constantinople.

"Yes, sir."

"You know what W.E.D. Enterprises is."

"Walter Elias Disney."

"Thatta boy," he said with genuine enthusiasm. "Where did you find that out?"

"My father, and at the library. I read a story about Mr. Disney's life."

"Har har har," he laughed. "And you haven't told the others, your father?"

"No, sir. They have not asked."

"Good. Good. Too many cooks, if you get my meaning. Was it your idea all along?"

"My father thinks Mr. Disney wants to buy a bean field on Salt Road."

"What are you going to do, son?"

"I don't know." And it was true.

The waitress returned with a tray she hooked to the door. Mr. Constantinople handed Callum his malted milk and stirred his black cow with a long spoon.

"Mr. Price is a vice president of W.E.D. Enterprises," he told Callum.

"I thought he worked for SRI."

"He did but he doesn't anymore. He has authorized me to offer you a bit more money for your land . . . if you are in the market to sell."

Callum sucked on the straw. "I am," he said, watching a waitress primp in the luster of the car's hood.

"He told me to offer you six thousand two hundred. It's a sweet deal."

Callum finished the malt with a gurgle. "Yes it is," he said.

"Well . . . ?"

Callum handed him the empty cup. "I'll have to see."

22

That Kinda Day

Bud was behaving as though something that he could not describe was owed to him. In those moments when he said anything anymore, he said he felt cheated. "Why do things have to work out this way?" he complained to Edith.

"You'll get over it," she told him.

"You don't understand, do you?"

"I guess I don't."

The real risk of taking risks, Callum told himself, was thinking you were owed the reward of success. He had tried to understand Bud's anger in this light. Walt Disney had not called him up to offer him millions for his bean field, and he now felt that the shooting star had passed him by. Callum wondered who owed Bud and why he should feel cheated? The mechanism was complicated but not *that* complicated. Failure was as difficult to be around as a person who was dying. Instead of setting an example, Bud was showing his friends a vision of their future in a coffin.

They were sitting in lawn chairs facing the empty parakeet cage in Milton's backyard. A few parakeets that had not returned to Mexico flitted in the branches. When Milton opened the *Santa Ana Register,* out of habit the budgies lighted on the overhead branch and pooped on the paper. Milton read doggedly through the hail.

"I got rid of the Vi-Bee-Beam," Roland told them.

Bud leaned forward. "No!" he said, putting little into it.

"Yeah. I put Buster and his dog back in the window."

"I thought the Vi-Bee-Beam was the future," P.O. remarked and propped his boots on the cage.

"I did, too," Roland said sadly. "But I discovered that the future just isn't what it used to be."

Gladys was sitting cross-legged on the ground in the shade. She was doing her yoga. Her hair was arranged in a knot on her head and her glasses were opaque as ever. She tucked her thumbs under her forefingers Buddha-like and rang a tiny brass dinner bell, which she then put down on a salad plate.

"Don't stop on our account," Bud told her.

Looking at Bud she said, "Milt told me your scheme didn't work out the way you thought it would." She didn't add that she was sorry or that life went on, any old bromide to ease the pain. She didn't say that she respected them for trying. Nothing of that nature. She was gloating in the presence of failure as vengeful people often do.

"You heard right," Bud said in a voice as flat as a table.

She breathed in, then exhaled with a hiss. "I'm not surprised," she said.

"Nothing succeeds like failure, huh, Gladys? The whole world loves a failure."

"Well, just look at it this way, Bud. You can't fall off the floor."

Callum bent down to look through her sunglasses. It was hard to read her meaning. In went a full lung of air and out again. She tinkled the brass bell for the second time.

"You can't fly like an eagle on the wings of a wren," she said and placed the bell on the salad plate.

"You sound like a damned Hallmark greeting card," Bud told her.

She tinkled the brass dinner bell again to annoy him and got up to go inside.

"What're you trying to say, Gladys?" Bud asked her, spoiling for a fight.

"Grow up," she replied.

"Is that something you say as part of your yoga?"

She had her hands on her hips and was looking at them all in a line. "Children believe that dreams come true. When they don't, they sulk. You believed your dream would come true. Maybe you still think it will. You sure can sulk. You aren't children anymore, fellas. You have children you are supposed to set an example for. My admonition to you is to grow up. Take your dreams like men."

"Is that all?"

"For now, yes."

"What is so great about being a grown-up?" Bud asked her.

"I wouldn't know," she replied. "I haven't seen one lately."

Bud's face paled as he watched her go.

"She's taking it hard," Milton told him. He roused himself from the folds of the overstuffed chair he had dragged outside from his workshop. He crossed his patrolman's boots at the ankles and shook his newspaper. The sports page was a pointillistic canvas of budgie shit by now. "Don't mind Gladys," he said, sounding wheezy. He swatted a gnat on his arm. "She's worse than a hag in a Greek chorus. I shouldn't have told her." He shrugged philosophically. "I thought marriage was to share the tragedies with the triumphs."

"I know what you mean," said Bud.

"I told her, you know, my opinion on marriage, and you know what she told me? She said if I brought her a triumph from time to time she might be able to bear a tragedy now and then. You think that's fair?"

"It's how she feels."

"That got me wondering. Do you remember your marriage vows, Bud?"

"Cripes, no."

"I don't either but I don't think I ever agreed that triumphs and tragedies had to be on a one-to-one ratio. I remember saying in sickness and health in front of the minister. Did that mean I can't have a sick day without having a healthy day first?"

"She's feeling sorry for us, is all," Bud said without believing it himself.

"So I was sitting here wondering," Milton went on with an audible sigh. "What the vow means is—in sickness and health, for richer or poorer?—what it means is, rich and healthy and up your kazoo if you are poor, sick, or a failure."

"Which would you rather be married to, Milt?" Bud asked, sounding tired.

He took off his patrolman's hat and examined a bird stain on the bill. He seemed resigned to the mess, as if being shit on were his due. "We keep tryin' to make things work but they don't, do they? It's not for want of trying. Trying doesn't count, I guess, with people like Gladys. She needs a bona fide bell ringer. I'll tell you, I've about run out of things to try. My tank's on low."

"All ours are," Bud said.

Doubting was too easy, Callum thought as he listened to them talk. That was the tricky part. Resist the doubts and the dreams came true.

"It was something, the dream," said P.O. "Just not everything."

"And when did you decide that?" Bud asked him.

"It wasn't that important. It was only a straw—"

"A straw that broke the camel's back," Bud added softly. "I'm sorry if I was to blame."

P.O. put his arm around his shoulder. "No one's ever to blame for that last straw. Who's to know which one it will be?"

"Only the camel."

Roland said, "All morning long I've been thinking of some words I memorized a long time ago. 'I dreamt the past was never past redeeming: But whether this was false or honest dreaming I beg death's pardon now. And mourn the dead.' That's really something, don't you think?"

"Jeez," Bud said, staring in the empty cage.

23

This for That

Bud was emptying a fifty-pound bag of rock salt in the new water softener, whistling the song from *South Pacific* about washing a man right out of his hair.

Callum had been waiting to catch him alone, and he saw an opening now and crossed the lawn under a weight he recognized as gloom. He did not fear retribution. He welcomed punishment as his due. He would give back his land to Mrs. Rodriguez, and Bud would no doubt praise that part of his confession. But what that left him with was nothing. No, less than that. He was paying a price for succeeding at what he should have left alone.

Bud shook out the bag and leaned against the tank.

"Dad?" Callum asked in a voice so small it wasn't even a whisper.

"I tell ya, nothing's easy," Bud said, swiping his forehead with the back of his hand.

"I tipped over Mrs. Rodriguez's smudge pot." Anticipating a beating, he took a step backward.

Bud reached his whole arm in the soft-water tank, stirring the salt. "Unhuh," he said, as if he had not heard Callum or had heard him and didn't care.

"I killed those trees."

He retrieved his arm and watched the salt water drip from his fingers. "I figured somebody did," he said, furrowing his brow.

"No, *I* did."

"I wouldn't worry about it."

"But Dad, I went there to kill them." He wanted to cry, but how could he if Bud wouldn't recognize his crime?

"Don't you have something to do? Go on, now." He handed him the empty salt bag. "Take this back to the incinerator."

Callum clutched the bag to his chest, his head bowed.

"Make yourself useful!" Bud said edgily. He walked inside the house. He wasn't whistling anymore.

He came back out a minute later, and Callum felt relieved to see him. He was going to catch hell, and he couldn't wait. Bud looked down at him and from behind his back he showed him the Rankin's box with Serena's scarf. "We're even," he said and walked away.

Callum opened the door on Ricky Constantinople and Buzz Price, who looked like they were expecting him. Their faces were no longer friendly, as though the time for understanding had run out.

"We were about to visit your dad," said Mr. Price.

"He's home if you want him," Callum told them, knowing that their talking to Bud would do no good.

"We're going to ask him to take charge of this matter," Mr. Constantinople said. "We can't fiddle around anymore. It was sweet at first. You're a sweet kid. But this waiting is starting to cost a lot of money."

Callum shrugged as if to say they could do what they wanted. Nothing could take his name off the deed unless he agreed. He would have thought that they knew that, but maybe they thought Bud would bully him. The thought dawned on him why Bud had excluded him when money made the dream serious. Adults thought with a certain logic that kids like him didn't share. This difference made them combative partners who could never share the same goals.

"We have to know, one way or another," Mr. Constantinople went on. "Are you going to sell us your land, or not?"

"That's why I'm here," Callum told them. "It's why I stopped by."

"Then you're going to sell?" Mr. Constantinople asked, almost feverish.

"Yes," Callum told him, "for a price."

Mr. Constantinople sighed with relief. "You don't know how much this means to me."

"Oh yes, Mr. Constantinople, I do," Callum told him deliberately.

Bud was slouched on a bench by the Spanish fountain in the park reading a book he had checked out of the library about Lourdes. The book's abundant illustrations of cripples and lepers and morons buoyed his spirits by showing that things could be worse. The book had actually started to make him feel better until he looked at the gurgling waters of the healing French fountain, thinking that the people at Lourdes at least had religious miracles to look forward to.

By chance, a bum shuffled by at that moment carrying a gamey odor as though it were a burden. Oblivious of Bud, he rested a moment on the edge of the pool surrounding the fountain, dipping his hand in the water. He leaned on his arm and looked up pensively at the sky. Only then did he notice Bud, and he got up to leave.

"Don't go," Bud told him. "Not on my account."

He sat back down and folded his hands in his lap, listening to the restful gurgle of water. "There's something nice about the sound, don't you agree?" he asked, and Bud looked at him, surprised by his intelligent tone and the interesting nature of his statement.

"I've always found it to be so," Bud replied, attuning his ears to the lapping of the water and, for the first time since he had sat down on the bench, truly relaxing. "I wonder why that is."

"Because we *are* water," the bum replied knowingly. "Ninety-nine percent of what we are, anyway, with a few minerals thrown in. The H_2O molecules in us relax when they hear the sound of their relatives nearby. They worry otherwise about drying up. It's why the sound of a desert scares them."

"Interesting," said Bud. "Remind me, what is the sound of a desert?"

"No sound at all."

Bud looked the guy over. His shoes had no laces, and he wore a cord belt, and where his skin was exposed on his neck and arms and, to some extent, on his face, he was dark as a Hottentot. He was about his own age, too old to feel sorry for and yet too young to be invisible. Bud looked him in the eye and again he surprised himself; he had expected to see madness or confusion. Instead, he recognized an intelligence dimmed by a pervasive sadness. "I suppose you live under the bridge across from the hospital?" he asked, aware that the bum's bridge was where all of them lived in cardboard shanties. Every few years a flash flood swept a torrent down the dry Santa Ana riverbed. Nobody seemed to care.

"When I'm not on the move I live there," the bum replied. "I'm on the move now, south. This cold snap stiffens my joints."

"I suppose you were once a millionaire," said Bud, testing the truth of a cliché.

The bum shook his head sadly. "No, but I dreamed of being one," he said in a gentle voice.

"I know what you mean," Bud told him, aware that his question inadvertently had cut to the heart of his own private woes.

The bum laughed explosively, and the sound echoed across the park.

"What's so funny about that?" Bud asked him.

"What you just said. If you knew what I meant, you would be under the bridge, too." He shook with a quiet laughter now, genuinely amused. "I apologize," he said after awhile. "I wasn't laughing at you, mister. I was just laughing. It's all a matter of degrees."

Bud misunderstood, figuring the guy was telling him he was a college graduate like Glumm, but worse. "What degrees would those be?" he asked him with a note of derision.

He ran his hand through the water, thinking. "Of wanting," he said.

Bud stared at him, wondering if he had heard correctly.

"I wanted a dream more than anything, you see," the bum explained. "I lost my family and my friends in order to learn that my dream had come true. I was rich. Not a millionaire, but rich. I assumed them. I didn't give their love the credit it deserved."

Something like that was what the gypsy on Olivera Street had tried to tell Bud, who had not believed her then but was beginning to now. He pushed himself off the bench and bid the bum goodbye and good luck, a bit relieved when he was not asked for dole. He tucked the Lourdes book under his arm and crossed the street feeling like he wished he were home. He walked behind Rankin's without realizing until he was standing at the meter, fishing in his pockets for the car keys, that he had parked in front of the pawn shop. He peered across the breadth of sidewalk into the window, thinking how strange.

He stepped over to the window and confirmed that the pawn shop owner had finally removed Edith's brooch from public view. Bud felt a strong sense of relief that one thing, at least, had gone his way, and he stepped inside. Closing the door behind him, he looked down the length of the shop wondering how many months he would need to save to buy back the brooch. He had almost decided to put the bean field up for sale. Walt wasn't going to call. Bud did not know how he could have believed he could outsmart Walt Disney. Then he remembered what the bum had just said about matters of degree. He had almost decided, but not quite. He still had his family and friends, and because of them a small part of hope still lived inside his dream.

He signaled for the pawn-shop owner's attention. "Thanks," he shouted over the racks of bongo drums and used LP records.

"For what?" he asked, recognizing Bud when he looked up from what he was doing.

"For taking my wife's brooch out of the window."

The owner wiped his brow hard like a man trying to erase a memory. "I'm sorry, mister," he said. "The brooch sold, just this morning. A guy came in and bought it, paid cash. Took it with him."

Bud walked outside, hurrying to the car, and when he was inside and the door was closed, he gripped the wheel in both hands and cried.

24

Zip Ah Dee Doo Dah

Callum peered through the venetian blinds in search of a silver lining. But a sight across the street confirmed his worst fears. Mr. Yaw, the jet-fighter pilot, was out on his lawn, his Hawaiian luau shirt dripping wet. He was seeding his dichondra, and Mr. Yaw gardened only on days that didn't have a ray of hope in the wild blue yonder.

Milton was in the kitchen at the table whisking powdered sugar off his chin. Cloud and Blue, in their pajamas, were stretched out on their beds browsing old movie fan magazines. Scooter was curled up asleep against the baseboard's heater. Over the hum of the Singer, Edith was telling Gladys that the black orchids on the fabric for her living-room drapes were hard to match. Bud was in the living room in the recliner looking introspective and moody, whistling "Oh, Shenandoah" through his teeth.

"The rain will cancel it, don't you think?" he asked Callum, who looked apprehensively at his wristwatch.

"You suppose that's what's holding them up?" he asked, worried that P.O. and Cheval, Mr. Wait and Roland, might not show up at all because of the rain. "When did you tell them to be here?"

Bud referred to the ceiling. "Yesterday. I told them yesterday, and they said all right, they'd be here. But it's raining. And it's supposed to rain all day."

"Can we call them just to make sure?"

"Give them a while," Bud advised, not caring himself one way or another what happened.

Callum paced the living-room carpet until Bud told him to stop. Listening for the doorbell, he went to his bedroom and changed out of his pajamas. From his closet he took the hanger with his Sunday flannels and the tweed jacket. In the dresser drawer he found a white shirt, a tie, socks, and clean underpants. He went to the closet and was reaching for the shoebox with the Bonerubs when his hand knocked the lid off the unworn Knapps with laces that weren't yet threaded in.

He slipped them on and looked down, thinking he might give them a try. He tied them up and was surprised at how they felt. He walked across the floor and squeezed the toes. Not bad, he thought, and checked himself in the floor-length mirror.

Last of all before leaving the room, he reached under the bed for his cigar box of valuables. The land deed in his name was on top where he had put it. He read his name written large, feeling the pride of ownership swell in his chest. At the sound of P.O. and Cheval's voices in the living room, he slipped the deed in his jacket pocket and left the room.

P.O. was dressed according to Callum's wishes in a business suit, a white shirt, and a necktie. Cheval looked conservative, for once, in a white ruffled dress.

"Are you going to tell me what this is about?" P.O. asked him. Callum shook his head no.

"I don't know about this rain," Bud said gloomily, glancing out the front window.

Cheval could see Callum's startled reaction. "We'll show up rain or shine," she said for his benefit.

A car horn beeped, and Roland waved through his convertible's window. Bud called down the hall for Edith and Gladys, and a minute later, dressed and ready to go, the women and Cloud and Blue came out discussing whether to carry an umbrella or wear rain hats. Edith helped Gladys on with the rabbit-paw stole that Milton had given to her. Edith wore Bud's long trench coat, and both women slipped on clear plastic rain bonnets at the door.

Bud looked at his watch. "I don't know about Mr. Wait," he told Callum.

"Should we wait for him?" Callum asked.

"No sense in that. You never know with him."

They went reluctantly outside and huddled in a small circle on the front walk, scowling at the clouds. Scooter started barking with rare insistence, having roused himself from his slumber, and pressed his nose against the front window at the sound of their leaving.

"He feels abandoned," Blue interpreted.

"For God's sake bring him!" ordered Edith, mincing across the lawn to the car.

"His fur'll smell," Cloud complained.

"Whatever . . . you girls will be the death of me," Edith swore and boarded the car.

Blue opened the door, and Scooter bounded over the grass and hopped in. A moment later, a caravan pulled out, with windshield wipers keeping pace with the beat of Callum's nervous heart.

"You're in charge now," Bud told him. "Where's this fandango going to be?"

"The entrance to Mrs. Rodriguez's driveway," he replied.

"What's going to happen there?"

"Now, Bud," Edith cautioned him. "This is Callum's moment, and he wants it to be a surprise. Can't you let him have a surprise?"

Callum told Bud where to pull off the road, and he parked behind two cars. When the engine was turned off everybody sat still. Bud looked at Callum, and Callum looked at his watch.

"Okay, then," he said. "It's time."

Their umbrellas popped and their hats went on. Under a sky that seemed low enough to touch they walked along the side of the road to the end of Mrs. Rodriguez's driveway. Water bubbled in the irrigation ditches along Mrs. Rodriguez's grove, and the leaves on the trees shone in the rain. Callum looked down the rows of living trees, haunted by the sight of the spidery reminders of his crime.

Heralded by Bob's braying, Mr. Wait appeared out of the grove on the opposite side of the road. He ambled along as if to him the day were bright. He said hi when he crossed the road, and he winked at Callum with the knowledge of their shared secret.

At the end of the driveway, Buzz Price and Ricky Constantinople stood under a black umbrella. Mr. Constantinople wore an English trench coat with brass hooks and bone buttons, and Buzz Price wore nothing waterproof at all.

"Looks like we're all here," Mr. Constantinople said.

"No we aren't, not quite," Callum told him. "I asked Mrs. Rodriguez and Serena to come, too."

"Let's give her a minute, then," Mr. Constantinople said and stepped forward to introduce himself to those he didn't know. Buzz Price held back, looking tense.

"Who's that fella?" Bud asked Callum, meaning Buzz Price. Callum pretended not to hear. He glanced up at the clouds as rainwater trickled down his neck. He did not want to start explaining who everybody was and why they were here. Time would tell. When he had set up this powwow, he had thought he knew what he was doing, but now he was not sure. He looked down at his Knapps. All the men were wearing them, but he felt as alone as the man on the moon.

Mrs. Rodriguez and Serena appeared in the drive, with Mrs. Rodriguez apologizing to Edith for being late. She smiled and laughed and was altogether in a festive mood. Serena stood beside Callum. She looked prepared for the deluge in a shiny red raincoat and yellow rubber boots.

"I thought about it," he whispered to her out the side of his mouth.

"I knew you would," she said, looking at him with an expression that was hard to read. "I'm glad you did."

Mr. Constantinople clapped his hands. "I think we should begin, don't you?" he said to Callum.

"That's not what we agreed on," Callum reminded him in a voice that caught their attention.

"Yes, you're right about that," Mr. Constantinople said. "Thank you for reminding me."

"Agreed on?" Bud, furrowing his brow, asked. He looked at Mr. Constantinople, hating that Callum had done business behind his back.

"Ask your son," Mr. Constantinople told him with a dismissive shrug.

Buzz Price stood in the middle of the road and stared up and down. He walked back under the umbrella and whispered to Mr. Constantinople, who furled the umbrella and, like everybody else, stood out in the rain.

Through the gloom in the far-off distance, a bright yellow Lincoln Continental approached with its fat whitewalls hissing and its chrome grill gleaming. The car slowed and pulled to a stop on the opposite side of the road. The driver turned off the engine, and steam rose from the hood, partly obscuring the car. A man climbed out and closed the door, staring at the grove as if he were appreciating its quiet beauty. He removed a broad-brimmed tan hat and, looking up, frowned at the scud.

As though the sky were his minion, the rain stopped, like that. The sky filled with an arcade of color as a single bright rainbow anchored itself in Callum's quarter acre. The sky changed all the time, Callum thought, but this was different. The heavens themselves seemed pleased to see the man in the Lincoln.

With his hair swept back and his brown mustache sparkling in the sunlight, with those big ears and that buck-toothed shy grin he was famous for, he walked out of their dreams. Standing alone on that side of the road, he was much bigger than life could ever be, in a jacket with a sash tied in front, an open-neck sport shirt, and gabardine slacks with a crease.

"Well, hello, folks," he greeted them in a familiar and comforting voice as he came across the road. He stuck out his hand to Callum. "Congratulations, son," he told him, then turned to acknowledge Buzz Price and Mr. Constantinople with a slight nod. "That's kind of a zip-ah-dee-doo-dah sky up there, wouldn't you say?" He smiled at the rainbow.

"It's showing off for you," Callum told him, feeling like laughing.

"Why, of course it is," he said. "Now that we've cleared up the sky, I understand there's something else I can help with here?" He looked inquiringly at Mr. Constantinople. "Tell me what I can do."

Bud stepped forward, his face drained of color. The presence of this man signaled the failure of his dream. "Walt Disney . . . ?" he asked as if he hoped that the sound of his name would make this man disappear.

"I'm sorry about the confusion, folks," Walt told them. "I hear that this W.E.D. Enterprises confused some of you. I wanted to call it Walt Disney Enterprises but my board of directors wouldn't let me. The truth is, my name isn't my own anymore. The board got darned upset when I called my new company that. Imagine! They said my name was taken."

"A man should own his own name," Roland pointed out.

"You folks seem to know pretty well about my idea," Walt told them. "My board thinks it stinks, if you'd like to know the truth. What do you think?"

"It's genius," P.O. said and stepped forward boldly to grasp Walt's hand.

"These men knew, I swear, knew before you did," Cheval told Walt. "The truth is, they think you're swell."

Walt blushed. "I thought I was being clever, too."

"Well, you *are* clever," said Roland.

"Not if you folks figured it out."

"Not us," Mr. Wait said. "The boy." He pointed to Callum. "We thought you'd choose a different place."

"I know," Walt said as he slipped a hand in his jacket pocket. "I didn't want land speculators pouring in, if you know what I mean. I may be well off but I'm no pharoah. I want to see my theme park built." Then he drifted off on a different tack. "Because of my work I've been lucky to save what you'd call a youthful quality. But sometimes, you know, I look back on how tough things were, and I wonder if I'd go through it again. I hope I would. When I was twenty-one, I was broke. I slept on chair cushions in my studio and ate cold beans out of a can. But I took another look at my dream and set out for California. An older person might have had too much common sense for that. Sometimes I wonder if common sense isn't another way of saying fear. And fear too often spells failure."

"Not to us," said Roland.

"When I heard about you folks I was truly amazed," Walt said.

"I thought I was the only person left in the world who still took a position on dreams. We think alike, you and I. Are there many like you?"

"More than you probably know," said Mr. Wait.

"We dreamed the same dream," P.O. said.

"Yes, we did, and that's just amazing."

"Mr. Disney?" said Mr. Constantinople in a respectful tone. "Callum has something to say, I believe."

Walt held up his hand. "I'll tell you right now my dream can't come true if my land has a hole in it." He looked fondly at Callum. "It's up to you, young man."

Callum stared at Walt, thinking how he proved himself by making dreams come true. Walt was the king of dreamers, Johnny Appleseed scattering the seeds of dreams from one end of the country to the other. His dreams took root in the imaginations of people like himself and Bud and the others. This new dream was so new his board of directors was scared to touch it. They had left it up to Walt whether to go ahead, and now Walt was leaving the decision up to him. He looked at Bud staring at the ground, his hands tucked in his pockets and his shoulders rounded in defeat. He loved Bud, and even if Bud had lost sight of what was important, even if he had guessed wrong, he had invented this dream. The dream belonged to him.

Callum took the deed out of his pocket and, seeing what he was about to do, P.O. stepped forward. "Hold on a minute!" he shouted. His face darkened with anger. "We damn well all should have a vote in what you decide, Callum," he said.

"Take it easy, P.O.," Bud told him, holding him back.

Callum handed Bud the deed. "This is your dream," he told him.

Bud stared at the parchment as if he already had decided what to do. He hugged Callum and held out the deed to Walt. "Your dream doesn't have a hole in it anymore," he told him.

"Well, thank you," said Walt. "Thank you. But first, what's your price?"

"You already paid us, don't you see?" Bud said.

Walt turned around. "You briefed me on this, boys," he told Buzz Price and Mr. Constantinople. "You didn't say we'd already paid these people for their land."

"We haven't," said Buzz Price.

Walt tried to give the deed back to Bud. "I have to know the terms. It's the way I do business."

"Don't you see?" asked Bud. "The terms have been satisfied."

Walt looked genuinely confused. "Is there something going on here I don't know about?" he asked Mr. Price.

"Yes, sir, I think there is," he replied.

"What is it?" Walt asked.

"*You*," Bud told him. "*You* are the terms. It's a gift from us to you, for free, in return for all you've given us."

Walt stared at Bud. "I heard how you put yourself out on a limb for this. I want you to know I understand limbs. I've climbed out on a few of them myself. When you're dreamers like we are it happens all the time. Whatever you do, don't stop climbing on limbs." He smiled at Edith and bent down, reaching in his pocket. He pretended to pick something off the ground and held out his hand. "I think you dropped this, ma'am," he told her in a voice that was so honest that Edith in that instant did not doubt the truth of his assertion.

She took her brooch from his hand without thinking that she could not have dropped what she had not worn. She stepped over and kissed his cheek. As she pulled away, suddenly the delicate muscles around her eyes slackened. In an instant she was able to see clearly, as if she had been a witness to the events herself; she knew what Bud had done behind her back and why, and her breath caught with the understanding of what risks this dream had forced on him. Another woman in her situation might have grown angry, but Edith did not have that in her. Indeed, she loved Bud more in that moment, and she smiled up at him not for the return of the brooch but for the thought of his courage and the flaring of wildness she had always fallen for. She rubbed the center of the brooch with her palm and handed it to him without a word.

Tears welled in his eyes. He tried to say something, but the emotion in his throat muffled the word, and he simply reached over and pinned the brooch to Edith's chest.

"By the way," Walt said to all of them, "I'll be needing a bit of bean field for this theme park of mine, won't I, Buzz?"

"Yes, sir, about an acre—"

"—or less," Walt said with a chuckle. "What do you think I will have to pay for this bean field?"

"There's been a fast appreciation lately in bean fields and this one is no exception," Buzz Price said, nodding slightly at Callum. "Ten times what its owners paid, I'd imagine. Am I right, Callum?"

Callum tried to nod his assent without the others seeing. But they weren't looking at him. They had turned their eyes to Bud, who had started crying with relief and happiness, unable to help himself. They turned away, sharing in some vague way his feelings that this dream was over, and while they had not won the way they had hoped, they had not lost either.

"Mr. Constantinople, come over here," Walt said in a sharp voice that got the realtor's immediate attention. "I understand you tried to hoodwink this woman here. Mrs. Rodriguez?"

Mrs. Rodriguez knew that Ricky Constantinople was not to blame. "He was doing what he thought was in your interest," she told Walt.

"I didn't want to get scalped, that much was true," Walt said. "But I told Mr. Constantinople to pay a fair price. I think he was being overzealous on my behalf and I am embarrassed. I apologize, Mrs. Rodriguez. I hope that you are satisfied with how things worked out?"

"Completely," she replied, looking over at Callum. "Thanks to him."

Callum had been waiting for a chance to get a word in and he took it now. "I kicked over the smudge pot, like Serena told you I did, Mrs. Rodriguez. I meant to do it. But I wouldn't do it again."

"Callum has made amends," Walt said to her. "He has told you himself and he is sorry."

"I'm sure you had your reasons, Callum," she told him.

"There is one last thing before I go," Walt told them. "Callum made it a part of our deal. I was happy to agree. I wish I had thought of it myself. Mr. Wait, Callum thought you should know what will happen to your grove. Will you please tell him, Mr. Constantinople?"

"The State Highway Commission is within a few days of condemning your property," he told him reluctantly. "I'm sorry to have to be the one to tell you. I know what your grove means to you."

Mr. Wait looked up at the rainbow, about to cry. "I saw it coming," he said to the sky. "Yes, sir, I saw it coming."

Nothing any of them could think to say could help Mr. Wait now. The news ruined all the good that had happened. Edith reached in her handbag for a hanky, and Cheval started to cry.

"The boy here," said Walt, "gave me specific instructions. He insisted. And he is right. We need a reminder of what this part of California used to look like. Pretty soon it will be parking lots and housing tracts and business centers. We need a place parents and their kids can visit to walk among the orange blossoms. Your grove, Mr. Wait, will remain as it is under my authority. The freeway is going in anyway but I've talked with the people in charge. The road will swerve around your grove. We will call it the Wait Bulge. Your grove will stay as it is from now until kingdom come." And with a sudden thought he added, "Even until *magic* kingdom come."

Bud reached over for Edith's hanky. He honked loudly and the others laughed as Bob, hearing what he thought was the call of the wild, started hee-hawing to beat the band.

"He was just like I imagined," Milton said as they walked into Mary Rodriguez's grove, still filled with the wonder of meeting Walt.

"Better," said Roland.

"I thought he'd be taller," said Mr. Wait.

"Now I know where his dreams come from," said Blue.

"Where?" asked Cloud.

"His eyes."

No one disagreed. His eyes had been soft and gentle and focused inward just as dreamers' were meant to be.

Callum was thinking of what to say to Serena, strolling by his side. A new thought dawned on him—that he did not have to say anything. Serena seemed content with that, perhaps in a belief that an utterance some day would connect her to him with a bond of emotion. In the meantime she could wait. It was meant to be. Waiting was what people did who were in love, waiting to catch up and slow down and keep in stride their whole lives.

The grove after the rain was lush. The leaves glistened, and the earth underfoot sighed a loamy scent that was lovely and right. A covey of mourning doves took wing as they approached. Cheval ran to catch up with P.O., who was walking all alone, regret darkening his handsome face. He spoke to her but really to all of them when he said, "Well, what does this leave us with?"

Callum wondered why no one had asked that question before this. He knew the answer for himself. A burden of conscience had been lifted that he would have carried his whole life. Serena and her mother had found an answer, too. They were millionaires. Mr. Wait was out of the woods. And Bud was off the hook with Edith. But the others? What did they have to show?

They soon found themselves in Callum's former quarter acre of dead trees without knowing that this was where they wanted to be, without knowing they had nowhere else to go.

"Well . . ." P.O. demanded.

Milton hooked his thumbs in his Sam Browne, and with a determined look he addressed the spindly branches high up in the tops of the trees. "You know," he said. "Montezuma buried a chest of treasure before he died."

"Where was that?" Roland asked, looking up brightly.

"The Ancients tell you about this, Milt?" asked Bud, giving him a playful wink.

"In Las Cruces, New Mexico, I believe, and no, Bud, not the Ancients. I read it at the library."

"Too far away," said P.O. Everyone turned to look at him. He was grinning. "Good idea, though, Milt."

"What about John Sutter's ring, the one he made out of the first Gold Rush nugget?" Bud asked.

"What about it?" asked Roland.

"It's been lost for most of this century."

"That'd be nearby," said P.O.

And with that they started to leave the grove with a collective spring in their Knapps—of old . . . and new.

ABOUT THE AUTHOR

MALCOLM COOK MACPHERSON, a former corre-
spondent for *Newsweek* and the author of several books of fiction and nonfiction, grew up a
couple miles from the grove in Orange County
that became Disneyland. He now makes his
home with his wife and two children in North
Carolina.

A B O U T   T H E   T Y P E

This book was set in Bodoni Book, a typeface named after Giambattista Bodoni, an Italian printer and type designer of the late eighteenth and early nineteenth centuries. It is not actually one of Bodoni's fonts but a modern version based on his style and manner and is distinguished by a marked contrast between the thick and thin elements of the letters.